BLOOD BROTHERS

Cover art by:
Ken Farmer
Back Cover by:
Warren Martin

BLOOD BROTHERS

BY

DORAN INGRHAM, BUCK STIENKE & KEN FARMER

timbercreekpress@yahoo.com

ISBN: 9780989122085 - Paper
ISBN-10: 0989122085

ISBN: 9780989122092 - E
ISBN-10:0989122093

Printed in the United States of America
Published by:
Timber Creek Press
312 N. Commerce St.
Gainesville, Texas 76240
timbercreekproductions@yahoo.com

DEDICATION

BLOOD BROTHERS is dedicated to all who proudly serve in the United States military and the men and women who work in the shadow world of Risk Management. The freedoms held dear are protected by their willingness to serve. Thank you for standing up when called and for your service. Let Freedom Ring!

TIMBER CREEK PRESS NOVELS

MILITARY ACTION/TECHNO

by Buck Stienke & Ken Farmer
BLACK EAGLE FORCE: Eye of the Storm (Book #1)
BLACK EAGLE FORCE: Sacred Mountain (Book #2)
RETURN of the STARFIGHTER (Book #3)
BLACK EAGLE FORCE: Blook Ivory (Book #4)

HISTORICAL FICTION WESTERN

by Ken Farmer & Buck Stienke
THE NATIONS
HAUNTED FALLS

SCI/FY

DAYS OF THE HARBINGER by Alex Cord

FAMILY

HOTEY by Josephine Bailey

COMING THIS FALL

LEGEND of AURORA by Ken Farmer & Buck Stienke
BLACK EAGLE FORCE: Fourth Reich by Buck Stienke & Ken Farmer

TIMBER CREEK PRESS

THE AUTHORS

 **Buck Stienke** – Captain – Fighter Pilot - United States Air Force, has an extensive background in military aviation and weaponry. A graduate of the Air Force Academy, Buck (call sign 'Shoehorn') was a member of the undefeated Rugby team and was on the Dean's List. After leaving the Air Force, Buck was a pilot for Delta Airlines for over twenty-five years. He has vast knowledge of weapons, tactics and survival techniques. Buck is the owner of Lone Star Shooting Supply, Gainesville, TX. As a successful actor, writer and businessman, Buck lives in Gainesville with his wife, Carolyn. Buck was Executive Producer for the award winning film, *Rockabilly Baby*.

 **Ken Farmer** – After proudly serving his country as a US Marine (call sign 'Tarzan'), Ken attended Stephen F. Austin State University on a full football scholarship, receiving his Bachelors Degree in Business and Speech & Drama. Ken quickly discovered his love for acting when he starred as a cowboy in a Dairy Queen commercial. Ken has over 39 years as a professional actor, with memorable roles *Silverado, Friday Night Lights, The Newton Boys* and *Uncommon Valor*. He was the OC and VO spokesman for Wolf Brand Chili for eight years. Ken now lives near Gainesville, TX, where he continues to write screen plays and novels.

Buck and Ken have completed four novels to date. The first was *BLACK EAGLE FORCE: Eye of the Storm*, published by Tate Publishing. *BLACK EAGLE FORCE: Sacred Mountain*, second

Return of the Starfighter, third. A historical fiction western, *The Nations*, the fourth and our fifth novel, this time back to the Black Eagle Force series: *Black Eagle Force: Blood Ivory,* all published by Timber Creek Press.

Contact: blackeagleforce1@yahoo.com

 **Doran W Ingrham** – Inactive USMC – Retired Risk Management/Close Security Specialist (call sign 'Zorro'). Extensive global experience dealing with terrorist threats. Has vast working knowledge of weapons, explosives, survival skills urban, jungle, desert and intel gathering methods used around the globe for covert (Black Ops) actions and Executive Protection. Combat Pistol competitor and International Sniper competitor. He has appeared in over 20 commercials, 15 television episodic and 40 films. Has written a series of film scripts based on his world-wide experiences. Doran now lives with his wife, Maria Mae, exact location undisclosed.

TIMBER CREEK PRESS

PROLOGUE

NAIROBI, KENYA

Mark Ingram winced as the curved suture needle made another pass in the two inch sword cut inflicted under his left arm by the very recently departed Japanese Yakuza kingpin. The tending physician was not actually a doctor at all—Rheinhart Fabian was a topflight close security operative who served as the head of security for President Mobutto of Kenya. The six-foot four, one-man wrecking team was powerfully built—245 pounds of solid muscle with the appropriate handle of *Rhino*. He glanced up at the much slimmer, but equally deadly Texan and grinned.

"An' I thought ya said ya didn't need any anesthetic, Zorro. Gonna use your Zen power of concentration, were ya now?"

Mark reached over to the center of the dining room table, grabbed his sunglasses and slipped them on. "Can it, you big gorilla. Sun's coming up and it hurts my eyes."

The blonde South African glanced over his shoulder and noticed the first yellow rays were streaming in through the window. "Sure…whatever ya say," he replied as he skillfully tied off the black linen thread and knotted it. He took a pair of forceps and lifted the last Steri-Strip that the two had applied shortly after the nighttime fight. "Almost done…Want another swig of Maker's Mark?"

"I'm good."

"Only two more to go…but it should hold a lot better than the strips…The lats get a lot of pressure put on 'em…Lucky you had that shoulder holster on…we might not be having this conversation."

"Kinda the worse for wear," he replied as he looked at the remains of the Bianchi X-15 rig. The bottom three inches of leather were severed, with only a single side of the clamping spring left attached. "Wonder if they still make this model? Got used to it over the years."

"Know what ya mean. Man in our line of work gotta have hisself some good equipment."

"Yup." He glanced over at the Halliburton attaché case. "What are we gonna do with the money?"

"I'm not touching it…With my boss' wife being involved, makes me look like I planned tha whole thing just to get tha three million."

"Conflict of interest? Okay, I can buy that…but I'm damned sure not turning it over to the KWS. My boss was up to his pencil neck in the smuggling thing…"

"*Ex* boss."

"Doesn't matter now. All three of 'em are crispy critters. Terrible crash...just one of those freak highway accidents," Mark said sarcastically. "They'll need DNA to find out who the hell they were."

"Yeah...Speed kills...Ya can let it down now...I'm done."

Mark lowered his deeply tanned arm after checking out the stitching. "I did a hellova lot better job on you."

"So?...Sue me. I still make house calls."

Mark grinned. "Thanks...for everything."

"Glad it worked out for ya...Tell ya what. Keep tha loot...Call it battle booty."

"I was kinda thinking the same thing...never know when it might come in handy."

Rhino nodded, stood up and stretched. "Don't know about you, but my tired is hanging out. Tha guest room is available if ya want."

"That's an idea. Think I'll deposit the cash in a Cayman bank after a little nap."

BEF FACILITY
EAGLE NEST RANCH
SOUTH TEXAS

The winter morning sun broke bright and clear as it usually did in wintertime in far south Texas. A light frost still lay upon the buffalo and grama grass that grew among the scattered mesquite and ancient live oaks. To the west, across the sluggish Rio Grande, lay the nation of Mexico with similar, if not identical topography—but there the similarity stopped. On the American

3

side, in what Mexicans called Del Norte, the three thousand acre ranch was not what it appeared to be.

The Eagle Nest Ranch served as the southern White House for President Annette Henry Thompson-Hermann. The property, owned by her husband Gunter, had been in the Hermann family since 1811 and had been the site of General Santa Anna's crossing enroute to the Alamo in 1836. The family referred to the passing of the Mexican army across their land as the *Trail of Misery*—all but one of the Gunter's progenitors had been slaughtered by Santa Anna and his troops.

The outward appearance of a peaceful cattle and horse ranch, its two story German-style native rock house with five hundred head of registered Beefmaster cattle and over fifty head of the finest blooded quarter horse stock in the southwest belied what was underground.

Three miles from the house and barn area, underneath a ten thousand foot paved runway built ostensibly for Air Force One, was the 17,000 square foot southern headquarters for the most deadly Above Tier One Special Ops fighting force in the world.

Created in 1976 by then President Ronald Reagan as an ultra-rapid deployment black ops strike unit that was not—and could not be—officially sanctioned and usually worked independently of the military for plausible deniability. The contract group was made up of mostly former special ops personnel from all branches—the unit was named the Black Eagle Force. Reagan made it an Executive Order for the civilian group's existence via contract with the DoD under *TOP SECRET NOFORN* status. BEF was set up as a corporation in the state of Nevada and was funded from the discretionary black ops funds in the DoD.

The massive underground facility was constructed using the Earthcom Blackhawk Dome configuration. A 60x34 foot rectangular aircraft carrier hydraulic elevator had been installed inside the top side hangar, had been salvaged from USS *Valley Forge* before she was scrapped in 1971. The hangar was large enough for the giant Air Force One and the BEF's specially modified C-5M *Super Galaxy* nicknamed *Mama Bird*.

Underground, in the operations room, Dare Phillips, the CEO—Colonel, USMC Ret.—COO Burner Stewart—General USAF Ret.—were discussing the recently completed mission in the Indian Ocean and the rescue of Senator Breitbart and his daughter with the team leaders of the BEF ground force, known as the Raptors.

"You've gone through the debriefing reports from all departments...Any questions, changes or additions?" asked Dare.

"Just be prepared to hear SecDef Baker scream when he gets the expenditure report...we won't even need a radio. We spent more on *Operation Firestorm* than we did on the Sacred Mountain and Chinese operations combined," said Burner.

"A great deal was spent on upgrading our Black Eagle fighters, adding the M800 troop carriers and the Raptormobiles, don't forget...All that went into inventory," answered Dare.

"I know, but it still took a hellova bite out of their black-ops budget."

"The SecDef will get over it...eventually...Anything else?"

Leroy "Bad" Poole, leader of Raptor Team Four, held up his huge black hand.

"Bad." Dare nodded to the giant former Army Ranger.

Poole turned to his compatriot and leader of Raptor Team Five, former SEAL Sean Baker. "Widowmaker, any chance of us recruiting that former jarhead friend of yours in Kenya, Mark Ingram? I think he'd make a great addition to the Raptors."

"Don't know, man. He's always been kind of a loner...but I've never seen him quite as excited...if you want to call a flicker of the eyes excited...when he saw some of our toys. He is a warhorse, I grant you that...Like I said over there, you really don't want to piss him off."

"Let's keep our options open, you never know when an opportunity will arise that we can talk to him...We'll leave it up to you, Widowmaker," said Burner Stewart.

***

CHAPTER ONE

WASHINGTON, DC
Dulles International Airport

The Boeing 767-400 turned off the parallel taxiway and into the international arrival ramp as the nosewheel taxi light reflected off the fresh snow that had fallen the previous night. The mid-January DC weather featured a bitterly cold northwest wind that cut to the bone. Safety observers, clad in matching blue hooded parkas, watched the majestic bird inch toward the gate as the marshaller signaled the captain to brake the huge aircraft to a stop. Ground crew members scurried to place the yellow wooden chocks behind the aircraft's main and nose gear as the marshaller flashed a thumbs-up as the captain directed the copilot to shut down the idling turbofans. Inside, the cabin crew made their final announcements to the 184 passengers who had flown all night from South America.

"Welcome to Dulles International Airport. Please check around your seat and in the overhead compartment for any personal items you may have brought on board. Thank you again for flying Avianca Aerovias." The flight attendant repeated the message again in Spanish for those passengers from Argentina. She hung the PA hand piece back on the bulkhead cradle and gave an *okay* signal to the gate agent, who promptly opened the forward entrance door.

The balding, portly agent grinned at the gorgeous raven-haired attendant. At five feet nine, she stood slightly taller than he, even without her high heels. He began his obligatory announcement directing the passengers to US customs and identified the baggage claim area where they would eventually be reunited with their luggage. She moved across the wide-body jet and approached the tanned blue-eyed man seated on the aisle in first class. Slipping a business card into his hand, she winked and smiled seductively.

"Next time you're in town, call me."

"Sure thing, miss," he said as he slipped the card into his shirt pocket and reached to the overhead for his carry-on bag. *Nice to be noticed...even when you're not in the market. Why is it always like that?*

A couple of minutes later, Mark Ingram, along with the first four rows of first class passengers, exited the jetway and stepped into the gatehouse. He was dressed in a dark charcoal-gray Italian wool suit purchased and hand tailored at Etiqueta Negra, a exclusive men's wear store in Buenos Aires,

Argentina, the day before. His sky-blue Egyptian cotton shirt contrasted nicely with a midnight-blue Thai silk tie. The Texas native had trimmed his premature silver hair—once long and ragged in the Kenyan bush—and wore it just over his collar. If not for the dark tan acquired from months in the hot equatorial sun, a casual observer would have thought that the slender, but well muscled man just another business traveler.

Mark had taken a roundabout route from Kenya, wanting to stop over in Buenos Aires and meet with fellow risk management operatives to check on possible new employment. His exit from Kenya had been swift—as often was the case when a contract ended or was cut short by circumstances beyond his control.

Buenos Aires was a stopping point for many who worked the trade. There were always a few familiar faces from the past in attendance at one or another favored drinking holes. Everyone in the gray world of security employment worked with numerous identities and were known by their *handle* or *call sign* more often than by their given name.

He checked his passport and credentials one last time insuring all were in order. The name Steve McCallister printed below his passport identification photo was one of several that he used to travel while living the life of a close security agent. The identity had been set up by a the American CIA when he had worked with them in Columbia. It still existed in the State Department data base, and the feds were happy to allow him to use it in case they needed his services at another time. In short order, he was entering the primary baggage claim area with hundreds of mixed international and domestic passengers.

Once inside, he proceeded to the carousel where the checked baggage for his flight would be seen as it rode up the conveyor belt and slide unceremoniously down the overlapping stainless steel panels that formed the oval shaped track. Dozens of unfamiliar black bags passed by before a large rollaboard with a bright yellow ID placard came into view. He stepped up to the rubber bumper lining the carousel, spun the bag around, snatched it up effortlessly by the handle and set it upright on the short gray Berber carpet.

Mark extended the carry handle, and then unfastened the small brass lock securing the twin zippers, reached inside and removed a small U-shaped metal hook attached to a sturdy nylon strap riveted to the top of the rollaboard frame. Eight bags later, a silver Haliburton attaché case spun down the carousel and bounced off the resilient black bumper. He smiled almost imperceptibly as he recognized his last checked item. Lifting it off the slowly turning conveyance, he hooked the case handle to the carry strap and headed toward the customs processing area.

He spotted the sign over the line identifying his status—*US CITIZEN WITH DECLARATION*. Mark was the second person in line and stood patiently awaiting his turn. The young black customs agent nodded as he spoke up,

"Next in line."

"Mornin' to you, sir. I see they got you out of bed early on this cold day in DC," Mark said with his usual west Texas drawl as he handed his passport and the customs declaration form.

"Got that right...Mr. McAllister," he said looking at the photo on the passport and comparing it to Mark's face. He scanned the magnetic card hidden under the front cover and noted the computer console light turned green accepting the ID as valid. His face screwed up into a visible question as he looked at the declaration form. "Amarula liqueur? That's a new one on me."

Mark smiled. "It's made with fruit from the marula tree. They call it *The Spirit of Africa*. A bit sweet for my taste, but it's a present for a special young lady. Has a bull elephant on the label."

The agent nodded as he stamped the form and dropped it in the appropriate *In* basket. He noisily marked the passport with the inked date/time stamp and returned it. *Whatever it takes to seal the deal.* "Welcome home, sir."

"Ya'll have a nice day, hear?" Mark walked briskly to the next agent who pointed to the second in a long series of lines for baggage inspection. He tossed his small carry-on bag on to the rubber conveyer belt leading to the x-ray machine It contained his books, iPad, international cell phone and a small bag of cherry-flavored hard candy. It went through without a hitch. He removed his jacket, shoes, belt and watch, placed them in a rectangular tub and sent them through. Lastly, he placed the suitcase and his attaché case on the belt and stepped though the metal detector when prompted by the security guard. He passed as expected without setting off the alarm, then grabbed his shoes and slipped them back on before retrieving his belt and jacket. He could see the facial expression of the x-ray technician change when they saw the three full boxes of .45 ACP rounds in the rollaboard. The grimace turned to a near panic as the familiar shape of a Colt Gold Cup and extra magazines nestled inside the smaller silver case.

The technician slammed his hand down on the stop button and reversed the direction of the conveyer. He called over to a supervisor and spoke to him in hushed tones. The supervisor lifted a small radio transceiver and spoke softly but hurriedly into it. The man eyeballed Mark suspiciously as armed DC police approached from two direction, their hands on their sidearms.

Well, here we go again. Mark thought as he slipped into his jacket.

After a several minutes inside a closed screening room where the customs agents examined the stainless Colt and recited chapter and verse about why no one was allowed to bring a handgun into the nation's capital, Mark grinned and simply said, "There's somethin' ya'll gotta see, before you go and make complete fools of yourselves."

"And just what the hell would that be?" asked a dumpy customs agent with a coffee stain on his tie.

"This," he said as he held up one finger and slowly reached inside his jacket pocket. He pulled out a small laminated card with his ID picture and name on one side and a brief statement on the back. Below the statement was a signature the senior agent recognized.

"Holy shit! Is this for real?"

"I reckon it is. George W. gave it to me…in person. If you like, hand me my phone and I'll wake him up back in Dallas…You can ask for yourself."

The five TSA agents and two DC cops huddled and spoke to each other hurriedly. Only one of them had ever seen a real *Get Out of Jail* card signed by a President before, but all had heard scuttlebutt about their existence. None was willing to risk their job trying to incarcerate the holder of one. If the man had the ear and trust of the Commander in Chief, he was not to be messed with. After all, the card did say *until revoked* upon it. The huddle broke up as the two DC police headed for the door. The dumpy customs agent closed the Haliburton case and handed it to Mark as the others replaced his neatly folded clothes and ammunition inside the black nylon suitcase.

"Sorry to have inconvenienced you, Mr. McAllister."

"Just doin' your job. No problem at all…I'll put in a good word to W. for you."

"Thank you, sir, uh…have a nice day, sir."

Mark scanned the crowd for any sign of Sarah Breitbart. He noted his pulse rate was up in anticipation of seeing her again. *Damn. Feel like a high school senior about to pick up his prom date, I do.* He relaxed, falling into a light Zen meditation to clear his mind and block out some of the noise and chaos of the rushing crowd of travelers. Several yards away, over the heads of the undulating humanity, Mark spied a small handheld sign with an arrow pointing down. It read, *Sarah Here!* A smile passed over his face as he made his way toward the sign and the young woman he had traveled halfway round the world to see again.

The five foot two Sarah, her dark hair pulled back in a pony tail, stood on her toes to see over the crowd. She still had the lithe figure and body tone of a competitive gymnast gained from years of practice. Her thoughts raced as she anxiously scanned the crowd for the man who had rescued her from the kidnappers in the Mount Elgon forest in Kenya. Her heart was beating a hundred and ten beats per minute in expectation of being in his arms again. When she saw Mark weaving through the throng toward her she could not help but yell, "Mark! Mark! Over here!"

The crowd seemingly parted at her call and she rushed to him, dropping her sign and leaping into his arms. The travelers flowed around them as they embraced. Time seemingly stood still as she whispered, "Oh God, I thought you would never come."

Mark gently released his grip and leaned back to look Sarah in the eyes. "I said I would…"

Before he could finish, Sarah pressed her lips to his in a urgent and passionate kiss. Most of the crowd that flowed past them only noticed for a moment, but a trio of Marines on leave, dressed in their green wool winter uniforms, shouted,

"Oorah! Get some!"

The gusty salute caused Mark and Sarah to glance to the young jarheads and smile. "Semper Fi, Devil Dogs," he said as he lowered her to her feet.

She took him by the hand. "Let's get out of this jungle."

He laughed at her reference to the throng of people. *Does remind me of a herd of wildebeasts at that.*

The drive from the airport went as smooth as could be expected considering the rush hour traffic and the light snow falling. Winter in nation's capital was a dreary sight with piles of dirty snow plowed off the roadways. Sarah drove directly to the Jefferson Hotel, less glitzy, but well-appointed five star hotel. Riding in her cherry red BMW was a far cry from the rugged vehicles Mark was use to driving. There was barely enough room for him in the front seat and his luggage was stuffed into the tiny compartment behind them. The Haliburton case in his lap added to the cramped ride.

He rarely allowed anyone else to drive and when he did it was another operative he trusted. Mark had to admit he was impressed with Sarah's ability to weave in and out of the tightly packed mass of humanity—all jockeying for position in an effort to arrive at their destination.

Mark handed the young bellman a fifty dollar bill after his luggage was deposited in the spacious sitting room of the Jefferson Suite. He removed a small electronic monitoring device—able to detect of all kinds of active radio transmitting devices—from his carry on bag and swept the rooms for surveillance devices as he made a tour of the suite. Mark obtained the device in Buenos Aires. Hans Schoepke built a thriving business catering to the needs of close security operatives. He had degrees from MIT and Columbia University in electrical engineering—some compared his inquisitive mind to Nikola Tesla—the electronic wizard invented and patented hundreds of items that were unique and essential to the risk management trade.

Mark moved through the suites amenities noting a table for two, positioned to take full advantage of the striking views while enjoying morning coffee; a separate formal dining room for 10 in privacy; a daytime sitting room; kitchen; study; as well as a guest powder room, and the Italian marble master bathroom window allowed in natural light and fresh air.

Satisfied the suite was clear, he removed his jacket, hanging it in the entry closet and sat down on the French provincial sofa next to Sarah. She moved closer and nestled against him, laying her head on his chest.

"I don't recall you telling me you were in the CIA…How many other secrets do you have?" Sarah purred.

Mark stroked her hair. "Never in the CIA officially. GW gave me the get out of jail free pass for doing some private work for him and Laura years ago. Acted as a baby sitter for the twins while they did spring break in Cancun."

"I see." Sarah gazed into his eyes. "What about the other secrets? Why did that TSA agent call you Mr. McCallister when he came out of the inspection area?"

"You ever hear about curiosity killing the cat?"

She lightly slapped him on the chest and started to pull away, but his grip tightened. She nestled into his grasp again and was amazed at how strong, yet gentle he was. It was comforting to be held and she relaxed to enjoy the moment. The cloud cover broke open as the sun came into view. The splendid view of the city, shrouded in snow, was bathed in its yellow glow.

"Father has made reservations for us at the Plume here in the Jefferson for dinner…Unless you have something else hidden in those suitcases, what you have on will be perfect. Most of his friends dine there regularly," Sarah said as she kissed Mark lightly on the lips, pulled away and moved to the door. "I'll see you in the lobby at 8:00 p.m."

"Sounds like a plan. I need a shower, shave and a little down time before the get together."

After Sarah closed the door, Mark picked up the phone and called the concierge, "I need a suit cleaned and pressed right away. There's fifty bucks in it for you if you get it done by 1900 hours."

"No problem, Mr. Ingram. I'll have a porter pick it up in five minutes."

Mark hung up the phone, took off his soft leather handmade Italian loafers and stretched out on the sofa.

NAIROBI, KENYA

Rhino lay back in a hot tub of Epson salts, bathing his aching, exhausted physique and mind. His massive body filled the tub. The last two weeks of cleaning up the details concerning the first lady's death and Mark's swift departure from the Kenyan Wildlife Service, had been both physically and mentally taxing.

He had been apprehensive about President Mobutto's reaction to the details of her death—it was his wife, no matter what a treacherous bitch she had been. His fears were ill-founded. Mobutto sat behind his large English walnut desk and read the folder on the events. Rhino stood by with his hands together below his waist and watched the President's face for any sign of emotion—there was none. *One cool customer*, he concluded.

The President closed the folder, stood up and secured it in a wall safe hidden by a large oil painting of a herd of elephants that hung behind his desk. He poured two Waterford crystal glasses of sixty year old Glenfiddich single malt Scotch whiskey from the well-stocked wet bar—neat, no ice. "Have a seat, Rhino," he said as he walked around the massive desk and nodded at two high-backed leather chairs set near the bookshelf. He handed him the glass and both of them sat down and took a sip.

A long silence passed as the two men savored the fine whiskey. It ended when Mobutto called out to his personal secretary, "Lutto, would you come in here please."

She was in her late 40's was still a stunning woman of the Kikuyu tribe, the largest of the tribes in Kenya, totaling about 5 million—twenty-two percent of the population. They lived in the fertile central highlands and dominated the country politically and economically. Mobutto's government consisted almost entirely of Kikuyu. At six feet, she was an imposing figure and a beautiful, desirable woman. She seemed to glide across the room like a big cat.

"Yes, Mr. President."

"Call the Chief of Police, the Minister of Defense and the Minister of the KWS. Inform them to be in my office at 0900 hours tomorrow." Mobutto still used the military terminology for time, a holdover from his duty in the Kenya Air Force.

"Yes, Mr. President. Anything else, sir?" she spoke with a distinct British accent though slightly lyrical due to her Kikuya background.

"Yes. Have a check made out to Mr. Fabian for the remaining months of his contract as well as a check for a two hundred thousand bonus. Use the US dollars account in the Kenya Commercial Bank for both."

Well, that's about it then. Rhino looked to Mobutto with a bit of surprise, which he immediately hid, taking a long slow swallow of the Scotch.

"Yes, Mr. President."

"I suspect there will be numerous ramifications to the events you presented me with today. I think it would be in your best interest...and mine for that matter, if you made a timely departure, Rheinhart," Mobutto said as he moved to the table and poured himself another shot.

"Mr. President, I'm at a loss for words," Rhino said in an uncharacteristically quiet tone. He had gained deep admiration for Mobutto during his time working for him, and especially respected him as being a man of his word—no matter what the consequences.

"I will forever be beholding to your friend Mark Ingram. Poaching fell nearly eighty percent during his tenure with the KWS...Bloody good show!" The President raised his glass in

19

salute and slammed the shot down. "As for you…I doubt I'll find a comparable replacement. You have performed admirably. I know it must have been difficult for you to present me with the documents concerning my wife…and her lover. She was not of my tribe, but you were already aware of that."

Rhino nodded as Mobutto continued, "Ours was a marriage of…political necessity…a merger if you will. With the support of her tribe, we easily outdrew the other candidates and my election was assured. We both got what we wanted, and I was rather fond of her…I really was. Somehow, my ambitions clouded my judgment, I would say in retrospect. I trusted her too much, and she used her position as First Lady to enrich herself at Kenya's expense. With her out of the picture, the coalition we formed may crumble. We must make contingency plans for that possibility."

"I can make some calls in your behalf, if you like, about a replacement. I know some very good men, sir."

"Splendid…Do that. See you at 0900," the president said as he turned to the window that looked out onto the immaculately trimmed grounds surrounding his office.

***

CHAPTER TWO

WASHINGTON, DC
Plume Restaurant

Mark admired the Jefferson's sizable collection of antiques, period artwork and original signed documents coexisting alongside the best of modern-day amenities as he and Sarah moved through the lobby to the restaurant.

With a guest list that read like a Who's Who of political and social circles, The Jefferson established a reputation as DC's most discerning hotel, known for its attention to detail, exceptional service and exquisite interiors filled with European and American antiques and Jeffersonian artifacts.

Of all the Founding Fathers I'd like to sit down with you and discuss your life and times, Mr. Jefferson...or should I say Mr. President, Mark thought as Sarah took his arm at the reservations desk.

Senator Breitbart stood up, as any gentleman would do, when the hostess led Sarah and Mark to their table. Thomas Jefferson was known for his love of fine wines and the award winning list of wines from around the world lay in the extensive cellar below.

Heads turned as Mark and Sarah passed through the room. A simple black dress complimented Sarah's athletic figure, a single strand of pearls adorned her neck and the black high heels elevated her five foot two inch frame to his shoulder. She looked every bit the vision of Audrey Hepburn in the film *Breakfast at Tiffinys* with her hair up in a tight swirl. Though he wore the Italian tailored suit well, Mark still carried the presence of a hunter, a predator among lambs. The crowd of Washington elitites measured the couple with varying degrees of interest.

Mark had changed his midnight blue shirt in favor of a light blue Thai silk shirt accenting his clear blue eyes. In staying with the protocol of Washington he wore a red tie—power symbol of the conservatives that worked on the hill.

"Great to see you again Mark," Senator Breitbart said as he shook Mark's hand.

"Pleasure's all mine, sir," Mark replied as he pulled out Sarah's chair.

A smile crossed her lips as she was seated and Mark moved the chair forward for her. *Everyone is watching and Mark is such a gentleman. Take that, you hypocrites.* "Thank you," Sarah said as she lightly touched his arm.

"How was the flight from Kenya? Long as I recall…Did you connect through Berlin or London?" Senator Breitbart asked.

"Buenos Aires actually," Mark replied after the hostess had left. "Had some business opportunities to inquire about before coming here…How's the steak?"

"Excellent. So is the Atlantic Salmon this time of year," Breitbart offered. "Thinking of working in Argentina now?"

"No, sir," Mark replied as he studied the menu.

"Let's not discuss business tonight, Dad…Please?" Sarah said. "He's on vacation. Aren't you Mark?"

"Yes I am…Senator, just to be clear, I came here expressly to see Sarah. My intentions…"

"I have no doubts as to your intentions. To be clear as well…I approve. The young men Sarah has introduced me to in the past were all…ah, shall we say…loafer wearing…"

"Father!" Sarah cut her father off, her face flushed with a pink glow of embarrassment.

The waiter arrived and defused the moment as the three placed their order.

"Bring us a bottle of your '95 Château d'Yquem, Premier Cru Classé Supérieur," Mark requested.

"Sir, we only have it in half bottles."

"Then bring us two half bottles…Unless either of you prefer something besides a fine Bordeaux." Mark looked to Sarah then her father.

"I usually have white wine, but I'll try anything once," Sarah replied. She began quickly scanning the wine menu. When she located the wine he had requested, she lost her breath for a moment and glanced at her father. Senator Breitbart seemed lost in the menu and did not show any recognition that Mark had ordered a thousand dollars of wine.

Once they all ordered, the waiter left the table confident he would be receiving a substantial tip. *Don't recognize this cowboy, but his taste in wine is impeccable.*

"I'm going up to the cabin to take some winter photos, Dad. I'd like to have Mark come with me. You know…In case any kidnappers were to show up," Sarah said without hesitation.

Senator Breitbart blew water out of his nose as he laughed. He used his napkin to remove the drops that ran down his chin. "Yes, by all means. There have been a rash of kidnappings in the Blue Ridge Mountains of late." He chuckled at his own joke.

Mark sat quietly, feeling slightly uncomfortable as the two worked out the arrangements and permission of the photographic trip.

"Mark? Mark Ingram?" Senator Coleman asked as he passed the table. Coleman stood six fee two; dressed in a tuxedo with the bearing of a leader stood beside the table. "My God man, I didn't know you were in Washington now. Why haven't you called me?"

Mark stood up, placed his left hand on Coleman's shoulder and shook his hand vigorously. "I just arrived you ol' jarhead. How've you been?…What are you doing here?"

Senator Breitbart stood up. "Senator Coleman and I serve on some of the same committees…Good to see you, Sam." As he shook Coleman's hand, he glanced at Mark with a newly

24

enhanced interest. *Just who the hell is this guy?* "How do you two know each other?"

"Gunnery Sergeant Ingram served in my company in Iraq and again in Afghanistan. Finest noncom I ever had the privilege of having in my command...Great to see you, son!" Coleman replied. "So, what are you doing here? Last time I heard you were in Colombia...or was it Peru?"

"Possibly either one...So, you're a Senator now? Congratulations! Uh...I'm here actually to see Sarah and her father."

"I knew it! The minute I heard about it, I figured that you were, no doubt, the crazy son-of-a-bitch that pulled their asses...ah...pardon my French, Sarah...Rescued them from the kidnappers...Cold dead hands, I suspect," Coleman said a little too loud and heads began to turn towards the table.

"I'm not at liberty to discuss the details, Sam...Good to see you again," Mark said and seated himself.

"I hope these two appreciate who they are having dinner with." Coleman turned to Sarah. "Mark has nearly as many medals as ol' Chesty himself. He single-handedly held off more than a hundred ragheads..."

"I'll call you before I leave, Sam...If you would excuse us, we have some details to attend to," Mark cut Coleman off. *He always likes to make too big a show.*

Coleman looked around the table, finally realizing he was interrupting. "Of course, I look forward to having a drink with you and hearing of your latest adventures." Coleman reached into his jacket, removed a card and handed it to Mark.

He returned to his table where seven other well-dressed and influential looking men and women were seated watching the interchange. It was clear that Coleman's visit with Mark and the Breitbarts was the center of discussion—as well as a point of interest for many of those dining at other tables close enough to hear.

"Sorry about that," Mark stated as he took Sarah's hand—a point noted by her father. "How long does it take to cook a steak here? I'm starving."

Sarah looked into Mark's eyes. "You certainly have some interesting secrets. Can't wait to hear about serving with old ramrod Coleman."

"Sam's a veteran and a patriot. He's done a great job defending the second amendment lately," Breitbart stated. "We need more like him…"

"Father, no talk of business tonight…Remember?"

HONG KONG
Langham Hotel

Ching Wu stood on the balcony of his suite overlooking the city of Hong Kong and the bay. He lived in the Presidential Suite at the Langham Hotel exclusively when attending to business off the mainland. The 3,320 square foot suite was as large as many homes and expensively appointed, including a spacious dining area for up to eighteen guests with a separate bar and guest bathroom. The adjoining study was fully equipped with the latest electronic business equipment and a rich dark mahogany desk left over from the British colonial period. The suite was serviced by a private elevator, made available by the hotel in appreciation of his leasing the suite year round—a small concession considering the $500,000 a year he paid, not including his generous tips. Additionally, the management and staff turned a blind eye to the coming and going of anyone who entered the suite's elevator, including the stunning young women.

Ching was only five feet six and a rather rotund man of sixty-five years. He was dressed in a white silk short-sleeve shirt, pants and gold satin slippers. He looked the part of a 1940's hoodlum in a Clark Gable or Humphry Bogart movie. His appearance belied the fact that he was actually the world's largest trader in illegal ivory and a significant player in the rhino horn and heroin trade as well.

The door to the elevator opened and a tall Japanese man entered the suite hesitantly. He scanned the room quickly to insure who or what might be awaiting him. His straight black hair was long, reaching to his waist and tied back with a single ribbon of red silk. On his left hand he wore a ornate gold ring with a symbol of a red dragon in the center.

"Join me on the balcony, Hayato," Ching called.

Hayato—Japanese for hawk—crossed the lavish living room toward the balcony, not missing the numerous invaluable Chinese artifacts that decorated the entire suite. He stopped five steps from Ching and bowed.

Ching, without looking back, said, "Come."

Hayato moved beside him and waited quietly.

"Your brother in Kenya is dead," Ching spoke softly. The news struck Hayato like a high speed train. He had suspected something was amiss since the flow of ivory had slowed to a trickle then stopped completely. Ching allowed the news to set in. "The man who murdered him is an American. He has left Kenya and is now in Washington, DC."

"With your permission, I will go and kill him myself," Hayato said with clenched jaw.

"No. As Sun Tzu wrote long ago, 'It is better to let your enemy come to you than follow him onto a battlefield of his choosing'," Ching replied quickly. "I have a better plan."

"I await your orders. But I and I alone must avenge my brother's death," Hayato said firmly.

"And so you shall...Now let us make preparations. I want the flow of ivory to resume immediately."

WASHINGTON, DC
The Jefferson Hotel Lobby

"That went better than I expected," Sarah purred as she and Mark strolled through the lobby.

"If you say so...When's this photo trip going to kick off?"

"Pick you up in the morning. Ten o'clock sharp." She noted the look on his face. "Sorry to disappoint you, but I can't stay here tonight. The stories are already flying around DC about you. Your friend Coleman was sitting at a table of inveterate rumormongers. I can't add to Dad's problems here by staying overnight with the great white hunter," she added with a smile.

"Yeah, I understand. Don't like it, but I do understand Washington…Tomorrow…Ten o'clock sharp it is." He extended his hand.

She took it and they shook longer than was necessary. "Tomorrow. Promise we'll have plenty of privacy at the cabin." She winked. "You'll like it I'm certain. It's a really rustic log cabin surrounded by a national forest."

Mark watched her as she left the hotel and then he entered the elevator to return to his suite. The solo ride up was quick. *There's that high school prom feeling again. Travel half way round the world to find out…tomorrow.*

NAIROBI, KENYA
Mobutto's Office

President Mobutto entered his office at precisely 0900 hours, followed by Rhino. The Nairobi Chief of Police, the Minister Of Defense and the Minister of the KWS were waiting as instructed. Everyone rose to their feet when Mobutto entered and made a slight bow from the waist, a show of respect in Kenya for authority.

Mobutto moved to his desk and sat down. "You may be seated gentleman." As the three men took their seats, he spoke in a direct manner, "Yesterday, Mr. Fabian brought me up to speed on the circumstances of my wife's accident. I'll not bore you with the details. The importance of his report is in the folder you are about to receive. It will not leave this room nor will any of the information within the report be discussed outside this meeting."

As Mobutto was talking, Lutto entered the room and handed each of the men a red folder and left the room. The men opened and began reading the sensitive information as he continued his speech. "Mark Ingram is no longer employed as the leader of the KWS Quick Reaction Force. When Rheinhart locates a suitable replacement, he too will be leaving Kenya. I am certain you will understand why when you have finished the report before you." Mobutto paused and touched the intercom button his phone. "Lutto."

Practically before he had finished calling, she entered the office with a silver tray and coffee service set. She appeared to have been reading his mind, having served him for years even before his election to the office of President. She placed the service tray on a small table to the right of his desk and poured a cup of coffee into a fine china blue cup, added the two lumps of sugar and cream. She looked to Rhino, who shook a brief *No thank you,* and then departed the room without a word. The implication of not offering coffee to the three other important men in the room was not lost on them.

Ten minutes passed as the men read the information contained in the folders. Rhino stood at parade rest near the door, ever watchful of the President.

The Chief of Police, a large stocky man weighing well over 250 pounds, was the first to speak, "I will immediately begin a full-scale investigation…"

Mobutto cut him off without turning to face him, "No, you will not." Allowing the statement to settle on the room for its full effect, Mobutto then turned toward the men sitting in front of his desk. "The matter is closed. What you *will* do is prepare a complete list of your staff, including all their banking details concerning them and any member of their families. I want it on my desk within forty-eight hours."

"Yes, Mr. President," the Chief of Police responded submissively. He could tell that Mobutto was in a dark mood and intended not to cause any further difficulties for himself.

"In addition, I want the same reported for all ranking members of the Department of Defense and the Kenyan Wildlife Service. Rheinhart will be responsible for a thorough review of each report so I suggest you be accurate and concise."

All of the three quickly replied, "Yes, Mr. President."

"You may go now, but leave the reports on my desk," Mobutto said in a quiet, yet authoritative tone dismissing the three men. The men rose, bowed and left the room without hesitation. None wanted any further discomfort to be directed their way.

Once the men had departed, Mobutto turned to Rhino. "Have a seat. Would you like some coffee now?"

Rhino moved to the coffee service and poured himself a cup of black coffee and then sat across from him.

"Review each of the reports. To expedite matters use a highlighter to indicate any discrepancies rather than write a report. Before you are relieved of duty, I want to eliminate anyone and everyone suspected of negligence or misdoing."

"Yes, sir," Rhino replied. "There will be a real shit storm once this gets out. May I suggest that I stay on for sixty to ninety days after a suitable replacement for myself is in place…act as transitional consultant slash personal body guard 'til the matter is resolved."

"Bloody good idea. I'll have Lutto prepare a contract to reflect this new position and duties for you. Any other thoughts?"

"This would be a good time to reconsider my suggestion concerning a team of four to six men to serve as personal twenty-four-seven body guards, sir. The men selected from your military forces that are currently working as the Presidential security team are all good men. I selected and trained them myself. What I suspect is coming may require another level of skill sets, Mr. President."

"I'd be most pleased if you could find men like Mark Ingram...Is that possible?"

Rhino smiled. "No...Zorro's one of a kind, Mr. President. But I can recruit some operatives I know he would approve of. Until my replacement is on board and the new close security team is functional...I want two men from the existing security force with you at all times. Eat, sleep, shower...every minute. They will rotate on eight to ten hour shifts to keep anyone from establishing a pattern."

Rhino left the President's office and walked to Lutto's desk. Two men of the Presidential Security Force stood on either side of the door inside her office, wearing beige suits, white dress shirts and dark blue ties bearing the Presidential seal. Each carried a H&K MP5KA1—a pistol variant of the ubiquitous submachine gun, firing the standard 9x19mm round, with no protruding buttstock—slung over their right shoulders underneath their jackets. A small bulge under their left arm indicating a pistol as well in a shoulder holster.

Rhino nodded at the two men then turned to her, "No one enters your office without being searched. No one enters the President's office without my knowledge. You will call me every time a new visitor arrives. Is that clear?"

Lutto stood up from her desk. "Completely. May I show you something?" She pulled out the top right hand drawer of her desk. Laying on a piece of red cloth was a Walther PPK and a spare magazine. "Will this be a problem?"

Rhino smiled. "You're familiar and well trained with the pistol?"

"Two to the chest. One to the head," she replied. Her dark eyes burned with a fire Rhino had not seen before. The matter of factness of her statement carried well her intentions. She would die before harm befell her President.

Rhino laughed at her comment as he turned to the two security guards. "No one is to be alone with the President." *If anyone gets past these two I doubt they will get past her.*

Both men responded in unison, "Yes, sir!"

VIRGINIA, USA
Interstate Highway I-66

Mark felt a sense of relief once he and Sarah had left the confines of Washington, and were traveling west toward the Blue Ridge mountains, noted for their bluish color when seen from a distance. Trees put the *blue* in Blue Ridge, from the isoprene released into the atmosphere, thereby contributing to the characteristic haze on the mountains and their distinctive color. The rat race of DC seemed to fade significantly with each passing mile.

Mark insisted on renting a GMC four wheel drive SUV rather than travel in her BMW. Winter driving in a small car was not high on his list of ways to encounter road hazards plus the SUV allowed him to carry and conceal his weapons. A quick stop at a REI outdoor sports store afforded Mark the necessary attire since none of the clothing he brought from Kenya was adequate for winter conditions.

Sarah's voice rose as she excitedly talked about her new camera. She was explaining all the features when a different thought hit her. "Oh! You should see all the great shots I got in Kenya, before…"

"I saw your other Nikon, all shot to hell…I assumed…"

"No!" She blushed a little. "See, when we were driving like mad…trying to get away from those poachers…"

"About the time you called me and I was out of cell phone range?"

"I was just so scared," she said as she couldn't help but relive the terror from the previous month. "Anyway, I thought about all those other great animal shots on that thirty-two gig memory card…A week's work all on one little postage stamp…"

"And you had the presence of mind to yank the card out and stash it? Wow…now I'm really impressed," he said with a big grin. "But, I detected a tiny little pink in your face when you started to tell me about it.…or was I imagining that?"

She smiled somewhat sheepishly and pulled both hands up to cover her cheeks, which were once again turning red. Sarah shot him a sideways glance. "Don't miss a thing do you?"

He shook his head. "Try not to…not and stay alive in my line of work."

"Promise you won't tell anybody else? Only my Dad and I know this secret."

"Cross my heart, " Mark said as he took one hand off the wheel and made a symbolic X over his chest.

"Okay, so…uh, I got the little memory card out of my camera and I didn't know where to put it…It's so small and all."

"Yeah."

"I kinda jammed it down in my panties and hoped for the best…I didn't know if they were gonna rape or kill me…They already had shot our driver…"

The look on Mark's face hardened at the memory of the merciless butchers. Then he realized his frown might be misinterprcted. "That's some really fine thinkin' under pressure. Those bastards would have killed you had they found out you had the evidence of their rhino poaching hidden on you…They shot the camera and assumed they destroyed the evidence." He smiled broadly. *My kinda girl.*

"I didn't want you to think I was…I don't know…lewd or crude or anything when you found out where I hid the flash card…I still plan to publish a book about the trip."

Mark shot her a look.

"Withholding certain sensitive information about the Black Eagle Force and you in the rescue...I know. Dad explained all that to me."

Mark nodded. "Give Robert and the Kenyan Wildlife Service the credit...Really looking forward to seeing those shots, by the way."

The time past quickly as she chattered on about the photographs she wanted to take and the beauty of the passing landscape. The tension of being alone, but not yet at their secluded destination, grew with each passing mile. He turned onto a small road that she indicated would lead to the cabin.

Thirty yards after the turn off, a small one-lane bridge crossed a mountain stream. The crystal clear water, bordered by two feet of snow, raced down the hill. A stone fence with a ornate metal gate sat just past the bridge. Mark eased the SUV to a stop while he studied the forest covered in its winter glory. He lowered his window and sighed as he gathered in the sound of the brook below and the silence of the forest all around them.

Sarah searched through her bag and retrieved a electronic gate opener. "Hope this is still working. We had some trouble with it last winter." She pressed the button and the gate opened without hesitation. "Awesome!"

Mark noted the strategic placement of the gate positioned at the end of the bridge and the steep banks of the stream blocking any other entrance other than this one. He recognized the security camera to the left of the gate and another one twenty-five yards further up the road just before it made a right hand turn into the forest. *If those two are working as well, we should have plenty of visitor warning. Or, someone now knows we have arrived.* He put the SUV in full time 4-wheel drive before moving on.

"See how beautiful it is?...Told you it was remote. I absolutely love it up here...We use to come up here every summer." She sounded almost like a small child again.

"It's nice. Hope the water's on and not frozen...or busted pipes flooding the whole place."

"Oh, no way...John comes up three to four times a week to check everything out for Dad. I called him this morning before we left to let him know we were coming. He promised to get by and make things ready...You know, turn up the hot water heater, bring some firewood inside, stock the frige and check the generator."

The road wound through the forest, crossing the stream twice on one-lane bridges before the cabin appeared. *Cabin? Holy Crap! This place is a mansion.* The two story, rustic log home with three car garage stood on a small knoll just above the stream with a clear field of view for a hundred yards in all directions.

Mark drove into the first stall of the garage. They entered through a door into a hallway with a stocked pantry on the left and the laundry room on the right and finally stepped into the designer kitchen—he recalled seeing kitchens in magazines like it. *Probably cost more than any house I've ever owned.* Marble counter tops, stainless steel appliances, Viking professional stove, exposed rustic beams overhead and a wagon wheel suspended over the butcher block counter with assorted copper and cast iron pots and pans attached.

She set down her luggage and leaped into his arms. Without further ado, she kissed him long and passionately. "See, told you we'd have all the privacy we wanted up here."

He carried her into the large living area and laid her down on one of the leather couches in front of the fire place. They stayed in each others arms until the sun was setting. The long awaited moment was theirs and they relished it slowly, exploring one another's body tenderly as they disrobed. Sarah was troubled by the first scars she discovered on his upper torso, caressing each one before moving on to the next. The latest one under his left armpit had the stitches removed just days before.

"Oh, sweet baby! Does it still hurt?"

"Not anymore."

By the time they had removed all but her lingerie, she was too excited to notice the scars on his buttocks and thighs.

Mark was the first to rise. "I'm going to start a fire. Mind getting us some wine?"

"Love to. Though we don't have anything like the kind you ordered last night…Hope that's okay?" she said with a sigh.

"As long as it's red, not sweet and you come with it, I'll be fine."

Mark noticed there wasn't any kindling, but rather a gas valve on the lower right hand side of the fireplace. He placed several logs on the grate, turned on the gas and used a extended butane candle lighter to start the flame. By the time Sarah returned with the wine and glasses, he had built a fledgling fire and was sitting on the leather couch again.

She walked in front of him and had put on a silk robe. Her slender athletic body silhouetted by the fire light.

"I know it's corny but I wanted to change into something more comfortable," she said with a twinkle in her eye. "You like?"

Mark, lost in the beauty of her image spoke softly as he pulled her down to him. "Yeah. I like."

***

CHAPTER THREE

HONG KONG
Chek Lap Kok Airport

A black Mercedes S550 limousine pulled up next to a jade green Legacy 650 private jet manufactured and customized expressly for Ching Wu. The jet, powered by 2 Rolls-Royce AE 3007/A1P turbofans, featured extended range via extra fuel tanks in the tail behind the baggage compartment and forward of the wing. It was certified to 41,000 feet, with a maximum speed of 450 kts and, with the modifications to Ching's specifications, could carry twelve passengers plus the pilot, copilot and flight attendant.

The thirty-five million dollar price tag was pocket change for Ching. What mattered to him was it cost more than the internationally famous actor Jackie Chan's personal Legacy 650 jet given to him by the manufacturer in return for acting as their spokesperson.

Four men stood at points surrounding the jet and limousine keeping watchful eyes on anything and everyone around them. Even the maintenance and fueling crew was subject to search. Another indication of Ching Wu's influence in Hong Kong; each man openly carried a H&K MP5SD6, a variation of the venerable MP5 with a collapsing stock, and a internal suppresser. Ching and Hayato sat in the comfort of the Mercedes limousine as the sun rose, discussing the final details of Ching's plan to resume the flow of elephant ivory and rhino horn from Africa.

Ching spoke quietly, "Follow my instructions implicitly Hayato."

"Yes, Mr. Wu. It will be as you desire…What of the American?"

"I have already set the wheels in motion. By the time you arrive, I will have further details." His expressionless features remained stolid as a marble statue.

A black Lincoln stretch limousine approached the private jet. The armed guards signaled it to halt. Four Japanese men and two women exited the vehicle and were searched. They then removed their luggage and bags from the limo and were escorted onto the plane.

"You are certain six is all you need?" Wu queried.

"They are the best I have. I'm certain they are more than enough for the job. The American and his South African friend will be dealt with swiftly."

"Call me when you arrive in Nairobi. I want daily updates on your progress. How is your family?"

Hayato bowed his head slightly as he replied, "Fine. Everyone is well."

"Time to go. I will check on your family while you are gone," Ching said as he touched a button on a console next to his seat.

The security guard sitting with the driver exited the vehicle and opened a door on the side of the parked jet. Hayato stepped out, walked to and boarded as Wu's Mercedes slowly drove off. Something in the final words of Ching Wu hung in the back of Hayato's mind as he moved to his seat. In the ten years he had worked for the Chinese kingpin, the man had never once asked about his family.

KENYA KWS QRF HEADQUARTERS

Robert Muwanja, Mark's number one KWS Ranger and compatriot in the rescue of Senator and Sarah Breitbart had been promoted to Operations Supervisor of the Quick Reaction Force, *QRF*. He assigned and dispatched three of his Ranger Units to locations in question as to recent poaching, and then sat back in his chair and viewed a map of Kenya with the National Parks and protected wildlife zones all outlined in orange. The areas most active with recent poaching events were tagged with small red flags. The country was quiet compared to the days when Mark Ingram first arrived. A small smile came to Robert's lips. *Hell had no fury like that Texan. Gone but two weeks and already I miss you too much, Bossman.*

A clap of thunder broke the moment of reflection—Robert moved to the window and saw a summer storm rolling in from the east. The dark blue clouds highlighted by white peaks and bolts of lightening approached in a fierce line that covered the horizon. Stepping out onto the covered wooden porch, he felt the slight chill of the cold air that raced ahead of the storm picking up dust and debris in its path. As the first drops of moisture began to splatter on the dusty ground and the metal roofs of the KWS compound a strange sense of uneasiness rushed over him.

Seeing several of the Rangers rushing to the horses in the corrals, Muwanja shook off the sensation and ran across the parade ground to join them. *Mark would skin us all if we did not get the horses safe.*

NAIROBI

Rhino reviewed the security tapes of the President's mansion and his office complex before viewing those of his own residence. There was a small glitch in the tape for his residence that he wrote off to the constant rolling brownouts.

He put on his suit jacket and opened the door to a small courtyard leading to the garage where he kept his prized Jaguar parked. It was still early and the oppressive humid heat was bearable. In another couple of hours Rhino's shirt and jacket would be soaked in sweat. He looked up at the sky and made note of the thick white clouds that floated lazily across the sky.

He removed a small black remote from his left front pocket and pressed the button to open the garage door, and then triggered another to start his Jag. As the vehicle's engine roared to life and began the sweet purring sound Rhino loved, he remembered a folder left on the entry table. He turned and made it to the front door when the Jaguar exploded violently. The explosion knocked him forward into the closed door and then to the ground.

He instinctively rolled behind a large cement urn filled with flowers and drew his Sig P220 from the shoulder holster under his left arm. A quick look around the base of the urn revealed the Jaguar and garage were engulfed in flames and a thick column of black smoke rose into the air. *Shit's in the fan now. Thank ya God for the remote start.* Rhino retrieved his cell phone and made a call.

"President Mobutto's office," the secretary answered.

"Lutto, Rhino here. Is the President in his office?"

"Yes he is. Would you like to speak to him?"

"First, either one of the security men stationed in your office?" Rhino overheard Lutto call one of the security team to the phone.

"Sergeant Onyango here, sir."

"Get the President to the safe room. Do it now!"

"Yes, sir!" He motioned to his partner to secure the door, then turned and entered the President's office without knocking.

Lutto came back on the phone. "What's happening? Your man just rushed into the President's office…"

"No time to explain…Go with the President. Take your cell phone and the pistol…Now!" The phone connection went dead practically before he could finish.

Rhino made another call, this time to the barracks where the rest of the President's security force lived. "I want every swinging fok to the President's safe room ten minutes ago! This is no drill," he said before replacing his cell phone in the carrier on his belt and took another quick look around the base of the protective urn.

Seeing no movement, he eased up to a kneeling position with his Sig at the ready, scanned the courtyard, and then the rooftops all around before moving quickly inside his residence. *Bloody hell! They are making a move!* Inside, he rapidly gathered together the necessary additional weapons he needed from his safe room before going out the back door to the small storage shed next to the cinderblock fence—constructed with broken glass shards embedded in its cement cap and further topped with concertina wire—that enclosed the back yard. He opened the double doors, entered and pulled the protective canvas tarp off Mark's 2008 dark green Harley-Davidson Softail Custom. *Forgive me, bro. I know you prize this metal beast nearly as much as a good horse. But it's all I got.*

He lifted the cover to the sissy seat, revealing the hidden compartment, and quickly stashed an ammo bag filled with 200 rounds of .45 ammo for his Sig P220 as well as 500 rounds of standard 9mm for the H&K MP5KA1 he carried under his jacket. *As Zorro always says...No such thing as too much.* Once the rounds were secured, he started the Harley, allowing it to warm up while he opened the small gate that lead into the alley.

After scanning both directions, as well as all the rooftops he returned to the bike, mounted and drove off slowly until he reached a main street then opened the throttle and raced to the President's office. Twice, when traffic hindered his progress, he fired a short burst skyward with his H&K to help clear the way.

When he pulled into the parking lot, he rode the Harley all the way up the steps to the surprise and no small consternation of the two Kenyan Army and two security guards stationed on either side of the large ornate teak doors that lead inside the Presidential Palace. The Army soldiers responded slowly and by the time they had their rifles at the ready Rhino had shut the Harley off and was walking past them.

"If anything happens to this bike before I return I'll personally shoot you," he said to the two soldiers as he approached the doors. Looking directly at the guards he barked, "Anyone enters through these doors before I come back, I'll skin your mompie asses." With that, he disappeared inside leaving the men staring at each other in disbelief.

MOUNTAIN CABIN
Blue Ridge Mountains

Mark and Sarah lay nude on the king-size four-poster bed watching the fire in the bedroom's private fireplace. Only the warm glow of the firelight lit the room. The panorama out the second story French balcony doors gave a perfect view of the snow falling outside.

"I'm going to the ladies room," Sarah said with a sigh of contentment. She picked up her silk robe from a chair.

Mark watched her, then rolled over to the hand-carved cherry bedside table and retrieved his cell phone. He dialed, then waited as the call connected. A familiar voice answered, "Goeie dag! Leave a message. If it means buck, I'll return your call. If not go voertsek. Ya jukka"

A smile crossed his face. *Always about the money.* When he heard the appropriate tone, he left his message. "Rhino…Zorro. Call me. Picked up some leads in BA. Funding in several banks." Mark hung up and was placing the cell phone back on the bedside table when Sarah returned.

"Business or pleasure?"

"Just checking up on Rhino. Haven't talked to him since I left Kenya.…Now about pleasure?"

She threw the robe off and leapt back onto the bed, landing on top of him. "You are insatiable, Mark Ingram." She kissed him long and passionately. "I like that," she cooed as he rolled over on top of her, returning her kiss with equal abandon.

WASHINGTON, DC
Senator Breitbart Office

Senator Breitbart sat at his desk, surrounded by framed photographs of himself and former presidents, dignitaries, professional athletes and family, reading a thick congressional document. He occasionally glanced up at one of the news stories on FOX. His attention become riveted when the anchor announced news in Kenya.

"We have breaking news from our offices in Kenya. President Mobutto has issued a Presidential State of Emergency. Several of his leading political allies have been assassinated. Information at this time indicates there may have been an attempt on President Mobutto as well. We will continue to bring you the latest reports as this story unfolds."

Breitbart immediately called his secretary on the intercom, "Elouise, come in here, please."

The attractive forty year old brunette came in. She was attired in dark blue pin stripe skirt and white long sleeve blouse appropriate for her position as a senior Senator's personal secretary. "Yessir," she said with a thick southern Georgia accent.

"Get me Sarah on the line immediately. She's at the cabin...Then get me Senator Coleman."

"Yessir." She could tell by the tone of her boss' voice that something was amiss.

Once she had departed, he began surfing the main stream news channels for further details about the incidents in Kenya. He discovered no one was carrying the story but FOX. *Color me not surprised.*

Elouise came over the intercom, "No answer at the cabin or her mobile. I left a message on both phones to call you back as soon as she can. Ahm fixin' to call Senata Coleman."

"All right...After you have him on the line I want you to keep calling Sarah until you reach her. Tell her I need to speak with her immediately...Then get me the Secretary of the Navy."

"Can do, sir." She released the intercom button, thinking her boss sounded even more anxious than he had on his first call.

Breitbart returned to FOX news just in time to see scenes of rioting in Kenya. Hundreds, if not thousands, of black men, women and children were caught in up the chaos of tribal anarchy. Bloody machetes were raised in the air by rampaging crowds—screaming women, running or attempting to protect themselves and their children from the slaughter. The burning vehicles and buildings caused him to shake his head in disbelief.

The transmissions showed shaky erratic images as camera crews rapidly retreated from the surging waves of angry mobs. Foreigners at the airport fought for seats on departing flights to anywhere outside of Kenya. The same frenetic scenes told the story of outsiders at the port of Mombassa clamoring to get on board any vessel that would get them clear of the chaos. Armed Kenyan military units guarded the airport, the port docks and government property.

"Sir, Senata Coleman on line two."

"Sam, thanks for taking my call. Have you seen the news in Kenya?"

"No. I've been in budget hearing committee since 0700. Egg-sucking sons-a-bitches want to cut some more military expenditures…What's going on?"

"I suggest you turn FOX news on right away. Then call me back."

The line went dead. Elouise came back on the intercom. "I have Sarah on line three."

"Baby, have you and Mark seen the news since you arrived at the cabin?"

"No, Daddy. We've been pretty busy…uh, taking photos," she replied as she lay on Mark's chest, lost in the warm glow of contentment, feeling his chest rise and fall and the beating of his heart.

"Check out FOX news, then call me back. I'm up to my ass in alligators… "

"Sir, I have SecNav on one," Elouise interrupted.

Breitbart hung up on Sarah without saying good-bye. "Admiral what's going on in Kenya? Where are our closest ships?"

Admiral Linedecker replied, "Senator, our intelligence is pretty sketchy at present, but it appears to be a real bloodbath over there. I've ordered one of our destroyers off the coast of India to get there flank speed to assist evacuating all American personnel and their families."

"Keep me in the loop, Admiral. I have some good friends there and let me know what I can do to support your efforts."

"Consider it done, Senator."

Breitbart returned to watching the newscast. *Shit! Sarah's not going to like this turn of events.*

KENYA
President's Mansion

A Kenyan Army Harbin Z-9 helicopter landed on the helo pad within the compound. Soldiers were already everywhere in full combat gear—hastily constructing sandbag emplacements, mounting .50 caliber machine guns—five mortar teams labored to set up positions on the grounds and the roof of the buildings. Four Puma APC 4X4s were positioned at strategic points and a trio of Mi-28 Hines attack helicopters circled the 10 foot walled compound providing support from above.

Rhino and Mobutto, followed by Lutto and a personal servant with two dogs in tow, exited the Presidential mansion and moved rapidly toward the helicopter waiting on the helo pad. Four of the President's security guard unit flanked them, weapons at the ready.

Rhino shouted above the noise, "Once we get ya to the safety of your summer retreat we can sort all this out, Mr. President. But first, we have to get ya out of here!"

"I understand your concerns. Surely there is room for my two dogs."

"I'll make sure they're on the next chopper. No dog left behind, sir." He attempted to reassure Mobutto with a little humor.

"All right then. I trust you to insure their safety. If my deceased wife were here I'd insist on Abasi and Adimu being evacuated before her." Mobutto laughed.

Rhino turned to the four members of the security force. "I want you two on this chopper...Tha rest on the next one out...Muzzle tha dogs and get them on board and secured. Show up without the President's dogs...shoot you myself! Understood?"

The two security men smiled and nodded as they shouted, "Yes, sir, Mr. Fabian. We be sure to bring the dogs."

As the helicopter began to lift off, one of the Kenyan soldiers building sandbag emplacements began running toward it with a grenade screaming, "Death to all Kikuyu!"

Rhino's hand snaked under his jacket and flashed back out with the Sig. The 185 grain hollowpoints did their job well—the first clipped the soldier's aorta and the second lifted the top of his skull and helmet sending it tumbling across the well trimmed lawn. His body crumpled forward, the limp right hand released the grenade.

Rhino grabbed the closest security man and tossed him to the ground like a discarded shirt as he bellowed his warning, "Grenade!" The other security operative dove for the turf as Rhino threw himself on top of the first. A second later, the grenade detonated, shredding the lifeless body of the attacking soldier.

Rheinhart looked up at the departing helo and got a thumbs-up signal from the pilot. He checked himself for injuries and then scrambled to his feet, cleared the area, holstered his weapon and then reached down and helped both of the still prone security men to stand.

"Mr. Fabian...you saved my life!" he said breathlessly.

"Day ain't over yet," he said as he turned back toward the Presidential palace. *This tribal crap is gonna get outta hand.*

MOUNTAIN CABIN
Blue Ridge Mountains

Sarah and Mark sat in the huge living room watching the Kenyan news events unfolding. She held his arm tightly. "You'll be leaving?"

"I have to...Rhino's my friend. I don't know what I can do to help...but I have to go." The horrific images were nothing new to him, but the fact that his best friend was there and certain to be in grave danger protecting the President caused his stomach to churn.

"The Kenyan military…" she started to say.

"Keystone Cops meet Laural and Hardy…Some good men there, but the jabber walkies at the top are spineless politicians…Sure to go with whoever appears to be winning."

She turned to him. "When?"

"Now."

Sarah got up and ran to the bedroom, tears streaming down her face.

He shook his head. *Dammit! Broke an iron clad rule. Never get involved.* Rising to his feet, he turned off the television and followed her into the bedroom.

NAIROBI
Mukuru-Kwa-Reuben Slum

Members of the Luhya tribe and their arch enemies the Kikuyu rampaged through the shanty town's narrow and twisted streets. Not much more than donkey cart tracks—normally dry, hard-packed earth or, in the rainy season, rain soaked mud that sucked the traveler's sandals off their feet—the perilous passageways now ran red with blood, both human and animal mingled together as the warring tribes indiscriminately slaughtered every living thing in their path.

Centuries of the primordial conflict between the Luhya and Kikuyu created a underlying seething hate that needed little to catch flame and bring on a massacre of either tribe. The bodies of men, women, children, dogs, chickens and donkeys lay strewn about like so much trash—mingled together in grotesque frozen poses of anguished death. Some lay sprawling with heads and limbs hacked off, others with their heads split open from crown to collar bone. Babies cried in pain, as they sat next to their dead parents. Mutilated males cried out, slowly bleeding to death from the crude removal of their genitalia. Nearby, females screamed from the unbearable pain of filthy sticks of smoldering firewood having been savagely inserted in their vaginas. Neither tribe spared anyone.

Older children suffered another atrocity before being murdered—male and female alike were gang-raped—sometimes for hours, sometimes for days—if the authorities did not intervene rapidly enough. Female victims as young as four years old to gray-haired women of eighty were passed around like a bottle of beer from one barbarian to another until they died. Even then, the rapes did not always end 'til their body grew cold and stiff from rigor-mortise.

Thick clouds of black acrid smoke from burning tires, shacks and piles of bodies, rose in the sky over Nairobi and wafted through the slum, burning the eyes and lungs of those who still lived. So dense was the smoke, it carried down wind of the Mukuru-Kwa slum, until it blocked out the sun.

Occasionally a marauding band from each tribe encountered each other, resulting in shirtless machete-welding black males hacking and chopping one another to death. Those incredibly violent encounters ended only when one side or the other was eliminated or fled in panic.

News teams dared not venture within the confines of the slum. The blood lust of the combatants was simply too high to attempt recording the event. Only two local news helicopters dared to fly above the horrible bloodletting, sending shocking images of the devastation back to their newsrooms to be aired on the six o'clock broadcast.

WASHINGTON, DC
Senator Breitbart's Brownstone

"I've made several calls to get you on a flight as soon as possible. But it seems very few flights are going into Kenya at present," Breitbert said.

"You have high level connections, don't you? Call them," Mark replied.

"I do...but I'm not sure this is within their scope of..."

"Call them...I need a flight and I need it now!"

Sarah sat listening nearly in tears. "Father...Mark's going to try and save his friend. Please make a call." She offered a shaky smile then left the room quickly to hide her tears.

"All right," he relented. "I'll call in the morning. It is after midnight."

"Now, Senator. Please...Every minute I'm not there is another minute lost," Mark said in a tone that Breitbart was unaccustomed to.

The bone-weary politician picked up his cell phone and dialed the number of Secretary of Defense Baker. After several moments, a groggy man answered. "Who the hell is this?"

"Baker. Breitbart. I need to call in a favor."

"You know what time it is? This had better be damned important," Baker said, still half asleep.

"I need a flight from Washington to Nairobi as soon as possible. Can you help?"

"Kenya's a blood bath right now. Why the hell would you want to go back there?"

Breitbart gazed steadily at Mark. "The man who rescued Sarah and I from the kidnappers in Kenya is sitting in my study. He needs to get back to Kenya as soon as possible."

"Let me make a few calls. This is highly irregular Andy. If I get this done, you owe me one…Maybe two."

"I understand…Contact me as soon as you know anything."

"If he can't get 'er done maybe those boys in the Black Eagle Force could," Mark said as he watched the news from Kenya on the BBC. He dialed his cell.

On the second ring a voice answered, "Tom Tallman, Black Eagle Force. How may I direct your call?"

"Get me Widowmaker, please. Tell him Zorro's on the line."

"Zorro? One minute," Tallman said with a bit of curiosity.

Five minutes passed, but finally, a familiar voice came on the line. "You Leatherneck dipwad. Have you reached a decision on the offer to join Black Eagle Force? The consensus all the way up the ladder to Dare Phillips, is you'd be a good fit…"

"Not yet. You heard about the shit storm in Kenya?"

"Yeah. Damn shame. We don't have any orders as yet…What's up?"

56

"I need a ride…Yesterday. My friend Rhino is sure to be up to his ass in machetes about right now."

"I don't know, man…Let me run this by the boss. What's a number I can reach you?"

"Seems every body has to run it by some body else," he said dejectedly to Breitbart.

The Senator dialed another number. "Sometimes you just have to take the bull by the horns."

"Andy, how are you? How's Sarah?" President Annette Henry Thompson-Hermann asked.

"Sarah's fine. Thanks for asking. Madame President, I'll be brief. You remember us telling you about the man who tracked our kidnappers down in Kenya, Mark Ingram?"

"Yes, I do. Why?"

"He's sitting here with me right now. It goes without saying Sarah and I owe him our lives."

"This *country* owes him, Andy. What are you leading up to?"

"I've always loved your straight-to-the-point attitude Annette. Mark needs an emergency flight back to Kenya. He needs it now. Any thoughts?"

"In what capacity would he be going to Kenya?"

"His best friend is head of security for President Mobutto. Since Mark is no longer a member of the Marine Corps he would be going in as…as a tourist, so to speak."

She laughed. "A tourist? Andy, you have a wicked sense of humor. I read his jacket. Call you back in a half hour…Tell Mark to pack his bags."

Ingram sat listening anxiously to Breitbart's side of the conversation. *The President...of the freakin' United States. Hell of a phone call. If this doesn't do it, I'm like, totally screwed.*

"Said she'll call back in a half hour. She also said to pack your bags...Now go up there and console my daughter."

***

CHAPTER FOUR

JOMO KENYATTA INTERNATIONAL AIRPORT
Nairobi, Kenya
Thursday

Wu's Legacy 650 rolled down runway 06/24, the single runway used for all landings and take offs, commonly referred to as 06. Rather than proceed to the new passenger terminal building, it taxied to the old one used for air freight cargo and a Kenya Air Force training facility. There was little air traffic as most commercial airlines had discontinued flights until the unrest settled down.

The Legacy taxied to a waiting black limousine flanked by two Kenyan Army Puma 26-15 4x4 Armored Personnel Carriers. The newly acquired APCs cost roughly $300,000 each and could transport a crew of 10, including the driver, the commander plus eight Kenyan Special Forces members. Their presence spoke volumes on how deep Ching Wu's influence went in Kenya and demonstrated the value of the resources awaiting Hayato and his team's arrival.

Sixteen Special Forces members were positioned around the Pumas and the limousine creating a security perimeter. The two commanders stood talking with the limo driver and his body guard as the jet taxied to a halt and the twin engines shut down.

Hayato deplaned first, practically before the ramp touched the ground followed by his team of six Yakuza assassins. Each member of the team had proven themselves many times and totaled over a hundred elimination's amongst them.

Hayato spoke briefly with the commanders, "It is imperative that we reach my brother's estate as soon as possible. I will brook no delays."

The trio of vehicles departed immediately after the bags and luggage had been loaded into the limousine. A Puma led and trailed the long black limo as they proceeded on Airport South Road and to the Mombasa Highway. Hayato and his team rode in silence, each man and woman making a final check of their weapons and occasionally looking at the chaos on either side of the highway. There was no haste or sense of urgency in their work—just a feeling of highly trained, well-tuned warriors preparing for action.

Chikako—Japanese for shrewd or clever—was a striking female who could easily grace the cover of any fashion magazine in Asia or the western world; broke the silence. "We will need more ammo."

The team chuckled at her comment—all except Hayato. He was fixed on the thoughts of revenge he would extract on the American once he had him in his grasp. *First the ivory and horn. Then I will avenge my brother's death. I should never have let you stay in Kenya, Akihiko. I failed you.*

A series of short bursts from the machine guns on the ACPs behind and in front of the limo broke his train of thought. The rampaging mob had come too close and the nervous gunners fired over the heads of the crowd to move them back.

MOBUTTO'S SUMMER HOME
Mt. Kenya

Rhino surveyed the area around the President's estate—located in the MacKinder Valley, just above the forest. It was semiarid alpine terrain and what little moisture there was, could be found only in the deep valley streams and rivers that cut through the mountains. Accompanying him on a previous unannounced inspection of the property, Mark had commented the flora reminded him of the high desert southwest in New Mexico and Arizona.

While the helicopter circled—starting three miles out from the compound—he scanned every tree, lobelia telekii plant, rock and clumps of grass looking for anything out of the ordinary. A herd of twenty or so rock hyrax scurried for cover when they detected the sound of the aircraft. The squat, heavily built adults and plump young were surprisingly swift. Reaching a length of twenty inches and weighing around eight pounds the rock hyrax a distant relative of elephants—even sporting a pair of long, pointed tusk-like upper incisors—was tasty fare if one knew how to properly prepare and cook them. Their thick light grayish brown fur was perfect camouflage, but the movement of the herd caught Rhino's eye through his twelve power binoculars.

Having satisfied himself the perimeter was clear of present danger, he signaled the pilot to take the chopper in for landing. As they made the final approach, Rhino turned his full attention to the dozen or so small houses, sheds and corrals outside the walls. *The staff homes look deserted. Lieutenant Kamau must have brought them inside the compound.* He spoke over the interphone, "Set her down."

The skilled pilot landed the chopper on the helo pad at the west end of the compound, just outside the four foot inner fence surrounding the swimming pool, tennis court and residence.

"Radio the President's chopper to stand by until we sweep the facility," instructed Rhino.

"Yes, sir."

Lt. Kamau, Kenyan for silent warrior, came out of the interior wall gate and headed straight for the helo pad. He ducked under the blades as they spooled down.

Rhino opened the side hatch and stepped out. "Status?"

"Yes, sir. Normally there would be a full compliment of twenty-five men, but five have not yet returned from their Christmas and New Year leave. That would give us a total of twenty-three including yourself and the two men you brought with you."

"There are two more choppers enroute. Another two men from his personal security team with the President are on board." Rhino stuck his head back inside the chopper. "Clear Falcon One to land."

"Ngie! Gupta! Get the President and Lutto inside," Rhino yelled over the noise of the gun ship. He then motioned to the pilot to refuel and depart.

Both crew members responded with a thumbs-up. They moved quickly to a small shed and an elevated 1,000 gallon fuel tank on a six foot metal stand next to the landing pad and made ready to refuel the chopper.

Lt. Kamau, wore his best tailored uniform, perfectly pressed and creased to meet the President. Only five foot nine and weighing 160 pounds, he did not look like the hero of the Somali border wars. News reports of his military exploits led many to expect a bigger man when first meeting him. Kamau, accompanied by two of the Kenyan Army Special Forces troops who stood duty year round at the estate, met Mobutto, Lutto and the two security guards at the gate.

"Mr. President!" Kamau said as he delivered a crisp hand salute. "All is made ready for you. Your staff is inside awaiting your instructions."

Mobutto returned the salute as he passed by Kamau. "I'll address them immediately...Prepare for the worst."

"Yes, Mr. President," Kamau replied before joining Rhino in the process of making an inspection of the exterior compound wall.

The entire facility was surrounded by a five foot native rock wall covered with a mixture of cement and sand for esthetic purposes. Every twelve feet, a two foot wide pillar—constructed of the same materials as the wall—rose another four feet with a wrought iron fence attached between the pillars. Atop each iron rod was a spike that resembled a Massi spear head. At each of the four corners, a twelve-by-twelve tower standing eight feet taller than the fence marked the boundaries of each section of the fortress-like enclosure.

Guard stations sited on top of the towers were open on all sides and covered with a sturdy pitched roof crowned with red tiles. The main entrance was doubled-gated with another pair of guard towers on each side. The outer was wrought iron and matched the sections along the fence. The inner was one inch steel covered with wood for esthetics. Both gates were electronically controlled and rode on sizable solid rubber wheels.

Lt. Kamau began to give a duty list of the troops under his command. "Mr. Fabian. The men here are hand-picked from special forces units and are highly skilled. Each trained at Fort Benning in the United States...Crack shots, all. I'd bet my life on everyone of them."

Rhino listened attentively as he continued to inspect the perimeter fence while Kamau gave his report. "I pray you're right. What I expect to arrive shortly will test your good faith to the limit." He reached up and grabbed a section of wrought iron fencing atop the cement wall. He gave it a stout push and caused it to buckle at the anchor points. "Shit! This iron is worthless!"

Lt. Kamau stepped back at the South African's outburst. "I'm not in charge of fencing here. I'll have…"

Rhino cut him off as he spun and began striding toward the residence. "Don't bother…We don't have time. Keep men in tha towers at all times. Have every other swinging brak saddle up. I want flags set at 100 meter intervals out to a 600 meters. One string at each corner and two strings between them out from the walls…Daylight is burning. Get it done before dark."

Lt. Kamau responded, "It will be taken care of, sir." He lifted a walkie-talkie off his belt and ordered teams of his men to start carrying out the instructions.

As Rhino moved toward the inner compound and the President's residence he glanced up at the sky. The heavy white clouds that he had noticed earlier in the day were beginning to thicken into a solid mass and turn dark gray. *Great. This cluster fok will be danced in the rain.*

ANDREWS AIR FORCE BASE
Virgina USA

Senator Breitbart's congressional license plates and personal identification smoothed the entrance to Andrews Air Force Base and he and Mark were parked beside the Gulfstream 550 jet that President Annette Thompson had arranged for transport to Kenya.

"Thanks. I appreciate what you did," Mark said sincerely as he exited the vehicle and moved to the trunk to retrieve his personal gear.

Breitbart followed him toward the waiting aircraft. "If I can do anything, and I mean anything, do not hesitate to call me. Day or night...You hear me?"

"You've done more than enough...Thanks again, sir," Mark replied as he shook his hand. He turned and climbed the stairs into the aircraft cabin and the doors closed.

The Senator stood watching as the jet taxied off and then climbed into the air headed for Kenya. *Go with God, Mark Ingram, go with God.*

YAKUZA COMPOUND
Nairobi Kenya

Hayato's limo and the two APCs entered the palatial estate of his late brother, Akihiko, just as the sun set. A light smog had settled over the entire city of Nairobi from the fires burning in the riot torn slums. Oddly, the estate had not been ransacked and plundered by the looters roaming around the city in the absence of police. Akihiko's death had not made the news and the locals had no desire to tangle with him or his thugs, preferring to prey on the helpless masses of unarmed Kenyan men, women and children.

Hayato and his assassins stood quietly looking at the deserted and dark house for a moment. The distinct sound of the special forces soldier's weapons being chambered echoed off the walls of the courtyard. The echoes of distant gunfire outside added an eerie element to the dark empty buildings and grounds.

"Captain! Get your vehicles positioned to guard the gates and walls in front of the house. Disperse your men as you see fit. No one is to enter," Hayato directed.

The ranking Kenyan officer immediately ordered his special forces troops to defensive positions that created interlocking fire and moved his two APCs to provide support.

Hayato turned, without speaking, gave a hand signal to advance and began to walk up the steps to the front door. He removed a key from the mouth of a eight foot red dragon—carved in relief on the left side of the massive double teak doors—and pulled his H&K 9mm pistol from a shoulder holster. Once the doors were unlocked, he and his team entered silently. The six assassins spread out like a well choreographed dance and began to clear the interior of the home.

Hayato stood in the huge entryway looking out across the spacious living area to the glass wall at the Olympic sized swimming pool. A series of sounds, each replicating one of different bird species found in Japan, informed him the team had completed their sweep and all was clear. He turned on the lights to the entrance hall and the vast living room beyond.

AIR SPACE OVER ATLANTIC OCEAN

Mark used his satellite phone attempting to call Rhino. The fact he had not reached him yet did not create any sense of comfort. Failing to do anything more than leave another message, he dialed Bert, a fellow operative who flew the personal helicopter for DeBeers Diamond Executive Vice President Georg M. Bakken in South Africa. *Haven't touched base with Bert since I high-tailed it out of South Africa. He may have intel on Rhino.* As expected, Bert did not answer. No reason he should, considering Mark's number was unknown to him. Mark left a brief message. "Zorro here. Call me."

Less than ten minutes later, Bert returned the call. "Devil Dog...how's it hanging?"

"Any word on Rhino?"

"Nothing. Doubt he has much time for chit chat though."

"I'm enroute to Johannesburg. Touchdown at 0100 hours. I need a lift into Kenya. Can you assist?" Mark said in clipped direct fashion.

"Thanks for the advance warning. See what I can do. On a twenty day off cycle. If I can find suitable transpo, I'll hump you in myself. Who else you got with you?"

"No one...yet. You got a number for Malakhi?"

"The crazy IDF joker? Yeah," Bert replied with a laugh. "Anyone else on your shopping list of misfits?"

"Crank...Last I heard he was holed up in Thailand. Be good to have another pilot in the mix. Tell 'em there's a hundred thou each in the deal."

"Crank? Might take more than a hundred to pry him out of Thailand. You've seen the staff. Holy smokin' hot passion flowers they are."

"Remind him he owes me...Bogota."

"Done...Anyone else?"

"Four is enough. Don't want to land with a crowd…Small is fast."

"Right."

"Thanks, Bert."

Mark started to remove the battery from his phone then paused. He quickly sent a text message: *Banjo. Zorro. ETA cement factory 0300 hours tomorrow. Prep Betsy II. Need tools and equip for 4.*

He turned off the cell and removed the battery before leaning back and gazing out the window at the star sprinkled sky and the moon reflecting on the clouds below.

ROME, ITALY
Malakhi's Villa

The dark-haired, well muscled man stood on a marble balcony over looking the Mediterranean Sea. The former Israeli Defense Force commando had just finished his martial arts routine when his encrypted cell phone rang. He wiped sweat from his deeply tanned brow and neck with a thick blue cotton towel as he viewed the number. *What the hell could Bert want? He's sitting sweet with that fly job in South Africa.* Glancing over at the tall blonde Danish fashion model reclining nude on a blue lounge chair, he answered the call as he walked across the balcony for privacy, "Yakco Bert? Where the hell is that spicy Afrikaans sausage you promised to ship me?"

"Mark has a gig. A hundred thousand to go into Kenya…"

"Kenya? You're joking my leg…See the news in Kenya lately?"

"He's going in to extract Rhino."

"Shit! I have a contract in two weeks…Pays a hundred fifty thousand for a month of sweet duty baby sitting a couple and their teenage kids visiting the Far East…I don't know, Bert…Who else is on?"

"Calling Crank next."

"That's it? Mark, Crank and you?" Malakhi said incredulously.

"You on or not?"

"One week…That's it. If it's not done in a week I'm gone."

"Yeah, right. Like you're going to be able to get your hairy arse out…Be in Johannesburg tomorrow."

BERT'S FARMHOUSE
South Africa

The tall thin chopper pilot walked through his isolated farm house situated in the secluded Klein Karoo valley surrounded only by natural vegetation, onto the verandah with views of the magnificent Swartberg mountains. The steeply pitched metal roof, additionally covered with a native woven grass for esthetics and insulation. The interior was accented by heavy wooden beams and copper lighting fixtures hanging from the cross timbers in the main rooms. The bedrooms and study ceiling were made of native wooden poles, reflecting South African custom. The foot-thick white stucco walls acted as background to an extensive collection of American Indian and African weapons, tools and artwork.

Bert personally selected each item and designed the layout himself—as a form of therapy after his wife passed away five years earlier.

Ladismith, the closest town in the western Klein Karoo region of South Africa's Western Cape province, lay fifteen miles to the east. His closest neighbor lived nine miles to the south. He chose this place because it reminded him of the Southwest United States with it's tough arid conditions, open vistas, mountains and sparse population.

Bert lifted a cold Castle Milk Stout—bottled in South Africa by the oldest brewing company in the country—from his verandah frige and moved to the northeast corner of the covered porch. He gazed off in the direction of Kenya as he called Crank. When the answering service picked up, he began a message, "Crank. Bert. Got a proposition for you…"

The former Navy SEAL at six one and 210 lbs of lean muscle with shoulder length blonde hair—originally from Southern California—broke in as Bert spoke, "Long time no chit chat, helo man…Hope your deal's a sweet one. Going a little stir crazy here in the land of Buddha."

"How exactly does one go crazy with the staff you got?" Bert chuckled.

"Ain't easy mi amigo. The first nine months were a breeze, but the last has been kinda trying…Still workin' out everyday, but I'm losing my game-time edge." Crank extracted himself from between two young naked Thai beauties sleeping beside him. He stepped over the bodies of two more sleeping on bamboo mats on the floor and walked out of the bedroom onto the balcony.

"Don't think dipping your piddle is considered workin' out."

"Whatever...Last time you came to visit, I recall you piddle dipping like a Arizona desert dog loose in the Redwood forest...What's the prop?"

"Zorro needs a hand extracting Rhino from a situation."

"What's the pay?"

"Hundred per man...Did I mention Rhino is in Kenya?"

"You did not...What's going on in Kenya?"

"You should give the dog walking a rest and check the news more often, my friend. Kenya is in a state of civil war...You know? Large crowds of black men with machetes chopping up the countryside. Pretty much the same go as in the missionary extract in the Congo back in '08."

"Fuck me running sideways...Where's the rally point?"

"Zorro lands in Johannesburg at 0100 hours tomorrow."

"Rang, you strong man, you come back to bed me," one of the girls called.

Crank turned back to the bedroom. "Som lone gig...Is this bring your own armory?" He moved back into the bedroom.

"No time to deal with customs. We weapon up here."

"Tell Zorro I'm in." He hung up his cell phone and crawled into bed between the two women. Both women began to caress and kiss on him as he laid back and relaxed. *Gotta be a fool to leave these little nymphos.*

WASHINGTON, DC
WHITE HOUSE

Gunter Hermann entered the private dining room inside the Presidential quarters, with his personal Secret Service agent assigned to him in trail. The silver-haired ex-Marine moved quietly to his wife's side and gave her a quick kiss on the cheek.

"Oh, good, you made it back in time for dinner." She smiled up at him as he took a seat beside her.

"Well, we finished up the weanin' and separatin' faster than I anticipated...They're makin' me feel unnecessary."

"To tell you the truth, Eagle Nest is certainly going to be a welcome change once my term is up."

"Got that right...Gonna enjoy bein' a real cowboy again."

A trim young brunette wearing starched black and white servant's uniform entered carrying a silver tray with a blue and white china cup adorned with the seal of the President of the Unites States. She place the hot cup of coffee on the saucer in front of Gunter. "Any special requests today, Mr. Hermann?"

"How about a good old fashioned greasy cheeseburger...all the trimmings?"

She grinned and nodded, then silently disappeared through the swinging door to the kitchen.

"So, tell me. What major world cataclysm has got your attention today?"

The President laid down her spoon beside the bowl of soup and looked him directly in the eyes. "Still having fallout from the Islamic world after our rescue of the Royal Pleiades passengers and crew. They have no proof linking us to the

Wrath of God campaign...Looks like the operation may eventually produce some beneficial results."

"Tell 'em to piss up a rope. If they minded their own business, they wouldn't be such a pain in the ass to the western world."

"If only it were that simple."

"I can see something else in your eyes. What's really gnawing at you, sweetheart?"

"I can't get away with anything with you, can I?"

"Hope not. We knew there were gonna be some tough times ahead when we married. You've got the hardest job in the world, and I promised to shoot straight with you...win lose or draw."

"And for that I will be eternally grateful," she said as she took a sip of coffee. "Okay, here it is in a nutshell...late last night, I got a call from Andy Breitbart asking for a favor. Remember that young former Marine that helped the BEF rescue him and his daughter?"

"Sure. Good man...hard charger. What about 'im?"

"He asked if I could help get him back to Kenya in a hurry, and I put him on a Gulfstream in the middle of the night."

"Okay? Nice of you to...wait a sec...isn't there some kind of civil unrest stirring up in Kenya?"

"It's far beyond unrest, my dear. Mr. Ingram went back to try to help his friend who is the personal bodyguard to President Mobutto...Things are looking pretty grim, I might add."

"A Marine running to the sound of gunfire...What you would expect...Like the man even better already. So, what exactly is the problem?…You've sent people into harm's way before."

"It's just that I'm concerned not only for the young man and his friend…President Mobutto is ally of the United States and believes in the democratic process. My concern is that he'll be deposed and some Idi Amin type will replace him…Uganda hasn't recovered from that debacle yet."

"So, Madame President, what are your options? Spend weeks trying to get the United Nations off its ass to actually do something but spend our taxpayers money for a change? Hope that the African Union will stand up for freedom?…Don't hold your breath."

"You can see what I'm dealing with, honey. Our hands are tied with international law vis-à-vis internal conflicts and even gunboat diplomacy takes time. And time is something we are running out of. The reported death toll is in the thousands."

Gunter sat back and held his coffee cup with both hands. After a few seconds silence, he sat it back down. "You know what you have to do to stabilize the situation? Given the current budgetary and geopolitical constraints, I would suggest you give Harold Baker a call. Dare and the team are probably chompin' at the bit, waiting for him to give the go ahead."

She gazed at his weather-beaten face and a slight sparkle came to her antique gold eyes. "How is it that you got so smart for a south Texas rancher?"

"Aw, come on, Sweet Pea. You didn't just marry me for my hot body and boyish good looks…did you?"

She leaned over and gave him a proper kiss, just like she had decades earlier when they were college sweethearts, and then winked at the Secret Service agent.

BLACK EAGLE FORCE HEADQUARTERS
Grayson County Airport
Denison, Texas

CEO Dare Phillips stood up from behind his desk and walked around to speak to Sean 'Widowmaker' Baker. He had considered the former SEAL's late night request for transportation for Mark Ingram and denied it out of practicality. The BEF had a couple Lears for administrative duty, but they were not particularly well suited for long range over water flight. The C-130 gunships would not substantially be faster than a commercial flight to an adjoining nation and a helicopter ride into the war zone that Kenya had become. Now only fifteen hours later, Widowmaker was asking for a leave of absence to travel on his own to try to assist Mark.

"You know I won't stop you if you really want to go," Dare said. "I think it's a little crazy, but believe me, I do understand. True friends are hard to come by, and you hate to lose one…particularly if there is a chance you can be the difference."

"So, guess you can just put me down as on vacation, Boss. Be back as soon as I can."

Dare extended his hand and Widowmaker shook it firmly as they exchanged knowing glances. He turned to go as the intercom system interrupted with a message. "Mr. Phillips, Sec Def Baker on line one."

"Hold on Sean, you may have gotten your wish after all." Dare lifted the portable handset and pressed the illuminated button. "Mr. Secretary, how may we be of service?"

Fifteen minutes later, the massive hangar doors of Warbird Restorations, Inc began to open as yellow flashing lights warned all personnel inside that the C-5M *Super Galaxy* was preparing to be towed out. Inside, on the bottom cargo deck, were two highly modified VTOL M-600/A *Eagles*, one M200/A *Hawk*, and one BEF M800/A *Condor*. Upstairs, two full twelve man teams of combat-ready futuristic Raptors were already strapped to their gray leather business class type seats, along with a full contingent of pilots and weapon systems operators. Two ray-shaped *Manta* unmanned reconnaissance fighters were magnetically attached—one beneath each wing between the inboard and outboard engines.

Aircraft Commander Gears Formby released the brakes and relayed the appropriate signal to the tug driver. In minutes, the four giant turbofans propelled the huge craft into the clouds, enroute to an uncertain fate over Kenya.

***

CHAPTER FIVE

KENYA ARMY BASE EMBASSY
50th Air Cavalry Battalion

General Janmohamed, commander of the Kenyan 50th Air Cav, stood at the head of a twenty foot conference table addressing a half dozen officers with perfectly proper British English. He was an imposing figure, standing six four and weighing 260 lbs, his black hair was closely cropped in tight military fashion. The illicit union between his grandmother and a British plantation owner caused his skin to have a light honey-brown complexion. His uniform was immaculately pressed and adorned with an array of medals. "President Mobutto has slipped out of our grasp and is now at his summer retreat...A sterling tactical move by the rogue bastard from South Africa who heads his security detail." He let the information register on his men before proceeding. "This in no way will deter us from our mission. Once we have Mobutto in our grasp, we will enact military law and regain control of our country."

The officers listened intently to his speech. Each was well aware of their high stakes gamble. Failure was not an option—losing meant certain execution by order of a military tribunal.

"Colonel Biwoot, commander of the Air Force Mi-28 squadron has declined to join us. Last night he suffered a fatal automobile accident and has now been replaced by Major Luvusti. I will be discussing the current state of the nation with him at 1100 hours today. He will assure that the Hines will not be available for Mobutto's use, therefore guaranteeing our victory."

"What if Major Luvusti refuses? The Kenyan Air Force is loyal to Mobutto as he was once one of them," one officer asked.

"Then I will approach his successor," Janmohamed replied. "I had conformation last night that Ranger D Company of the 20th Parachute Battalion is with us. I am certain everyone is familiar with the 20th. Additionally, this morning, the General Service Unit responded they too are on board. These two units plus our companies from the 50th are more than enough to place the President in our hands. You have your orders. Lead your men wisely…Overcome all obstacles with extreme prejudice. All of Kenya will sing praises to our victory!" Janmohamed turned and walked sharply out of the room.

MOBUTTO'S SUMMER HOME
Mt. Kenya

Lutto admitted Lt. Kamau into the study where the President sat watching live newscasts of events in Kenya on three huge flat screen televisions. The room lights were off and the flickering images on the monitors cast odd shadows on the many trophies and artifacts on the wall.

"What is it Kamau?" Mobutto asked without looking away from the horrendous images.

"I have just been informed that Colonel Biwoot died in a automobile accident in Nairobi. Seems he was enroute from the military headquarters to Embakasi. No other details at this time Mr. President," Kamau rattled off in a rush. He was well aware that Biwoot and Mobutto were long time fellow officers in the Kenyan Air Force and close friends.

"Have Rheinhart come in," Mobutto said heavily.

"As you wish, Mr. President. Be advised Mr. Fabian is out of the compound at the moment. He went to run a one mile perimeter inspection. I expect him back within the hour."

"Until he returns, please arrange transportation for the staff. I want them safely away from here. Do we have the vehicles to accomplish this?"

"Mr. President…no one else is leaving, sir. I attempted to do as you suggested yesterday…I was able to get their families to leave. The staff informed me they would not depart under any circumstances and if forced, they would return as fast as they could."

A smile crossed Mobutto's face. *I am blessed with such great people. God help them...help us all if Rheinhart is right.*

Forty-five minutes later, Rhino entered the study. His shirt and waist band to his khaki trousers were soaked in sweat. "You wanted to see me, sir?"

"There is a small garrison not twenty kilometers from here. If it is still manned, there could be sixty men there. I suggest we send the helicopter crew and Lieutenant Kamau out to recon the base as well as have a couple of our trucks headed that way to requisition men, weapons and ammunition...He can act as negotiator and radio the men in the trucks to continue or return here if the base is no longer standing."

"We're short handed already, but I think you have a good plan. I'd feel a lot better about our chances if we had another sixty men...Loyal men." Rhino paused. "Our munitions are not going to hold back any serious assault. If the men are unwilling to join us...I suggest we take what ever we can carry."

"Agreed. If the patrol departs within the hour they could be back by midnight." Mobutto turned off the televisions, clicked on an end table lamp and faced Rhino. "Any word on the last flight as yet?"

Just as he finished the question, the faint sounds of helicopter blades in the distance were heard. Rhino moved through the study onto the verandah. He lifted the binoculars still hanging around his neck from the perimeter sweep and began to scan the sky to the south. As Mobutto joined him,

Rhino spoke, "Incoming now, sir. That will bring us up another seven men."

"And two dogs."

Rhino looked to him and the two men shared a chuckle. "And two dogs...Nothing can stop us now."

The helicopter settled onto the grass next to the helo pad as Rhino and Mobutto strode to the gate of the inner compound fence. The chopper door opened and two Presidential security guards stepped out, followed by Abasi and Adimu, both straining at the leash as they saw their master and headed for him. Abasi broke free from the grasp of his handler and charged across the open lawn. Adimu's handler released him as well to join the race. The two dogs bounded and jumped around Mobutto like a pair of puppies as he knelt to embrace them. Rhino was certain he saw tears in the President's eyes before approaching the newly arrived security guards and helo crew.

"Top your bird off," Rhino ordered. "You men join the team inside the President's home. Get yourself cleaned up and chowed. Report to me within the hour for further duty assignments." He lifted a radio from his belt. "Kamau, select eight men for a road trip. Best two trucks we have. See me in the southwest tower."

The radio crackled. "Yes, sir, Mr. Fabian."

Rhino walked briskly across the outer compound grounds to the corner tower and climbed the dimly lit well-worn wooden stairs to the upper observation deck. With only a casual nod to the sentry on duty, he began to scan the horizon for the enemy he knew was coming. In a few minutes he heard the engines starting in the motor pool and turned to see two long-bed Toyota 4x4 pickups pulling out to the elevated gas tank for fueling. *Damn good bloak. Wheels turning in less than five.*

Kamau climbed into the observation deck while Rhino continued his inspection of the landscape in the direction he most expected the enemy. "Your orders?"

"President Mobutto informed me there is a small garrison twenty kilometers from here. He has ordered a recon and resupply mission. You will take one of the helicopters and two of your special forces and get there on the quick time. If the base is still intact, enlist the unit to join us...If not? Scrounge any weapons, ammunition, food, medical supplies still serviceable," Rhino continued to scan the horizon as he spoke.

"What if the garrison is still there but elects not to join us?"

"Commandeer all ya can carry in the two trucks and the chopper and get back here as fast as ya can." Rhino lowered the binoculars and looked the man directly in the eye. "Use what ever force necessary, including elimination with extreme prejudice...Is that clear?"

"Yes, sir." He snapped to attention and saluted crisply.

ATLANTIC AIR SPACE

Mark's watch gently vibrated against his wrist, alerting him he was half way on his sixteen hour trip from DC to Johannesburg. Looking around the passenger compartment of the Gulfstream 37B he spied the burly master sergeant loadmaster asleep in a rear seat. He unbuckled his seat belt and stood up to stretch.

Glad I took my loafers off. Hate it when my feet swell up. After several moments of easing the body fatigue from sitting for seven hours, he moved to the cockpit door and knocked.

"Come," a voice commanded.

He opened the door and leaned in. "Want some coffee?"

"Black for me, all dressed up for Gus. The fixings are in cabinet above the coffee maker in the galley," the aircraft commander, a trim but muscular major, responded without looking back.

Mark made a fresh pot before pouring up four cups and returning to the cockpit. "Nothin' like some Joe on a long flight," he said.

One copilot nodded as he took his and asked, "How long's the layover in Johannesburg?"

"Layover?"

"Our orders are to fly you to Johannesburg. Layover 'til you're ready, then deposit you safely in Nairobi," the A/C responded.

"Well, first class service all around. I have a team forming up in Johannesburg and expect to be ready within twenty-four hours of landing...Who gave you the orders?"

"The President," Gus answered. "Said you had a important date with chaos," he added with a slight chuckle. "She asked me to give you this after we took off." He handed Mark a sealed manila envelope with his name on it—the seal of the President of the United States emblazoned on the upper left corner.

He took the envelope and returned to his seat. *What the hell?* A single sheet of paper, with the Presidential letterhead on it was all that he found inside.

I don't know you. You never received this letter. It doesn't exist. President Mobutto is a important American ally in Africa. I read your Marine Corps jacket, very impressive, I might add. Senators Breitbart and Coleman speak very highly of you. We know you will do what is necessary to insure his well being continues. At present, I am unable to assist you any more than the transportation of yourself and whomever you decide necessary to complete this mission. Godspeed, Mark. PS: Return this communiqué package to the aircrew after reading.

The message was imply signed *Annette*. Mark placed the letter back in the envelope and laid it on the seat next to his. *After meeting those Black Eagle Force boys and seeing what they did to the Muzzies, I don't think I can do anything she's not aware of.* Mark smiled as he got up to get another cup of coffee.

CAPE TOWN
DeBeers Helicopter Pad

Bert landed his personal MD 500 helicopter on the pad normally used by Debeers Executive Georg M. Bakken, climbed out and walked briskly to the waiting SUV. *Last time I saw Zorro was here. Delivered Bakken after the terrorist kidnappers made the wrong call of tangling with him.* Without pause, he entered the passenger side and the vehicle rolled off immediately.

Alf, as everyone called Ian Courtney, was a former Royal Marine Commando and British Secret Intelligence Service operative. He drove the vehicle at the posted speed limit. Selected personally, he had taken over the security duties for Georg M. Bakken when Mark had to suddenly depart South Africa. "I'd be looking for details," Ian said in a heavy Irish brogue.

"Thanks for coming on such short notice. Here's the long and short of it. He's landing at 0100 hours in Johannesburg. I need to see this captain friend of mine at a SDF base and arrange for some firepower off the books...Then meet up with Zorro to finalize the dance. We're good after you drop me off."

"And?"

"He's putting together a team to go into Kenya and extract Rhino."

"I've a lad here in Johannesburg. He's lookin' for employment if'n you'd be needing another."

"Give me his contact number. Is he up for it?"

"He was a bit of a friend in the Royal Marines...Top lister he is. Right handy in a firefight. Faith an' bloody good with a knife with a bit of a death wish, if truth be known...Tell him Alf would be sending you."

"I'll pass it along."

SOUTH AFRICA
SDF SPECIAL OPS BASE

Captain Albertus Schoeman drove out the gate in a command vehicle and proceeded down the dirt road for a mile before coming to the small shanty town, Uraia. It was nothing more than a few bars and two brothels that existed only as long as the

SDF base was located where it was—if the base moved so did the bars and brothels. The rusted tin roofs and clapboard walled buildings with peeling white paint on first view would be considered uninhabitable. Rustic rough-hewn tables, chairs and bar—nothing more than planks on fifty-five gallon steel drums—did nothing to amend the opinion once inside. Bare dim electric light bulbs hung on exposed wires. The ceiling was little more than the corrugated underside of the metal roof. A trio of fans nailed to the rafters rotated lazily, barely creating any air movement at all. The pungent stench of human sweat, urine and split beer reeked like any third world dive where soldiers gathered to kill the drudgery of daily life in the bush.

Schoeman pulled up to the last building on the strip. A garishly painted sign—*The Jade Earring*—hung slightly askew above the entrance. Alf and Bert's SUV, covered with dirt from the two hour drive down the unpaved road was parked in front. He opened the front door and paused for his eyes to adjust from the bright South African sun to the dim lighting.

"Over here, you jackabee," Bert called.

Schoeman turned to his left and moved toward the sound, stumbling into a chair laying on the floor. "Shiat!"

"You'd be watchin' your language…there's ladies about," Alf said with a laugh.

At the end of the rough bar, two tall slender black women, wearing brightly colored loose dresses with artificial flowers in their hair, sat with vacant eyes. At a table near the back, three more short plump black women played dominos—attired in shorts and blouses rolled up exposing their ample stomachs, but barely covering their huge breasts. One of the women responded, "He can say what ever he likes if he pays me fee." All the women laughed and agreed in a chorus of voices spiced with slang and cursing.

The bartender, a sixty year old white man with half his teeth missing and the remaining stained brown from tobacco or blue from rot, set down three bottles of luke-warm local beer he brewed himself in a shack behind the bar. "Brought you another round o' me finest."

"I drunk camel piss 'n Iraq tasted better than your finest," Alf replied.

The bartender departed without responding, shuffling back behind the bar where he busied himself with washing glasses in a tub of cold gray-brown water.

"Bring me a shopping list?" Schoemen asked before taking a swig on the bottle of beer—He made a face and spit it out on the floor.

Bert, Alf and Schoemen laughed as they clanked their bottles noisily together and saluted, speaking in unison, "To those who are about to die!"

Bert pulled an envelope from the side pocket on his fatigue pants and handed it to Schoeman. "Need this by 0600 tomorrow...There's a bonus if you have everything."

Schoeman sat reading the list silently for several minutes, then thumbed the money without removing it from the envelope. "Well hell, ya dun't want much do ya?" He folded the list and placed it in his back pocket before buttoning it down and slid the envelope with the cash into his boot. "See what I can do. Where? And what's the final tally? I only count five."

"The old concrete factory in Johannesburg...East side... Panay Road. There's a three story building," Bert replied. "The remaining forty-five thou upon delivery. I'll throw in a bottle of twenty-five year single malt as well."

Schoeman rose from his chair and walked out without another word.

As the sound of his vehicle driving off faded, Alf said, "You'd be trusting him?"

"It's hell doing business with the devil...But he's the only contact I've got that could possibly deliver on such short notice."

"It would be another three hours to Johannesburg before a hot shower an' clean sheets," Alf said as he stood up. He placed several bills on the table before starting to the door. "Let's be for moving."

KENYA
KDF BASE - 127

Kamau's helicopter circled the base, a tawdry affair consisting of two dozen tents, a thatched roof building—locally called mescal—with open walls. Nearby were a twenty foot tall observation tower and a pair of forty foot shipping containers covered with sand bags—all within a wire mesh fence topped with razor wire. After completing several circuits around it, he ordered the pilot to set it down on the parade deck. His recon of the installation revealed no movement by any troops stationed there, and all but one of the 6x6 trucks were gone.

Kamau, and the two special forces men stepped out of the craft and into the swirling dust, weapons at the ready. Once the blades had stopped rotating, the pilot and copilot joined them. There was a uneasy silence only broken by a radio faintly playing native music coming from one of the tents.

The Lt. spoke to the crew, "You two stay with the chopper. Be ready to get us the hell out of here if need be." Turning to the two special forces he barked brief instructions, "Headquarters first. Stay alert." He moved off toward a single wooden building.

As they neared the structure, a voice called out from inside, "It is Quara. I am coming out."

Kamau and the two guards stopped. Both guards knelt and panned to the left and right looking for any sign of danger. Quara opened the door and walked on to the porch his weapon held over his head with one hand on the buttstock, the other on the forend.

"It is good to see you Lieutenant."

"What happened here? Where is the rest of the unit?" Kamau asked as he moved forward. "You can put your rifle down Corporal Quara."

"I was on a three day patrol. When we came back everyone was gone," the tall slender soldier replied. "We were going to leave in the morning."

"Where are the rest of your men?"

"Inside." He turned and yelled to some other unseen soldiers remaining in the building, "Come out!...I know this man. I served with him in Somalia."

Nine men, members of the regular KDF, slowly came out of the door and joined him.

"What is your alliance to the President?" Kamau asked.

"His cousin is married to one of my sisters. I met him once at a family marriage ceremony. I am tied by blood loyalty," Quara replied.

"Do you have the keys to the munitions bunker?"

"No, sir. The captain had the only key and he took it with him."

"In two hours, a couple of trucks will arrive from President Mobutto's summer home. I want to get everything of any use ready to transport. Use whatever is necessary to get the bunker open without blowing it up. Assign two men to the observation tower with binoculars...Double time!"

Quara ordered one man to join him in opening the munitions bunker, two men to the lookout tower and the others to assemble everyone's personal equipment on the porch of the headquarters building.

HONG KONG
Wu's Suite

Wu lifted the light 400 count cotton sheets off himself and the beautiful fifteen year old Filipino girl, exposing her head and shoulders, revealing her earnest efforts to provide pleasure with her tongue. He lay back enjoying the visual as well as physical

91

pleasure when his red iPhone rang. *My first report from Kenya comes at a unfortunate time.* Grabbing the girl's head and pressing her to him, he rolled on his side and picked up the phone. The child giggled as they turned on the bed, but never missed a stroke while he answered the call.

"Yes," Wu said followed by a low moan of pleasure.

"I have secured Akihiko's residence and will use it as our base of operations. I met with our new KWS contact this morning. A shipment of ivory will be departing in twenty-four hours," Hayato announced proudly.

Wu rolled on to his back again, the Filipina still working to provide for his enjoyment, and stared at the gold tapestry ceiling. "Well done, Hayato."

The Yazuka continued, "I have a meeting tonight with our contact in the Ministry of Law Enforcement to insure business agreements are honored."

"Again, well done."

"What news of the American…"

Wu shoved the willing concubine forcefully off the bed and sat bolt upright. "Do not ask me about this matter again!" he bellowed. "When the time is right I will tell you what, when and where you will extract your revenge."

The nude, large breasted Filipina cowered on the floor beside the bed rubbing the back of her head where it had impacted the wall.

A short silence lingered before Hayato answered, "Yes, Mr. Wu. What are your instructions?"

"Follow the plan I gave you!" the naked Chinaman growled.

AIR SPACE OVER THE ATLANTIC

Mark sat on the floor, his legs crossed, attempting to relax through meditation. Unfortunately his conscious mind continually brought back thoughts of his brief time with Sarah at the mountain cabin. *Got to get this stowed away. Not going to help where I'm going.* Just as he felt the quiet beginning to slip in place, the memories of his wife Lydia and son Josh flashed forward and burned his heart with images of their vacation at the beach just before he deployed to Afghanistan. *Shit! Now this?* Mark shook his head to clear it, and then stood up and began doing a series repetitive martial art moves designed for defense and assault in an attempt to rid his mind of any thoughts at all.

His first kata, a guttural— "Keyaa!" —at the end of a three step woke the burly loadmaster sleeping in the rear with a start.

"Jesus man!" he uttered through heavy lids as he saw him moving down the aisle.

Mark paused, turned and performed another three step—this time moving away from the grumpy master sergeant.

"Hell of a way to wake a man," the loadmaster muttered to himself as he unbuckled his seat belt and moved to the lavatory.

Mark ignored him and focused on the defensive and offensive moves, determined to rid himself of the distracting thoughts and images from the near and distant past. His moves became ever more aggressive until he looked like a Tasmanian Devil moving about the passenger compartment.

Ten minutes later, he sat down on one of the front row seats and held his head in his hands. *I'm sorry Lydia....Josh...I'm so sorry.*

The loadmaster moved up the isle and paused two rows behind, not exactly sure of his state of mind and not wanting to get too close until he was. "You all right, mister? Need anything?"

Mark, without looking up, still holding his face in his hands replied, "Ghosts...Just tryin' to stow some ghosts."

The sergeant then slowly moved past and entered the cockpit, securing the door behind him. "Our passenger's a few bricks short of a pallet, I suspect."

"We thought you had started square dancing back there," the copilot said with a nervous smile.

"Said he was dealing with ghosts."

The three shared curious glances with one another before Gus responded, "Keep an eye on him. Last thing we need is a PTSD Marine going postal on board."

***

CHAPTER SIX

KENYA
KDF BASE - 127

"Two trucks are approaching!" one of the tower sentries yelled. Kamau exited the munitions bunker followed by Quara and two of the KDF soldiers, each carrying a case of ammunition. "Toyota trucks with the President's emblem?"

"Yes, sir!" the sentry responded.

"Corporal, does that 6x6 work?" Kamau asked.

"The reverse gear is out."

"Good enough. Get it over here and load every thing it can carry except for the MK 19 grenade launchers and ammo. We'll haul two of them in the Toyotas. The third 19 goes in the helicopter along with ten belts of grenades. Once the munitions are loaded on the truck, throw the men's personal gear on top."

As the soldiers moved the large truck to the bunker and began loading it, a large thunderhead to the east rumbled. Amau turned to view it, estimating its time of arrival to be less than two hours. *This will complicate things, but will also help cover our movements.*

"Call Rheinhart and inform him we will be underway in thirty minutes," Amau yelled to the pilot. He then turned to his special forces troops and ordered them to load a MK 19 into the chopper. *Bloody good show here. Not much food but a bounty of weapons and munitions.*

As the men found places to ride on the trucks, Amau looked one last time at the three forlorn mongrel camp dogs. *Mobutto and Rhino are not going to like this.*

"Get the three dogs on the 6x6," Amau shouted.

NAIROBI, KENYA
Serena Hotel

General Janmohamed handed the keys to his BMW to the valet and entered the spacious lobby of the hotel. Despite its pivotal central location, the Serena Nairobi hotel remained true to its title, offering an oasis of serenity amidst the bustle of one of Africa's most vibrant capital cities, even during the turmoil raging through the streets.

The interior décor reflected an entirely pan-African theme featuring art and inspiration from Ethiopia, the Maghreb, West Africa and East Africa. Janmohamed moved directly to the renowned *Mandhari* fine-dining restaurant and spied the Minister of Defense sitting alone at a table in the back. Once seated and having placed his order with the white clad waiter, he spoke quietly with the minister, "All is in place. I have successfully arranged the alliances we needed."

"Excellent, General. I again assure you that the position of Minister of Defense is yours once Mobutto is disposed of."

"I look forward to the day," Janmohamed softly answered. *Like hell, you fat pig. Once the coup is complete I will be the new President. You will join Mobutto with a hangman's noose.*

"What progress have you made with an Air Force alliance?

"None. They are too close to Mobutto. So...I enlisted a captain in the 20th Parachute Battalion to render all aircraft at Laikipia and Moi Air Bases unflyable. With the jets and attack helicopters out of commission, there will be little support for the President to call upon."

"What about the other helicopter units?"

"They're stretched far to thin dealing with the civil unrest to come to his aid, either."

"Get this done quickly. A slow coup is death to those who attempt it."

YAKUZA COMPOUND
Nairobi, Kenya

The midday sun had all but two Yakuza assassins inside to avoid the oppressive heat. The sun bore down and reflected off the swimming pool and the marble deck casting a glare on the ceiling-to-floor glass window that overlooked the pool from inside the house. One male killer and Chikako swam laps, passing each other at the center of the Olympic pool.

When she reached the end of the pool, she lifted herself out effortlessly and stood gleaming as the water drained off her muscular well-rounded body. The fact that her grandmother had married a American GI during the reconstruction after WW II accounted for her ample breasts and hips. Many a man had fallen to her alluring appearance and social charms. Her record for successful target elimination was unblemished. It stood at twenty-eight for twenty-eight, including the five women killed at Hayato's orders.

She moved gracefully across the hot marble deck into the shade of a cabana umbrella and lifted a thick white towel with an embroidered emblem of a red dragon from a chair and began to dry off. Feeling eyes upon her, she looked toward the dark interior of the living area where Hayato sat, reclining on a long low couch. Unable to see into the dark interior, she turned her back to the window and finished toweling off before sitting down on the pool chair. She retrieved a dark blue band from her bag and pulled her beautiful waist-long ebony hair back into a single low pony tail.

Hayato watched her with both admiration and distrust. She had questioned his methods two months earlier concerning the removal of a corporate executive in Tokyo. Several months prior she had challenged the elimination of a politician, his wife and two children in Java. She was his most accomplished assassin and her fringe benefits complicated his decision to eliminate her. *The pleasures you provide are without equal, Chikako. But you never join me completely. Always holding something back, you bitch.*

98

She gazed up at the sky, aware of the burning stare. *This is the time...this is the place. I can feel it. I will implement my escape here in this dark, dirty country and never look back.* She laid her head back on the lounge chair and closed her eyes. Chikakto longed for a man who could equal her prowess and appetites for pleasure. She allowed her imagination to soar, slipping deeper into the joint dreams of freedom from the deadly grip of the Yakuza and the embrace of the lover she desired. Her body began to warm and tingle with erotic anticipation—so much so that she stood and walked rapidly to the edge of the pool and dove back in, swimming the length of the pool under water before surfacing for air. *I will either escape or die here.*

Hayato's cell buzzed, indicating a text had arrived. Opening the message, he viewed the GPS coordinates and directions to the KWS QRF headquarters. A dark wicked smile crossed his face as he rose from the couch and moved to the sliding glass door leading to the pool area. "Chikako! Get dressed. I have an assignment for you."

Relieved to hear 'get dressed', she swam the length of the pool, climbed out and gathered her things before entering a door that lead directly into the bedroom she was assigned—one adjoining his with a door that connected them. Not knowing exactly what her mission would be, she showered quickly, put on a pair of black knee length cargo shorts, long sleeve red blouse and hiking boots. She quickly packed a small travel bag before picking up her black cordura weapons case and moved to the living room.

"I forwarded a text message. Take two men of your choosing and eliminate anyone you find at the location."

"May I take Raku? We make a good tandem…"

"No! I have another assignment for her," Hayato snapped back. "I am weary of your questioning me! Two men."

"As you say." She left the room. *Soon…Have to leave soon*

KWS QRF HEADQUARTERS
Kenya

Robert, Mark's number one Quick Reaction Force Ranger, watched as the three trucks and horse trailers drove out of the base and onto the dirt road. Having dispatched all but one Ranger to investigate the latest reports of poaching, he considered his new position and the responsibilities he had inherited. *I liked being number two much better.*

Entering the office, he lifted the base radio handset and called the remaining Ranger to his office over the public address system. The man came in the office shortly smelling like the stables he was mucking out.

"Yes, sir," the Ranger said as he snapped to attention in front of Robert's desk.

"At ease. I want you to saddle up and take the horses out to the north lake…All but Mark's horse, Lakota Moon. I will ride him out and join you before sunset to bring the herd back in. They will appreciate the tender new grass."

"Yes sir."

A half hour later Robert heard the horses galloping off with the Ranger following behind. *Those bloody horses know exactly where to go.* He grinned as he glanced out a window and watched the animals racing for the lake, snorting, kicking and nipping at each other.

Robert, his rifle in one hand and wearing his big Guatemalan straw hat—a parting gift from Mark—as he stepped out of the office onto the covered porch. He saw a cloud of dust approaching from the direction of Nairobi. *Wonder who that is? Probably some lost tourist seeking directions.* Lakota Moon whinnied and pawed the ground as he stood tethered to one of the supporting posts.

Robert approached the Toyota 4 Runner that pulled to a stop in front of him. The rear passenger window began to lower. He turned to see the muzzle of a suppressed handgun pointed at his chest.

Phssst! Phsst! Phsst!

He fell back against one of the wooden poles—two holes in his chest and one in his forehead. The last thing he saw was the azure blue Kenyan sky as he drew his final breath.

Lakota Moon sidestepped as he fell but showed no real fear of the incident. Chikako stepped out of the rear passenger door and moved to stand over Robert. *Twenty-nine for twenty-nine.*

"Check the barracks and the stables," she ordered.

The two men drove first to the barracks and entered, weapons drawn. She came back out of the office as they exited the barracks and cautiously moved to the barn.

101

Chikako sat down on the long wooden bench waiting for the men to finish their work and unscrewed the suppresser from her H&K UPC pistol—one she had taken off a dead US Marine on the island of Mindanao several years before. Looking around Robert's lifeless body she spotted the three spent brass .45 casings and picked them up as the two men headed back to the office.

The front passenger window lowered. "There is no one else here."

As Chikako began to enter the rear door, the man in front of her stepped out and emptied the thirty round magazine from his MP5 into Lakota Moon. The horse reared and thrashed on the end of his lead rope before falling to the ground breathing his last gasps for air—pink froth pouring from his nostrils. His lead rope still tied to the post stretched his head up at an awkward angle.

She stepped back out of the vehicle and smashed the shooter in the face with the butt of her pistol. "What did you do that for?"

He staggered to his knees then used the open door to stand, "The file on the American who killed Hayato's brother…said he rode a buckskin horse with black stockings. What better way to send a message…"

"Get in the car before I beat you to death, you fucking animal!" Chikako hissed softly as her eyes burned through the man. *I'll kill you before I leave.* She stepped to the dying horse and placed a well-aimed round behind his ear.

KENYAN ARMY BASE
50th Air Cavalry Battalion

General Janmohamed watched as the troops loaded onto the seven AS332 helicopters, sixteen men to each aircraft. *The first wave.* As the troop transports lifted off he turned to the officer behind him. "The coup has begun."

"Yes sir, General Janmohamed."

"Have the next units stand by. I want them in the air as soon as the transports return and are refueled.

The officer saluted, spun and headed to the troops barracks.

The General checked his expensive Swiss watch. *Second wave will lift off in four hours. Just enough time to visit Enika.*

He entered his staff vehicle and gave the driver the address. *A little pleasure is good for a man's soul.* He smiled as he lit a large Cuban cigar. Once lit he drew deeply and exhaled a series of smoke rings that floated lazily to the ceiling.

MOBUTTO'S SUMMER HOME

The summer sun was setting as Lt. Kamau's helicopter landed inside the compound walls. All the exterior lights were dark, only a dim glow from several windows with drapes drawn tight showed any indication of life inside.

Kamau was the first to exit the chopper as Rhino approached. "We have *bloody* good success! I have a surprise for you." He motioned to the soldiers to remove the MK 19 from the passenger compartment. "I call them game changers."

Rhino's face lit up as he recognized the weapon. "That it is, Lieutenant. That it is."

"Two more coming on the Toyotas. We commandeered a 6x6 as well, loaded with ammunition, a couple cases of grenades and food."

"Get this to the southwest tower. I expect the assault to start there...Well done!" Rhino turned and walked to the President's quarters to share the good news.

***

CHAPTER SEVEN

YAKUZA COMPOUND

Chikako entered the foyer followed by the two Yakuza. Not seeing Hayato in the living area, she left them and proceeded to her room. Once inside she removed her clothing and tossed the blouse and shorts on the chair in the corner, lay down on the bed and closed her eyes. She heard the sounds coming from Hayato's room next door of he and Raku having sex. *Wonder how many little blue pills the bastard took this time.*

Realizing Hayato might call her into the room to join them She dressed quickly, choosing a pair of white slacks and a blue blouse. Grabbing her light travel bag, she placed her H&K PS9; two additional magazines; her numerous identification cards inside and quietly slipped out into the hallway.

She walked briskly to the ornate front gates and ordered the KDF soldier on duty to let her out.

At the first intersection she waved down a Isuzu taxi cab—one of the few still trying to make a living in the riot torn city—and instructed the driver to take her to a currency exchange bank.

SAROVA STANLEY HOTEL
Nairobi

Leaving the bank, she looked around and saw the upper two stories of the Sarova Stanley Hotel over the buildings that surrounded her. The three blocks passed quickly as the streets were empty except for the occasional passing military vehicles.

Chikako walked into the lobby and crossed the black and white tile floor, past the dark brown leather circular centerpiece seat with a tall slender carved teak staff rising above it. At the top of the staff, a large circular double-faced clock displayed the time. She carefully scanned the room as she moved to the main desk.

"May I help you?" the tall white man manning the counter asked.

She smiled and handed him a Taiwanese passport and driver's license in the name of *Lucy Woo*. Both were created and paid for without Hayato's knowledge. *No way he will find me now.*

"Miss Woo, certainly. Welcome to the Sarova Stanley. I do not see a reservation...but we do have rooms available. Will you be staying with us long?"

"At least a week…maybe longer. Are any of the suites available? Something quiet," Chikako asked, flashing her engaging smile once again.

He returned the smile. "Well…yes…how about the Windsor? Top floor."

"Perfect."

"Do you need help with your luggage?"

"It has not arrived yet. Could you recommend a decent clothing store? I have no idea when it will turn up." She brushed her hand across her hair.

"The Swanson is just down the street. Two blocks west. You cannot miss it."

"You are a Godsend. Thank you so much."

Once registered, which did not take long due to the vacancies caused by the ongoing turmoil in the city, the stunning Japanese woman walked past a pair of eight foot tall hand-painted wooden giraffe statues to an elevator. She rode alone to the top floor, stepped out and turned right on the rich golden brown carpet with intricate dark brown designs and entered the elegant Windsor Penthouse Suite. *Ah, this will do.*

The pale sand-colored inner curtains allowed for daylight to illuminate the room without the lights. Chikako moved to the windows and closed the dark brown inner drapes allowing only slender slivers of light to enter the room on either side. The temperature set for seventy-two degrees seemed cold compared to the heavy humid heat on the street.

She laid her blouse, shirt and lingerie neatly on the king-size bed and removed her pistol and cell phone from the travel bag.

She walked into the spacious bathroom, turned on the vanity lights, laid the weapon and phone on the rich teak countertop and ran her bath water into the brushed burnt-copper jet spa tub. Waiting for the bath to fill, she studied her reflection in the large mirror behind the double brushed copper sinks. At five nine, she was taller than most of her peers.

Chikako lifted her 36 C breasts, slid her hands down and over taunt stomach, firm hips and tight buttocks before running her fingers over each of the four scars that revealed damages incurred from her profession. She lingered longest on one that ran the length of her left thigh, to just above the knee. A plastic surgeon in Hong Kong had performed a miracle in scar revision, but the slender line never tanned and stood out against her hard muscled leg.

Before she slipped into the tub she turned off her cell phone and removed the battery. *Go to hell, Hayato.*

MOBUTTO'S SUMMER HOME

The trucks entered the gates to the outer compound at 2000 hours. Lt. Kamau met them and directed the driver of the 6x6 to proceed to the security details quarters and the two Toyota pickups to the front of the president's home. He stepped onto the back bumper of the second truck and rode along, jumping off when the vehicles halted.

Rhino climbed down from the southeast tower and jogged across the grounds, arriving just as the drivers turned off the trucks. "Outstanding! Download every thing but the MK 19s and grenades and get the supplies inside. We're going to turn these two dinky troks into our mobile launchers." *Have to run a few through these. No idea why they were left behind unless they are broke-back bitches.*

Lt. Kamau relayed his orders before moving inside the home to over see the disposition of the supplies. Rhino remained with the trucks and personally attended to the placement and securing of the full automatic grenade launchers. For the first time since the evacuation, he was filled with a palpable sense of purpose. *At least we have a fighting chance of successfully defending the compound.*

Completing the preparations of his new mobile defense weapons Rhino addressed the men, "Get some chow."

As he walked onto the front verandah, he heard a sound that sent a chill down his spine.. The *thump, thump, thump* made by distant helicopters. Quickly pulling the radio off his belt he shouted, "All hands to their stations! All hands to their stations! This is not a fokin' drill!"

Men poured out of the barracks and mess hall scrambling toward the defensive positions Rhino had assigned earlier.

As Lt. Kamau ran out the front door he yelled, "Two men on the 19 and one driver…Stand by!"

"Kamau! Get two more men to the launcher in the southwest tower." He turned toward the men manning the two towers. "Close the gates! Lock 'em down!"

Moments before the lights of the approaching helicopters carrying the men of the 50th Air Cavalry could be seen, the defenders were in positions to repel them.

"Get those choppers up!" Rhino shouted at the two crews. "Move three clicks northeast. Set down and wait for my call."

The pilots and copilots ran to their birds, started the engines and lifted off, flying away from the incoming 50th to safety. Rhino watched them fade into the night sky. *Sitting ducks here. Have to keep 'em out of harm's way for now.*

Kamau broke the silence. "I count six...no seven."

They watched the helicopters disappear behind a ridge two clicks away. Moments later they lifted off and flew back in the direction of Nairobi.

"First wave is on the ground," Fabian said to Kamau. He then pulled the radio off his belt again. "Stand by. Ready the flares. Launch on my command only."

"Just a suggestion ol' boy, but...I command the walls. You command the mobile MK launchers."

"I'm good with that...I need to talk with the security guards. Call me if anything happens before I return...Good luck." Without waiting for a reply he walked off toward the President's home.

YAKUZA COMPOUND

Hayato, wearing a pair of red silk pants, his chest glistening with sweat, opened the door between his and Chikako's rooms. He saw that she was not there, turned back to Raku lying nude on the bed behind him. *Wore that bitch out. Where the hell is Chikako?*

He moved into the hall from his favorite pleasures room, looked about and saw the ballistic nylon weapons case lying open—the pistol gone. He checked the room again and realized the charger for her cell phone and her light travel bag were missing as well.

Hayato moved through the house, anxiously checking all the rooms as he went before stepping out onto the pool deck. She was not there either—he strode through the living area again and out the front door. A man on a mission, he crossed the parking area and to the KDF soldier on duty at the front gate. "Has anyone left?"

"I just came on duty. No one has passed through these gates in the last hour."

Hayato turned and stormed back across the courtyard to the servants quarters where the other KDF soldiers and officers were billeted. He slammed open the front door and entered the main room with a force that shocked the men inside.

"Who was on duty last?" Anger was evident in his voice.

"I was," a guard said hesitantly.

"Did anyone leave on your watch?"

"One of the women...several hours ago," the guard replied. Beads of sweat appeared on his forehead as he looked up at the enraged Japanese.

Hayato glared at the guard for a moment, and then wheeled and headed out of the building.

Back inside the main home, Hayato called all the male Yakuza to join him in the living area. After they were assembled, he paced back and forth in front of them slowly.

"Who saw Chikako since she returned?" he asked quietly but the anger was simmering for all to see.

No one answered. Each man remained upright, his eyes locked straight ahead.

"You and you. Take the Toyota and search for her. Now!"

He returned to his bedroom, picked up his cell and called her number. The voice mail answered on the first ring. "Chikako. I am waiting for your call." Looking at Raku laying on the bed he continued, "If I do not hear from you *soon* I will punish Raku."

He hung up and called another number. When the voice answered he said, "Track Chikako's cell phone."

"Yes, master."

A minute passed. Then another before the voice came back on the phone. "I can not locate it, master. "

"Baka! How can that be?" Hayato growled.

"If she turned off the phone and removed the battery it is untraceable, master."

"Shimatta Teme!...Run your scan every thirty minutes. Call me as soon as you find her," he hissed through a clenched jaw before terminating the call. Raku moaned and he glanced over at her. *Too bad for you.*

He picked up a black leather satchel and laid it on the dresser. Removing several lengths of cotton rope, he moved to the bed and prepared each with a slip knot loop. As she slept, he carefully placed each of her hands and feet inside a loop and secured her to the bed—spread eagle.

She awakened as the last rope was being tied to one of the posters of the bed. "Hayato? What…" Realizing her situation, she struggled, attempting to free herself—to no avail. "Hayato? No…Please!"

He never broke his lecherous gaze into her eyes—took a small ivory pill box from the bedside stand, removed two small blue pills. He washed them down with a shot of sake.

Her eyes went wide in terror…

JOHANNESBURG, SOUTH AFRICA
Tambo International Airport

The Gulfstream 550 touched down lightly and rolled to the second high speed taxiway, where it slowed and then joined the parallel. It taxied back to a series of hangars opposite the passenger terminal. One was marked with a circle filled with four stars placed in the form of a cross. Under the logo, the words Southern Cross Aviation were painted in darker blue. The sliding doors of the gray steel building opened, and a ground marshaller directed the crew to taxi inside.

"Looks like we were expected," Gus commented.

"Five will get you ten, it's a CIA op," the copilot added.

Once inside, the ground crew signaled for them to set brakes and shut down.

"We're here, Smitty…let the man off

"You got it, sir," he said as he unlatched the entry door lock and opened it. A set of stairs deployed out of the fuselage as the hydraulic system activated.

"Welcome to Africa," the loadmaster said he stepped back from the doorway.

Mark descended the stairs and walked over to Bert and the dark blue SUV rental vehicle. "Hey, Bert. Good to see you, my friend." The two engaged in a hearty bear hug.

"Good to be seen, I think."

"Sir, here are your bags," the master sergeant said as he set down the roll aboard bag and the ever-present silver attaché case.

"Appreciate it, I'll see you guys after I take care of some minor details. I have Gus's cell number."

The loadmaster nodded and left to discuss refueling options.

Mark loaded the bag in the back, and took the passenger seat in the left front. He set the metal case behind his seat as Bert slipped into the right side driver's position. The SUV pulled out of the airport onto R21 headed south. In a matter of minutes it turned left onto M12 West.

"I contacted Schoeman and delivered the shopping list and where we need it. Alf suggested we contact one of his associates if we need another op." Bert handed him the information from Alf.

Mark studied the name and number for a moment. "I know this guy...Has a death wish to the ninth degree."

"Exactly how Alf described him. Your call...Four seems to be a light team for what you intend to do,"

"I'll call him. Hand me your cell."

"What's up with your phone?"

"Had to turn it off. The young woman I went to see in DC has called twenty times since I left. Sent thirty text messages as well. I can't keep focused…"

Bert cut him off, "Never let a woman inside buddy…Get you sidetracked in a New York minute."

They shared a look then began to laugh.

"She's a twenty-two on a scale of ten…Lifelong gymnast and can get in positions…"

"Lock that shit up…Get yourself killed…get us all killed."

The two rode in silence. Mark opened his silver Haliburton case—removed the brown leather horizontal shoulder rig and put it on. He lifted out his prized Colt 1911 Gold Cup from the case, dropped the magazine, inspected it before returning it and effortlessly chambered a round. The solid metal-on-metal click reverberated sweetly inside the passenger compartment. Bert glanced over admiringly at the sound of the weapon being chambered for action.

"Pull over…I'll drive the last leg," Mark said.

"Sure?"

He nodded. "Been sittin' on my thumb for the last sixteen hours."

They rode another half and hour before he turned onto Panay Road headed north. "Do you remember an op called Black Bear?"

"Yeah. Worked with him in Peru. Heard he bought the farm in Java."

"Not exactly. Hal put him out to pasture after Java though. He's a caretaker now...We're going to rally at his vault location."

"Does Hal know?"

"'Course...I sent Banjo a text message after you and I talked yesterday."

"Banjo?"

"Hal's one strange Scotsman. Everyone has a code name. That's how I ended up with Zorro. If anyone gets injured and can't continue field ops...and he thinks your worth it, you get a caretaker gig till you hit thirty years...But your handle is changed to some weird-ass name of Hal's choosing again."

"Never worked directly for Hal myself. Any flying gig I took that involved his ops was by the numbers."

"Taught me seventy-five percent of what I know. Landing at one of his safe houses will cost me big time."

DESERTED CEMENT FACTORY
Johannesburg, South Africa

Mark parked at the double chain link gates facing the deserted looking cement factory and powered up his cell and sent a text message—*Zorro has landed*. Five minutes later, a dirty tan Land Rover pulled out of a small building near the main three story manufacturing structure. As it approached the gate, they could see the beaming smile of Banjo behind the wheel. The vehicles soon disappeared into an open double-wide door of the run down facility and pulled into a small bay half way down the cavernous building.

The three men exited their vehicles and shook hands all around—they had a shared history.

"Sweet Lord! You be a sight for sore eyes," Banjo said to Mark. "And you...you as well, sky pilot." Banjo walked with practiced ease on his high-tech prosthetic limb.

"Hard to tell you're a peg leg Bear...uh, Banjo," Mark remarked as he admired the man's mobility.

"They calls it a C-Leg. Dis sumbitch is microprocessor controlled. Has dis remote control that allows me to switch the settings in a flash for walkin', runnin', bicyclin', inline skatin'...hell I can dance better than any white man with it."

Mark and Bert could not help but burst out laughing as Banjo did a bit of hip hop dancing.

Another man carrying a scoped rifle in his prosthetic hand began to descend the steel stairs from the third floor.

"Didn't know you had an assistant now. Care taking gettin' to be too much for your sorry one-legged Alabama self now?" Marked asked.

"That's Harmonica, used to be Puma. He showed up last week fer me to train his happy ass. I o-fficially hit thirty years tomorrow. Gonna take my raggedy black butt to Dumaguete, eat some good foods an live the life of leisures."

"Dumaguete? Isn't that where Pinoy Joe was from?" Mark asked.

"Sho 'nough is. I waz with him on that op when I lost my foot. He took me to his home to recuperates. I plumb fell in loves with dat place."

As Harmonica joined them, Mark and Bert could see clearly the high tech replacement bebionic3 myoelectric hand. It looked fully functional holding the Springfield M1A.

"Look like a real life terminator," Bert commented.

"Ya'll would be amazed. It has fourteen grip positions, microprocessors continually adjusting the individual motors for each finger...hell I can type and pull a trigger, they so finely tuned. Selectable thumb positions, speed controls...only thing I cain't do is spank my monkey...Latest model," Harmonica said as he proudly demonstrated the limb.

"Gezz! How much did that set you back?" Bert asked.

"No idea...Hal paid for it."

"Harmonica, I likes to interduce you to a couple a salty dogs, Zorro and Bert."

"Your name precedes you, Zorro. Privilege to meet a legend...Bert, heard some tales about you as well."

"I don't know who you've been talking to, but suggest you take to wearing taller boots the next time...Hal's the legend. I'm just a leatherneck Texan lookin' for a place..."

"Shit! He cries his self to sleep ever night since you went out on yer own, he does."

"The man's the one that said it...Flashed your photo on the screen first day new ops orientation. Said to be the best and we'd have to measure up to you," Harmonica added.

"First thing you need to know about Hal...he's the biggest liar you'll ever meet. And I say that with all due respect for the crotchety ol' Scottish bastard. And if he *ever* says the op is a piece of cake...run like the hounds of hell are behind you."

They followed Banjo and Harmonica up a series of metal stairs to the second floor where they entered a room once used by the operations manager. Dust covered the desk, empty file cabinets and book cases. On the desk, a blue Igloo ice chest rested next to several bags of groceries. Bert opened the cooler and removed two cold bottles of spring water.

Zorro inspected the food and selected a bun, a length of boerewors, and a bottle of local mustard. After taking the first bite, let out a sigh of enjoyment. "Man I missed this. Any naartjie?" he asked looking through the bags.

"In the cooler...Tangerine and satsuma," Harmonica answered as he removed a map of Africa from a leather satchel sitting on one of the file cabinets.

As Bert picked out his food. "I'm still waiting on confirmation for a ride..."

"Cancel it. The fly boys with the Gulfstream have orders to drop me...us off in Kenya."

"Who'd you have to blow to arrange that?" Harmonica asked incredulously.

"Up yours...Senator Breitbart called the President of the United States. She waved her magic wand and away I went."

"Yup. Move along now, folks. No legends to see here," Banjo said to his trainee.

"So our insertion is government sanctioned?" Bert asked as he curbed his hunger—bits of bread crumbs falling on his chest.

"Oh, Hell no! Once we step off the Gulfstream in Kenya, we are on our own. We'll need transpo to wherever Rhino and the President are though…Reminds me…need to call him."

Waiting for the phone to connect to satellite service he grabbed a chilled satsuma—citrus unshiu, a seedless and easy-peeling citrus species, also known as cold-hardy mandarin, satsuma orange or Christmas orange.

Rhino felt his cell phone vibrating as he lay sound asleep on a cot in the southwest guard tower. Rather than rest inside the President's luxurious home, he had chosen to remain where he felt would be the likely site of any attack. *There's that same number.* Rhino answered the call, "Who the fok 're ya? What the hell do ya want?"

Remembering that Rhino did not know his new number, Mark answered in his best she-boy voice, "I'm calling to inform you, Mr. Fabian, that your order with Victoria's Secret has been shipped. The tracking number is…"

The blood vessels on Rhino's neck pulsed out. "What? Ya bloody domkop brak! I never placed any damn order…"

The sounds of Mark and the other operatives laughing gave him reason to pause, "Who the bloody fok is this?"

"Zorro, dick wad." Mark laughed.

"You moffie mompie! I ain't got time fer any o' your loskop sat piel! The whole of Kenya's 'bout to come down on me here."

"Figured as much…I'm in Johannesburg. Have a team together early this mornin' and enroute to you ASAP. What's your twenty?"

Rhino's mood improved immediately. "Mobutto's summer estate. You 'member it, right?"

"West slope. Mount Kenya. Text the GPS coordinates to Bert…Details as I know them."

"Bert? Who else?"

"Malakhi, Crank and Ian O'Rielly."

"O'Rielly? He's crazier than Crank. Well, if'n dyin's his dream, he's comin' to the right place, he is. Expect more friggin' pop-up targets than we saw Afghanies in '05."

"Hang in there…Cavalry's on the way, buddy. Keep us updated on your tac sit."

"Just another head's up for you. Word has it, the Yakuza moved back into the Jap's estate in Nairobi," Rhino cautioned.

"Yakuza?…Jesus. Well, hell…the more the merrier." Mark hung up, a frown on his brow .

"Yakuza?" Banjo asked.

"Ivory pipeline mules to the far east. Before I left Kenya, I parted their boss from his head," Mark said. "No harm, no foul if you want to check out now, Bert."

"Oh, I wouldn't miss this one for all the tea in China."

"Funny, but I'm beginning to think that's where I'll end up before this rodeo is over."

MOUNTAIN CABIN
Blue Ridge Mountains

Sarah sat on the four poster bed in the master bedroom wearing sweat pants and shirt. She was propped against the ornately hand-carved cherry wood headboard staring at the wide screen television. Images of the carnage in Kenya ran in what seemed to be a never-ending loop on the BBC. Her youthful face, devoid of makeup, was red and her eyes puffy from crying. She turned off the sound and picked up her cell phone—dialing the number once again. *Please answer this time, Mark. Please!*

His voice came over the phone sounding distant and cool, not like the tender voice she remembered while they held each other and made love. "Hello, Sarah."

"Mark! Oh, my God! Where are you? Are you all right? I love you!" The words rushed out like the mountain stream roaring below the cabin before she could stop them.

"Easy girl...I'm fine."

"Where are you? I'm so worried," she said with a bit more control of her emotions.

"I can't tell you that now...I'm safe. Where are you?"

"I'm at the cabin. I missed you so much...I came back here to feel close to you again..."

"I don't know when...or if I'll be comin' back..."

She started crying again. "Don't say that...I love you! I need you!"

A long silence hung like a dark heavy storm cloud over her as Sarah waited for him to reply. "Mark?"

"We'll talk when I'm finished here. I can't allow myself the distraction…"

"Distraction?" She choked back her tears. "Distraction! Is that all I am to you?"

"No…I have to go now. Please don't call me again. I'll call you when…"

She hung up and buried her face in the covers as her sobs racked her body. *Distraction? Oh God. What a fool I was…I am. Damn you, Mark Ingram.*

DESERTED CEMENT FACTORY
South Africa

Mark replaced the cell phone in his pocket and turned to the map Bert had pinned to the wall. They stared silently for several moments in silence.

Bert broke the uncomfortable moment. "You know, Maggie's the reason I took the fly gig for DeBeers…Changed my life for the better, she did. Home cooked meals, clean sheets, a warm lover every night who understood my nightmares."

Mark lifted a red marking pen from the top of the filing cabinet and placed an circle in the vicinity of where his memory told him Mobutto's summer estate lay.

"You could start a new life, my friend. Get some cushy consultant position in the states…Never look back…"

"First, we extract Rhino. Not sure what comes next. Hong Kong seems to be calling my name. What ever happens…I don't know if I could…you know…start all over again."

"Sure you could. If this little cream puff cares about you, and from what I could hear off your cell she does...All you have to do is walk away and never look back," Bert responded with the tone of a friend.

"Yeah...The lookin' back part would be a bitch. There's still a bounty on my ass in Colombia. Probably one here in South Africa for that matter...What kind of life would it be? Always lookin' over my shoulder."

"Stupid bastard! You're already looking over your shoulder! Duh."

A tan Toyota 4 Runner followed Banjo's Land Rover into the cavernous open area and parked in a bay next to Mark and Bert's SUV. Malakhi stepped out and surveyed the area cautiously.

"Up here," Bert called down from the walkway outside the small office room he and Mark had set up as a operations command center.

Nodding acknowledgment, Malakhi removed his gear from the back of the 4 Runner and climbed the stairs and looked around. "Any tools yet? I feel a little naked only carrying Ariela." He removed his light blue jacket and exposed his IMI Desert Eagle in .44 magnum—the one he called Ariela or *lioness of God*—nestled in a shoulder rig under his left arm.

"Hell, Malakhi! That Eagle could take out a friggin' tank," Bert responded.

"Maybe, but I'd feel better with a H&K for back up...if you know what I mean."

"Banjo will weapon you up. Give him your dream list," Mark said. "Glad you could make it…Hungry?"

"Starving. Airplane food sucks big time," the former IDF special forces member said. He fell on the food like a starving lion.

They returned to the map of Kenya and the notes they were making on Bert's laptop while Banjo wrote down the items Malakhi wanted to carry.

The sound of a motorcycle reverberated heavily in the open manufacturing area as Crank rolled in on a four cylinder Kawasaki. He shut down engine and looked around for signs of Mark and Bert. Harmonica parked the Land Rover and started up the steel stairs motioning him to follow.

As Crank entered the small command center he said sarcastically, "Nice digs. I expected more."

"Where did you rent that crotch rocket in Johannesburg?" Bert asked.

"Didn't…bought it," Crank replied with his crazy grin. "Going to ship it back home when we're done…Imagine tooling around Chiang Mai on that beast? Babe magnet deluxe."

Bert glanced at Mark, then replied, "Like you have any need for more…"

"Hey! You have to rotate 'em…Frequently…Like tires. If not they go flat on you," Crank replied with a laugh.

Mark looked up from Bert's laptop. "Chows in the bags. Beer and water in the cooler…if Malakhi left any."

"A man has to eat. When do we resupply? There's going to be nothing left when surfer boy here finishes," Malakhi replied.

"Harmonica, you guys make a grocery run. Crank, you stay here…While you're out, Bert, call the weapons man from a pay phone. Get current intel on delivery," Mark said.

"On it, Boss. Let's go, Jewboy." Bert slapped Malakhi on the shoulder as he walked out of the room.

Crank wolfed down the last of the food as Mark spoke, "Good to have you with us. How's the recovery?"

"Done. Hell I was riding waves off Siargao five months ago…Knarly post tsunami opuus. Got bent more than once but had more bonzer glides than not…Some *outstanding* jazz glassing."

"Un-uh?"

"I'm not joking man! Friggin' eight to ten foot breaks you could ride for a mile. Cold as witches tit…but the hot LBFMs warmed me up every night."

"How many women back home now?"

"Four."

"Jaka still with you?"

"Nah…started getting possessive, nest building. You know? Had to cut her loose…How 'bout you Grandpa? Have a little nester now, do you?"

Mark ignored his personal question. "Give Banjo your weapons list, then take your bike and do a sweep around the area…Back here in an hour."

After Crank left, Mark stood up and stretched. "Lets visit the vault, Banjo. I'd rather have the weapons in here than have the team see the safe room."

***

CHAPTER EIGHT

DESERTED CEMENT FACTORY
Johannesburg, South Africa

Harmonica, Bert, Malakhi and Ian O'Rielly stepped out of the SUV just as Crank roared in from the opposite end of the factory's main floor. Sliding his motorcycle to a stop, Crank hopped off, booted the kick stand down and crossed to Ian.

"Ian! You Irish header!" Crank said, again with his crazy grin.

"Boyyo. Ye broke away from going at it, I see. When I heard ye were on this one, I asked meself bloody why. You're as useless as a wee chocolate tea pot," Ian said with a thick Irish accent.

The two men embraced in a bear hug—each attempted to out-squeeze the other. Satisfied neither would win, they broke and shook hands heartily and punched each other's shoulders.

"I heard you bought the farm over in Borneo...Or was it Java?" Crank sparred.

"It'll take more than few little mussies to do meself in, laddie...What's up with the bazzer...ye be lookin' like the old man Zorro," Ian jousted back.

"You're not looking any better...With that beard of a flaming leprechon...Phew!...when's the last time you took a bath?" Malakhi asked.

"Bite me bollox, ye Jewish bitch bag," Ian responded as he shoved Malakhi.

Bert was half-way up the stairs when he turned. "When you kids get through with comparing Johnsons, bring the supplies up." He couldn't help but smile as the three men continued to insult each other while they grabbed the bags and boxes from the back of the SUV.

Mark greeted the newest arrival as he had all the others. "Good to have you on board, Ian."

"I came soon as I heard ye were formin' up a right good bucket of snots. That and the fact ye'd be goin' into Kenya...Faith and a good place to ply ye trade it is."

Mark turned to Bert. "Intel on the delivery?"

"0400 hours. Once we check the gardening supplies we're off to your fancy sky taxi and on our way."

"Ye gotta sky taxi now do ye?" Ian asked.

"Hell, he's got the damned President of the United States' private jet!" Bert exclaimed.

Ian, Crank and Malakhi all looked to Mark in disbelief.

"Temporarily...Once we land, we're on our own. That's where it gets a tad complicated," Mark said with a sly grin.

"I've got the GPS coordinates now. Rhino sent them while we were collecting chow for the kids," Bert said as he moved to the map of Kenya. After studying it for a minute, he remarked, "Couple hours by air. Impossible by road, I suspect."

"Still have a connection or two in-country." Mark also moved to the map and marked a circle with a black marker. "The David Sheldrick Wildlife Sanctuary...His widow runs it now. She'll get us in the air."

SAROVA STANLEY HOTEL
Nairobi

Chikako woke on the first ring of the courtesy phone. She looked at the face of the six inch round clock sitting on the dresser across the room as she rolled over to lift the receiver. As she held it to her ear, the computer voice informed her it was 4 AM, temperature 27 degrees Celsius, and began to list the hours that the various dining establishments in the hotel opened for breakfast.

She hung up yawned, stretched and rolled out of bed. For a moment, she flexed her toes, then moved to the lavatory and started the hot water running in the free standing glazed glass shower. Before entering, she went back to the large room, picked up a desk chair and jammed under the entrance door handle. *Should have done that last night.*

Once in the shower, she leaned over and let the hot water run over her head and shoulders. Sitting down on the floor, she reached up and increased the flow of hot water to compensate for the free fall cooling of the invigorating moisture. Five minutes later she stood, washed her hair, applied conditioner and then bathed her body. She turned off the shower and stepped out onto the cool tile floor.

At the front desk, Chikako rang the small silver bell and waited for an attendant to appear. Looking around the empty lobby she marveled at the huge oil paintings of African animals in their native settings. She stepped over to take a closer view of a bull elephant, ears flared out, nose down with magnificent curved tusks. *Damn shame…Killing these creatures for their ivory.*

A sleepy looking attendant from behind the desk, addressed her, "Yes, miss. How may I assist you?"

"I need a cab," she responded still gazing at the painting. "I know it's early…"

"No problem, miss. Give me a moment," he replied as he picked up the phone.

YAZUKA COMPOUND

Chikako stepped out of the cab two blocks from the compound and watched it drive off. She had only walked a few yards when three black men stepped out of an alley in front of her.

"Oh my! Look what we have here," the larger man said with a wicked smile that exposed his gold capped teeth.

"Going to be a good day," the smallest man chimed in, his face contorted with carnal desires.

She continued to walk toward the men as if they did not exist.

"I'm gonna consider keeping this one," the larger man said with lusty interest.

As he reached out to her, she grabbed his hand and twisted it violently back while delivering a viscous side kick to the smaller man's chest—breaking several ribs, puncturing his left lung and knocking him to the sidewalk. His head smashed into the concrete with such force, blood immediately pooled on the dirty cement. Holding the larger man's hand, she took him to his knees as the third man slashed at her with a machete. Chikako whirled, pulling the larger man's arm forward. The blade sliced through his forearm just above the wrist, causing the artery to pump out his life's blood in spurts.

"Ahhh!" the man screamed in agony.

The third man looked on in disbelief. She delivered a powerful forward knife hand to his throat—grabbed his esophagus, ripped it and his tongue out. The man dropped the bloody machete, fell to the ground holding his neck in both hands; gurgling to breath through his own blood and vomit.

She stepped to the obviously unconscious smaller man, crushed his throat with a downward kick, driving her heel with such force the man's eyes literally popped out of his head.

Chikako continued walking to the Yakuza compound without looking back. The entire event took little more than fifteen seconds. *You fucking black bastards bloodied my white pants.*

She quickly reached the Yakuza compound. Standing at the gate, staring at the sleeping KDF guard, she realized a bit of good luck was hers. "A-hum!"

The guard jumped from the chair to his feet and fumbled with his rifle. Realizing who stood outside the ornate red wrought iron gate, he quickly looked back to the house and servants residence to see if anyone was aware of his misdeed.

"Open the gate. Say nothing of my return and I will not mention how I got in," she said softly, flashing a sly smile.

The guard stood frozen as he considered his options. A look of both fear and confusion was on his face.

"I'm waiting…Or would you rather someone else see us?" She eyed the man with contempt.

The thin black odoriferous guard, his suit rumpled and soiled from wear the previous three days, removed a key from his pants pocket and unlocked the gate.

"Good choice." She walked through and continued on to the main house.

Chikako quietly moved through the darkened hall and carefully opened her bedroom door, closing it quietly. Slipping silently across the room she stopped by the connecting door and listened. She removed her clothing and stuffed them between the mattress and the box springs before placing the battery back into her cell phone and lying it on the bedside table.

She took her pistol out of the travel bag, lifted the sheet and light blanket and lay down on the bed. *If I even think he will touch me…he's dead.*

Twenty minutes later Hayato awoke to the sound of his cell phone vibrating on the beside table. He rolled over the still secured Raku and retrieved it. Seeing who was calling, he answered, "Where is she?"

"She is in the compound. I believe she is in the bedroom next to yours," the voice said.

Hayato charged into the room. There, lying on the bed, he saw Chikako. "Where have you been?"

"I went to find a Buddhist Temple. You were busy with Raku when I left, so I did not bother you," she answered softly.

"You will never...*never* leave without my knowledge again. Is that clear you chikushou?"

"Yes."

"Yes, *what?*"

"Yes, master," she answered with a cold gleam in her eye.

DESERTED CEMENT FACTORY
Johannesburg, South Africa

Bert and Mark stood in the center of the vast open room as the BMW one and a half ton South African military truck drove in following the command vehicle. Mark stood at parade rest, hands behind his back, holding his Gold Cup. *Never trust a thief.*

Bert held a briefcase in his left hand and had his Beretta in a leg holster, the safety strap off and folded back, his hand on the grip.

The rest of the men lay in positions surrounding the delivery site, weapons ready—if anything went amiss.

The vehicles pulled to a halt, stirring up a light gray cloud of cement dust. Captain Albertus Schoeman stepped out and walked to Bert and Mark briskly. "Let's see the money," he said with authority.

"We'll inspect the weapons first," Mark replied with equal authority.

The three men stood for a moment measuring one another. Any time money and stolen weapons were exchanged there was always the chance of foul play—no one blinked.

Finally Schoeman spoke, "I remember you...You're the bloody bloke that murdered a gang of nigga revolutionaries last year in Cape Town."

"It was a fair fight," Mark stated flatly.

"Fair? Christ, man, there were what...Six or seven of 'em as I recall...Right?" The South African Captain said with a laugh.

"Didn't stop to count...Look, you came recommended by a former employer, Hal McCambell. Said you could be depended on if the money was right...money's in the case...Let's see the weapons."

"Yeah, sure...Right this way." Schoeman turned and waved for them to follow him to the back of the truck. He pulled back the tarp and exposed the crates. "Everything on the list."

After Schoemen, his men departed, Banjo stepped out of the shadows and joined Mark and Bert. "If'n yer takin' any mo volunteers I be on da list."

Mark turned to him with admiration in his eyes. "Be proud to have you, but you're retiring…The land of coconut milk and little brown fuckin' machines…"

"One mo op, Zorro. Dat's all I'm askin'. I can keep up. Dis space-age foot won't be no problem."

Mark placed his hand on Banjo's shoulder walking away from the weapons. "Never thought it would, old friend. But…this has all the signs of a one way trip…Be a shame to deprive those sweet Filipinas of your charms and oversized endowment."

Banjo laughed hard before responding, "So yous were checking out da tool in da shower all dees years!"

"Hangs between your knees…Sorta hard to miss."

"Up yours, cracker!…So…seriously…I'm in?"

Mark studied his black friend's face. He recalled the time in Chile where Bear had carried him—broken ankle and all—through the jungle as he fired magazine after magazine at the Shining Path insurgents pursuing them. He saw the earnest desire in Banjo's eyes. "One *last* op, my friend…one last op."

JOHANNESBURG, SOUTH AFRICA
OR Tambo International Airport

The team arrived at the Gulfstream discretely parked inside the hangar.

"Heave to girls and get the gear loaded," Mark ordered. "The faster we get in the air the better. Don't want some rent-a-cop stumblin' on us. Poor bastard's certain to have a wife and six kids…Bear, your post is up by that corner of hangar.

Bert, you got over there in the rear. Crank, Ian, Malakhi…on me." Mark stepped out of the SUV.

Ten minutes later, the jet was taxiing, awaiting takeoff clearance from the tower.

Mark immediately used his cell phone to call the Sheldrick Wildlife Sanctuary to arrange for transportation when they landed. Three rings later, the voice of a young woman answered.

"Sheldrick Wildlife Sanctuary, Malute speaking."

"Good morning Malute. Mark Ingram. Is Dame Daphne around?"

"Oh! Hello Mark! Let me get her on the line. She'll be thrilled to hear from you," she said with a distinct tone of joy.

Several moments later Dame Daphne came on the line. "Mark! How are you?…Where are you?"

"I'm doin' fine. Four hours out of Nairobi, Darlin'…need a little help. Don't know who else to call."

"Certainly…Anything you need, young man."

"Can you get my friends and I from the airport to the sanctuary?…Do you still have that ten passenger van?"

"Yes, I do…There's ten of you?"

"No, but we have…uh, luggage."

"I'll have Stephen pick you up. You said four hours?"

"There about…Pick us up at the Wilson Airport. Give Stephen my cell number and I want his so we can coordinate after we land, if you please."

Mark wrote down the number before thanking her and hanging up. "All set," he said to the team. "That was easy."

After takeoff, Mark and each man began a final inspection of his weapons and gear in his own fashion. Self-employment allowed them to wear what they liked—how they liked. One man might prefer a hip or drop-leg holster, while another would elect to wear his sidearm in a shoulder rig or cross draw on his vest. Mark preferred to carry his extra magazines in a shoulder bag while Malakhi wanted his strapped on the front of his chest.

Each weapon was fully disassembled, cleaned, lubricated and reassembled by the man who would use and depend on it.

The clothing was a hodge-podge of South African uniforms and civilian clothing suitable to the rugged demands of the African terrain. Everyone brought their own boots and socks. Camouflage BDUs were generally the same from one country's military to the next—only the pattern varied.

Ian, Crank and Malakhi kept up the good-natured insults and conversation. Only when asked for an opinion or to settle a dispute did Mark concern himself with the banter.

Zorro field stripped, cleaned, oiled and reassembled Betsy II, his back-up to Betsy I left with Rhino for safekeeping. *That worked out well...not.* Betsy II, a Springfield National Match M1A, .308 rifle with black composite stock would do fine. Opening a hard plastic foam-lined case, he lifted a Nightforce B.E.A.S.T. scope. It featured a 34mm diameter tube and world class 5-25x56mm glass with target turrets. It was attached to a Springfield M1A/M14 factory made fourth generation all-steel

138

mount. Steel weighed more than the lightweight aluminum alloy ones, but when removing the scope and remounting, it would still maintain a constant zero. The scope itself cost more than the rifle at $3,300.00—but was well worth the price. Once the scope was attached to the mount Mark slid it back into the padded nylon case and attached it to his chest carrier.

He selected a shoulder bag that would carry six 20 round magazines. Another—designed to secure twelve grenades—he filled it with a mixture of fragmentation, phosphorous, smoke and flash bang.

He pulled two bandoleers loaded with 7.62x51 ammo in stripper clips out of a metal ammo can. *Bright clean South African ammunition.* He emptied two boxes of Winchester National Match .308 onto the seat beside him and jammed them into ten round magazines and stripper clips marked with a black X. *The military ball would do fine out to 500 yards but the Winchester rounds would be dead on even out to 1,000.* Finally he filled a pair of stripper clips with AP or Armor Piercing, and another pair with API and marked them appropriately.

He had cleaned his Colt on the last flight and only loaded two of his extra Wilson Combat magazines with 8 rounds of US military ball and two with 185 grain FTX Critical Defense.

The CamelBak hydration pack was new issue. *I'll drink from the supply of anyone on this team. But not some unknown mofos.* On the lashing straps, he attached several small pouches—first aid, weapons cleaning kit, fire kit and one with two dozen one tenth ounce Krugerrands. *Barter is good, but gold is king.*

In the three day recon pack, he added four pairs of clean socks wrapped in plastic bags. A dozen MREs, poncho liner, a spare empty hydration bladder and a one pound bag of refined sugar went in the main compartment.

In the three small outside pouches he loaded his medical supplies.

Satisfied with the pack, he lashed a poncho on the top and set it aside. He then checked a chest carrier for defects and placed the Armor500 molded bulletproof plates in the front and back pockets. *God knows I wish we all had one of those BEF sci-fi suits, but this will have to do.*

Stacking everything in the floor and seat next to him, Mark retrieved a Haliburton case from one of the crates—*Zorro* stenciled on the face in black letters. Opening the case he studied his second favorite handgun, after his Gold Cup, a Smith & Wesson 5906 stainless steel 9mm. *The question is not if the SHTF...but rather how many times.*

"You look like you're ready for just about anything..." the big Air Force loadmaster quipped, eyeing the pile of gear and weapons as he passed headed to the cockpit. "...except a dinosaur."

"Need a Gunga Din...you interested?"

"Oh, hell no! I just fly the friendly skies. Getting my boots dirty is not in my MOS," the master sergeant said without even the hint of a grin.

***

CHAPTER NINE

AIRSPACE OVER AFRICA

Bert spent the least amount of time in preparation—he had brought everything he knew he would need from home. Living in South Africa meant only a short drive to the rally point.

He preferred a Colt M4—he was never much of a long range shooter, but very handy with the little black rifle when needed. He, like Mark, carried a Colt 1911, a Model Mk IV, with five magazines for his side arm. The parkerized finish he had applied himself twenty years before was showing signs of wear due to the age and use of the weapon. He carried only four 30 round carbine magazines due to weight—his concern was that he would have difficulty keeping up with the younger stronger men if he packed too much.

As the best trained EMS of the group, he carried the medical bag—considered a Level V bag—and could do just about any field surgery necessary. Since he kept his own weapons ready 24/7, he spent most of his preparation time inventorying the bag that would mean life or death to any of the team wounded.

Malakhi—call sign *Boom Boom*—disassembled, cleaned, oiled and reassembled his trusted Desert Eagle .44 Magnum and five 8 round mags. He chose a Galil R4—manufactured in South Africa—as his rifle from the weapons stored in the vault at the cement factory. It was chambered for the 5.56 ammunition and similar to the weapon he used while serving in the IDF Commando Unit Shayetet 13—the naval commando unit, equivalent to the US Navy SEALs.

As the explosives expert on the team, he inspected all the Claymore mines before handing each of the team a M7 bag with two mines each. He carried an additional two himself. *Nothing says hello so rudely as 700 one-eighth inch steel balls traveling at nearly 4,000 feet per second.* When a M28A1 Claymore detonated, the explosion would drive them in a 60° fan-shaped pattern that was a little over six feet high, fifty-five yards wide and out to a range of 100 yards, with fifty yards being considered optimum.

Boom Boom would carry a pound of C4, and a dozen detonators. He, like most demolition experts, preferred C4 for simple reasons—stability, insensitive to most physical shocks and cannot be detonated by gunshot, very important to the carrier in a fire fight. He also carried a bag with assorted grenades. *Never have too many grenades.*

"These Armor500 plates are money in the bank, you guys," he remarked to the team as he loaded chest carrier.

Crank, a black skull cap over his blonde hair pulled back in a low pony tail, broke ranks on the 5.56 and selected a Vektor SS77, 7.62 general purpose machine gun. He rigged two shoulder bags, each with a 100 hundred round belt and would carry the weapon with a two hundred round belt. He then rigged another two shoulder bags, one each for Ian and Bear to carry as back-up.

For a sidearm, he chose a Smith & Wesson Model 629 .44 Magnum revolver, 7.5" barrel in stainless steel with a matte finish.

"How'd you get that hand cannon into the country?" Bert asked.

"Bought it here a couple of years ago working a contract. Keep it in a safety deposit box at the bank."

Satisfied with his machine gun and side arm readiness, he began filling his three day pack.

Ian, his red short-cropped hair gleaming with a light sweat, chose the only H&K, a MP5SD, with a removable integrated suppresser and a Aimpoint Micro Sight T-1. He wove together a group of pouches for 30 round magazines and altered them to carry across his chest.

Bear carried another M4 with a M203 grenade launcher for his battle rifle.

The four hour flight passed quickly and the loadmaster entered the passenger compartment to alert Mark they would be starting their descent.

"Thirty minutes. Hot Joe in ten," the burly master sergeant said as he passed by on his way to the laboratory.

"Rise and shine girls. Thirty minutes till you start earning you keep," Mark announced in his best DI voice.

"Shit man! I just closed my eyes," Crank said groggily.

"You snooze, you lose…and vice versa," Zorro shot back.

"Huh?"

WILSON AIRPORT
Nairobi

Thirty-five minutes later, the plane approached the Wilson Airport, located on the east side of Nairobi—originally named Nairobi Aerodrome. Due to wide spread corruption, land surrounding the airport was illegally developed resulting in only thirty meters clearance at the end of runway 32 for a buffer. Any aircraft that overran the runway would crash into the houses.

"Nobody home on the tower freq," said Gus as Mark crouched between and behind the two pilots in the cramped cockpit.

"Tell you what…make a low pass parallel to three-two at, say…fifteen hundred feet. I'll check out the area and make certain the runway is not barricaded."

Gus glanced back and saw he was carrying a small pair of Leica binoculars. "Not your first goat ropin', I see."

"No, sir. Try to plan for almost all contingencies…Two hundred knots will do. No sense in making a big-ass slow movin' target if we can avoid it."

"Speed is life," the copilot said as he looked at the smoldering ruins of the shantytowns surrounding the city. "You guys sure you really want to do this?"

"Yeah, guess I'm kinda warped that way. Got a good friend down there…and he'd do it for me."

Both pilots nodded in agreement. Each knew the Air Force spent many lives and millions of dollars trying to rescue downed fliers—they understood the concept. The A/C clicked off the autopilot, pulled the throttles to idle and made a shallow turn to the north. Drifting smoke indicated the prevailing winds to be from the west. He rolled out of his turn and selected a heading of 320 degrees.

"Flaps five."

The copilot moved the flap handle to the desired position and confirmed the indicator moved to the first index mark. He pointed at the gauge as he made his verbal crosscheck, "Flaps to five."

Mark scanned the area as the sleek aircraft continued its descent and leveled off. Nothing was out of the ordinary, save a few burnt-out remnants of cars in the almost deserted parking lots. The tinted windows in the control tower were shattered and the top of the building was blackened with soot from a looter's fire.

"The assholes are like pet coons…what they don't fuck up, they shit on," Mark muttered as he continued the scan.

"See anything?"

"Looks like the rampaging masses have come and gone. At least the runway is clear...Hello! Looks like our ride is already in place." The familiar logo of the Sheldrick animal sanctuary could be seen on the van. Stephen was standing outside, waving one hand at the white jet as it passed abeam him. A slight smile came to Mark's face. "Boys, that's about a good as it's gonna get...Put 'er down."

Ten minutes after touchdown, Stephen drove the passenger van carrying the team and their gear out the gate and onto the highway. Mark looked back to see the Gulfstream clear the housing development and streak northwestward.

MOBUTTO'S SUMMER ESTATE

The defenders of the compound had spent a long night waiting and watching as three flights of helicopters came in and landed just out of sight in an alternating light downpour and torrential rain. Flashes of lightening only enhanced the surreal image of the warbirds operating in the distance. Unbeknown to the small group of men inside, the first wave of the 50th Air Cav had forced marched most of the night and were positioned in one of the many ravines to the east of the compound.

The total force preparing to attack numbered 336 crack troops. Veterans of the Somali wars, they were well trained and battle hardened. All they were waiting for was General Janmohamed himself and the fourth wave of 112 men to arrive.

Rhino stood in the southeast tower scanning the south horizon and occasionally the east—purely from experience. Lt.

Kamau manned the southwest tower and swept the west and south side relentlessly for any movement. *Bloody bastards are takin' their time.*

Rhino felt his cell phone vibrate, pulled it out of his shirt pocket and saw Mark's number. "You're going to miss the party, bro," he mumbled as he kept his eyes on the focused on the perimeter.

"The fox has landed. We are enroute to Sheldrick's Sanctuary to hitch a ride...ETA...three hours."

"Keep your cell open. Estimate 300 plus Air Cav troops. Two clicks out. Holdin' positions out of sight...No idea what the fok they're waiting on."

"How many men do you have?"

"Thirty-nine."

A moment paused as the dire straights Rhino was facing sank in. Mark glanced at the team as they bounced along the rough streets driving through Nairobi.

"How many did ya bring?" Rhino said breaking the silence.

"Six...Have an idea...The Brazilian Ball Buster."

Rhino smiled, remembering a operation they had pulled off several years earlier. Lowering his binoculars, he yanked a damp bandana from his left rear pocket and wiped the moisture from his eyes. "Keep you appraised. Shaping up like the southeast flank would be the one."

"10-4...Call as soon as we're in the air." Mark hung up. He turned and looked out the window at the passing destruction along the streets to avoid letting the others see his concern. *300 friggin men. Holy shit! Shades of the Alamo.*

Rhino entered the President's study and found Mobutto reading his bible. "Sir, any word from the Air Force?"

"I am told all fighter and attack helicopter squadrons have been sabotaged. Best estimate is twent-four to thirty hours before the birds will be operational again."

"Shit!...My apologies Mr. President..."

"None needed. My sentiments as well."

"When it comes, both you and Lutto need to get in the safe room. Ngie and Gupta will go with you. Don't open the door unless you hear the password."

"What will that be, Mr. Fabian?"

"Timba."

YAKUZA COMPOUND

Hayato, Chikako and four male Yakuza drove out of the compound in two black Land Cruisers, each with a small red dragon emblem on the front fenders and rear door. A pair of Puma APCs provided additional security for their trip.

The first shipment of ivory would leave a warehouse on the south side of town and travel through the Nairobi riot zone before continuing on to Mombassa and the ship waiting at the port. Hayato planned to personally escort the three transport trucks carrying shipping containers loaded with lumber and ivory and see them off.

Raku had been left behind, still recovering from the ravages of Hayato's pleasures and rage.

No one took note of the Sheldrick passenger van passing on their right as the Hayato's convoy and Mark's team passed like ships on a storm tossed sea.

The drive to the warehouse proved uneventful as did the trip through the riot torn city with the transport trucks. Once out on the open Mombassa Highway, the convoy picked up speed slowed only by the occasional tribal road block. Due to the PUMA escort, the convoy passed without event at each one, but the delay infuriated Hayato nonetheless.

SHELDRICK WILDLIFE SANCTUARY
Kenya

Mark instructed the driver to drop him at the headquarters building and take the rest of the team directly to the helo pad. As he stepped out, Dame Daphne walked out onto the verandah.

"Mark! So wonderful to see you again...And so soon."

"Privilege is all mine, ma'am."

The two met at the steps and Mark took the elderly woman in his arms and embraced her.

"I'm afraid I have some sad news, Mark."

Mark pulled back and looked into her eyes. Something was wrong, terribly wrong.

"Robert is dead," she said softly.

The unexpected jolt hit him like a heavyweight contender's shot to the gut.

"What?...When? How?"

"No one knows for certain. He was alone at the QRF headquarters. When one of the Rangers out grazing the horses heard some shots, he rode back and found him."

Mark's eyes narrowed. *Damn! Professional hit.* "Who's in charge now?"

"Qunto. He brought all the Rangers and horses here. We have been grateful to have them."

"Robert was a good man. I'd like to see Lakota Moon before I go."

"Mark…they killed him too."

Mark was torn with emotion. A seething rage built within him, but he forced it to stay contained—at least for the present.

"Long Shot!"

Mark turned to see Qunto step out onto the verandah.

"Good to see you, my friend."

They shook hands.

"The helicopter is fueled and ready for you as requested. I understand you are in a hurry."

Mark nodded—unable to think of anything else he could say. "I've gotta go. Thanks for the use of the chopper. Promise to bring it back in one piece."

"Don't worry about that flying machine. Just be careful for yourself and your friends," Qunto replied.

Minutes later the KWS Sikorsky S-76 Mk II, lifted off with Bert and Crank in the cockpit. All of the nonessential KWS gear had been stripped to allow room for the six men and their equipment in the open bay compartment.

"Figure out what to toss if we pick up any bogies. We're so heavy now she feels like a pregnant goose," Bert called over the intercom.

Mark used his cell phone. "Rhino, in route. ETA two hours. What's your tac sit?"

"No contact as yet. Bit of good news I forgot to tell ya. We picked up a trio of Mark 19s."

"Any way for us to get one delivered to the Brazilian Ball?"

"Yeah. Couple of the President's choppers are positioned two clicks north. I'll have one delivered."

"Outstanding! Keep us appraised. Out." Mark turned to the team, "Anyone have hands-on with a Mark 19?"

"I was an instructor at Fort Benning," Bear replied with a huge grin.

"You the man Bear. Rhino will special deliver one to us when we land...Here's the plan." Mark laid out a topo map on the floor of the helicopter.

MOMBASA SEAPORT

The convoy transporting the first load of illegal ivory in weeks, pulled into the maze of warehouses. Mombasa's port, the only one of any importance in Kenya, was busy year round. Cruise ships, carrying mostly sex seeking travelers, used the harbor as well. The appearance of the trucks escorted by APCs would have created special interest if it were not for the unrest raging across the country.

The Pumas set up across the roadway, blocking any vehicle traffic and the KDF special forces troops leapt out and sealed off the area to foot traffic. Satisfied the perimeter was secure, Hayato and his people got out of their black Land Cruisers and positioned themselves next to the trucks. Hayato met a man dressed in khakis and short sleeve shirt with the words, *Port Authority*, printed on the back in large letters.

"You are just in time. The last containers are about to be loaded," the slender ebony skinned man said in perfect English.

"Here are the shipping documents."

The port authority employee opened the folder and read the enclosed papers before speaking. "And the money?"

Hayato handed the man a 5x7 manila envelope that appeared about to burst at the seams. "I will be back next week with another shipment of lumber. You will receive a call with details."

The supervisor waved his hand at the first driver, motioning him to pull forward to the unloading area. The container was lifted by crane to the deck of the cargo vessel—one bearing Hong Kong registration and flag.

An hour later, the convoy was back on the Mombasa Highway returning to Nairobi.

AIRSPACE OVER TUNISIA

The BEF's C-5M *Super Galaxy* had switched on the visual stealth mode the team called *LIZARD* shortly after liftoff from the underground base in North Texas. All exterior surfaces of the huge four engine craft were coated in RAM as used on the B-2 *Spirit* bomber, but the genius engineers, who happened also to be crew members had gone Northrop Grumman one better.

An additional specialized coating, using a proprietary photo-chromataphor membrane had been added over the radar absorptive material. Coupled with a sophisticated computer and literally hundreds upon hundreds of light-sensing charged capacitor devices—and tiny lens of the size in cell phone cameras—allowed the bird to actually sense the background in 360 degrees and display whatever was on the far side to anyone who viewed the aircraft from any angle. In effect, *Mama Bird* could become invisible to outside observers.

Gears Formby and his counterpart, Blaze Hermann, had studied the ubiquitous chameleon and discovered its secret of changing colors. They adapted the reptile's organic biochemistry to an electromechanical system and named it after the gentle creature. Not content at making the combat carrier invisible and stealthy, the two designed special curved panels that fit inside the giant intake shroud and exhaust tailpipes of the four turbofan engines. Each was electronically mated to the sound outputs of the exposed fan blades as well as the exhaust notes. By generating a white noise precisely 180 degrees out of phase with the engine generated frequency, the result was astounding. The bird was silent when observed from more than a thousand feet away.

Inside, the crew was in various states of readiness as some slept, others prepared to come on duty, and still others were deep in planning their initial contact with the rebel forces encroaching the Kenyan President's summer estate. Former Air Force General Heater McElhenny was about to go off duty as Deputy

Mission Commander. He took an intercom message over his headset at the MC station.

"Heater, incoming call from NSA analysts on one."

"Got it, thanks…" He pressed the illuminated button on his console. "McElhenny, go ahead, over."

A three second delay occurred as the transmission had to bounce out to a MILSATCOM geostationary satellite secured voice channel, then get relayed to another over the mid-Atlantic and then get beamed down to Washington, DC.

"Mama Bird, be advised we have picked up a significant buildup in what are assumed to be Kenyan rebel forces in three quadrants surrounding the Mobutto compound, over."

"What is the force disposition and strength? Over."

"Preliminary estimates are three full companies of infantry, no armor visible at this time. We have live NEOS feed available for three more minutes before horizon passages, over."

Heater processed the information as his heart sank. *Christ. Poor bastards don't have a chance.* "Mama Bird copies all. Send current feed and any stills your people have analyzed. We're just under five hours out and flying at max cruise speed as it is. Over."

"NSA WILCO, next available NEOS in ninety one minutes. NSA, clear."

Burner Stewart approached the mission commander station with a fresh cup of coffee in his hand. He had just awaken from his crew rest on the nineteen hour flight. One look at his Deputy Commander for Operations told him most of what he needed to know. "That bad, huh?"

Heater reached up and removed the combination wireless earpiece and boom microphone and set it on the console. He nodded and rolled the kinks out of his shoulders from sitting in one place too long. He turned the swiveling leather seat around until his eyes met Burner's. "Yeah...three hundred infantry, plus or minus, to the thirty or so defenders. Washington is sending some live feed and their stills...not lookin' good for the home team. Kinda looks like the Alamo."

Burner took a sip and glanced at the digital clock current time and ETA displays in the corner of the flat screen above their station. *Five hours is an eternity in a firefight.* "We'll have Widowmaker and his team review the intel photos. Perhaps they can figure something out...That's what they do."

Heater unbuckled his lap belt and shoulder harness and stood up. "Have a seat...I'll go let him know what's up."

MOBUTTO'S SUMMER ESTATE

The summer sun climbed high in the sky after the heavy nighttime rains had moved farther west. A breeze from the east help dry out the top surface of the soil, but underneath, it was still a sodden mess of red clay. The weary defenders looked out anxiously, but saw no sign of the troops they knew were awaiting orders to advance. Lt. Kamau heard a familiar whistling sound coming from the south and immediately sounded the alarm, "Incoming!"

The barrage of 60mm mortar rounds landed both inside and outside the compound. One round struck the south tower at the front gate blowing the structure to pieces, showering debris and moist body fragments of the defenders across the grounds below. Another landed on the 6x6 and sent hot steel shrapnel in all directions before the fuel tank exploded repeating the deadly rain of metal. Three men defending the north wall were killed instantly. Another ran across the yard burning, covered in fuel by the first explosion and set on fire by the second. Badly wounded men lay screaming in agony as their life's blood drained.

Chunks of earth and rock flew up along with plumes of muddy earth covering the entire compound with choking, blinding debris. The screams of the injured and the moans of the dying mixed with the whistle of incoming mortar rounds, deafening explosions, the *zip* and *crack* of passing shrapnel struck terror in the defenders who had never experienced combat before. Some men cowered on their knees, hands over their heads, screaming for it to stop. One man bolted and ran from his protected position—not that there was any place safe to go—and was struck with a direct hit. His body disintegrating in a spray of pink mist mixed with the tortured red African clay.

Rhino had scrambled down the stairs three steps at a time. As he exited the doorway, an explosion lifted him with such force he could not breathe and throwing him back into the room from which he had just come. None of his multiple cuts and abrasions were life threatening. He rolled over and using the stairs, pulled himself to his feet and staggered to the door way again. Looking across the compound, he suddenly realized...*So this is what it's like to be on the other end of a barrage.* In all his years with the SADF he had been on the sending end, never the receiving.

As he stood leaning on the entrance door, two mortars hit the main house—one on the front porch, the other in the area where the President's study had been. Flames leapt up from the building as Rhino moved forward on wobbly legs. His sense of hearing was instantly impaired, the sounds around him seemed distant, muted, dull, as if his ears were filled with warm oatmeal. Reaching up to clear them, he first felt the warm moisture on his neck. Looking at his hand, he realized it was his own blood.

He circled the home to the north side and, using his rifle butt, knocked out the remaining glass of a shattered window and climbed in to find the staff huddled in the corner of the kitchen under two large solid wood tables. Seeing him covered in dirt and blood, two women screamed in horror. He motioned for them to stay down and proceeded into the hall and to the entrance of the safe room. He found it locked securely from the inside and moved through the house checking for other survivors. In the study three Presidential security guards, their crumpled bodies—torn and bloody, their shredded clothing still smoldering—lay in positions a body cannot attain in life. *No way for a man to die, God damn it!* In the front living area he discovered two more guards dazed but, like himself, not seriously injured.

As suddenly as the attack began, it ended. Rhino left the building through the back door and walked past the swimming pool, now shattered and leaking from a direct hit. The tennis court had two craters and the net was hanging from the chain link fence on the south end, blowing in the breeze like a fluttering holiday banner.

"Rheinhart! Come in!" Lt. Kamau called on the radio. The sound seemed distant and muffled.

"Rheinhart here."

"Thank God! I feared the worst. They will be coming in now. How many men did we lose?"

"Too damn many. Walk the west and north walls...I'll take the east and south. Report as soon as you have a count."

He moved off toward the northeast tower to take inventory of the damages. Finding two men in it unharmed, but shaken, he proceeded to the other. One man stationed there, though alive had been blinded by the explosion that destroyed the south gate tower. He helped the man down the stairs and handed him off to one of the Base KDF soldiers to be taken to the guard barracks.

The south gate tower was nothing more than a smoldering shell. The direct hit had not only taken it out, but severely damaged the two gates, both bent and twisted allowing the enemy easy access if they assaulted from the east. *Shit! And damn us to hell!*

Rhino used his radio. "The front gate's been breached. Get some men over 'ere to shore 'er up." He continued on to the southeast tower, his legs beginning to regain strength with each step.

"On it!" Kamau responded. To a small group of men outside the northwest tower he barked out orders, "Jump right smart and get the gate patched up...Hurry along now."

Four KDF soldiers took off at the run—well aware that an open gate meant certain defeat and probably a slow painful death to anyone captured.

The second and most devastating blow came as Rhino turned to walk the south wall. Two entire sections were gone. Direct hits had torn a pair of ten to twelve foot wide openings, killing three men and wounding two others. *That about bloody tears it then. Holes big 'nough to drive a tank through.*

He squatted down on his heels at the first breech and stared out at the southern horizon, certain the assault was about to come. Glancing to his left, he noticed a chunk of dark red, purple and black human flesh clinging to the wall three feet off the ground. It took a moment before he realized there was an eye hanging there—lifeless, yet staring back at him.

***

CHAPTER TEN

GENERAL JANMOHAMED'S FIELD HQ

General Janmohamed stepped out of his personal helicopter shortly after the fourth and final wave of 50th Air Cav troops disembarked their choppers. He was wearing crisply starched and pressed combat fatigues with his five most important medals attached to his left front jacket just below the pocket flap. Like so many military men in Africa, he wore medals wherever he went, no matter what the uniform. A large woven maroon and gold parachute cord aiguillette on each shoulder and the bright maroon berét gave him a image of authority, though be it comical to military men from other continents and cultures. Five gold stars on each epaulet and another five placed just below the crest of his beret, further enhanced his look of cartoonish self-importance. A handmade black leather holster held his sidearm on his right hip and over his left shoulder he carried a H&K MP5A3—9mm with a collapsible metal buttstock.

He was followed by a camera crew of five and a three person sound crew, a videographer who was constantly filming on a handheld Canon EOS-1D X camera. It had cost nearly $7,000—mere pocket change for the corrupt general. They only paused to take occasional still shots on a Canon PowerShot.

A small frail Englishman, his personal secretary and keeper of all things important for the book Janmohamed intended to write about his illustrious career, danced around nervously making entries incessantly on his pink covered iPad. He was sweating profusely from his anxieties rather than the morning heat.

The arrogant psychopath had kept in constant contact with his junior officers through out the all-night process of deploying troops from the base in Nairobi to their hidden positions—out of view of the men inside Mobutto's estate.

All the while, he relaxed with his concubine—a sixteen year old blonde Danish sex slave—in air-conditioned comfort, drinking Louis VIII rare cask cognac. He smoked water-purified hashish—often called bubble melt hash—in a hand-carved ivory hookah and partook of his sexual pleasures with the unfortunate teenager.

He was now on the field of battle—a drunken drug addled strutting peacock about to order his men into the pages of history—his personal glory and ascent to the Presidency.

"General! All is ready for you orders, sir!...The mortar barrage was an overwhelming success. The President's estate is practically destroyed," a young colonel shouted above the noise of the departing helicopters.

"Where is the command tent? I wish to speak to the men."

"This way, General." The colonel pointed to the garish canopy in plain view and started off ahead of him. *Is the old man blind?*

The film and sound crew had proceeded to the HQ tent and were busy setting up their equipment to record the event—two Red One state-of-the-art video cameras, tripods, silks, scrims, a small lighting package, as well as a silent electric generator. They scrambled to complete their preparations as the general approached, making a final sound check on the audio equipment before attaching a lavaliere to his jacket.

Once under the 20x30 foot maroon canopy—trimmed in gold with the emblem of the 50th Air Cavalry emblazoned in real gold wire—the general took a seat in his personal field chair. It was a director's chair—as used on a motion picture film set—with maroon fabric and five gold stars on the back. "Men of the glorious 50th Air Cavalry. Today, we will make history...Songs will be written about our heroic actions...Kenyans will toast our bravery for ages...Go forward and conquer!"

The general's voice was projected onto the crowd of soldiers by four large 100 watt speakers, each with their own six foot tall stand, all steadied by guy wires attached to steel stakes driven into the ground.

162

In Somalia, a speaker stand had collapsed during one of his speeches. The accused culprit was executed on the spot for the embarrassing offense by the general himself.

He turned back to the young officer. "Mortars."

The colonel started to repeat the upbeat news of the previous attack; reconsidered, and then relayed the general's orders. The mortar teams dropped their first rounds of the second barrage into the tubes. *Whomp! Whomp! Whomp!* The whistling sound of the rounds in-flight grew quieter as they arced away from the firing positions. Only five more volleys were fired, expending the last of the rounds brought by the teams.

Satisfied the barrage was enough, the general stood up and raising his hand, motioned for the ground troops to advance.

The colonel relayed the orders to the commanders of the forces positioned on the west of the estate and the first line on the south. He and the men stationed around the command tent watched as the first wave of troops marched over the crest onto the open plain surrounding the President's compound.

Simultaneously the troops positioned on the west moved forward as well. Two hundred and twenty-four men began marching to a hero's destiny and glory—or so they imagined.

MOBUTTO'S SUMMER ESTATE

Shortly after the last airlift landed to the south, the defenders of the compound could vaguely make out the words of the rogue general. Unable to understand the full message, they knew full well the time had come and the enemy would soon be upon them.

As the second mortar barrage began, everyone sought what cover they could. The only serious strikes delivered were the destruction of one of the helicopter fuel storage tanks and a third hit on the President's home.

Rhino walked along the interior of the south wall offering encouragement to the survivors. "Steady men, the worst is over," he lied. "Now we've got the braks where we want them." He checked and adjusted some of the sand bags now laid two high atop the rock fence behind the wrought iron grate. To keep the men busy, Rhino had previously had them fill sand bags and place them on the fence to add height and provide a steady rest for their rifles. After the first mortar barrage, additional bags had been hurriedly filled and stacked three feet high in the two breaches.

"Pick your targets. Single fire. Make every bloody round count...Keep your heads down. Wait for Lieutenant Kamau's command to fire." He brought the binoculars to his eyes. Lines of infantry fanned out across the open plains. Another line appeared behind them. *Now I know how those bloody Texans felt at the Alamo.* He swallowed hard and checked his men again. All eyes were upon him. He took in a deep breath and let it our slowly. "Watch your wind flags...Stay calm. Easy boys...Easy."

He moved to southeast tower, entered and climbed to the observation deck. He slipped the radio from his belt and spoke to the teams manning the Mk 19s which had miraculously been missed. "Steady men. Fire on my command...Then give 'em bloody hell!"

At that moment the first waves of troops appeared on the western horizon, advancing surely, but steadily, toward the compound. They moved forward line abreast as they had done so many times in Somalia, crushing ill-trained rebels with superior firepower and discipline. They moved with the unmistakable confidence of warriors undefeated in battle.

At a distance, easily noted with the flags Rhino had the men install, Lt. Kamau ordered five men with accurate rifles to commence firing, "Sharpshooters! Range five hundred! Take your targets!"

The men adjusted their sights. Five rifles fired in rapid succession, each sending a 7.62x51 NATO round downrange into the ranks of the advancing enemy. Three men fell like rag dolls and lay still. Again, five rifles fired. Two more men fell immediately—another pair staggered forward a step or two before sagging to the ground.

The advancing troops broke into a trot and begin to zigzag as they advanced, slipping and sliding on the rain soaked ground beneath their fect. A blood curdling yell rose from the rebels and floated across the plain into the compound of the defenders.

"Steady boys…I want them in closer," Rhino called to the Mk 19 teams.

"Range three hundred…Fire at will!" Lt. Kamau ordered as the advancing men hit the 300 yard markers. Every man on the south and west walls began firing.

Thirty seconds later, Rhino spoke evenly into the radio. "Range one hundred. Open fire…Rake the field."

All three of the Mk 19s roared, sending a steady stream of M1001 40mm high velocity canister cartridges and high explosive rounds into the rebel lines at sixty rounds per minute. The effect was devastating. The open ground turned into a killing field for the assaulting troops—the advance abruptly stopped. Men hugged the earth attempting to hide from the shrapnel shredding the air around them and churning the earth in great chunks. Hot steel, earth, rock and cordite fumes blended into a huge cloud of debris obscuring the field. Bodies lay as they had fallen...pieces of men; arms, legs, contorted carcasses littered the ground. The screams of the wounded mingled with the moans of those too weak to scream.

"Cease fire!" Rhino and Lt. Kamau called almost simultaneously. Kamau's command was unnecessary as the riflemen had ceased firing and stood in awe of the destruction being wrought on their countrymen in front of them.

As the smoke settled, a scant few survivors could be seen fleeing from the field of death and destruction. Those that were able, were hobbling as best they could, staggering after those who ran in terror ahead of them. A few tried to crawl, but most of the initial wave were still or writhing in agony, screaming for help, crying for their mothers...

Janmohamed stormed around the headquarters area, fuming with unmasked anger. No one wanted to be near him and everyone made moves to avoid his presence or contact with his glowering eyes. *The Mk 19s were indeed game changers.*

"Get Colonel Shaiti on the line. Order him to bring up the rest of the 50th. I want every man...every Puma here *now*! Contact Lieutenant Colonel Guadf immediately with the 20th Parachute...Inform me when he is on the line!" the raging general bellowed.

With shaking hands, and his voice cracking with fear, the young colonel did as ordered.

MINISTER OF DEFENSE OFFICE
Nairobi

A frantic wide-eyed aide entered the minister's office with a dispatch in hand. "Sir! This was just intercepted. General Janmohamed has called for the remaining units of the 50th Air Cav and called in the 20th Parachute Brigade."

Injera Daar took the document, put on his reading glasses and studied it for several moments. A deep worried frown crossed over his tired face. He had not slept for the previous two nights concerned about the outcome of the impending coup. "Get that arrogant bastard on the horn. Now!"

"Yes, sir."

Daar moved from behind his desk to the large map of Kenya on the wall to his right. Placing his left fore finger in the vicinity of Mobutto's summer estate, he said softly, "How the *hell* does anyone screw this operation up with the entire 50th under one's command? How?...How?"

YAZUKA COMPOUND

"Mr. Wu, I am most pleased to report the first shipment of lumber was loaded and has left the port for Hong Kong," the leader of the group said into the satellite phone.

"Very good. Most excellent news, Hayato."

"I will prepare for next week's shipment but I must tell you the civil unrest here is disrupting the distribution of all goods..."

"I am certain you will be successful. I have some news for you...An associate informed me that the American you wish to meet is back in Kenya."

"Where?"

"At last contact, he was departing the Sheldrick Wildlife Sanctuary enroute for the President's summer home. Another source informed me that a larger force of Kenyan military are gathering there as well."

"I will investigate this matter thoroughly. If necessary, I will await his return before introducing myself." A hard smile played across his face.

"That would be wise. He is most enamored with protecting the Kenyan wildlife. Consider using some leaked information to lure him into your web. And...like the patient spider...collect him at your leisure."

"Yes, sir. Sage advice. On the other hand...I have a woman who specializes in eliminating problems like the American...I may have her deliver him to me. As you say...at my leisure."

"Keep me appraised of the next shipment."

The phone went dead, leaving Hayato sitting by the pool in a dark, but expectant mood. *Chikako...one last assignment before I rid myself of you.*

AIR SPACE OVER KENYA
KWS Helicopter

"Ten miles out," Bert informed the team.

"Circle to the east...Rhino suggested the southeast flank," Mark ordered.

"Copy."

Mark dialed his cell. "Okay boys...eyes wide open. The tangos should be visible soon to the west," he told them as he waited for an answer.

"'Bout damn time...What took ya so long?" Rhino asked.

"Good to hear you too. We're ten miles out and closing. Pulling up on the east. Get us the Mark 19..."

"Too late for that. Hit us with a bloody mortar attack followed by a ground assault near an hour ago...No bloody way to get a chopper in and out a 'ere now."

Mark listened to the update with growing concern. "How many did you lose?"

"Eleven dead...Four critical wounded....Seven walkin'. But we bloodied the bastards...Never saw the 19s comin' 'til we opened up on 'em...Been quiet since."

As the helicopter continued its inbound course, Bert came back on the intercom, "Look! Down there...must be over a hundred tangos in that ravine."

Mark leaned over Crank to get a better look out to the west. In the distance, he spotted the troops that Bert reported—lying in a deep cut in the landscape below. Beyond, he could see the smoke rising from the President's estate.

"Rhino. Be advised we have visual on a light company to your southeast."

"Jesus Christ, mate! They came at us from the south an' west last time."

"We're gonna hook up with the two choppers you said are north of your position. Can you alert them we are incoming. KWS helicopter, blue and white."

"Done…Then what?"

"Have to get back to you on that one, buddy."

Mark hung up and spoke to Bert, "Maintain your present heading…Keep a good distance. Don't wanta spook 'em. Continue north a couple three clicks and then west. Rhino says there are two of the President's choppers out there somewhere."

"10-4. North three then west."

MINISTER OF DEFENSE OFFICE

A voice came over the intercom, "General Janmohamed is unable to take your call at this time, sir. Said to inform you he is winning. Will contact you when the President is in hand."

Daar slammed his left hand down on his desk as he picked up the phone hand set. "Call that stupid son of a bitch back and tell him I will speak with him *now* or I will override his orders for any further troops!"

"Yes, sir!"

The scheming bureaucrat picked up his cell and dialed. He got up and walked to the large bay window and looked out across the smoke filled sky line of Nairobi as he waited for an answer.

"Hello," the voice sounded as if it were coming from a echo chamber mingled with static.

"Mr. President. I am calling to inform you that General Janmohamed has gone rogue and taken some of the 50th Air Cavalry with him. I am unsure of his intentions or exact location at this time but I suspect he has illusions of enacting a coup…"

"That would explain the military forces attacking my home, Minister. My question for you is…what are you going to do about it?"

President Mobutto's voice sounded much calmer than he expected. "Attacking your summer home?"

"Wrong answer…I asked what are you going to do about it."

"I will marshal a force immediately to relieve your position. Do you have the forces to resist until they arrive?"

"That remains to be seen. I suggest you *marshal* your forces post haste…Mr. Daar. If you will excuse me, I have a call coming in from the President of the United States."

As the call went dead the aide called over the intercom, "General Janmohamed on line three, sir."

Picking up the phone, Injera spoke in measured terms as his mind raced, "What is your situation, General?"

"Everything is going well. We have destroyed much of the estate and many of the defenders…"

"Then why in the hell are you calling for more troops?"

171

"One difficulty, sir. The defenders are armed with several automatic grenade launchers. Additionally, it appears KDF soldiers, most likely from Base 127 have joined Mr. Fabian and his presidential guards," Janmohamed lied to bolster his reason for unsuccessfully overrunning the estate.

"I just got off the phone with Mobutto. He informed me he is talking with the President of the United States. I suggest you conclude this situation quickly or you will be swinging from a hangman's noose this time next week."

Janmohamed's voice changed from cool and collected to one hard and cold, "I have this under control, do you understand? I will contact you when I am victorious."

The line went dead. Injera Daar stood looking at the phone receiver for several moments, not believing the turn of events. He tried to swallow, but his mouth was suddenly filled with cotton. *Damage control is the priority now.*

MOUNT KENYA NORTH OF ESTATE

"Have the choppers in sight. Down in two," Bert announced as he banked gently to the left.

"Make a pass to insure Rhino cleared us for landing," Mark replied. "Don't want those boys taking pot shots at us."

Mark and the team jumped from the S-76 helicopter onto the rocky ground as the four crewmen of the President's choppers moved to meet them. A stiff wind blew across the switch back to the north and raced down into the canyon below while Mark, Bert and the four airmen conversed and the team unloaded their gear. The shadows of a dozen European black kites passed over the men causing all to look up. The kites, commonly known as hawks, stared back down at the men showing no fear. Suddenly the birds of prey veered from their path and circled the men and machines below. The raptors, unlike most species of hawks, often travel in flocks, especially when migrating as these were. Without warning the largest of them swooped down—fluttering its wings in a near stall—directly over Mark and stared down into his eyes.

"Aiiiee!" one of the copilots yelled as he hit the deck on one knee—his arms crossed over his face, joined quickly by everyone but Mark.

He stood still sharing a moment with the magnificent bird of prey. *"Ta?yá? Yahí. Wayác hi yac hí?"*

The men stood up as the hawk ascended skyward again.

"So...now you talk with birds?" Bert asked incredulously.

"Yeah, sometimes. Said welcome...would you like to dance with me?...Lakota Souix...to the best of my memory."

"That one seemed to take a liking to you," the elder pilot—his hand across his forehead to shade his vision from the sun—said as he watched the squadron of hawks fly away. "In all my years, I've never seen a live one so close."

"The American Indians considered hawks good omens," Mark remarked.

"How many more of you are coming in?" the youngest pilot asked as he attempted to knock mud off his uniform.

"This is it. Six and done. You boys have combat experience?"

"I do," one replied.

Mark turned to the other three. "Well, you're about to get your feet wet. There's a company of tangos laid up southeast of here. I suspect they'll go in on the next assault. Two of my team will go with each of your choppers. Bert and I in the KWS bird...Once we're up...we do fly bys...Take out as many as we can."

"All we have are our side arms and a pair of AKs," one of the copilots said anxiously.

"No problem...We came to play," Mark stated with a sly smile.

"No shit," the youngest blurted out.

"Stash the munitions in that cluster of boulders. Cover them with the camo netting," Mark ordered.

Watching the team work the elder Kenyan pilot remarked, "Damn! Looks like death comes calling."

Mark briefed the four chopper pilots, "When we go in on the tangos, I want you to fly like those hawks you just saw. Dive in...and pull out with a turn. Circle and repeat...Crank! Bear! Load up this chopper. Boom Boom! Ian...that one."

As the team and chopper crews made ready, Mark called Rhino with details of plan B.

YAKUZA COMPOUND

Chikako, responding to his summons, found Hayato sitting by the pool under one of the large beige umbrellas. She approached with trepidation, unsure of his intentions, but certain she would choose death over another session as his pleasure toy.

174

"You wanted to see me, master?"

"Yes." Hayato removed his dark sunglasses and ogled her body rather than making eye contact. "I have an assignment for you."

A sense of relief rushed over her, but she did her best not to let him see. To appease him and play to his incessant need for dominance she answered, "Yes, master."

"I will have one of the men drive you out of the city to the Sheldrick Wildlife Sanctuary. Let them think you are a wealthy benefactor coming to make a donation to their cause. While there, find out when the American is returning."

"Mark Ingram?"

"Yes, Mark Ingram." His voice grew harder, and cold as a jagged chunk of ice falling into the Arctic sea. "There is an envelope on the desk in my bedroom. Twenty thousand American dollars. That should be enough to loosen their tongues."

"Yes, master." She turned and quickly left the man she abhorred deeply, not wanting to be in his presence any longer than absolutely necessary.

Chikako got dressed in a suitable pair of white cotton slacks, a jade blouse and walking shoes. She carefully applied a light application of makeup, not looking to seduce, rather to impress. Collecting her H&K pistol, magazines, a few personal items and the cash envelope she headed down the cool dark hallway to the front entrance.

SHELDRICK WILDLIFE SANCTUARY

Arriving at the sanctuary Chikako instructed the driver to park in front of the visitor's center and to remain with the vehicle. As she walked up and onto the open verandah, one of the armed QRF Rangers standing on either side of the front door stepped forward.

"What is your business today?"

"I came to make a donation…A sizable donation. Might I speak with one of the administrators?"

At that moment Malute, hearing the conversation through the screen door, stepped out. "Good afternoon. I oversee daily operations here at the sanctuary and act as Dame Sheldrick's first assistant…"

"I've read about Dame Daphne…What an amazing woman. Is she here? I would so love to meet her," Chikako remarked giving Malute her most endearing smile as she extended her hand. "My name is Lucy Woo."

"Lucy Woo? The famous actress?"

"No. I'm afraid I am far to shy to be in the movies. We just share a similar sounding name."

"Come in…Thank you Laita. I'll take it from here." Malute opened the door as they entered the building. "Dame Daphne is presently out with our newest orphans. We had three juveniles come in four days ago. She likes to visit them every day until they acclimatize…Follow me."

The young black woman lead the way to a small office off a long hallway. Once inside, she motioned to a wicker chair. "Have a seat. Would you like some tea?"

"Ice tea would be nice. I am still trying to adjust to the heat here. Such a beautiful country, but so much hotter and humid than where I am from," Chikako said as she studied the many framed photos of people and animals at the sanctuary. More than one captured Malute and Damn Daphne with a lean, tanned Caucasian man with haunting blue eyes and silver hair falling onto his shoulders. In each, they were interacting with baby elephants.

Malute used the intercom to order beverages, then settled into her chair behind the desk.

"Who is that you are with? The man with the long hair?"

Malute turned to the photo that she was pointing at as a big smile lit her face. "That's Mark Ingram. He's very special to *all* of us here. Up until a few weeks ago he was the head of the KWS QRF..."

"QRF?"

"Quick Reaction Force. They go out and investigate poaching incidents. While he was here poaching fell dramatically."

It was evident in her voice and body language Malute was enamored with him.

"And where are you from?"

"Taiwan. I am here for a few months to oversee some computer upgrades for your government agencies."

"We have not had much news out here the last few days. What with the riots and all."

"It was quite awful. I was totally in fear for my life driving through Nairobi. The company sent a driver with me, but I felt like we needed to have armed guards," she said feigning fear and concern.

A small heavy black woman in her late fifties, wearing a flowing brightly colored dress, entered with a wooden tray, a pitcher of iced tea, two glasses and a bowl of sugar. Placing the tray on the desk, she departed without speaking a word.

As she poured and prepared their tea, Malute continued, "You said something about a donation?"

"Yes. I have a small one," Lucy modestly replied while digging through her travel bag. Finding the envelope, she laid it on the desk and pushed it gently towards her.

Malute picked up the package and looked inside. She took a deep breath. "A small donation? Exactly how much is here?"

"Twenty thousand...American. I thought they would be the easiest for you to exchange..."

"Twenty thousand?...Oh, my." Malute removed the money and laid it on the desk. "This is...is very gracious...of you Miss Woo."

"I only wish I could do more. When will Dame Daphne be back?"

"Laita! Please go to the new arrival nursery and ask Mrs. Sheldrick to come here as soon as she can. We have a benefactor she should meet personally," Malute called out.

The ranger departed quickly, leaving the two women drinking their tea and making small talk. Ten minutes later, Dame Sheldrick entered, using a knurled teak cane.

Lucy stood up and extended her hand in greeting. "It's a great privilege to meet you. I have read so much about you and the incredible work done here."

As they shook hands, Malute interjected, "Miss Woo wants to make a donation…a twenty thousand dollar donation."

Daphne looked at her with obvious surprise then back to Lucy. "Sweet Lord in heaven. You are indeed an angel, young lady."

"I wish I could do more."

"Please consider having dinner with me tonight Miss Woo. I'll see that the driver outside is fed as well."

"I'd be honored."

"Malute, please inform the staff we will be having a guest tonight for dinner."

She nodded and disappeared down the hallway to the back of the building.

"Would you like a little tour? The most precious new babies arrived a few days ago. They are still in mourning, but we also have a dozen others that are feeling right at home now."

The normally cold-blooded killer felt a slight tinge of professional pride in the ruthless effectiveness of her deception. But, deeper inside, a strange feeling of kinship with the multitudes of orphaned elephants began to stir—a bond perhaps she shared from her tumultuous captive relationship with her Yakuza *friends*. She knew intellectually that the greed of the man she worked for was the real reason those innocent young pachyderms were there inside the sanctuary in the first place. The framed pictures with her nemesis and target, Mark Ingram, had likewise touched her in a way she never thought possible. She fought to never allow her face betray the slightest hint of her inner turmoil.

"I would *love* that," she replied with true sincerity.

***

CHAPTER ELEVEN

REINFORCEMENTS ON THE MOVE

General Shaiti and the remaining units of the 50th Air Cavalry, a dozen Puma APCs and ten two-ton troop carrying trucks began to roll down the highway headed west out of Nairobi. Several hours later, the procession pulled up a hundred yards from the command tent. Senior officers stepped out of the rear crew door of the lead APC and began barking orders. A gaggle of dusty, rather disorganized infantrymen slipped out of the canvas covered trucks and gathered behind the troop carriers.

"Move it! Fall in! General Janmohamed is waiting! Go! Go!" Shaiti yelled. "Major! Inform the General we have arrived."

Eventually, an organized line of armored personnel carriers was created, and the reserve companies broke into their assigned squads. The NCOs doubled-timed their men into the stifling hot metal vehicles. General Shaiti climbed into the command vehicle with a white star painted on the cupola and gave the order to stand at the ready.

Captain Xavier Mandoda and Ranger D Parachute company, 20th Battalion deployed to Mobutto's summer estate in answer to General Janmohamed's call for reinforcements. The original D Rangers, the only military unit designated as commandos, had been trained by US Army Rangers—their creation funded by $40 million in US aid. Their first deployment had in the Mt. Elgon area in 2008 to put down a civil war between numerous tribes and insurgents—they were immediately accused of torture and illegal detentions of the local Kenyans.

"Captain, I just intercepted a communications from General Shaita. He is on the ground and moving," the copilot called over the communications headset.

YAKUZA COMPOUND

Hayato viewed his phone before answering, "Yes, Chikako."

In the background he could hear the sounds of elephants trumpeting as they were being fed.

"I have been invited to stay for dinner."

"Again you work your magic." As he waited for a reply he overheard Dame Daphne inviting her to stay the night.

"I was just invited…"

"I heard. Who invited you?"

"The owner, Dame Daphne Sheldrick. I will stay with your approval, master."

"Return first thing in the morning. Bring me news of the American. Better yet...bring me the American."

"Thank you, master. Good-bye."

SHELDRICK WILDLIFE SANCTUARY

"Who in the world were you talking to young lady?...Master?"

"It was my boss. In our culture it is considered respectful to address one's employer as master."

"Lord have mercy, child. Well...never mind. Look, I think this new one is taking a liking to you."

Lucy turned to find a three month old juvenile standing behind her, reaching out with its trunk to smell her. As the animal explored closer, its trunk touched her softly and moved across her breasts to her face, gently drawing in the scent of her.

"Oh my god! How sweet." Her eyes begin to moisten.

"They are so precious...each and every one of them. I've tired but for the life of me I can not understand how anyone could kill them for their tusks," Daphne spoke softly, not wanting to break the moment.

The orphan sniffed the top of her head, drawing in several strands of her long black hair before releasing them unharmed. Lucy gazed into the intelligent eyes of the chest-high elephant. Tears begin to stream down her cheeks as she reached out and touched the baby's ears; moved to the top of its head and then continued to feel its exploring appendage. The juvenile shook its head and raised its trunk high above her before turning and ambling off to join the other orphans at the feed trough.

MOUNT KENYA NORTH OF ESTATE

Mark watched as the sun began to drop from the sky to the western horizon. *Couple more hours, it'll be dark.* "Change of plans. Not gonna wait for the tangos to assault the estate. We go now," he informed Ian and Malakhi in chopper number two. "Follow my lead 'til we hit the bastards then dive and cut alternately. Don't get lined up...Don't give them a steady shot...keep moving. Once you've expended your grenades, we rally back north...Opportunity presents itself...we go in hard and fast with the light arms and strafe the bastards."

Moving to chopper three, Mark gave Crank and Bear their orders, "Stand off to the east. Lay down suppressive fire with the Vektor. Be prepared to cover any ship that goes down and pickup survivors."

The men in each helicopter replied with a thumbs-up.

Mark ran across the muddy, windswept ground and climbed into the KWS chopper with Bert. "Let's rodeo!"

They lifted off and began a wide swing to the north then turned south with the other choppers behind him flying 300 feet higher.

"I want a low pass at two hundred. Do your best zig zag all the way down. Incoming gets heavy...pull out. We'll regroup and go to plan D...my dick is bigger than your god," Mark announced over the radio as he attached web straps to his harness. *Be hell to fall out.*

"Roger that. 10-4...Zig and zag."

"Make it rain grenades 'til you're out...Resupply at the munitions dump."

"Gonna mess 'em up, Buckos," Ian answered.

"Pineapple rain," Bear chimed in.

"Lightin' 'em up here, boss," Crank responded.

"Out go the lights!" Boom Boom added.

Mark opened the sliding doors on both sides of the chopper before pulling the pins and carefully placing his grenades in the gear pockets on the back of the copilot and pilot chairs. From past ops, he knew the slender rubber bands he had placed on the arming spoons would hold them down— rendering the grenades safe until they hit the ground. Then they would release as the grenade impacted amidst the unsuspecting troops. *Hello baby! Good-bye balls!*

SOUTHEAST OF THE ESTATE - 50th POSITION

"Tangos. Two o'clock," Bert alerted the team.

"Sit on your helmets if you have one," Mark added, knowing full well that no one did.

Bert nudged the stick over and initiated a steep descent that brought his helicopter over the north flank of the unsuspecting men below. The first thing the members of the 50th saw was a bright blue and white KWS chopper headed toward them—for many it was the last.

Mark grabbed and tossed grenades with both hands as the helo swept over the exposed troops below. As soon as the first pair were released, he snatched up two more and repeated. By the time he started to pick up the third pair, the startled men below were returning fire. *Ping! Tink! Phsit! Phsit! Crack!*

Crack! Crack! Rounds were impacting the helo with alarming regularity.

Bert jerked the stick to the left and rolled away, diving as fast possible to gain cover from the canyon rim between the bird and the soldiers below. Mark threw the third pair of grenades as hard as he could at the enemy below.

The first Presidential chopper, the number two helo, was slicing down over the battlefield right behind the SF 76 Mk II. Malakhi and Ian sat on either side of the cargo floor, each chunking grenades in tandem. The incoming fire was already heavier than when Mark had attacked, but they managed to get off four grenades each before the chopper pulled out to the right.

One of the hundreds of small arms rounds directed at their helicopter hit the copilot in the buttocks and traveled upward through most his body—piercing his intestines, liver and a lung—before lodging in his spine just below the neck. His head jerked violently and slumped forward, blood and froth oozing from his nose and mouth. Multiple rifle rounds impacted the chopper—one cut a hydraulic pressure line and hot fluid sprayed over both Ian and Malakhi. The pilot took a round to the right thigh and hand. Switching hands, he struggled to keep the damaged aircraft flying and banked hard left—greasy black smoke billowed in the rotating downdraft of the blades.

"Number two's hit…Looks like he's done…Two, come in!" Bert said with cool measured words as he switched over to the UHF. *Crap. Just another run like Nam.*

"We're hit...copilot dead. Attempting to get back to the munitions dump," Boom Boom answered.

"Set her down...We'll pick you up," Mark ordered. "Follow 'em Bert!"

Up in chopper three, Crank laid down a devastating barrage—a steady well-aimed series of three, five and seven round bursts of 7.62mm—every tenth round a tracer. Hovering at 1,200 feet above the chaos, they were too far out to receive much of the enemy's AK fire. The majority of shots taken at their ship were erratic and ineffective. One shot found its mark. Bear felt a dull thump on his right leg as a rifle round pierced the deck of the chopper and hit his artificial limb before spinning out the open door. "Shit! I'd be a hurtin' puppy now...if I wasn't already crippled," he said, flashing Crank a wicked smile as he continued to feed the belted .30 caliber ammo into the Viktor machine gun.

On the ground, the battered light company of the 50th lay decimated with nowhere to hide. Before the attack, one hundred and twelve men awaited their assault orders. Afterwards, only thirty-five were fit for duty. Around them, strewn in the mud, fire and smoke, forty-six lay dead and another thirty-one seriously wounded or dying.

The NO77 WP grenades Mark dropped, did the most damage. It was fitted with a fuse referred to as the *always,* due to the reliable percussion ignition—it lit off every time, no matter which way the grenade hit the ground. Once it exploded, the hellish white phosphorus scattered—igniting as soon as it touched the air—burning whatever it touched at 5,070° F. The horrific damage that the WP grenades caused was due not only, from the enormous heat it produced, but also from the chemical itself. The human body, once exposed, would absorb the poisonous phosphorus, leading to organ failure.

DOWNED CHOPPER

The damaged chopper carrying Ian and Malakhi lost altitude and came in hard, but remained upright as it slid to a stop in an barren plain—the two skids digging deep furrows in the red mud, As the rotors spooled down, Ian leapt out, yanked open the crew door and began unbuckling the harness of the wounded pilot. "Bloody good flyin', Boyyo! Easy now...gonna get ye outta here."

Malakhi scrambled out and checked the copilot for a pulse. He looked at Ian and shook his head.

They carried the injured man away from the chopper, while Bert touched down some thirty yards away.

"Let's go! Move it!" Mark yelled, motioning to the three men. He disconnected from the web straps and helped lift the wounded pilot onto the cargo bay.

The third aircraft flew closer and hovered nearby. Crank leveled his machine gun back in the direction of the decimated enemy, watchful of any who might try to climb out of the canyon.

"Boom Boom! Hang a bag of Willie Petes on the north side of the downed bird...Make it visible from that ridge," Mark yelled pointing at a low rise crowned with a jumble of gray boulders.

He ran back to the downed aircraft and followed Mark's orders. Once finished, he sprinted quickly back to the waiting chopper. Sweat poured off his chiseled arms and ran down his face as he dove into the crowded cargo bay.

Mark and Ian slammed the sliding side doors. Bert lifted off and turned toward the munitions dump.

"Drop us on that ridge!" Mark yelled out as he clambered up to the cockpit. He indicated a rocky outcropping dead ahead. "Don't come back 'til I call."

He hovered at two feet as Mark and Boom Boom dropped to the boulder-strewn crest of ground. The two scrambled to find a suitable position, and then settled between a pair of house-sized granite boulders with a perfect line of sight to the disabled helicopter. He pulled Betsy II from its drag bag and began affixing the Nightforce scope.

"Range me." He handed a small brown padded field case to Malakhi. "Jack be nimble, jack be quick...Any boy scouts coming to play, my guess is it will be soon."

Boom Boom opened the case and pulled out a Leupold RX-1000 TBR—true ballistic ranging laser range-finder. He looked through the seven power eyepiece and pressed the activation button once he had steadied it on the damaged chopper. The device indicated 430 yards in a digital display superimposed over the image. "Oh...I gotta get me one of these...Range four hundred thirty."

Mark laid his three-day pack down in front of him and rested the rifle on it before settling in behind.

MUNITIONS DUMP

Back on the ground at the original staging area, Bert shut down the engines and climbed from the pilot's seat into the cargo bay and began giving the injured flyer medical aid. "He's going to get a medal for this one…Maybe two."

"Faith and a miracle it was. Being shot up like that and all," Ian remarked as he held pressure on the man's thigh wound.

As the bird carrying the others landed, Crank jumped out and jogged to the munitions dump. He threw the camo netting off and grabbed two ammo cans containing belted ammo for his Viktor. Bear, meanwhile, swept spent brass out of the cargo area with his good left foot, cleaning the floor space to insure positive footing.

"Lash these down, Bear. I'm gonna check with Bert," Crank said as he tossed the two metal cans into the chopper. He turned and sprinted over to the KWS chopper.

"How is the lad?' Ian asked.

"Lost a lot of blood…Not good," Bert replied.

Crank arrived and surveyed the scene. "Is he gonna make it?"

"I stabilized the bleeding…looks like it missed the artery…"

"What the hell is Zorro up to?" Crank asked as he climbed inside the helicopter.

"No idea…Somethin' crazy, most likely," Bert answered as he injected the pilot with morphine. He tossed the empty syringe to the dirt and began to clean and bandage the man's shattered hand. It did not take long for the morphine to show its affect.

The Kenyan's eyes began to dilate and his head sagged off to one side.

DOWNED CHOPPER

Five KDF soldiers finally appeared as they crawled over the canyon rim and began to cautiously move toward the downed helicopter. Though badly shaken by the surprise assault on their position they still maintained good fire team tactics as they advanced.

"You listen to the Stones?" Mark asked.

"Oh, hell yeah, 'Spider to the Fly'," Malakhi said before he broke into song in a rich baritone, "Sittin', thinkin'…sinkin', drinkin'…wonderin' what I'd do when I'm thru tonight…"

Mark picked up as he snuggled Betsy II's stock into his shoulder, "…smokin'…mopin'…maybe just a hopin'…"

"…some little girl will pass on by…don't want to be alone," Boom Boom started laughing as he sang.

Mark carried on, "…don't say hi…like a spider to a fly…jump right ahead…" then he relaxed and exhaled half a breath. His finger squeezed rearward on the 2 ½ lb pull trigger.

BAMM!!

The soldiers that just arrived at the downed bird never heard the sound of the rifle before the API round impacted one of the WP grenades—detonating them all and creating a brilliant white shower of phosphorus fire followed by a huge explosion as the chopper's fuel supply went up.

"…and you're dead," Mark finished the tune. "Damn, what the hell did you put in that bag?"

"Couple ounces of C4. Figured the phosphorus would ignite it…Hey! Look…a rabbit," Malakhi said.

Mark dropped the ten round magazine loaded with API and pulled another stuffed with national match grade ammo and rocked it up into the Springfield's well until he heard a reassuring click. He cycled the operating rod once to eject the unfired API round. "Range me."

"Wind value three quarter, push three left," Malakhi said as he judged the drifting smoke. "Range 470…490…515…I *definitely* have got to get me one of these…530…"

BAMM!

A half second later, the fast moving soldier threw out his arms and launched face forward like a sledge hammer had hit him in the back.

"Tagged him runnin' flat out at 545!" Malakhi muttered, looking over at Mark with a new sense of respect.

GENERAL JANMOHAMED FIELD HQ

The young colonel approached the general with the communications from the 50th commander positioned on the east perimeter. He was apprehensive to be delivering the bad news—he paused at the edge of the awning, considering his options. Janmohamed finished his speech to the camera extolling his exaggerated accomplishments during the battle for Mobutto's estate.

He stood up, waving the film crew to follow him, and marched off to receive the newly arriving troops. "Now we shall take the President. Grenades will not stop my Pumas!"

The nervous colonel placed the disastrous news about the unit on the southeast in his right front pants pocket and followed the general and his entourage to meet the arriving reinforcements from the 50th.

MOBUTTO'S SUMMER ESTATE

Rhino stood in the southeast tower scanning the eastern horizon. He had watched as the three helicopters made their run over the enemy position and saw one chopper streaming smoke drop from sight. He figured it was a full four minutes later when the cloud of black smoke rose in the sky—well before the sound of the explosion.

Lt. Kamau's voice came over the radio, "What is happening?"

"Zorro."

"Zorro?"

"An old friend has arrived. He just hit the forces on our southeast flank...From the sounds of it, he did some damage."

"I see smoke."

"One of the President's helicopters went down."

GENERAL JANMOHAMED FIELD HQ

At the very same moment the defenders of the President's estate heard the explosion—the general and his troops did as well.

"What was that? Who ordered those men to attack?" the general bellowed.

The colonel knew the time had come. Pulling the crumpled communications from his pocket he stepped forward. "General. This just came in from the commander. A unknown force has attacked them by helicopter."

Janmohamed snatched the paper and read the damage report. "God damn it!"

Colonel Shaiti looked to the aide with a question in his eyes. The man simply shrugged his shoulders and shook his head.

"We attack one hour after dark!" the angry general yelled as he strode back into his HQ. "Make ready all units! Get me Guadf on the radio!"

"Yes, sir!"

"Colonel Shaiti, I want half your APCs to move to the southeast flank and link up with the remaining forces of the 50th. Take command of that unit personally. Contact me as soon as you are in position." He turned to the film crew. "Get that stupid camera off me, idiots!"

AIRSPACE OVER LIBYA

Sean "Windowmaker" Baker, Mickey Williams and James "Ten Ring" Weber reviewed the latest near earth orbital satellite pictures sent from the NSA offices in DC. The photos were high resolution—any object six inches or better could be easily discerned—albeit taken at a oblique angle as the rapidly traversing spy tool cleared the horizon from the north northeast.

The three Raptors surrounded a high def flat screen laid into the top of work station built for the team's tactical planning sessions. Baker pointed at a corner of the Mobutto compound wall, where the distinctive shape of a MK-19 automatic grenade launcher could be seen underneath the overhanging roof of the reinforced position.

"Tell me that's not a Mark Nineteen! So that's how those sumbitchs kicked the rebel's tails."

Mickey put a finger on the far left side of the screen. "Here's another one in a pickup." He studied the shattered structures of the compound and makeshift repairs to damaged walls. "My God...the bastards caught hell from mortars or artillery..."

"Too small for artillery, I'm thinkin'," Ten Ring said. "A 105 would have made a bigger hole." He pointed at an obvious miss.

"Agree," observed Baker. "Didn't make any difference to the dead guys." He pointed to a row of neatly laid out corpses of the undermanned defenders.

"Can't get killed deader than dead," Mickey said.

Widowmaker scrolled on to the next picture. It was only slightly different than the first. Searching for any sign of Mark, he became slightly depressed as none of the visible defenders were white. He expanded the third shot to encompass most of the battle zone and silently began to try to count the dead rebels splayed across the killing field. *Holy crap! There are hundreds of them.* "Guys...must be several companies of stiffs."

"Somebody down there knows what the hell they're doin'," Mickey said. "Wouldn't have given a plug nickel for their chances..."

Widowmaker shot him a look. "You know, it really sucks to be hours away from a battle where you got a bud in the shit."

"Heard that," Ten Ring said knowingly.

Sean fast forwarded through a dozen more frames as the satellite rose higher and arced over the location. He froze it once again and backed out to the widest point of the camera's imaging. "Lookie here, boys...Now ain't that cute. The rebels have a command tent set up...Too bad the president's men don't have artillery..."

"Zoom in. I think there's something written on it."

"Mickey, believe you're right," Sean said as he placed a box around the target area. He made a couple commands on the keyboard and brought the image to full scale. He twisted his head to read the letters. "Fiftieth Air Cav...Need to have Blaze do some research on their organization."

"I'll handle it," Mickey offered.

Widowmaker returned to the full screen and slowly clicked through another forty pictures.

"Hey! Hold it there...chopper!"

Sean glanced at the area where Ten Ring pointed and strained to see what the sniper was so excited about. Nevertheless, he boxed the target area and enlarged it. The distinct image of a Kenyan Presidential helo emerged. "Son! Got some peepers on you, I'll grant you that."

"Twenty twelve," Weber said casually. "It's a gift...you can call me eye god if you like."

"Don't hold your breath...They came in kinda hard...look at the drag marks from the skids," Mickey noted.

"Wait...are those enemy soldiers?" Widowmaker asked.

"Can't tell. They look like they are crawling toward the chopper...The rotor is either not turning or moving really slow, The image is too clear."

"Think you're right. I'm gonna fast forward a few frames. This crap is already ancient history as far a combat goes," Baker said with a hint of sadness in his voice.

Frame by frame the soldiers moved closer to the downed helo. No one said a word until they were almost on top of it.

Mickey had a thought. "Guys, there must not be anyone inside the chopper. Nobody is moving out and the infantry is really close."

The other two merely nodded. The next three frames showed the infantry reaching the bird. None were prepared for the fourth.

"Sonofabitch!" they exclaimed simultaneously.

The blast filled the entire screen with white and pieces of the shattered fuselage. A stunned silence followed as the three elite Raptors shared nervous glances.

"Whaddaya think? Remote detonator? Timing was too damned good for a fuse..." asked Widowmaker.

"Back up a frame," Ten Ring suggested.

"Okie dokie." Sean tapped the command.

Weber scrutinized the close-up of the chopper just before the detonation and ignored the approaching soldiers. "Uh huh…Fast forward ten seconds then enlarge to five hundred meters."

"You saw something, didn't you?" Baker asked as he complied. He compared the time date stamp of every shot then using the terrain as a guide, gave Ten Ring what he wanted.

Weber scanned the available terrain and his eyes came across a boulder strewn ridge. "Zoom in here."

The Team Four leader complied and a pair of figures appeared as they rose from their hiding spot. One had the tell-tail gray ponytail and carried what appeared to be an M-14. "Zorro!" he cried out as he glanced up at the slightly smug look on Ten Ring's grinning face.

"How the hell did you know?"

"Sniper's just know," he said cryptically as he received a high five from Mickey. He leaned in to Sean and whispered, "Actually, saw a small bag hanging on the chopper. A shooter had to be on the same side…And your boy can shoot."

SHELDRICK WILDLIFE SANCTUARY

The sun began to set as Lucy, Dame Daphne and Malute sat down on the verandah. The deep red, yellow, pink and peach colored sky offered a dazzling show as a soft cool breeze picked up and caressed their skin, blowing mosquitos away.

"I love this time of day," Dame Daphne said as she settled back on her chair and began to gently rock.

"Amazing sunset," Lucy added.

"You haven't said much about yourself...Are your parents worried for you? Have they seen the news about what is going on here in Kenya?

"My parents died when I was five."

"My condolences," Dame Daphne replied while studying the woman closely.

They sat in silence for a time. The rich colors in the sky became more brilliant as the landscape became darker until the trees and buildings turned black against the painted sky. In the distance, the ominous sounds of a hyena pack could be heard calling. The roar of a solitary lion echoed across the plain. Elephants trumpeted to one another. One of the QRF horses snorted and the sounds of their hooves stomping indicated the nightly herd pecking order was being discussed.

"The American...does he come here often?" She halfway hoped the answer would be no.

"He was here the other day...Quiet a surprise too. He had gone to America to visit the father and daughter he rescued from those despicable kidnappers."

"Rescued?"

"Yes. They were on a photo safari near Mount Elgon and stumbled upon some rhino poachers...quite by accident. Turned into a terrible nightmare for them. Mark was in the area and discovered the site of the poaching incident...He tracked the group to the salt caves and rescued them from a fate one can only imagine." Dame Daphne told the story without embellishment, much like reading of the event from a newspaper.

"Mark is…different," Malute continued. "I dare say he's not like anyone we have ever met before. He is very polite and respectful. Well spoken…One gets the feeling he could hardly hurt a fly, but his actions toward poachers say otherwise. He seems to be…carrying a cross…a…I don't know…How would you explain it Dame Daphne?"

Lucy sat listening attentively to Malute and turned to Daphne as the conversation was passed to her.

The older woman gazed at the sky for some time before speaking. It was difficult to tell if she was even aware of Malute's question. Then she shook her head, ever so slightly. "What ever troubles him is in his heart…I have lived a long life. I have seen that look in a man's eyes who has experienced the horrors of war…But there is something else. What ever it is…he has been a wonderful friend to us here and the animals of Kenya." There was a long pause before she leaned forward. "I haven't told anyone else this…only Malute knows and, since I have already sold it and put the money to use…before Mark left, he gave me a diamond ring to assist with our expenses. A one hundred and eighty-three thousand dollar ring."

MUNITIONS DUMP

Bert set the chopper down and shut off the engines. Mark and Malakhi stepped out and rejoined the team.

"Get everything loaded onto the KWS chopper. As soon as it's dark, we're going in…Get 'er loaded, then chow down…Crank set your gun up there above the munitions. Anyone comes callin'…light 'em up."

The team fell in on the task of moving the ammo as well as the wounded pilot onto the helicopter. When finished they broke out the MREs and ate heartily, not because the food was that great, but the emotional adrenaline rush of combat can stir a mighty hunger—especially if you are on the winning side.

One dead and one wounded compared to a near annihilation of the rebel troops in the canyon was a heavy blow. Besides, the team knew as well as Mark, there was absolutely no telling when another opportunity to eat would present itself.

"How much fuel we have left?" Mark asked as he spooned up the last of his chicken fajita main dish. He picked up a package of cooked refried black beans and stirred it into one of Mexican rice.

"Enough," Bert replied as he worked on a serving of spaghetti in meat sauce.

Bear gathered up his trash and stuffed it all into the main meal wrapper before pulling a small silver flask out of his pack. He unscrewed the lid slowly, well aware the eyes of Ian and Crank were on him. After taking a short shot, he replaced the cap and placed the flask back in the pack.

"Ahhh man! Ain't you gonna share?" Crank asked.

"Eah, boyyo! How 'bout a snort for your lads?" Ian added. "A bit o' whiskey…"

"Blow me," Bear retorted. The two badgered him for a taste as he dug around in his pack and proceeded to pull out five other silver flasks and tossed one to each man on the team. "Who da best one-legged vault keeper ya eva knowed?"

Ian, Mark, Malakhi and Bert caught their flasks in midair. Crank fumbled the pass and missed as both of his hands were already full. He quickly picked up the errant flask and took a small pull at the warm whiskey.

"You the man," Bert said with a knowing grin.

The others quickly added their agreement.

"You boys play nice now. Have to share wit our new friends," Bear said motioning to the president's surviving crew members.

Mark smiled at the team's antics as he put his flask into a pouch on his pack. *Rhino could use a shot I suspect.* He checked the sky, then his watch before calling Fabian.

"You coming to the party or what?"

"Tell your men we'll be coming in from the north, lights off, thirty minutes after sundown."

"10-4 that. Keep the rotors turning. I have a plan."

Rhino has a plan. Wonders never cease. Mark smiled again remembering the cluster the big man had come up with in Peru. *Monkey humpin' a basketball, it was.*

DEFENSE MINISTER'S OFFICE
Nairobi

Injera Daar busily gathered documents from his floor safe and placed them into a pair of small black rollaboards. He flinched when his cell phone rang, but made no move to answer it.

Once the small safe was empty, he moved to a wall painting and swung it open to reveal a larger wall vault. After opening it, he removed cash, jewelry and passport, which he placed in a dark brown leather shoulder bag.

A knock at the closed door, followed by the voice of his aide came as he finished, "Sir, your car is here."

"Come in."

The aide entered the room with a look of uncertainty in his eyes. The volume of phone calls had been four times as many as usual and some of the callers did not sound pleased.

"Take these two bags to the car," Daar said while going through the drawers of his desk.

"Yes, sir."

***

CHAPTER TWELVE

MOBUTTO'S SUMMER ESTATE

Built to provide security in the eventuality of numerous threats, the 20x30 foot room was more than adequate for Mobutto, his personal security guards, Lutto plus his two dogs. With a state-of-the-art air filtration system designed to counter even a nuclear, biological or chemical threat, the constant flow of fresh clean air protected the occupants from the rank odors above ground in the mortar ravaged compound. The water purification system tapped into a spring ten feet below the ground. Stores of food and drink for a month provided a variety of dining choices. A bank of industrial grade batteries and a silent generator in a separate closed room supplied the electricity needed to keep everything running and the environment comfortable.

The impacts of the mortar attack had been barely heard, no more than mere thumps since the twenty feet of earth above the room absorbed the sounds.

Mobutto dialed his cell phone calling the commanding general of the Kenyan Air Force.

"Yes, Mr. President."

"What is your ETA, General?"

"I am told we will have a pair of F-5s in the air within four hours. The maintenance crews are working nonstop to cannibalize other aircraft and outfit those the least damaged by the terrorists."

"Get whatever you can in the air immediately! Kenya is depending on you."

The tired president hung up and placed his head in his hands. "Dear Lord, I ask you to be with us now in our time of great need. Protect and comfort those above who now stand in harm's way. In your name we pray…Amen."

Lutto sat down beside him and placed her arm around his shoulder. Mobutto leaned into her embrace and the tall elegant woman gently wrapped both arms around him.

The guards shared a knowing look. Rumors had circulated for years that she was more than his personal secretary. The circumstances of the day washed away all pretense that the two were not deeply attached to one another.

AIRSPACE OVER UGANDA

Gears Formby set 12,000 feet in the altitude window of the Flight Management System, and then selected Flight Level

Change. The nose of the big bird pitched over almost imperceptibly as the aircraft initiated a programmed autopilot descent to the deployment altitude for the BEF's fighters and Condor. "Mike Charley, we're starting down. Distance to target is one five zero."

Burner noted the distance and quickly computed the time. "Copy that AC. Thirty minutes out." He swiveled to his left and glanced over at the two *Manta* control stations. "Launch both URFs."

A flurry of activity began as the two crews initiated their checklists to get the pair of ray-shaped drones launched and heading into position to provide the highest level of real time intelligence, command and control experienced by any American fighting force. The highly advanced reconnaissance packages could designate, track and target up to two hundred enemy soldiers, ground emplacements or vehicles at one time. Its onboard laser system supported JDAMS as well as provided targeting information to the *Eagles* and *Condor* air to ground missiles.

Burner turned to Dare Phillips. "We haven't been able to raise either of our contacts on the ground. The last shots we had before the NEOS crossed the horizon indicated the defense team is holding out...but just barely. The rebels have brought up some APCs, but we don't know the reason they have not been engaged as of yet."

"Got it. We'd best start getting ready for launch. If there's any update, have Blaze relay it directly."

"Good luck, and good hunting," he said as he extended his hand.

Dare grasped it firmly. "Thanks, we may need it." He took a couple steps and placed his hand on Blaze's right shoulder. "Time to go, sweetie."

She unstrapped and swiveled her seat around from the Weapons Station. Her green eyes showed concern, but were dry and clear. "Come back safe...and keep an eye on those newlyweds, would you?...Last time we let them out of our sight, all hell broke loose."

He smiled and kissed her gently. "I'll do what I can." He touched her face with his hand for a brief moment, winked and turned around. Dare stepped over to the crew rest seats assigned to the primary VTOL crews. "All right boys and girls...it's showtime."

The seven other flight crew members brought their seats upright electrically and began to pull on their boots. Mike Hermann led the procession to the crew lockers to retrieve their helmets and combat survival vests. He and the M200 pilot, Jill McElhenny Hermann, stopped by Blaze's station to say their good byes.

"Be back before you know it sissy...keep the coffee warm," Mike said with his characteristic joking manner.

"I'd warn you that it would stunt your growth, but looks like I'm a little late for that," she replied as she gave him a hug. "Watch yourself out there, sis," she said to her brother's new bride. "Sorry you guys didn't get to finish your honeymoon."

"There will be lots more time for that later," she said as she winked at her sister-in-law.

Mickey Williams, husband of Maria Sanchez Williams, stepped out of the changing room where he had already slipped into his Dragonskin lined body suit worn by all the Raptors. She was waiting outside for him, holding her helmet bag. He embraced her and kissed her passionately. "You'll do a great job, I know it," he said when the two separated.

She beamed at the show of confidence—coming from a former Green Beret and Secret Service agent, she knew he was the real deal. "Thanks, hon...I promise not to let Mike get us into too much trouble."

Mickey laughed. She was a former Marine Corps F-18A pilot and could handle about any situation he could imagine. She turned to head to the forward stairs leading down from the monster C-5M's upper deck. He swatted her playfully on the rear.

"Mickey! What am I gonna do with you?"

"I've got some ideas," he said with a smile.

MOBUTTO'S SUMMER ESTATE

Rhino hit the send button on the president's safe room communication device. "Timba."

A few moments later the door opened revealing a guard with his H&K leveled at the opening.

"Get everyone ready to move…five minutes," Rhino barked. "Take food and water for three days. Sleeping bags and comm gear."

"Yes sir."

Precisely five minutes later they came out into the rubble of the once immaculate and stately home.

"Ya will be picked up by helo and moved to Shipton's cave. The staff is already at the north wall…Let's move it!"

"What about you and the men?" Mobutto asked.

"We stay. If the choppers can make another run, those of us still standing will join ya."

The group entered the security detail's barracks to find the staff gathered, all carrying meager possessions of food, water and blankets. There was a freshly blown hole in the north wall large enough for two people to pass through abreast.

They heard the sound of incoming helicopters in the distance growing ever closer, but not visible in the darkness. As everyone moved outside the walls of the compound, they discovered a dozen of the estate guards forming a perimeter around the exit route.

Mobutto grabbed Rhino's arm. "Rheinhart I must protest. I cannot leave you and the men…"

"Yes you can…an' you will Mr. President. Kenya is going to need you even more when this clusterfuck is over. Whoever is out there will think you are still 'ere. The cave is our last line of defense," Rhino spoke directly as he swung his huge arm up out of the president's grasp and wrapped it over his shoulder.

"Mark Ingram is coming in with two choppers...He brought a team of hard men. You will ride outta here with the staff. I'll come get ya."

"I know you are right but I feel like I am..."

"Wrap your arms around your feelings at the cave."

"What about my dogs?"

"No dog left behind, sir...They go too."

As the two helicopters landed, Mark and the team began dragging the munitions off. Satisfied the choppers were empty, he turned and walked toward the group standing against the compound wall.

"Who the hell's runnin' this circus?"

"That would be me, ya brack," Rhino yelled. "All right let's go! Everybody on a chopper!"

As the group hustled into the helos, blades still rotating, Mark and Rhino met face to face. They stood silently eye-balling each other for a moment—each understanding the gravity of their situation. It wasn't their first time.

"Did you bake me a fokin' pie?...Surely ya did?...Time it took ya to get 'ere ya coulda baked a dozen," Rhino yelled to be heard over the helo noise.

"I did. But the boys ate 'em in flight."

"The hell ya say?"

The two men embraced each other hard as the two birds lifted up into the star studded night sky. Once they were off and moving away from the compound, the men remaining began moving the munitions and themselves back through the hole in the wall and into the barracks building.

Crank punched the South African in the shoulder. "Here to save your ass again, Rhino."

"I don't recall you ever saving my ass, wave rider."

"Brazil. Up to your neck in communist insurgents when Bert and I hauled you out."

"Ah...*That* ass saving."

"There's a trend here, gentile...I had to pull your butt out of the Congo myself," Malakhi quipped as he passed by carrying one end of a wooden crate.

"Shit 'n me pie, Jew boy."

"Where's the best place to position the RPGs?" Mark asked as the munitions were being hauled in.

"We have two holes in the south wall," Rhino replied.

"Bear was a Mark 19 instructor back at Benning. Which one is his?"

"Southwest tower." Rhino shook Bear's hand as he passed.

"Malakhi. Ian. Get the RPGs set, and then get outside the walls and place Claymores," Mark ordered. Studying the layout of the compound he added, "Save some for the inner wall...Second thought, Boom Boom...rig a C4 surprise in that opening and another in the door leading to the compound yard."

As the men moved to complete their assigned duties, Rhino lead the way to the southeast tower. Once on the observation deck, Mark dropped his pack, retrieved the silver flask and handed it to Rhino.

"Damn right, mate!" He took a long pull before handing it back. "We seen some tight spots before, bro."

"Now don't go all slobbery on me. You said there were 300 jack jaws out there...so we each kill our fifty and go home."

Rhino laughed. "Better odds than the mussie dance in Borneo. How much did ya offer the team to saddle up?"

"A hundred each...Suspect they would've come for nothin'...You know...one more tale to tell."

"Sheet me a river, why don't ya?" Rhino put his hand on Mark's shoulder. "We get out a this one? I owe ya big."

"Add it to your tab."

They stood in silence as the full moon began to rise, casting muted shadows across the ravaged landscape. Below them, they could make out Malakhi and Ian setting the Claymores. Inside, the exhausted men who had repulsed the first assault were visible at their stations.

"What ever happened to that Colombian woman?" Rhino asked reflectively.

"Which one?"

"Don't ya be buggerin me...The captain's wife."

"Oh...the one built like a brick house with two kids?"

"Jesus, mate. You know exactly who I'm talkin' 'bout."

"She's in Brazil now. Her, the kids...and her parents..."

"How da hell did she afford that move?...Oh...that's right...Zorro the protector of women, children...animals large and small."

"Up your six. Couldn't leave her in Bogota...Her husband's step-brother murdered him when he flipped to the

Tupac…Certain to have her whole family on a death list as well."

"You ever see or hear from her?"

"When time looks short, men tend to think of women they have known or would like to have known. Huh?"

"Oh, would 'ave loved to know her, all right…Top of my list for women scorin' a ten."

"Pretty much lost track of her."

"Bullshit! Ya be squirrelin' her away somewhere for your retirement days, I'm bettin'."

"Marta Maria was something."

"You did her didn't ya? Well damn! Just like ya, Zorro, send a man to his grave knowing you nailed his dream."

"Never did…She was in mournin'. Never do a woman in mournin', my friend."

A gentle breeze began to blow in from the east as the big yellow moon continued to rise, illuminating the terrain more clearly. Mark passed the silver flask back to his friend again as the two stood in silence, taking in the beauty of the landscape with the dark outline of Mt. Kenya in the distance.

AIRSPACE OVER EASTERN UGANDA

Inside the tiny M-200 two-seat fighter, Jill was busy with the last of the pre-departure checklist. Her WSO, the venerable Glenn "Bug" Haug was completing the final challenge and response procedures when a radio call came from the leader of the BEF.

"All units be advised the situation on the ground appears to be critical. Break formation and proceed with attack plan Bravo. Acknowledge with ident."

"That does it," Bug said as he tapped the yellow illuminated key on the comm panel. "Poor SOB's ain't got a Chinaman's chance if the boss can't wait to form up."

"Don't be so sure...You recall how things turned out down in Texas?"

"How could I forget, Lucky? I got a scar on my butt to show for it. You thought it was great sport to duke it out with a Ma Deuce on that Mexican APC."

"My bad...but we did kick the cartel's ass and saved the Hermann home place."

"Yes'um and I put a Hellfire into that ass wipe that tagged me...served him right. Besides it gave you a chance to marry that big good-looking jarhead husband of yours."

"Yeah...Where are we on the checklist?"

"Final item...gear and weapon's safety pins..."

"Right...removed and secured," she said as the crew chief held up the *Remove Before Flight* landing gear and missile pins. He snapped a crisp salute that drew one in return from the blonde fighter pilot.

"Before Takeoff Checklist complete," announced Bug.

The tractor chain inset in the cargo floor of the C-5M began to move once again. From the side of the wraparound canopy of the 200, Jill and Bug could see the figure of loadmaster Gunnz Garner as he controlled the movement of the compact deadly fighter. He wore a blue jumpsuit that looked more like a dove gray in the reduced red lighting of *Mama Bird's* cavernous bay. He stopped the drive mechanism, held up both hands, made two fists and rolled them downward at the wrist, signaling *set brakes*. Jill pressed down on the tops of the combination rudder pedals and brakes assemblies and pulled up on the small parking brake knob. A tiny red light confirmed the set position, so she responded with the appropriate hand signals.

The loadmaster nodded and signaled for her to run up power for takeoff.

"Here we go," she said without much emotion in her voice. Her pulse rate told another story. Launching in the night from the extended cargo ramp at 250 KIAS was not for the faint of heart. The five nacelle futuristic VTOL had power to spare. But the physical layout of the *Super Galaxy* tail and clamshell doors offered only a four scant feet from the top of the Skycar V tail to the bottom of the mother ship. She knew she had to be at the best of her game to make the takeoff work as planned.

Jill eased forward on the single throttle. The ten Rotopower engines—two twinned together in each of the five nacelles—were computer controlled and the flight computer made electronic inputs to the two front and two outside nacelles to cause them to rotate up forty-five degrees. Louvers at the rear of the ducted fans flexed downward another fifty degree as the eight engines whined like angry hornets.

Haug eased a hand behind hers as a precaution—call it self preservation—but he, like other WSOs, was a top notch pilot in his own right and he never forgot that his life was in the hands of the pilot in command as well. He could hear her breathing pick up as the oxygen system regulator cycled faster along with the RPM. "Approaching ninety-two percent," he noted as the engine instruments on the flat screen neared the computed takeoff power.

The craft bobbled slightly and lifted off the main gear first followed by the nose. A small *weight on wheels* green light extinguished.

"We're flying," he noted calmly.

Gunnz motioned to continue the takeoff and waved two muted red wands signaling for Jill to back up. She gingerly pulled aft on the stick a fraction of a pound. The M200 vanes modulated slightly sending the bird drifting toward the end of the ramp. She focused on him as he stood still at the center of the ramp's hinge point, tied to the aircraft with a long black two inch wide safety strap.

"Just like backin' the truck out of the garage," Bug said.

If you say so, she thought but said nothing.

The align LED lights laid into the end on the ramp finally came into view. The loadmaster snapped a salute, indicated *Eagle Three* was clear of the mother ship. Jill eased the stick forward as she transitioned into the cockpit with her gaze. Outside, the world was mostly black. She continued the descent until the craft felt the first impulse of the boundary layer around *Mama Bird*.

The turbulence was immediate and strong. Gears had maintained a less than optimum airspeed of 260 knots to cut the arrival time as much as safely possible. The small VTOL rocked left and dipped sharply down. She over controlled slightly and rolled right into a twenty degree bank before she recovered and leveled out.

"Fifty feet," Bug announced.

Jill knew the air would smooth out below that point and began to gradually push forward on the stick as she increased power. The fifth nacelle engines—mounted between the canted vertical stabilizers came up to speed, accelerating the M200/A to its top speed of 500 KIAS.

"Gear up, after take off checklist," she called as she tried to swallow the cotton that had formed in her mouth.

"You got it, young lady. Now let's go kick some ass."

MOBUTTO'S SUMMER ESTATE

Lt. Kamau climbed up to the observation deck. "I suggest we send some scouts out to gather intel."

"No. We already know where the hell they are. Best spend tha time filling sand bags...Oh. Lieutenant Kamau...Mark Ingram," Rhino said. "Never better on my six."

"I heard stories of your adventures with the QRF. Well played, sir. Well played."

"Thanks. Pale reading in comparison to your exploits in Somalia...How are the men holding up?"

"Bloodied, but still in the fight."

"My men and I will support you, but they operate under my command. Hope you understand. We...hell, there's no way around it...we function best as operatives."

"Glad to have you aboard," Kamau responded. "Rheinhart, we only have a couple of belts each for the Mark 19s. I issued all the rifle ammunition, three hundred rounds per man."

"Everyone have a shovel?" Mark asked.

"Shovel?" Kamau asked.

"When they get inside the walls, a shovel beats a knife, machete or bayonet every time. The most feared weapon back in the day of swords and shields was the ax…Make sure everyone has a shovel," Mark said as he unstrapped the short double-bladed battle ax from his pack and spun it in his hand.

Malakhi called up from below the tower, "Claymores set, Zorro."

"Set the inner compound mines, then you take the east wall. Tell Ian to take a position at one of the breeches on the south wall. Find Crank and send him here."

The Jewish warrior spun and sprinted away.

"Did ya see tha look on Kamau's face when ya said shovel?" Rhino asked.

"Did not."

"Puzzled he was, 'til he saw your ax."

Below, Mark could see Crank trotting toward them. He moved like a big cat across the torn muddy ground.

"Zorro…You rang?" he called up.

"Get an RPG and three KDF with machine guns inside the inner wall. Disperse as you see fit. When we have to fall back, cover our retreat."

"Aye-aye…El Capitan!" Crank replied, giving a Benny Hill salute before running off to gather the men.

"Crazy he is," Rhino said. "Not as crazy as Ian, the red headed potato farmer, but…crazy."

"I'm going down and man the second breech. Pass the word. Taking Ian and a couple of soldiers out. Collect some AKs and ammo before the rodeo starts again."

The moon provided ample light for the weapons collection expedition. All four of the men with Mark had a three or four Kalashnikovs slung over their shoulders and magazine pouches as well from the fallen men of the 50th Air Cav lying sprawled across the battleground. As they started back, the running lights of the APCs flashed in the distance as they crossed the ridge headed toward the estate.

"Move it!" Mark yelled. "Go! Go! Go!"

As Ian and the KDF soldiers ran for the walls of the compound Mark turned and knelt facing the advancing troops. Then, he noticed to his left more advancing Pumas. *Jesus!* He ran back to the bodies of the dead and set a parachute flare in the harness of one and stretched a trip wire to the body of another. Sprinting down the line, he repeated the process before turning and running as fast as he could over the muddy ground toward the compound. *Gonna light up this dance floor.*

Mark hurdled the wall of sandbags and hit the ground, rolling to his right just as the machine gun fire from the advancing Pumas began to tear into the walls. Chunks of plaster and rock flew all along the wall as the .50 caliber rounds impacted with solid *thunks*.

He picked up an RPG-7 launcher and loaded an armor piercing grenade round before leaning it against the wall. Looking to his left he could see Ian and Malakhi doing the same. Mark then arranged the control boxes for the Claymore mines in front of his position as a .50 caliber round penetrated the sandbag wall and impacted the ground inches from him. *Shit*! He rolled further to his right stopping behind the rock wall as a dozen more rounds chewed up the sandbag emplacement.

Rhino ordered his team of Mk 19s to open fire. The three automatic grenade launchers began to pump 40mm HE projectiles into the advancing soldiers following the APCs at 400 yards in slow, controlled bursts. One grenade hit a Puma dead on, but did not halt its advance. A second hit beside the right front wheel and disabled it. On yet another Puma—the luckiest shot of all time—passed through the driver's view window, knocking out the bullet proof glass like it was wet toilet paper, and ignited the ammunition inside. As the surviving crew members and troops struggled to get out, the personnel carrier exploded in a huge ball of fire.

Closer in, Ian fired his RPG and scored a direct hit on another much nearer Puma, as did Malikhi on the east wall. The APCs began to zig-zag as they advanced. Mark led one and fired, hitting the left rear tire, disabling it.

Time seemed to slow down—it always does—as the defenders and the attackers battled for victory. Advancing on three fronts, the men of the 50th were closing on the compound rapidly. Mark glanced to his right at the very moment a hail of .50 caliber rounds shredded the southwest tower observation deck. He could see Bear and the two men with him ripped to pieces. *Damn it! Never should have let you come.* He watched as Bear's bullet torn body lifted off the tower and tumbled to the ground, his lifeless limbs fluttering in the wind. *No time for soliloquies.*

He reloaded his RPG and took aim on a Puma when a .50 cal projectile hit the stone wall, showering him in fragments of rock and fine dust. Jerking back, he struggled to clear his vision. He peered around the wall again, two trip flares went off, arcing high into the night sky, then floating beneath their parachutes—illuminating the landscape with ghostly images of men and their shadows waving eerily back and forth. *Never that good with math, but if that's only 300 men, I'm Jesus.*

The rifles of the defenders fired as their individual targets became clear. The reinforced advancing troops, numbering six hundred, kept coming like a tsunami of black devils.

Suddenly, Mark felt a hand grab his shoulder and shake him. Turning he saw Crank kneeling beside him.

"Jumpers landing to the north. Hundreds of 'em!"

Looking past Crank, he could make out the silhouettes of the descending men. "Get back to your position! Falling back after we detonate the Claymores."

"Fall back," Lt. Kamau repeated the order to the defenders over his handheld bullhorn.

Mark used hand signals to tell Ian and Malakhi to hold their position as he held up one of the control boxes for the Claymore mines. Both men signaled thumbs-up.

As Rhino and the KDF soldier manning the southeast tower ran out of the building, a volley of .50 cal fire raked the ground around them. The soldier took two direct hits and lifted up like a piece of plastic trash floating on the breeze before hitting the muddy earth in a pile of his own intestines.

Rhino continued to run down the line toward Mark—hunched over to offer a smaller target. As he passed Ian and the opening in the wall a 7.62mm round struck him in the buttocks, causing him to spin and fall. Mark watched anxiously as his friend crawled to safety behind the rock wall and signaled an okay.

When the advancing force came within range Mark detonated his Claymores, followed by Ian and Malakhi. Thousands of steel balls tore through the ranks of the attackers shredding all who were in their path, bringing the advance to a halt.

Mark grabbed Betsy II, his RPG, a pouch of grenades, his battle ax and ran to Rhino. He arrived to find Ian applying a pressure bandage to the wound.

"Get him to the inner compound!" Mark yelled over the chaos.

"Ye get him…I'll be coverin' your six," Ian bellowed in reply.

The two men locked eyes. Both knew whoever stayed, was dead. Just then, Malakhi joined them.

"Get him up! Let's go!" Mark ordered.

They jerked Rhino to his feet and he wrapped his arms over their shoulders. Mark gave one last look to Ian.

"Move your bloody arses lads!" Ian hollered with a wicked smile. He began tossing grenades over the wall.

Miraculously, Mark, Rhino and Malakhi made the inner wall. With adrenaline pumping, they tossed the injured man over the four foot wall before joining him and the last defenders.

"I suspect you two 'ill be wanting a shiny medal now," Rhino said through clenched jaw.

Mark took a quick look over the wall and saw Ian engaged with a half dozen men at the wall breech. Overcome, the Irish madman went down in a hail of lead. As the attackers rushed over him, two grenades fell from his lifeless hands and exploded killing and maiming another dozen men.

"Ian's done," Mark informed Rhino and Malakhi.

"Out the way he wanted," Malakhi said.

Crank and the three men manning the machine guns no longer fired in controlled bursts, but rather swept the field in long strings of fire. Those who had made it back to the last line of defense fired their weapons or one of the captured AKs on full auto as well. Mark fired another pair of flares.

A Puma began to ease through one of the south wall breeches. Mark took it out with a direct RPG hit to the left front tire and as it tilted forward over the sandbags. The crew members scrambled to exit the disabled vehicle, but Mark picked them off, one by one, with rapid aimed shots from Betsy II.

"Come on assholes!" Crank yelled in a killing-crazed voice. "Gonna fuck you up!"

"Get me up…Give me a weapon!" Rhino shouted.

"Load me!" Mark screamed back, tossing his bandoleers and two empty twenty round M1A magazines to the wounded man. "Malakhi!…Claymores!"

Both men triggered them on the south wall. Malakhi ran to the west and triggered the mines there and started to the arming devices on the north side when a 7.62mm caliber round struck his right thigh, throwing him first into the wall and then to the ground. He pulled a tourniquet from his pants and wrapped the leg above the wound before crawling toward the Claymore triggers. Another round struck him in the back pushing him face down in the mud. The Armor500 plate saved his life, but the impact of the AK round knocked the wind from his lungs.

A violent explosion rocked the north wall. *C4 Surprise!*

Crank picked up his Vektor and ran to Malakhi, grabbing him by his harness. He drug the injured Israeli to the Claymore triggering devices, and then trained his machine gun on the barracks open door.

Mere moments passed, though it seemed like an eternity, before the first paratrooper appeared in the doorway. As the rebel soldier charged forward he tripped the arming wire to the second C4 trap. The explosion tore the front of the building off, and collapsed the roof.

"Now *that* was purty!" Crank yelled at Malakhi.

Mark grabbed his grenade bag and begin tossing one after another over the fence as fast as he could. Seeing Rhino laying against the wall, busy loading stripper clips of 7.62x51 into the M1A magazines, he tossed the grenade bag to him.

"Just chunk 'em over the wall. You can't miss...Joke you not!"

Rhino happily complied—the constant din of noise from the frequent explosions almost masked the anguished screams of rebel fighters ripped apart by the lethal bits of hot steel—almost.

The advance halted once again as the rebel forces took cover behind the estate's outer wall. Mark emptied his last M1A magazine at the tangos as they peered over, and then laid his rifle against the pockmarked rock. He pulled an AK to his shoulder, firing the entire thirty round mag in short bursts. He ducked down as returning hot lead splattered against the wall and cracked over head. He rammed another into the well before he popped up, emptying it too.

Without another AK magazine, Mark pulled his Gold Cup and continued to fire as he worked his way to his right and then back to Rhino. *Never use the same firing position if avoidable.*

"We got 'em now!" Mark yelled with a crazed smile as he looked down at Rhino. He dropped the magazine and reloaded. Quickly emptying the eight rounder, he tossed the 1911 into Rhino's lap, along with a loaded fifteen round magazine. "Load me!"

With a fluid motion gleaned from years of practice, he pulled the S&W 5906 from the drop-leg holster on his left thigh and began to fire rapidly into the mass of men now advancing on their position again. A stream of 9mm brass flew from the ejection port. Bodies stacked up as one after another rebel took hits to their center mass.

Rhino pulled himself up on his good knee and opened fire with Mark's Colt. "The hell ya say!" He dropped six men with his first eight shots—but still more came.

A pair of Air Cav soldiers jumped onto the wall a few feet to their right and began to spray the estate defenders with full auto fire. His back-up pistol empty, Mark grabbed his ax and hacked the closest man's right foot off at the ankle, then swung the bloody weapon a second time into the other man's groin. Both screaming men fell backwards off the rampart. He placed the leather strap on the ax handle around his right wrist and proceeded to feed another double-stacked magazine into the S&W.

"Didn't fokin' see that comin', did ya?" Rhino blurted out while laughing hysterically.

Mark pulled a pair of fifteen round magazines for the Gold Cup free from the carrier and tossed them to his injured blood brother. As he did, Rhino leveled the .45 caliber pistol toward Mark and fired a pair of shots. The dead body of a Air Cav attacker fell on top of Mark, knocking him to the ground. As he rolled out from under the body, a rebel corporal leaned over the wall and shot him twice in the chest at point blank range. The impacts did not penetrate the Amor500 plate. The shooter turned toward Rhino as Mark fired, hitting the man in the forehead—lifting off the top of his skull and vaporizing his brain into a thick pink mist.

Mark staggered back to his feet as he struggled painfully to catch his breath. Another Puma rolled past the last that he had disabled and he watched helplessly as the turret spun around to line up its death-dealing .50 caliber machine gun on their position. He glanced down at the nearby RPG launcher. *Sumbitch!* It was empty—no rockets left. Taking in what he though was his last breath, he lifted his handgun defiantly and fired the last four rounds at it.

A brief streak of light from above preceded the explosion that demolished the APC with a distinctly metallic sounding *clang*. Mark stood there for a second, trying to process exactly what the hell had happened when another *clang* sounded outside the wall—followed quickly by six more. Mark snapped out of his momentary daze and snatched up an AK from a fallen rebel paratrooper and helped himself to several full thirty round mags. *Don't guess you'll be minding,* he mused as he looked at the blank stare on the rebel's face.

He ran to Rhino's side and handed him the assault rifle. "Cover me, while I get Betsy back into the fight." Mark gathered up a double handful of empty M1A mags and began to feverishly thumb stripper clips of shiny ammo into their waiting cavities.

"How'd you do that?" Rhino asked as he checked that the weapon's chamber was still full. He snapped the rifle to his shoulder and fired at a soldier who was topping the wall some forty yards away. The man grunted and fell back in the direction from which he came.

"I thought…"

"Don't look at me," Rhino said as he shrugged his shoulders.

Suddenly the sky lit up with a faint blue glow as hundreds of hypersonic rounds streaked downward at a relatively shallow angle. The blue glow disappeared as quickly as it came—the sound of human bodies exploding nearby echoed outside the compound walls. *Blap! Blap!...Blap! Blap!...Blap!*

Mark's hands flew as the third 20 rounder was filled to capacity. He rocked it into Betsy II's magwell and slammed the bolt forward into battery. A figure appeared on the far wall on the compound, firing at the defenders. Mark engaged it and snapped the trigger as the crosshairs floated across the rebel's chest. The man exploded, leaving a ragged cloud of dark red mist where his body had stood only seconds before.

Mark stared curiously at the strange blue flash of light, but it had disappeared as suddenly as it came. Rhino's jaw dropped open slightly.

"Dammit, Zorro...I'm seeing that with ma own eyes!"

Sixteen hundred feet overhead, Dare Phillips made a radio call on the Black Eagle Force secure operations frequency. "Eagle One, off south." He nudged the fly-by-wire stick and the nimble M600 rolled right and pulled up to make another pass.

Weapons Systems Operator Bull Gaspar commented dryly, "Nice shot, bossman, but ya gotta admit...he was standin' still."

"I'll let you show me how it's done on the stragglers," Dare replied.

"Eagle Two, in hot from the west." The call from Mike Hermann matched what the other attack crews saw on their large flat screens in their *disposition of forces* cockpit displays. Both *Manta 1* and *2* unmanned reconnaissance fighters had assigned red target indicator icons to all combatants outside the embattled summer estate. The first two passes from each manned fighter, coupled with the missile attacks from the two sophisticated drones did more than break the backs of the attacks. With the rebel's armored personnel carriers destroyed, the mere sight of their comrades disintegrating in front of them caused a major panic. The ghastly deaths looked beyond spooky in the flickering yellow flare light. Survivors broke and ran, only to die tired as the *Eagles* pounced again and again with their multi-barreled electromagnetic coil guns.

In the BEF command ship, the *Manta 1* operator turned to General Burner Stewart. "Sir, it looks as if the only concentration of enemy forces left is in what appears to be a command tent." He pointed at the display that had been enlarged to show the fancy organizational emblem of the 50th Air Cav. Infrared returns of a dozen high ranking officers and a few support people were clearly in evidence.

"I see…Blaze, I believe we have something on board to take them out all at once, if memory serves me."

"Right you are, sir. One fuel air bomb coming up…" she switched her headset communication switch to interphone. "AC, Weapons."

The call back instantly. "Go ahead, weapons. What can I do for you?"

"Come left to 165 degrees. Maintain current altitude and speed."

"I think we can do that," he said as he turned the heading select knob on the flight director. He pressed a button marked *Heading* on the autopilot and discontinued the racetrack pattern he had previous set up on the FMC. The huge C-5M rolled into a shallow turn to follow his command.

Blaze set up the on-board target laser system to get the exact global coordinates of the targeted tent. In a couple of seconds, the flat screen display over her battle station showed a rectangular box beside the tent—the appropriate latitude and longitude inside. Her fingers flew over the weapons station keyboard as tiny red enemy icons scattered like ants from the vicinity of the President's estate. She right clicked an icon causing a drop down menu to appear and selected a 2,000 pound smart bomb from it. Using her mouse, she dragged and dropped the tent's lat/long into the bomb's memory chip.

Once she touched *enter*, a magenta circle appeared around the target, indicated the bomb release parameters in which the guidance system on the tail of the fuel-air bomb could fly it to the target upon release. She rechecked that the two sets of GPS data were exactly the same. Once the bomb was released, there was no way to recall or redirect it. Blaze calculated the time until the *Super Galaxy* reached the edge of the circle. "Weapons ready…thirty seconds, Burner."

"Engage when able."

General Janmohamed almost stumbled when the frantic radio calls ordering a retreat came over the tactical radio. He spun around in the brightly lit tent as he bellowed his displeasure. "Who the hell gave that order? I want that coward's name!" He glared at the executive officer of the 20th. "Colonel! Was that one of your men?"

If the XOs skin had been any color than coal black, Janmohamed might have seen the man blanch. As it was, he only saw his eyes grow wide as he shook his head. "No, sir! Our motto is *Never Surrender* at the 20th!"

"Give me that handheld!" the big narcissist yelled. He snatched the radio out of his aide's hand and screamed into it, "Who authorized a retreat? Who said that?"

Janmohamed never heard the solenoid open on the lower outer sidewall of huge transport, four miles above him. He never heard the thermobaric weapon fall as it accelerated to supersonic speed, coming in almost vertically. It deployed it's explosive gas mixture in a large gray jellyfish-shaped cloud that enveloped the tent and all the rebel commanders. The detonator flashed brightly, but the resulting blast rivaled the sun itself for an instant—but he never heard it.

Zorro helped Rhino to his feet. "Gotta get you to better cover, dog."

"Who you calling dog?…ya skinny little shit. I'll can still kick yer scrawny ass."

"If you say…"

A brilliant flash came from far outside the compound. All the defenders looked on in awe.

"What the bloody hell?" Rhino muttered. The concussion of the distant blast echoed off the surrounding hills.

Mark looked overhead, searching without success for the source of the offensive weapons that had turned the tide for the beleaguered defenders.

***

CHAPTER THIRTEEN

AIRSPACE OVER MOBUTTO'S COMPOUND

Mike Hermann, piloting the *Eagle 2* aircraft blinked his eyes and tried to regain his night vision after the blinding flash. "Whoa! Baby sister could have given us a little more warning…"

"Copy that," WSO Maria Sanchez Williams replied. "Instrument panel backlighting coming to full." The former Marine F-18A *Hornet* pilot turned a small knob on the cockpit sidewall, increasing the interior lighting dramatically.

"That's more like it. Appreciate it, Double D," the older of the two Herman siblings said as he leveled off from the shallow dive.

"Can't have you flyin' us into the ground again, can we?"

"Never gonna let me live that one down, are you?"

"Oh, sure. Someday…You can bet on it," she lied.

"Hold on…think I see a target bearing two five zero at eight hundred. Is that tango moving?"

"Can't tell for sure…let me zoom in…"

The flat screen in front of the WSO position expanded the God's eye view from one of *Manta 1's* powerful cameras. The greatly magnified scene clearly showed a single soldier running, and then he stopped and tried to hide behind a lone giant goundsels tree.

"Good eyes, hammer hands."

"Bite me." He rolled the VTOL into a bank, dove and lined up the red tango target icon in the center of his infrared laser boresight. At the short slant range, the drop of the 13,000 feet per second ferro-magnetic projectile would be negligible. He tickled the trigger on the stick, sending a dozen of the hypersonic 7mm bullets out the six barreled coil gun mounted in the tip of the Skycar's aerodynamic nose.

Both flyers heard a slight mechanical buzzing sound as the rotary feed mechanism cycled twice, sending another half dozen round into the breach of the non-revolving weapon to prepare it for the next target. Intricate sequential wrapping of carbon fiber nanotubes encircled each of the stationary 7.62 caliber barrels and supplied the electronic pulse required direct from the M600/A electrical system. The tubes were filled with liquid mercury—a substance that acted as a superconductor and created hyper-intense magnetic fields around the barrels. The slightly smaller projectiles were levitated within the chambers and flew freely, without touching the bore's inner lands and grooves—a factor that reduced friction and allowed the finely tapered bullets to reach almost unimaginable velocity. A momentary blue flash accompanied each salvo of six tungsten alloy bullets—the product of a plasma field generated by the intense air friction. The twelve rounds fired all arrived within a fraction of a second.

The rebel sergeant literally vaporized as three rounds impacted and created an instantaneous hydrostatic shock wave within his body. Blood and tissue—being constituted primarily of incompressible water—transmitted the almost immeasurable forces within his body—stretching the man's skin like a balloon until it burst. The destructive shock wave fractured and crushed the man's skeleton as well—leaving little to bury, save a stub of leg bone sticking out of an overturned combat boot.

"That's a kill," Maria confirmed, looking at the screen.

Mike pulled the nose up and leveled off at fifteen hundred feet above the battlefield. He selected *Altitude Hold* on the autopilot and engaged it before pulling the throttles to idle. The futuristic craft slowed and came to a stop—hovering over the northern side of combat area. "Weapons, Eagle 2," he radioed to the Offensive and Defensive Weapons station aboard *Mama Bird.*

"Eagle 2, Weapons, go ahead."

"Eagle requests Manta 1 or 2 do a moving target search. I don't see any active tangos outside the compound."

"Copy that, Cowboy. Stand by."

Blaze looked over at the two URF controllers. Both nodded that they had received Mike's transmission. Lauren Jones,

Manta 1 pilot, quickly sent the appropriate commands to the sophisticated software. The infrared returns identified with a red tango icon were filtered against a second third and forth snapshot of the same area. The images were electronically overlaid to compare the exact terrain over eight seconds. Any that showed no motion were removed from the final image.

"Weapons, Manta 1, negative tangos."

A couple of seconds later another call came over the intercom.

"Manta 2 reports negative contacts.

Blaze quickly acknowledged the reports and switched to tactical frequency. "All Eagle aircraft, be advised Mantas report no tangos moving at this time."

"Mike Charlie, Eagle 1," Dare Phillips called.

"Eagle 1, Mike Charlie, say your request."

"Mike Charlie, do you want us to initiate contact with the survivors?"

Mission Commander Burner Stewart had anticipated the request and immediately replied, "Negative, we will make one more attempt to make phone contact, then send in the Raptors. Hold your positions."

"Eagle flight copies. Standing by."

Burner called Communication Specialist Niki Layton and made his request. She rang the number an eighth time since the BEF deployed the *Eagles* during the battle.

MOBUTTO'S COMPOUND

Lieutenant Kamau moved from position to position, checking on his dead and wounded as well as heaping praise on the surviving brave men who fought with him. He approached Mark and Rhino and tossed the weary Texan a canteen. "Looks like you could use this...think maybe we beat them back for a while...No?"

Mark took a deep draw and poured a stream across his face to wash the grime and dust from his eyes. He handed the canteen to the South African. "I think you broke the code, Lieutenant...Damned fine show from your men...They fought like lions..."

"And died like lions as well...We are really starting to get low on ammunition..." Kamua said until Mark held up his hand.

"Hold that thought...somebody's trying to reach me on the dang cell phone." He fished inside his left thigh pocket and took hold of the vibrating device. He didn't recognize the number, but guessed it really didn't matter at that point. "Ingram."

"Mister Ingram!...General Phillips is calling. Hold on while I connect you."

Who? He wondered as he heard the woman's voice.

"Mark, we're glad you made it! You had us worried for a second."

"A second, hell!...I was worried for a lot longer than that! Who is this?"

The general laughed. "I guess we never actually met, sir...I'm General Jack Stewart...Black Eagle Force Mission Commander...overhead your position."

Mark looked up in the night sky, but heard or saw nothing. He took a filthy hand and wiped the remaining drops of water off his eyelids. "If you say so, General. I knew somebody was up there, besides God, giving us a big hand."

"President Thompson sends her regards. Is President Mobutto safe?"

"Yes, sir. We moved him to a safe location."

"That's great news. Our sensors indicate that the threat around you has been generally neutralized at this time. I'm sending in a ground team to assist. One of them is an old friend of yours. Tell your team to stand down."

"Copy that, sir. We'll be looking forward to it."

AIRSPACE OVER MOBUTTO'S COMPOUND

"Team Five, stand ready," barked Widowmaker over the tactical radio as *Mama Bird* circled back over the battlefield at eighteen thousand feet. The bird had been depressurized and all crew members wore supplemental oxygen masks. Once again, the lights in the otherwise empty cargo bay went from bright white LEDs to red as the loadmaster received clearance to lower the ramp.

The Raptors—as the ground troops deployed by the BEF were known—looked like futuristic apparitions with their head-to-toe high-tech gear. Their Kevlar helmets—resembling a full-face motorcycle helmet—completely covered their heads, including the mouth and jaw area, and featured an internal HMD to allow each member to view real-time imagery from *Manta*. Additionally, acoustic and optical magnification systems gave the them ten times the hearing and visual acuity of a normal warfighter. Strapped to their harnesses, they carried a variety of weapons designed to defeat specific enemy threats in addition to their personal choices of rifles, carbines and handguns. Under all that gear was the latest in ballistic armor, overlapping discs of lightweight ceramic layered with titanium called Dragonskin under a impenetrable formfitting suit made with graphene. It resembled a scuba diver's wet suit, but was far more comfortable. Flexible carbon-fiber nanotubes filled with nitrogen, ran throughout the entire outfit, keeping the wearer cool with a battery powered circulation system.

All that defensive capability protected the Raptor from small arms fire and minor shrapnel. The suit itself could even withstand a .50 BMG round, although the impact would likely kill the unlucky person. What really differentiated the BEF system from contemporary military competitors was the incorporation of the *Lizard* cloaking device borrowed from the group's aircraft. The concept worked the same, but the requirement for a battery powered control system placed some operational limits that the fighters were well aware of and included in their briefings.

"Thirty seconds," advised Gunnz Garner as he relayed the interphone update from the weapons station.

"Lizard up!" barked Baker as he tapped on the small green icon on control pad on his left wrist.

The others followed suit. All twelve Raptors had long since completed their final gear security checks as they jostled in two columns onto the first ten feet of the ramp. Behind the C-5M, the stars lit up the night skies as distant clusters of lights from small Ugandan villages looked like scattered points of light on a dark milieu. The craggy peak of Mount Kenya to the west was barely visible in the darkness as the moon had just cleared the eastern horizon. Patches of snow capped the second highest peak in Africa. At 17,057 feet above sea level, the rocky precipice was less than 1,000 feet below the altitude of the aircraft.

Widowmaker stopped fifteen feet from the end of the ramp as cold winds whipped around the open fuselage. He focused on the job at hand and waited for the amber light to change color in the jumpmaster's control panel.

"Go, go, go!" Gunnz called out as *Mama Bird* overflew the drop coordinates.

The Raptors didn't really need to be told more than once. They were underway at the first syllable and dove with arms extended overhead into the blackness below. Once clear of the aircraft, each man arched his back to help stabilize himself as he fell. The smoke of the burnt-out summer estate was visible far below as a gray haze drifting slowly away. A few fires, mostly burning APCs, generated their own narrow bands of denser black smoke, clearly giving signs of the light prevailing wind.

Wind whistled over the straps and harnesses of the team as they hurtled down at almost 120 mph. Mickey Williams, lead man in the second element, checked his altitude in his HMD. He was already passing 12,000 feet and his adrenaline had kicked in. The sensation of free-fall was not really like falling—the wind pushed back against his outstretched gloved hands, arms and legs. He—like virtually all the other Raptors—was an admitted adrenaline junky, but had learned to focus on the job at hand and used the extra energy that kicked in to analyze the potential threats below.

Widowmaker monitored his descent and pulled his D-ring at 1,500 feet above ground as briefed. The drogue chute instantly deployed and tugged the main out of the back of the MC-4 harness. At terminal velocity, the opening shock was considerable—he was yanked upright firmly as the black ram air canopy inflated with an audible pop. Sean grinned before he even looked up to check, as experience had taught him that the opening had been a good one.

In rapid succession, the other team members pulled theirs as well, stacking up laterally as well as vertically. None wanted to freefall through another's canopy in the event their primary didn't work. All twelve maneuvered to land within two hundred yards of the main gate of the compound. *Manta* had shown the tangos below to be stationary. That, however, did not insure that they were dead.

Mickey touched down a few seconds before Widowmaker, as he carried a few more pounds of muscle on his frame. He set down fifteen yards from the hulk of a burned out APC.

Baker had to pull down on both risers to hop over and glide past a jumbled pile of bodies as he landed. *Christ! They're everywhere.* He touched down gently at a walk and rapidly spilled his chute. Instantly, his hands flew to the harness as he shed himself of the rigging and grabbed for the padded weapons bag. He unsnapped the cover over the zipper and slid it down part way, exposing the Blaze G3 carbine. The tiny coil gun outwardly resembled the bullpup design of the Steyer AUG, but it was vastly more deadly than the 5.56mm weapon. Like the G1 sniper rifle and the *Eagle's* six barreled cannon, it fired a 7mm tungsten alloy projo at hyper velocity.

Widowmaker charged the weapon, moved several yards closer to the compound and took a knee. He tapped a command on his wrist control pad and watched the rest of the team land in the God's eye mode from *Manta.* Switching his optic to ten power, he scanned the compound walls for signs of life. He could make out a couple soldiers wearing the same uniform as the dead men littering the field around him. *Oh yeah…civil war* he thought as the sight disturbed him for a second. *They all wear the same uniform.*

Widowmaker scanned the battlefield for live rebel combatants. He saw a couple of wounded men eighty yards away and dispatched them with a single shot each. He checked HMD again and made a radio call. "Team Five, check in with ident."

Seconds passed and all of his eleven men responded electronically as mission ready. *So far, so good.* "Be advised, rebel survivors in the area.…Move on to the objective."

Like wraiths from a Machiavellian nightmare, the twelve invisible Raptors pressed forward, taking no chances with any rebel soldier. They had dispatched over thirty by the time Mickey, Ten Ring and Widowmaker reached the demolished main gate. "Form a defensive perimeter. Three of us will establish contact inside."

Widowmaker eased past the burnt-out Puma, the one taken out by one of the *Eagles* with a PASSM. He spotted four men standing near another prone figure and recognized the old friend from his Marine Corps days. He and Mickey approached directly and Ten Ring circled around.

Crank was sharing a canteen with Lt. Kamau. He took a swig, sloshed it around and turned to spit it out A footprint magically appeared in the red dirt next to the spot he chose, followed by another a few inches away. He wiped his eyes with the back of his dirty hands as he looked again. Suddenly, a black clad warrior appeared next to him. Crank reacted with a start. "Son of a bitch!"

"Hey, Zorro!" came a voice from inside the closed helmet.

Lt. Kamau reached for his sidearm, but another BEF fighter materialized and grasped his wrist as he screamed. "Ghosts! Pepo wabaya! Pepo wabaya "

"Sean the Widowmaker!" hollered Mark as his face broke into a full smile for the first time in several hours. "So nice of you to drop in."

Mark and Crank, surrounded by the other Raptors, were in conversation with former SEAL Andy "Doc" Long, the team's corpsman.

"Checked your buddy's wound, cleaned it and put a fresh dressing on…Too bad I don't have him in my facilities on board Mama Bird…got some stuff that'll heal it right up, but he should be fine in a couple of weeks or so…Told him at least he got shot in the same place Audie Murphy did," reported Doc.

"What did he say to that?" asked Mark.

"You really don't want to know."

Mark and Crank both nodded and grinned.

"Zorro, you give any more thought to hooking up with the BEF?" quizzed Baker.

"Well, not as much as I should…been kinda busy."

"Yeah, noticed."

"Why don't we put that on hold for a while? Got some unfinished business to tend to…Alright?"

"Figured as much. Can do…Brought you somethin'. Gift from Dare." He motioned back to Hannity.

Kyle came forward with a medium sized drag bag and handed it to Mark. He took the black heavy canvas carrier and looked back up at Widowmaker.

"Well, open it, jack wagon."

Mark pulled the heavy brass zipper and lifted out a Blaze G3 electromagnetic bullpup style carbine. "Kiss my rusty! Didn't figure there was a chance in hell I could get one of these when I asked…but looky here."

"There's a thousand rounds of 7mm double ogive tungsten projectiles for it in the bag too...just don't use 'em all in one place...Oh, there's a charger for the battery and Blaze wrote a short instruction manual in there too."

"Tell Dare and Burner I appreciate it. Promise I'll take good care of it."

"Goes without sayin' that you don't remember where you got it," Widomaker cautioned. "Don't let it fall out of your hands...we don't want the bad guys gettin' hold of somethin' like this."

"Of course."

Widowmaker punched an icon on his wrist. "Dare, you can send the taxis down for us. We're done here."

"Roger that. Eagles Three, Two and One will set down on the helipad in fourty-five seconds," came the reply.

"How many of those things did ya'll bring?" asked Mark.

"Mama Bird can carry four...that's all we usually need."

"No shit," added Crank.

"Dare's sending down our 800, it'll carry eight plus gear and the 600s can carry three each. We can infil and exfil with them, unless we're in a hurry to get on the ground...like tonight."

"Right." Mark just grinned and shook his head.

MOBUTTO'S SUMMER ESTATE
The next day

Shortly after dawn, Bert, followed by the remaining President's chopper, landed outside the north wall of the estate. The two presidential security guards exited first and took up positions on either side of the exit door. The President and the rest followed as the rotors spooled down.

Smoke from the destroyed buildings still drifted across the landscape. Surviving KDF defenders had collected their dead and placed them in neat rows covered with ponchos just outside the guard's barracks. Wounded soldiers offered care for those more severely injured as best they could.

Mark and Crank stood near the large hole in the wall that mere hours before had provided an escape route. Both were bloodied and bore the look of men who had stared death in the face up close and personal.

"Mark! Good to see you survived…Where is Mr. Fabian?" Mobutto asked as he shook hands.

"He's with the wounded, Mr. President."

"How badly?"

"He'll live, sir," Crank said.

"Lieutenant Kamau?"

"He's seeing to the dead," Mark replied. "Bert…could you take a look at the wounded?"

"On it," he answered as he returned to the helo and retrieved his Level V medical bag.

"How in God's name did you men do it?" Mobutto asked as he walked into the compound ahead of Mark and Crank.

"President Thompson sent a rescue force, sir. But they were never here, no one saw 'em…and they don't exist."

The President first gave Mark a confused look, and then said, "Oh, of course."

They continued to walk, ending up with the wounded. He spent a moment with each man. He stopped with Malakhi and Rhino last and sat wearily down beside them. Rhino lay on his side. Malakhi leaned against the stone wall for support.

"Kenya owes you a great debt, my friend."

"Right now, I'd settle for clean sheets an' a pretty young nurse ta tend my backside," he joked. "And the checks you offered before it hit the fan."

"First I will have the loyal troops round up all those who sought to throw this country into a dictatorship. Then I'll gladly sign your checks. And one for each of your friends."

"I believe you owe a great debt to that man over there as well," Mark said nodding at Lt. Kamau. "He pretty much ran this show. The rest of us just did what we could to assist him." Mark glanced to Rhino and winked.

"He'd be a perfect candidate for your new head of the presidential security," Rhino added, grimacing as a spasm of pain shot through his body.

"Yes...I concur. I shall speak with him right this minute," Mobutto said as he stood and moved toward Lt. Kamau.

"We gotta get the President's entourage, you and the rest of the wounded back to a secure base. Then I'm going to return the KWS chopper and scout around for some Yakuza ivory runners," Mark extended his hand as he spoke, handing both men a slightly broken cigar. "I'll check on you at the hospital, bro. The fat lady has done sung...Light 'em up."

Rhino took his hand in a vise-like grip. "Give me a couple days...I'll be right as rain an' we'll search out the little slant-eyed bastards together."

"Rhino...you're still a piece of work," Mark replied as he strode off toward the helo. "I'll check on you at the infirmary."

Crank started to follow, then turned back. "Come spend some time with me in Thailand when you're up and moving. I'll have a pair of sweet young things to tend your every need."

"Right bloody fine bloke ya are...don't care what any one says of you."

"Hey! What am I...invisible?" Malakhi added.

"You as well...you Jew bastard." Crank smiled, again offering a Benny Hill salute before trotting off after Mark.

SHELDRICK ANIMAL SANCTUARY

Lucy wandered around the new arrival nursery watching the antics of the juvenile orphans more acclimatized to their new home than the latest arrivals. Wearing a pair of khaki cargo shorts and shirt borrowed from the wardrobe of a QRF Ranger she blended in with the men, women and boys working with the young elephants.

Only her shoes gave away the fact that she was an outsider. She frequently paused to snap a photo on her cell phone when a particularly endearing image presented itself. Her long silky black hair was up in a tight bun covered by a Ranger bush hat to protect her face from the glaring midday sun.

The phone rang with the tone for Hayato. She walked away from the others and answered, "Yes, master."

"It is now noon. Where are you?"

"I was informed the American might return today."

"I see. I will be there by 6:00 PM…"

"I suggest you wait, master. Your presence here now would only blow my cover."

A long pause hung heavy. "Call me as soon as he arrives. Remember…Raku will pay for your failure." The phone went dead.

She held the phone to her breast for a moment before placing it in her shoulder bag. *Forgive me, Raku for what I am about to do.*

"Oh…there you are young lady. Malute told me you were at the nursery, but I could not find you," Dame Daphne exclaimed with a hint of motherly concern.

"Good afternoon. I was answering a call from my employer. How are you today?"

"As good as I can be for an old woman. Would you like to take a ride? Peter is going to drive around the sanctuary a bit and check on things…Please say yes…I'd love the company."

"I would be honored to join you."

One hour later the extended bed open-sided Range Rover carrying them pulled to a halt on a low ridge overlooking a vista.

"My David loved this place," she said softly. "Look…over there by the lake. That's Eleanor's family."

"You know every elephant's name?"

"Goodness no, dear. But Eleanor has been with us for so long…she's the matriarch of all our efforts."

Just then the vehicle radio squawked. "Peter. Come in Peter."

"Peter here. Come back, Malute."

"Please inform Dame Daphne that Mark has called and is arriving today."

Lucy felt a surge of excitement course through her resulting in a light blush on her cheeks. *The Great White Hunter returns.*

The silver-haired lady took the radio handset from Peter, "That's wonderful news, get the staff to prepare a dinner for Mark and his friends. We will start back now."

Lucy detected a glow about Dame Daphne like she had seen on a mother learning her son is coming home.

Peter dropped them at the visitor's center and proceeded to the motor pool with the Range Rover. Malute barged out the door to meet the two women.

"I informed the staff…and the Rangers…I hope you don't mind. I think the boys in the QRF were more excited than I am to see Mark again."

"That's wonderful. Let's get everybody together for dinner. We'll treat Mark and his friends to a banquet they will not forget."

"If you would excuse me I want to inform my employer I will be staying late today and I'd like to clean up before the event if you don't mind."

"Late? I won't hear of it, Lucy. You just stay here another night. If your employer has a problem, have him call me. I'll set him straight," Daphne stated adamantly.

"I took the liberty of having your clothing cleaned while you were out on the property, mamsell," Malute added.

"You are all to kind to me. How ever will I repay you?"

"Oh…nonsense, young lady. You are such a joy to have here. Now you run along and get ready. We have things to do for tonight. And make sure your employer calls me if he gets pissy with you."

Once back in her room, she moved directly to the bathroom and lifted the cover on the toilet water tank. A feeling of relief washed over her when she saw her H&K pistol still there. *Have to deal with my driver before Mark arrives.* She extracted the zip lock bag, laid it on the counter, and then removed weapon. Between the mattress and box springs, she recovered the silencer and attached it. She slipped it into the small of her back and covered it with her khaki jacket.

She knocked on the driver's door, *I know what he wants. Let him think it's happening.*

When the door opened, she showed the him an inviting smile and suggested they take a walk somewhere private to talk. As expected, he jumped at the offer—failing to retrieve his own weapon from the glove box.

Just over a small hill north of the sanctuary complex she turned and began to unbutton her jacket. His expression revealed his surprise and instinctive urge. As she revealed her ample breasts covered by a black lacy bra, the man could no longer contain himself and quickly moved to embrace her. His arms wrapped around her shoulders. His eyes went wide as he felt the cold steel suppressor under his chin—it was the last thing he ever felt.

She hid the body in a dense stand of thorn bushes, throwing dead branches and clumps of grass on top to further obscure it. Satisfied it would not be found before morning, she walked back to the headquarters by a roundabout route.

Bert landed the helo on the pad and shut down the engines. As he ran the final checklist, Mark and Crank, still dressed in their combat attire, stepped out to the waiting crowd of KWS personnel surrounding the landing pad. Word of the rescue had already been forwarded to Dame Daphne by President Mobutto himself. Every person in attendance held a lit candle in honor of the men's accomplishment.

"Holy shit, man. Who's the Asian chick?" Crank whispered as the group surged around them.

"Jesus, does your motor ever shut down?" Mark kidded him.

"Oh, it shut down at the compound. But it's back up and runnin'. Damn…she looks de…li…cious."

Lucy had purposely held back as the others rushed to greet the men. Standing in the distance wearing the white cotton pants and jade blouse, her hair flowed over her shoulder down to her waist.

"Young man, you and your friends come with me and get cleaned up. We have a something special prepared for you." Daphne took his arm and lead him through the crowd.

A half hour later, freshly showered, shaved and wearing borrowed QRF uniforms, the men joined the crowd under a large thatch covered open-air pavilion. Mark and Bert's attire fit them well enough, but Crank's gave him a comical appearance, due to his massive chest and long knuckle-dragger arms. It did not stop him from making a beeline for Lucy.

"Hey, Babe! How you doing?"

"Fine. You look much better cleaned up," she replied.

Crank, certain he was making headway smiled broadly. "Yeah. A little tight but, hey, they're clean…So…you work here?"

"No. Just visiting. Dame Daphne invited me to stay for the celebration."

"Glad she did. Want a beer?"

"I don't drink. An ice tea would be nice."

"One ice tea comin' up," he replied before moving off to the refreshment table.

She immediately walked over to the group surrounding Mark—Dame Daphne introduced her.

"Mark, I'd like for you to meet Miss Lucy Woo. She is a new and generous supporter of our efforts here at the sanctuary."

"Nice to meet you, Miss Woo. You live in Kenya?"

"No. I'm here on business. Just arrived a few days ago and came out to make a small donation personally. Dame Daphne invited me to stay for the festivities."

He noted the correctness of her English, but detected a light inflection. "Japanese?"

"Yes," she answered, then realizing her mistake. "But, I work for a company based in Taiwan."

Crank arrived with the requested beverage. "Your tea."

Mark studied her as she interacted with Crank and Malute. *Japanese. Just arrived.*

The dinner ended and most of the guests returned to their duties at the sanctuary or went to bed. Only a few remained chatting under the clear moonlit sky.

"Have you known Mark long?" Lucy asked as she stared into Crank's eager eyes.

"Yeah. Long time. He got me in the business."

"And what business would that be?"

"Security...Personal security. You know...protecting people from those who want to kidnap or kill 'em." *She digs me. I can feel it.*

"I enjoyed talking with you very much, but if you would excuse me I must say goodnight to Dame Daphne. I have an early departure tomorrow morning."

Crank's eyes followed the beauty as she crossed the lawn and joined Mark and the matriarch of the sanctuary. *I'll be up early...you can lay odds on that, sweet thing.*

"Mark...it is Mark, right?" she asked, looking directly into the clear blue eyes of the man she had come to seduce.

"Yes ma'am."

"I haven't been able to visit with you all night. Would you walk me back to my bungalow?"

"Of course. You'll excuse us Dame Daphne…Malute."

As they walked toward her quarters, all eyes followed the couple.

"She's seriously smokin'," Bert said as he stepped beside Crank. "You ever notice how hotties draw to him like moths to the flame?"

"Would you mind if I take one last look at the orphans tonight?" she asked.

"Not at all…I haven't paid my respects since I arrived."

As they turned toward the new arrivals nursery, she reached over and slipped her hand under his arm.

Bert continued to needle Crank. "Bet he'll be goin' deep in tang before they make it to the bedrooms."

"Damn, Bert! Give it a rest," he grumbled as he stomped off toward their quarters.

Unable to help himself Bert began to sing, slightly off key, "He's a smooth…operator…smooth…operator…coast to coast…LA to Chicago…north then south to Key Largo…"

The more adjusted of the orphans stood in a large five acre pen with an older mentor female for companionship. Mark and Lucy stood at the pipe rail fence watching the little ones flap their ears to keep cool and fend off insects.

"What's your business here in Kenya?" he asked softly as not to interrupt the juvenile's relaxation.

"I was sent here to kill you."

Mark felt a icy chill run up his spine. *Too close to avoid a hidden knife blade and she has a hold on my right arm.*

"Is this when you get it done?"

"I *was* sent...to kill you...But, I have another option."

Mark turned, her face mere inches from his—he could smell her sweet breath and feel the warmth of her body. "And...?"

"Hayato, the brother of the man you beheaded near the docks in Mombasa is here to restart the flow of ivory and horn. He hired me to come with him, not to assist with the flow...but to avenge the death of his brother."

"I still don't see the option."

"Patience...patience," she whispered, placing the fingers of her right hand on his lips. "I want a new life...You help me. I help you."

They stood in the moonlight, eyes locked, for a long moment—each studying the other for any indication of truth or subversion. Finally, Mark reached up slowly and moved her hand away from his lips.

"Why should I trust you?...And...how do I find this...Hayato?"

"Trust me? I just told you the truth...you see it in my eyes...Yes? First, you promise to help me escape...Then I will take you to him. Together we will kill him and his men."

"His men?"

"One of them is already dead. He rests over that hill behind us. There are still three men and a woman with Hayato in Nairobi."

"I want the main honcho…I cut off the snake's head here once…and already, there's a new snake taking his place. You take me to the man in Hong Kong…I'll help you."

Mark sat under the pavilion, out of the morning sun, with Bert and Crank drinking strong Kenyan coffee, eating sweet breads and discussing the new turn of events. The muggy humid heat caused sweat to form down the middle of their backs and under their arms staining their shirts with moisture.

"You're out of your ever lovin' mind, Zorro," Bert exclaimed.

"She came here to kill you, bro…and you want to help her?" Crank added.

"I say we get the hell outta Dodge and let the locals deal with the Yakuza," Bert continued. "Jesus, man!"

"Here she comes now," Crank muttered, looking askance at the approaching woman he had such desires of bedding the night before.

Mark turned to watch her striding across the open grounds wearing the khaki shorts—revealing part of the long scar on her thigh—and a QRF shirt. "I'll trust her like…a cobra in my shower stall 'til she proves herself…You two in or out?"

"Hey…I joined up to extract Rhino…" Bert said.

"Same here. Yakuza and Chinie in Hong Kong ain't on the contract I signed."

"Fair enough. Check in on Rhino before you bug outta Kenya."

The men all stood as Lucy joined them.

"Good morning," she said as she pulled her hair back, securing it with a red elastic band into a pony tail.

"Mornin'," Mark replied. "I'll take your offer."

"Good. Let's get started."

"I need to make one stop in Nairobi before we go see your boss. Couple of tools I need to pick up."

"Never meet your enemy on the field of his choosing...Sun Tzu," she responded.

"'Keep your friends close and your enemies closer', Mark Twain," he countered.

As they stood studying each other intensely, Crank chimed in, "Why don't you two just get a room?"

Without breaking her look to Mark, she replied, "Business before pleasure."

Bert broke out laughing. "Touche! Come on, Crank, Let's roll."

"Ya know...I changed my mind, helo man. I'm gonna stick around. Gotta see how this plays out," he replied as he picked up his cup of coffee and took a long swallow.

"Suit yourself...Zorro...'til we meet again." Bert extended his hand.

Mark took Bert's hand in his own then pulled him close into a hug. "Hell of a job, dog, hell of a job." He moved back. "Funds are in your account...Had it wired it this morning...Take the time to look in on Fabian...and don't tell him what's goin' on. Don't need to baby-sit Rhino on this op."

KENYAN HIGHWAY

"By the way, my name is actually Chikako, Lucy was just a cover."

"Works for me," Mark said as he glanced over at her in the shotgun seat of the Land Rover.

"You brought your armor?" Mark asked Crank sitting behind him.

"Oh, yeah! Wishing I had a sci-fi body suit like those Black Eag..."

Mark flashed Crank a hard look in the rearview mirror, halting his comment about the BEF before he could finish.

"We're gonna stop by Rhino's home and pick up some tools. Then...*we party*."

"You are very cavalier about this. You realize there are five of them, including Hayato?" she commented while looking out the side window at the passing Kenyan landscape.

"So, we each kill our...what?...one point six and go home," Mark quipped with a sly grin.

"I've never even seen a Yakazu. Always heard how bad ass they are," the former SEAL said.

"Hayato is five times better with a Katana than his brother," she said, turning to gage his reaction.

With his dark aviator glasses on, there was little to see or read other than a slight flexing of his jaw muscles. "No time for sword play this time. In and out...then on to Hong Kong."

She nodded. "By the way, we should stop off and buy some different clothes for you two. I think you look a little *mercenary*, if you don't mind me saying."

"Wouldn't mind finding something that actually fits," Crank replied.

"I know of a couple stores near Rhino's crib…If they're still open," Mark added.

***

CHAPTER FOURTEEN

RHINO'S HOME

Mark circled the block, noting the burned out roof of the garage and the open front door through the wrought iron front gate. After a second pass he pulled into the alley and parked just inside the open back gate. The double doors of the shed revealed his prized Harley missing. *That's gonna cost you big, Rhino.*

The three exited the vehicle, wearing casual dress clothes after the short shopping trip. As they proceeded to the back door, Mark drew his .45, holding it at the ready. Chikako placed her hand inside the light shoulder bag and gripped her H&K. Crank slid his massive .44 magnum revolver free from its holster and took up a position at the rear, scanning the rooftops and the open gate to the alley.

"Big gun," she remarked.

His face took on a sarcastic demeanor, repeating her words without sound while moving his head left and right, like a child mocking the perceived insult.

Mark stepped inside the darkened back entrance and paused, listening for any sound that might indicate the presence of looters or squatters. Satisfied no one was moving about, he signaled the others to *hold* before cautiously advancing inside. "Clear."

"After you," Crank said with a sweep of his empty hand.

Inside, Mark pulled a lever hidden behind a row of books on the top self of a dark brown wooden bookcase. The sound of a mechanical device clicked and reverberated through the empty room. As they looked on, Mark grabbed the right side of the bookcase and pulled it forward, revealing a steel door. Using a electronic key pad, he entered a series of numbers. The massive door sprang open and the vault behind it automatically lit up.

"Sweet...Rhino's the man!" Crank said after seeing the extensive array of weapons and munitions.

Cases of ammunition and explosives lined the back wall and were also stacked beneath a centrally located work bench.

"Bring in Betsy II and the other weapons."

"Yeah, boss."

She followed the him into the weapons room and uttered a low whistle. "Impressive. Your friend is well prepared."

"See anything you like...grab it," Mark said as he picked up his Colt five magazine pouch and laid it on a bench in the middle of the room. He lifted a metal ammo can from under the bench, opened it and began to fill the fifteen round magazines with military ball.

"This?" she asked, holding up a Walther P7M45.

Mark glanced over and seeing the weapon. "Anything you like. Nice piece. .45 ACP...oil-filled cylinder instead of a gas..."

"Delays the recoil based on an interesting adaptation of a artillery mechanism to a hand gun," she added. "I like. Ammo matches my H&K...Spare mags?"

"Wooden cabinet...back left corner." Mark gave her an admiring look as she moved to the cabinet in search of extra magazines. *Knows her weapons.*

Crank entered the vault carrying all the weapons they had used at the President's estate. "I'm trading in the Vektor for..." He scanned the walls looking at the numerous weapons. "...for *this*." He lifted a H&K M5N from its hooks and held it like a long lost treasure—as he should—he carried the Navy version during his years as a SEAL and felt great respect for its capabilities. It was fully coated for operations in sea water, had a ambidextrous trigger group and a threaded barrel.

"Suppressor?" the surfer asked.

"Cabinet marked *ssshhh*." Mark pointed as he continued to load the Colt magazines.

Once the trio was outfitted, and all the hardware loaded into hard cases, Mark closed the vault door—which automatically locked—before sliding the bookcase back in place and manually resetting the locking mechanism.

"Man…I'm starvin'," Crank said as they loaded the vehicle.

"I know a great little sushi place. Doubt it's open now…"

"The Sarova Stanley's open 24/7," she offered.

"Good call. We'll do chow and get a game plan together."

SAROVA STANLEY HOTEL

Mark parked the Land Rover. "Crank, stay with the tools 'til I can arrange for a room…I'll call you on the cell…"

"No good. My cell bit the bullet…literally…yesterday."

"Take mine. I'll call you from a land line. Use the service entrance and elevator. No need making folks nervous with all the toys on display."

"Got it covered boss."

Chikako and Mark entered the lobby and proceeded to the front desk.

"Miss Woo. So glad to see you again. We were worried for you not having seen you for several days," the front desk attendant said with a huge smile. "Nice to see you again as well, Mr. Ingram. So you know Miss Woo?"

She looked at Mark; surprised to learn the man behind the desk knew him by name.

He, in return, was slightly taken back to find out she was known to the staff as well, and recovered quickly. "Yes…Yes I do. Nice to see you again as well."

"Could you be so kind as to get my room key. And have a triple order of sushi sent up right away…Oh, and a tray of fresh fruit and tankard of ice tea," she said with charm dripping off every word. The effect on the attendant was visible.

"Absolutely Miss Woo. Right away," he replied. "So…Mark are you as big a fan of Miss Woo's films as I am?"

"Fan?" Mark answered. Then understanding her deception, "Why, yes…Huge fan. Especially liked her work in *Hard to Find* with Banderas…Very believable as a beautiful Asian assassin."

As the attendant handed her the room key, she stepped on Mark's foot. "You are such a dear. Please have the food sent up as soon as possible."

Crank arrived with a luggage cart stacked with the cased weapons. As he pushed it into the living area, he gazed around at the posh surroundings. "Livin' in style, we are. How'd ya swing this layout, Zorro?"

"Didn't…She did."

At that moment, a knock came at the door. Chikako moved and peered through the peep hole. "Room service."

"Tools out of sight…Now!" Mark ordered and motioned toward the bedroom.

After the porter finished laying out the service platters, Mark handed him a fifty dollar bill and escorted him out the door.

"Ah man! I was thinkin' of some steak and a big ol' baked potato with all the trimmings," Crank complained.

"Call it in. Miss Lucy Woo has a tab runnin'," Mark answered.

"How do you pull that off? Masquerading as Lucy Woo?"

"Pocket litter," she answered matter of factly.

Mark and Crank exchanged knowing looks of surprise and admiration.

"We should eat. Get our plan down. Catch some sleep. I suggest we go in after midnight," she said as she lifted the cover off the serving platters.

"She sounds just like you. Business…Business…Business," Crank joked as he lifted the phone receiver to order his steak.

YAKUZA COMPOUND

Chikako parked the Land Rover at the end of the block and silently exited the vehicle. As she closed the door, she whispered, "Ready?"

"Born ready," Crank replied as he go out.

She looked at Mark and rolled her eyes.

He had decided to carry his H&K UMP—it was easier to handle in confined spaces. He checked the chamber one last time to insure there was a round loaded before slipping a bag holding six spare mags over his shoulder.

All three quietly attached suppressors to their weapons as they walked down the alley toward the Yakuza residence.

"When I left, there were two armored personnel carriers and a couple dozen soldiers in the front of the compound. They were sleeping in the servant's quarters on the east side of the front door," she softly rattled off the intel.

266

The moon would not be up for another hour—none of the electric lights on the streets were functional due to the rioting and infrastructure shut down.

"Crank, slip around front and light 'em up if they stir."

"Not weaponed up for APCs, Zorro."

"Improvise."

"What'd you say this gig paid again?"

"Didn't."

"The in-and-out to extract Rhino was a hundred K...and it turned into a royal cluster worth two-fifty plus...Make it another hundred and we'll call it square," Crank said softly.

"Done. Use a mag of the M39/b on the APCs."

Crank immediately switched magazines.

As they neared the back wall of the Yakuza estate Chikako held up her left hand closing it into a fist.

"I'll try the code, but it will alert Hayato to our presence." she whispered.

Mark grabbed her hand as she reached for the key pad. "No...We jump the wall. Any security cameras?"

"Dozens," she replied, noting the gentle yet commanding grip on her wrist.

Mark turned loose. "To hell with any unannounced visit then...Crank shake a leg and get back to the front gate. We'll hold for five then breech this one."

"Aye–aye...El Capitan," Crank whispered and moved off.

"Where did you find that joker?" she asked as they watched him disappear down the alley.

"At the gates of hell. He has his quirks...but he's a good man."

"Hayato is mine."

Mark recognized the tone and meaning of her statement. *Reminds me of when I went for his brother.* "No problem."

"And Raku...if she is still alive...she leaves with me."

"Anything else?"

She looked to him as he peered through the wrought iron gate into the backyard of the estate. *Damn. Why does this man make me feel so...off center.* "That's it."

"In position," Crank's voice announced over their comm. "No APCs...and no sign of any KDF."

"He's ready. Says the front is clear," Mark relayed.

She entered a series of numbers into the key pad and a light click could be heard as the lock opened. She pushed the gate inward slowly and slipped inside followed by Mark.

A series of flood lights around the pool area flashed on, illuminating the entire area still lightly clouded by smoke from the riots. She methodically used her silenced pistol to eliminate them again throwing the estate grounds into darkness.

Damn! She's good. He gently tapped on her shoulder, and then indicated by hand signal he would move to the left and for her the right.

She acknowledged with a single nod and slipped off silently into the darkness.

He made his way along the left perimeter of the pool area, paused periodically to scan his front and right. Reaching the back wall of the house he stopped and whispered into his throat mic, "Crank."

"Yeah, boss."

"She wants the head man and the woman for herself...but kill whoever you find."

"Let God sort 'em out."

"Just don't kill her...I need her in Hong Kong."

"Always gets complicated around you, Zorro."

"Breach the front. I'm goin' in the back in three."

"Roger."

Mark tried the handle to a door. Finding it unlocked he pushed it open while standing to the side and waited for a moment before entering the dark interior. Once inside he slipped quickly to his left and dropped to one knee, weapon ready, to allow his vision to adjust. Hearing and seeing no one, other than his own breathing and heartbeat, he moved across the room to an interior door and positioned himself with his back to the wall. He listened for movement before reaching over, and feeling for the door knob and slowly turned it....

Chikako slipped into the dimly lit master bedroom and found Raku lying nude on her back, her hands and legs still bound. Her eyes were open, but the cut on her forehead and red marks on both sides of her neck and throat spoke volumes of Hayato's violence. She kept an eye on the closed bathroom door as she laid two fingers against the still warm neck of her friend—her heart sank. *Sadistic bastard! You'll pay for this!*

She moved across the room and set up in the shadows just outside the bathroom and waited. She felt her heart beat faster with each passing moment. Her rage was almost uncontainable as she glanced back across the room at the body of her lifelong friend.

A burst of full auto fire ripped through the door from the far side just missing Mark. A pair of splinters impacted his left hand before he could pull back. The hollow *clank of* an empty magazine hitting the floor in the next room indicated whomever was behind the door was ready again. With his back to the wall, he reached out until his H&K carbine was in front of the door and fired three short bursts through it at different angles. The sounds of a low moan, a body impacting the floor along with shards of broken glass or pottery, indicated several rounds had found their mark.

He counted to five as he slid down the wall to a squatting position, listening for any other sounds on the other side, before opening the door swiftly. When no further gunfire erupted he took two quick looks, duck-walked through and took up a position to the left.

The bathroom door flew open as Hayato reacted to the gunfire. He had thrown on a black sleeveless shirt with a deeply cut V-neck. He was once again wearing his signature red silk pajama bottoms—their front still tented out from the obvious effects of the three blue Viagra pills he had taken earlier. The man stood much taller than Chikako, was well muscled and his long black hair hung loosely over his shoulders. A tattoo on his chest confirmed for all to see that he was a made man and a lifelong member of the Yakuza criminal organization. He was highly skilled at several forms of martial arts and deadly with a blade or a gun. None of that mattered to her.

Without warning, she snap kicked the object of her rage and landed a solid blow to the big man's crotch—breaking the penile shaft and crushing one testicle.

He lurched over in searing pain as the sound of her shoe contacting his flesh echoed though the bedroom. His scream did nothing to soothe the torrent of hate flowing though her veins. She spun quickly, landed a vicious kick to his face that broke his nose, and stood him upright once more. He fell back against the wall as his eyes watered and blood spurted from his nostrils.

From the front of the house, Mark heard the *pfsit pfsit* of a suppressed weapon being fired. "Crank," he called softly into the comm mic.

"Yeah, boss."

He began to slowly work his way forward, swinging the muzzle of the carbine from side to side as his eyes searched for any sign of threat.

Crank moved to the body of a wounded male assassin and poked him in the eye with the tip of his suppresser. The downed killer moaned and flinched—he pulled back on the trigger and placed a single 9mm round in his brain. "I thought you Yakuza mofos were super Ninjas or somethin'."

Hayato recovered from the two blows enough to put the smaller Chikako on the defensive. The sight of the woman who had defied him enraged him almost as much as the pain she had inflicted. He lunged forward and threw a series of kicks and chops at her head. She parried them expertly, but one connected with her right wrist, sending the pistol flying across the room. She moved back out of reach, quickly spreading her feet apart to regain her fighting stance as they sized each other up. Both knew only one would live to see the dawn.

Hearing a sound from the expansive living area, Crank moved quickly to a marble column and crouched—taking a series of quick looks around both sides. Not detecting any movement, he silently pulled a flash bang grenade from the cargo pocket on his left leg, pulled the pin and tossed it underhanded into the middle of the room. The sheet metal spoon flew off and landed on the hardwood floor with a slight tinny sound, as the hissing grenade rolled to a stop. He turned his back and covered both ears with his hands.

BOOM! The explosive delivered a blinding light, illuminating the whole room and hallway for a moment.

He darted to his right, taking cover behind another column as the room filled with smoke. He counted to three, and then sprayed the room with the rest of his thirty-two round magazine as he softly sang, "Runnin' with the devil."

A dozen rounds swept across the foyer as the hearing impaired Yakuza sought to eliminate Crank—another dozen followed.

"Gonna mess you up asshole," Crank yelled with a grin as he rolled into the room, stopping prone behind a leather couch.

Silence permeated the room as the smoke settled and each sought to locate the other's position. The metallic sound of an empty magazine being dropped by the Yakuza echoed through the room—simultaneously, the lights came on—followed by a burst of fire from Mark's submachine gun.

Crank peeked around the couch to see the Japanese fall to his knees holding his guts in his hands—he placed a final round in the man's forehead.

As suddenly as they had come on, the lights went back off.

At the sound of the stun grenade, the bleeding Hayato had bull rushed his opponent. They grappled at each other's arms and tried to gain any form of leverage. They struggled mightily and moved closer and closer to the pool deck glass walls.

"Crank...You hit?"

"Not a scratch. That's three...right?"

"Yup. Leaves..." Mark's words were cut off by the sound of breaking glass.

Both men rapidly moved to the back of the living area, taking up positions on either side of the large glass wall. Looking to the pool area, they spotted Chikako and Hayato rolling across the marble deck.

The two combatants separated—he pushed himself to a standing position and she flipped upright effortlessly. As they circled, the leader of the Yakuza group assumed a martial arts posture while she kept her arms down like Muhammad Ali, as if daring him to attack. Hayato wiped at the blood from his broken nose with the back of his hand. He snorted and blew a stream of crimson that ran down across the pale skin of his chest.

"I will take great pleasure in killing you, busu yariman...after I have enjoyed your many pleasures one by one."

"Ugly dog slut? That the best you can do? Kisama kusottare...you shit dip, have never known my pleasures. Besides, I don't think your *love dragon* is ever gonna work the same again," Chikako said laughing in the killer's face.

His face flushed with anger and then hardened as he advanced throwing a series of punches and kicks. She deftly deflected the hand strikes with blinding speed and avoided the kicks by spinning out of their path or ducking under as they moved across the marble deck.

As he slipped past her, she landed a side kick to the small of his back and sent him flying forward into a tall sculptured plant in a heavy clay pot—she backed away and waited.

Hayato pushed himself off the thorny foliage, his face, neck and arms bleeding from numerous cuts and wheeled about as if expecting his adversary to attack. Seeing he was wrong, he stood tall and again assumed his martial arts stance before he advanced.

"Noroma, the longer you resist...the longer I will torture."

"Assuming you win, yowamushi."

"Ahhh!" he screamed as he attacked, again throwing a series of vicious kicks and punches, this time with more force and speed. He appeared visually to be an out-of-control death dealing machine, hands and feet merely blurs as they flew like a whirling dervish.

Chikako's defensive moves became a blur as well as she ducked, blocked, spun retreating and danced out of the way of each and every blow.

"Damn!...Bitch is good," Crank remarked as he and Mark watched from the shadows.

"Yup." He studied her moves and techniques. *Better than good.*

As Hayato passed, she landed a palm smash to his right ear knocking him to his knees, again lightly stepping back, bouncing gently on her toes, allowing him to recover.

As he regained his footing, he reached under his black silk shirt, pulled a seven pointed throwing star from a pouch on his belt. He spun to face her raising his arm to throw...

Baamm!

The sound of Mark's S&W barked, followed immediately by that of shattering glass hitting the marble deck. The shot through the thick glass deflected the 9mm round slightly—it still found its intended target.

Hayato staggered for a moment as the razor-sharp black *shuriken* fell to the marble with a *ping* and tinkled to a stop. He gripped his throat with both hands as blood from his carotid artery spurted through his fingers and ran down his chest. His eyes grew wide with a mixture of surprise—then fear.

Crank flinched at the unexpected sound of the gunfire and glanced toward Mark before returning his gaze to the dying assassin. "She's gonna be pissed, Zorro."

"I need her ass in Hong Kong."

Chikako watched her former boss and tormentor raised a hand toward her as he dropped to his knees, his eyes going glassy as he fell—his body face planting on the decking before bouncing and rolling into the pool. Crimson stained the crystal clear water as the body began to sink—casting macabre shadows from the underwater light. She continued to stare at the dead man until she heard Mark's voice.

"Where's the woman?"

She spun toward him with fire in her eyes. "I *told* you he was *mine!*" She began running toward Mark like a charging leopard and leapt into the air, intent on delivering a flying roundhouse kick to his head.

Mark waited till the last possible moment, then ducked as she flew over him. She landed behind him on her side, righted herself and turned to face him again.

"If he had killed you, I would have had to kill him anyway." Mark held his right hand up, closing it into a fist. "Then I'd be screwed," he spoke softly as he stood up and turned slightly to see her out of the corner of his eye. "Where is she?"

"Dead…The bastard tortured her to death."

Neither moved for several moments. She begin to tremble, then wheeled and walked back through the shattered glass wall.

Crank moved to join Mark. "Wouldn't want to piss her off. That dead man there...never laid a finger on her."

Mark gave his buddy a look of agreement, and then followed her into the house.

She was placing a sheet over Raku's body when he found her. He watched quietly as she removed the cotton ropes from the battered woman's hands and feet, then sat on the bed and gently moved strands of bloody hair from her face and closed her eye lids.

"She saved my life in Malaysia," she said very softly.

Mark waited silently, understanding her inner turmoil.

"She and I...we never...we met at the orphanage. That is where Hayato's father found us," her voice cracked as she spoke, motioning with one hand indicating her need for privacy.

"I'll be outside," Mark said. *I'll be damned. She does have a heart.*

HOTEL SAROVA STANLEY

Mark and Crank sat on the balcony patio sharing a bottle of top shelf tequila. Neither spoke as they squeezed a slice of lime into their shot glass and sprinkled salt between their thumb and first finger before licking it off and throwing back the burning liquid in one fluid motion.

"To Bear and Ian," Mark said as he prepared another shot.

They touched glasses and downed the fine tequila.

Chikako sat in the shower allowing the hot water to flow over her head and body. The room filled with steam creating a visual sense of being in a rain cloud. Neither the running water nor the ghostly visibility did anything to ease her anger and pain. *Forgive me Raku.* She began to cry uncontrollably and the anguished tears of loss mingled with the running water.

Mark was at the wet bar when the barefooted Chikako entered the living area wearing a thick white bath robe, her damp hair wrapped in a large cotton towel. He watched her in the mirror as she walked through the room and onto the balcony like a graceful panther and sat down beside Crank. He joined them with a bowl of freshly sliced limes.

"Want a shot of tequila?" Crank asked.

She took a piece of lime, placing in her mouth sucking out the juice before chewing off the moist pulp, and then picked up the bottle and took a long hard pull. "Ohhh…that burns good."

Crank and Mark exchanged a look.

"Guess you did," Crank joked.

It was evident from her red and swollen eyes she had been crying. Neither man made mention of it as the three sat and viewed the skyline of Nairobi. The majority of the rioting had subsided and only the smoke from the slums still blew across the city. Fortunately the prevailing winds carried it and the stench away from the hotel.

"I want her cremated."

"I can arrange that. Pretty certain the President himself will insure it happens," Mark replied after a long pause.

"Thank you...Once it is done I will take you to Wu."

"Couple of days at most to arrange transport...Give us time to prepare," Mark said and downed another shot.

She stood up and moved to the railing. "I could have taken him."

"Oh...we have no doubt of that. But..."

"Never let it get personal...Gets you dead," said Mark.

She removed the towel from her hair and began to dry the long silky black strands. "Is that what happened in Mombasa?"

Crank gave a nervous look to Mark. Not feeling too comfortable with the woman he had seen toying with Hayato only hours before, he stood up and moved behind his chair. He reached over and casually picked up a empty bottle of tequila as if to remove it. "What happened in Mombasa?"

"You didn't tell your friend?"

"No."

"Your buddy here met Hayato's brother, Akihiko, down by the loading docks and engaged him in a Katana duel." She turned with a cold gleam in her eyes. "The second best man with a Katana in all of the Yakuza...Did you know that?" She fixed her angry eyes on Mark.

"Nope." Mark squeezed a slice of lime into his glass. "But I believe you."

"Zorro, you are one seriously insane Texan!" Crank exclaimed. "A sword fight? Let me guess...it was night?"

A sly smile came to Mark's face. "Yup."

"So...personal?" she said, not letting go of her original question.

Mark nodded as he stood up facing her. "Dame Daphne told me you cried when you were with one of the orphaned juveniles at the sanctuary...So, tell me...Did you?"

She held his gaze for a long moment, and then concentrated on her hair as she dried it. "Yes...I did."

"*That* kind of personal." Mark turned and left the patio.

Crank and Chikako stood awkwardly in silence for several moments. Neither made eye contact, but were uncomfortably aware of the other's presence.

"You ever surf?" Crank finally asked.

"What?"

"Surf. You know ride a board...shoot a pipe line...roll a curl?"

She started laughing. "What the hell does surfing have to do with anything?"

"Nothing...but, it got you to laugh."

***

CHAPTER FIFTEEN

RHINO'S HOME

Mark, Crank and Chikako were busy field stripping and cleaning weapons when the Texan's cell phone rang. The ring tone itself announced the caller's identity.

"Have to take this one," he said as he stepped into the front courtyard.

"Hal, old buddy! How goes it?"

"That's what I want to fucking know! You show up at the concrete safe vault, take off with my equipment...*my* op man...and not even a fine howdy-doody to me! What the *hell*, Zorro?" The voice of his former employer blared over the cell phone speaker causing Mark to hold it away from his ear.

Years of dealing with Hal had built a special relationship with the big Scottish-American and Mark could tell he was on the verge of reaching through the phone and ripping his throat out. *Same old Hal. Could ass chew a twenty year Marine DI and never break a sweat.*

"Let me explain…"

"Explain, my ass. How the *hell* do you think you can just two-step into my facilities and take whatever you damn well please…then go gallivanting off into the sunset without even a 'by your leave, sir'?"

Mark could not help but smile as he listened to the crazy Scotsman rant. "Ease up there, big dog…Breathe…"

"Breathe?…You owe me for every *God damn* penny of equipment you stole!…And where the hell is Banjo? I'm gonna rip him a new asshole big enough to drive a Mack truck through when I find his sorry black ass."

"Bear's dead."

"What?…How?"

"Ease up a minute and listen…Rhino was working security for the President of Kenya. I gathered up a few men and dropped in to extract his butt. Bear begged to join us…"

"Shit fuckin' fire!…The man was all set to retire."

"Yeah…I know. But he asked…and wouldn't take *no* for an answer."

"Aww, damn!" Hal said in a slightly more gentle tone. "What about my equipment?"

"I'll return what we did not expend. Pay you for the rest…"

"Bull shit! You owe me now, you skinny son of a bitch!"

Owing him was the last thing anyone wanted to do. That proposition always ended up costing ten times as much.

"Have to wait on payment then. Have a piece of business to finish in Hong Kong…"

"Hong Kong?"

"Reminds me…can you get a couple of us out of Kenya and into there on the low-low?"

"Jesus, Zorro! What do you think I am…the Bank of Scotland?"

"Nah…you got more money than they do." Mark laughed. "So…day after tomorrow?"

"You'll owe me two times…Call me at 1800 hours. See what I can do."

"Thanks. I'll owe you…double. Oh…take Ian O'Reilly off your books. He bought it with Bear."

Mark re-entered to see Chikako and Crank admiring his two Katanas. She held the ancient sword he had taken off the dead Yakuza ivory smuggler in Mombasa.

"I recognize this one," she said admiring the fine craftsmanship.

The older of the two swords was indeed a treasure. Made in 1710, the three century old masterpiece was crafted at the pinnacle of Japanese sword making. It had once belonged to a powerful Samurai who served a warlord in the northern province near the current city of Komatsu and was a total of twenty-eight and one half inches in length. The blade itself was formed of hand-forged *Tamahagane*—jewel steel in Japanese—folded over itself sixty times and beaten back down in the heat of a charcoal fire to add the strength of carbon. The

283

tempered edge displayed a *hamon*—a wavy milky colored line resulting from the tempering process which allowed the highly polished instrument to hold a true razor's edge.

The handle was covered with pebbly black ray skin and wrapped in finely woven blue silk that matched the lapis lazuli colored lacquer finish of the lightweight sheath. A heavy bronze hand guard was pierced in a decorative pattern and had small dragons carved in bas relief. The sheath itself was not adorned, but did have a belt-like sash called an *obi* neatly tied up for storage. The sash allowed the user to wear the formidable weapon in a horizontal fashion on his off side with the blade edge turned up. A skilled samurai warrior could draw the sword and strike his adversary in a single, fluid motion.

Chikako pulled the curved blade from the sheath very slowly—almost reverently. She gripped the handle with hands spread apart appropriately and performed a perfect and swift downward Dotan followed by a series of Yoko horizontal moves. It was clearly evident that she knew how to use a Katana. Crank took a couple of steps backwards, distancing himself as much as the vault room would allow. As she turned and repeated the moves—adding a pair of spinning Tabi-gata at the end—the cold steel blade hissed through the air. Chikako ended with a slight bow to the blade itself before returning it to the antique sheath.

"Practice much?" Crank asked with a look of admiration mixed with concern.

"Not lately," she replied with a certain air of sadness. "This one's from the *shinto* period, right?"

"Yes, ma'am. The maker's *mei* is engraved into the *nakago* under the handle...You do know your stuff."

She raised one eyebrow as she studied him with interest. *How does he know so much about Japanese culture? Hayato's brother was a master swordsman, yet he defeated him at his own game* "I knew the man who used to own it. He was quiet good with it."

"Uh, huh...I've got thirteen stitches to vouch for that," Mark said as he reached for the weapon. He quickly pulled the blade out once again and wiped it off with small cotton cloth soaked in a preserving mixture of mineral and clove scented oils. He slipped it back into the sheath and stored it correctly—blade side up—on its wooden display rack. "That was an old employer of mine on the call. He's gonna arrange transport..."

"The angry Scotsman?" Crank asked.

"None other...Says I owe him twice...one for the equipment loan and one for the transport."

"Ahh shit, man...never, ever owe Hal."

"Too late...Let's get this done and get out the hell outta here."

KENYAN NAVY SICK BAY
Coast Province

After maneuvering through the various legal and administrative hoops, Bert, accompanied by a slender yet well-figured nurse, arrived at the semiprivate room where Rhino and Malakhi were recovering. Ngie, looking rested and cleaned up after the battle, stood at the door fully armed with a submachine gun and pistol.

"Good to see you again," Bert said.

Ngie only nodded.

The room, though sparse, was not unlike military hospital rooms around the globe. Malakhi lay reading a book, *The Nations,* by a couple of American authors about the old west. Israel, like most of the world, had a huge fascination about the American west, or the Old West as it was commonly referred to. Rheinhart lay on his side, unable to put any pressure on the bullet wound to his butt cheek, watching a episode of *Walker, Texas Ranger*—he was a big fan of Chuck Norris. Both looked up as the door opened.

"'Bout fokin' time someone showed up ta see if we were still breathing," Rhino said. The huge smile on his face indicated he was definitely glad to see Bert. "Hey sweet thing...how much longer till my next shot a no pain?"

"You are not due for another four hours Mr. Fabian," the pretty young black woman said as she checked his chart. "And curb your tongue. No cursing allowed," she continued with a stern look.

"No way..."

"Yes, way. I'll be back when your shot is due...Until then, tough it out," she said with a smile and a wink.

"The pain is killin' me, I tell ya," Rhino exclaimed, attempting to sound in far more pain that he actually was.

She ignored the comment as she moved to Malakhi's bed. "How are *you* doing?"

"I'm good Leski...and you?"

"Pulling a double today. I'll have a better idea of how I am doing in about…nine hours."

"How's the food in this joint?" Bert asked.

"With MREs being at a three on a scale of ten…I'd say a solid seven," Malakhi replied.

"When are you scheduled to get out?"

"Not fokin' soon enough."

"Language!" The nurse said as she checked Malakhi's chart. "I suspect both will be released in ten to fourteen days."

"Well, Zorro asked me to check in on you before I head home…I did."

"Where the hel…" Rhino stopped himself catching another disapproving look from the nurse. "Where is he? Too busy ta come see how we're doin'?"

The nurse started for the door. "Ten more minutes, then out. These two scoundrels need their rest."

"Yes ma'am," Bert replied, waiting for her to leave before answering the question. "He and Crank…and a friggin' Yakuza we met at the wildlife sanctuary are probably doing some fung goo danceathon in Nairobi as we speak."

"Yakuza? The fok ya say?"

"I'm missing something here?" Malakhi asked.

"Long story short…Mark evidently lopped the head off some son of a bitch…"

"Damn straight he did! I was there…" Rhino piped in.

"The dead mofos brother is in Kenya to get the ivory pipeline flowing again and has brought a gang of slant eyes along to terminate Zorro…with extreme prejudice…"

"How many?" Rhino shouted loud enough for Ngie to look through the small glass window into the room.

"According to the bitch…half dozen."

"Mark's teamed up with one of the Yakuza?…*And* she's a woman?"

"Redundant, Rhino. But yes…the Yakuza with Zorro and Crank is a woman. May be the hottest Asian woman I ever laid eyes on…"

"…and Zorro has Crank along to baby sit? Oh, this just gets better every minute." Malakhi laughed.

"I gotta get outta here!" Rhino threw back the sheet and started to roll out of the bed. "Ahhh!" He exclaimed as he fell back holding his wound.

"Like you would be any help," Bert remarked. "You just rest your sorry ass 'til you heal. By the time you could find them it'll be over…May be over already."

HOTEL SAVOY STANLEY

Mark joined Crank and Chikako on the balcony patio as they were finishing a hearty breakfast of steak and eggs. He had completed his daily Zen meditation and martial arts three steps and was famished. She stood up holding her glass of fresh-squeezed juice and moved to the guard rail. She wore a thin yellow cotton sarong—her loose hair hung down to her shapely hips.

Crank nudged Mark's shoulder as he reached for the tea pot and nodded to the beautiful woman standing in front of them, her body silhouetted through the light material and shook his head as he whispered, "Ouch."

Mark turned and couldn't help but admire her image. *Holy smokin'...scorchin' hot!*

"What's the plan?" she asked without turning.

"I have a plan...trust me...I *have* a plan," Crank said before he could stop himself.

Chikako stiffened slightly and looked at Crank from the corner of one eye. "And that would be?"

"Ah...well...I...ah..." Crank stuttered, looking to his friend for help.

Mark was amused at his discomfort and allowed him to hang, swinging in the breeze.

"Should I proffer a guess?"

"Crank has a...difficulty...he has a strong...some say incurable...admiration of the female form. I just overlook it and go on," Mark replied, smiling at Crank.

"A difficulty?...A pecker head difficulty I suspect."

Mark blew tea through his nose as he laughed. After wiping the warm liquid from his face. "Yup."

"Hey! You flaunt it...I can't help but...but..." Crank raced to defend his comment.

"I prefer older men...Got that, surfer dude?" She turned to face them. "Stable...esperienced...little if any drama or baggage."

Crank stood up, bumping the table and spilling water, juice and tea from the glasses and cups. "Never cared much for high maintenance bitches...pain in the ass."

"Easy now. Easy." Mark stepped in to defuse the confrontation. "The plan is very simple...Hal gets us to Hong Kong...you take us to this Chinga dingy Wu...I kill him...we ride off into the sunset."

Crank stood staring at her the veins on his neck and face bulging. As he spoke he threw his cotton napkin on the table. "Sooner the better! I know a sunset where split-tails know their place." He then turned and stormed off the patio, through the living area and out the door, slamming it with such force a framed picture fell to the floor, breaking the glass.

"You got under his skin big time," Mark remarked as he began to slice his cold steak.

"Wasn't that hard," she replied. "Your plan is...flawed. Ching Wu lives in a top floor suite at the Langham Hotel. He has a private elevator guarded on the ground floor by no less than three Triad Big Circle soldiers." She sat down facing Mark and poured herself another glass of juice. "The elevator is in the main lobby. There are security cameras there, inside the elevator and his suite. Another three, sometimes more goons inside. Riddle me that one...Zorro." She ended with a bemused gleam in her eyes.

Mark broke the yoke on one of the three over easy eggs and wiped a piece of steak in it. "Any other good news?"

"He has a emergency call buttons all around the suite. Triggers one and an army of Traid will ascend to his place in a matter of minutes."

"Ascend? Now *there's* some good news. We land on the roof...rappel down...pop in for a visit." Mark took another bite.

"...rope climb back to the roof...and Crank picks us up by helo."

"That could work," she mused as she watched him eat, seemingly completely at ease when confronted with the impossible task. "You said Crank picks us up...So you trust me now?"

Mark paused and poured more Thai tea into his cup before leaning back in his chair and fixing her in a gaze with his ice blue eyes. "Yup."

"Just like that?"

"Just *like* that. You showed your heart back at Hayato's compound. You let down in the tough girl act."

Chikako, unable to maintain a direct look into his steady eyes, turned her head and looked over the city skyline. "I told you I want out...I'm done." An expression washed over her face, making her look far older, tired and sad.

"You help me...I help you. Finish this and I'll make it happen. The crazy Scotsman has the means to help you disappear."

Long heavy moments passed as he watched her staring off into the distance. A single tear rolled down her left check and dropped onto her breast.

Crank returned several hours later to find them gone. He searched the suite thoroughly before stopping in her bedroom. Carefully inspecting her meager possessions, he found a small photograph of two young girls dressed in identical uniforms. Their white blouse's bore the crest of the orphanage where

Chikako and Raku had met and lived as innocent children. Just as he replaced the photo inside the cover of a notebook, he heard them returning. He slipped out of the bedroom and into the living area and sat down on one of the leather covered couches, feigning sleep.

"Look...sleeping surfer," Chikako joked.

"Shhh...let him. I need to call Hal for travel arrangements," he said softly as they moved out onto the balcony. He dialed Hal's number and waited. "Any news on HK?"

"Spoke to Harmonica. He's sending the list of equipment you stole, Tex," Hal replied forcefully. "Hong Kong? I have a transport arranged. Tomorrow, 0500. Wilson Airport. Operative code word...Jackass."

"Thanks..."

"Don't thank me yet. First repay is a contract to provide security for Global Energy. Your skinny ass will be living in Honduras for six months. You put the team together..."

While Mark listened, Chikako made hand signals to indicate she was going to clean up—he nodded.

"Honduras? Damn, Hal! Murder capital of the planet?"

"You want the transport or not?"

As she walked to her bedroom Mark could not help but follow with his eyes. *Lydia forgive me for what I am thinking.*

He paused, letting the reality of his first debt payment sink in. *Never owe Hal.* "Yeah. I want. You heard about..."

"Take it or leave it. I told the client you would be available in 30 days.

"One last thing...you still have a solid contact in HK?"

"Does a bear crap in the woods? Tech or field?"

"Field. Need a helicopter off books for a night."

"I'll have him call you. Code word...Jackass."

"What's up with all this love for Jackass?

"You like that? Good, cause I'm thinking of changing your call sign to Jackass permanently. If I find out you're headed to HK for the reason I think...I *damn* sure will."

Mark attempted to respond as the line went dead. He looked at his phone for a moment. *What the hell?* As he pondered the meaning of Hal's last statement, Crank joined him.

"I'm going to order up a massage. Feel the need," he said stretching his arms and rotating his head.

"Get a room. Don't need any sloppy finish moans and groans around while I finish the travel details," Mark replied with a knowing tone.

"Whatever....'Til I get paid for the Rhino cluster it's your nickel..."

"Check your bank account? Paid you the same day I paid everyone else. So...get a room...get a massage...bonk your brains out. We split this joint at 0300."

Crank followed him to the wet bar. "Yeah...you'd like that, wouldn't you? Just you and the chick here alone..."

"Give it a rest."

"I knew it! I damn sure knew it! You dig that kung fu bitch, don't you?"

In her room, Chikako lay on the bed with a cold wet hand towel over her eyes listening to his remarks. *Have to watch that kid. May be good on his six...but nothing but testosterone on mine.* Her muse brought a sly smile to her lips.

"All right then. If that's how it is I'll get a room. You can call me at 0200 for a wake-up," he said as he picked up his travel bag and walked out the door.

Jesus, Crank. Get a grip, he thought as he stood at the wet bar pouring a shot of tequila.

Don't let the door hit you in the ass on the way out! She heard the end of his rant and the door slamming. She lifted the cool cloth from her eyes and looked at the clock sitting on the dresser. *Eight hours 'til departure. Ummm?*

Mark poured another shot, and then looking in the mirror, paused and placed the shot glass back on the counter. Moving on into his bathroom, he started the hot water running in the shower and began undressing. He again looked into the mirror, studying his scared features as a light steam began to fill the room. Turning to his right he lifted his left arm and touched the still slightly red scar. *Damn, still sore.*

Chikako got up from her bed and moved to the door listening for any indication he might be moving about in the living area. Hearing nothing, she gently opened the door a crack and again listened. She opened the door fully and looked into the living area, and then onto the balcony—nothing. She moved to Mark's room, placed her ear to the door and recognized the sound of running water.

He opened the shower door and stepped into the cascading hot water. He let the coursing torrent wash over him as he adjusted the temperature. Satisfied, he turned his back to the shower head and leaned his forehead against the glazed glass. A few moments later the shower door opened. As he turned, a nude Chikako stepped in and pressed her breasts to his back, wrapping her arms around his waist. *Didn't see that coming.*

Her soft silky warmth pressed to his back caused a surge of mixed thoughts and impulses to rush through his mind and body. "I have a difficulty…"

"Shhhh…" she whispered as she moved her hand up onto his chest and slowly slid her breasts across his back.

"I'm not good at long term relationships."

"Like you actually expect to survive Ching Wu's den of death? Focus on…now…That's all we have."

The hot water flowed over their bodies as the room filled with steam adding to the intense physical sensations.

Mark relaxed, tilting his head up as he reached behind and gripped her hips gently but firmly in his hands. *She's definitely no saint…But neither am I.* He slowly turned to face her. She looked up, looking for acceptance or rejection—he gently kissed her lush lips then leaned back to look into her almond shaped obsidian eyes. As he leaned forward again she grabbed the back of his head and eagerly returned his kiss.

Time stood still. If not for the constant flow of hot water in the hotel the shower would have gone ice cold as they grappled in the confines of the glass stall. Rotating in one another's arms, she placed her arms around his neck; lifting herself up and wrapping her legs around his hips. As she did, a foot hit the shower door and knocked it open allowing a rush of cooler air to flow over the two lovers. Both laughed even though kissing passionately.

"Bed…Now," she growled.

He at first fumbled with the shower water valves then gave up and carried her to the bed, leaving the water running full force.

They fell onto the bed and rolled back and forth before settling with him on top. Disengaging from the long kiss that lingered from the shower to the bed, he looked deeply into her eyes. Leaning down, he kissed her neck, shoulders then returned to her waiting lips.

WILSON AIRPORT
Nairobi Kenya

The black Land Rover pulled to a stop near a dark blue civilian Gulfstream 550 corporate jet surrounded by KDF Air Force police. The aircrew was kneeling on the tarmac with their hands behind their heads. The officers immediately moved to surround the vehicle as well.

"Looks like security is beginning to return to Kenya. Stay in the truck while I deal with this," Mark said as pulled a leather pouch from inside his jacket and removed a letter. He opened the front passenger door and got out.

"On the ground! Hands behind your head!" a tall heavily muscled soldier barked. He wore lieutenant butter bars and leveled his MP5at Mark's head.

"Easy…I have clearance from President Mobutto…"

"On the ground! *Now!*" the officer repeated more forcefully as he approached.

Mark dropped to his knees as a sergeant rushed forward and shoved his face down on the deck before ripping the document from his hand. Without bothering to read it, he passed it on to his commanding officer. The man studied the letter with a look of surprise.

"Stand down Sergeant…This is Mark Ingram."

He started to get up. Both airmen assisted him to his feet.

"My deepest apologies, sir. We are just starting to get regain control of our country and everyone is suspect until we do."

"Understood," Mark replied as he brushed the grit off his clothing. "That aircraft and the crew are with me…So are the two people in the Land Rover."

"In compliance with the document you carry from President Mobutto, I stand ready to assist you in whatever manner you need. And furthermore, I would consider it a privilege to shake your hand personally for what you did at his estate."

Mark extended his—the KAF officer grinned and pumped it vigorously. "Let me and my associates get on the plane and be on our way. We have some urgent business to attend to."

"Sergeant, see that everything is loaded immediately."

"We'll move our own gear, thank you," Mark said as he motioned to Crank and Chikako. "Could you let the crew go now? They can't very well fly us kneeling on the asphalt."

The big Air Force officer signaled the release the pilot and two copilots. "Have a good trip, Mr. Ingram."

Chikako lowered the passenger side front window and called out, "Good to go?"

"Pull the truck over to the plane and let's get this circus off the ground," Mark replied before walking back to the flight crew.

"Damn glad you showed up when you did," the pilot said. Those bastards were about to haul us off. Call me Sparrow, this is Hummingbird and Robin."

"Nice to meet you boys…Now, fire this bad boy up and let's get airborne before they change their mind," Mark replied as he held his index finger up and gave the universal signal to start engines.

Twenty minutes later the G550 taxied to the end of the runway and prepared for take off. Mark looked back at Chikako and Crank. Each had taken one of the ten identical first class sleeper seats. He winked at both of them and signaled a thumbs-up.

***

CHAPTER SIXTEEN

WILSON AIRPORT
Nairobi, Kenya

Sparrow eased up the throttles as he released the brakes. The whine of the two engines filled the cabin with a low humming sound as all three passengers were pressed firmly back into their seats by the surprising acceleration. The experienced pilot gently pulled back on the yoke, allowing the nose to gradually lift off followed by the main gear.

"Positive rate," Hummingbird dryly announced as he cross-checked the vertical speed indicator to insure the aircraft was in fact climbing.

"Gear up."

The copilot raised the tiny lever to the up position. "Coming up." He noted the black and yellow in-transit indications before the three panels turned black indicating all were up and locked.

The two raised the flaps on schedule as Sparrow made a climbing turn to the east. "Glad to see Nairobi in the rear view mirror."

"Yeah, hate guys with guns pointed at my head."

AIR SPACE - INDIAN OCEAN

Once the jet reached the filed cruising altitude, the pilot-in-command reached up and turned off the fasten seat belt sign. Hal's ultra-long-range business jet was powered by a pair of enhanced Rolls-Royce BR710 turbofan engines and could fly up to 6,750 nautical miles without refueling. That enabled it to cruise non-stop from Nairobi to Hong Kong over the Indian Ocean—the third largest of the world's oceanic divisions encompassing approximately twenty percent of the water on the Earth's surface.

Mark unbuckled and eased up to the cockpit. "Are we there yet?"

"You bet. Step outside and say hello to Hong Kong for me."

"What's the story, guys?"

"Fifty-one hundred miles or seventeen hours and…ten minutes," Sparrow said looking at the Flight Management System. "Seven hour time zone change, so we should be in about 0500 local…any other questions?"

"Hal still stocking the galley with grub?"

"Yes, sir. Your personal preference dining profiles were still active. We added three types of meals for the third pax."

After a brief conference with the pilot and copilot, Mark moved through the cabin toward a seat at the far back. As he walked by Crank, he noted he had already fallen asleep. *Partied too hearty, me thinks,* Mark mused as he considered dropping something into his open mouth before thinking better of it. *For all your quirks, you're a great friend.*

Chikako sat curled up in her seat, reading a small book covered in rich maroon leather. Next to her on the adjoining seat was a jade vase, carefully strapped in with the remains of Raku. He was not as fluent in Japanese as he would like to be, but was conversational due to a couple of contracts that kept him in Japan for six months. Mark was able to make out the title of the book. *Hmmm, full of surprises.*

"Buddha?"

"Yes, you know Buddhism?"

"Most folks in Japan refer to Buddha as Shaka. It's a religion that claims there is salvation and an after life like Christianity. Other than that…don't know much."

She placed a bookmark where she was reading, closed it and looked directly at him. "I am Buddhist…and you? Are you a Christian?"

"Once…a long time ago. Now…I don't know."

"A man…or a woman should know what they are."

"Oh…I know what I am…just don't' know if any religion would have me," he replied, grabbing the back of a seat for balance as the aircraft bucked in some light turbulence.

They held eye contact for a moment, then Mark broke off and looked out the window. "I was raised Southern Baptist...But seem to have lost it over the years."

She held her gaze, which he suddenly realized, for the first time in many years, made him feel somehow uncomfortable. He glanced back. "I'm going to crash."

She reopened her book and began to read as a sly childlike smile crossed over her face.

HONG KONG
Langham Hotel

Ching Wu allowed Hayato's number to ring until voice mail picked up. It was the fifth call he had made in an hour with the same results. "You have not answered me repeatedly. I shall check on your family and see if they know what has become of you."

"Zhang!" The rotund leader called out firmly.

In seconds, the stocky, balding leader of his personal security group responded, "Yes, master."

"Pick up Hayato's family. Take them to the warehouse."

"Yes, master," Zhang said as he bowed slightly.

The merciless guard moved to the elevator doors and spoke to one of the Triad soldiers in whispered tones. With a bow of his head, the killer called for the elevator.

Zhang returned to report, "I have dispatched Tan. He will call when he has the family."

"Do not harm them...just yet."

"Yes, master."

AIR SPACE - INDIAN OCEAN

Crank awoke and stretched out in his reclining seat. *Damn! My head is pounding. Shoulda laid off the booze.* He looked back and saw Chikako kneeling on her chair looking to the back of the cabin where Mark lay fully reclined in a fitful sleep. His body was contorted, his face frozen in a ugly scowl.

"Pssst!" he whispered.

Chikako turned and shrugged her shoulders. "What's going on? Should we wake him?"

"Nooo..." Mark mumbled. "Jes...us..."

Crank took a seat on the armrest on the seat across the aisle and spoke quietly, "He's having the dream."

"What dream?"

"The bad one." Seeing the question in her eyes he went on, "Mark was married...Had a young son. While he was doin' a second tour in the sandbox, he got word they'd been killed."

"And?"

"The Marines sent him home for the funeral...Two week family emergency leave. Turned out they were killed in a drive-by...Some drug cartel gang-bangers gunning down their competition. His family just happened to be in the wrong place at the wrong time. He's had the same dream before...many times."

Suddenly Mark, still deep in sleep, slammed a fist overhead as he mumbled, "Die..."

"He's gettin' to the part where he went Marine postal down in Mexico."

"His family was in Mexico?"

"No, they lived in San Antonio. The cartel was in Mexico...
He found out from the investigating LEO that the bastards who
killed 'em went back to their base in Ciudad Acuña. When he
learned nothing was going to be done about it...he
ah...basically, he invaded Mexico."

"By himself?" she asked incredulously. "Just marched into
the home turf of the cartel?"

"Don't be fooled by what you might think you see. Zorro's
not a big guy, but he's one serious inactive US Marine killin'
machine."

"So...what?...A couple of Mexicans drive to San Antonio,
kill his family and flee back into Mexico...Mark follows them,
finds them, kills them and then runs back to the US?"

"Ha!" Crank laughed out loud. "Oh...he killed 'em all
right...Tracked 'em down with a license plate number to Acuña,
then rented a car and crossed the border...Asked a few
questions and discovered the name of a bar where the cartel
muscle liked to hang out. Dropped in for a visit...wrecked the
joint extracting the intel he needed...In the process, he acquired
some no longer needed weapons..."

"He went in *unarmed*?"

"Like I said...he ain't much to look at, but he's a total killin'
machine when motivated...Suggest you don't' ever motivate
him...Well, when he started to leave the bar, a couple of
carloads of Los Zetas showed up...probably tipped off he was
wreakin' the place...looking for *them*, most likely...He killed
all but three..."

304

"How many were there?"

"Oh, a dozen or so in the bar...He killed two women inside who tried to pop 'im...Outside? Another dozen or so...Let me tell you..."

Mark continued to writhe about, pounding the seat with his hands and feet, causing both of them to look back again.

"...somehow, he captured three and drove 'em to an abandoned site in the desert outside town. Performed a little down and dirty interrogation. I think he slit one's throat to make a point...must have worked. After he learned who the big boss was, he shot the other two...feet, knees, hands...you know? Then he cut their throats and went back into Acuña..."

"Where were the police while all this was going on?"

"Oh, yeah...the police and military in Mexico have taken corruption to a high art form. Don't think they were all that interested in Zorro...Especially after he killed a half dozen local cops and Federales that made the mistake...or had the misfortune of crossing his path." He stood up to check on Mark who had slid down out of his seat and onto the floor.

He continued as he walked back a couple of rows to get a better view, followed closely behind by Chikako. "Night fell before he located the kingpin's hideout...bad news for the Zetas. Mark's a documented night fighter deluxe...You may have noticed back at the compound the other night. He slipped in like a wraith and eliminated the whole damn bunch of 'em...kid you not. The friggin' news reported forty-five dead bodies...not sure if that included the three stiffs in the desert."

She began to formulate a new perception of the man.

Mark apparently slipped into a deeper sleep as he stopped thrashing around and only sobbed and mumbled incoherently.

"He's about done."

"Should we wake him now?"

"Oh, *hell* no! You prod him now, and you'll pray for God to save you...I made that mistake once...If Rhino hadn't choked him down, I'd have been dead meat."

"And you know all this...how?"

"We were on an op in Colombia years ago. After the gig we hopped down to Buenos Aires and got knee walkin' drunk. Rhino asked him about the fits."

"And he told you all this?"

"Did I stutter?...We were seriously drunk...rip roarin' drunk. Four sheets to wind...fall down pukin', commode huggin'..."

"I got it...He seems to be waking up."

Mark began to reach up on the seat beside him and pull himself to a sitting position.

"Time to take a seat...No need to let him know we watched him make a fool..."

"Nightmares make no fool of any man." She returned to her seat.

As Crank passed, he said softly, "Hey...apologies for yesterday. I...ah...sometimes, I let the...little head take the lead."

Chikako looked up at him as she spoke, "I'm told I have that effect on men."

HONG KONG
Langham Hotel

Ching's phone rang with a distinctive tone that informed him the Kenyan Minister of Defense was calling. "Yes."

"Mr. Wu…I need…assistance. Operation *Eliminate* failed. I am in Mombasa…"

"Why have you not contacted Hayato?" Wu asked in a tone that hid his anger as he ogled the young Thai woman laying nude on his bed.

"Hayato…he's dead Mr. Wu…I just learned of it."

"You are certain of this?"

"Yes. A source…a trusted associate in the Ministry of Law Enforcement confirmed it. With Haya…"

"What assistance would a man in your present situation need from me? If your coup failed…you are now hunted. What value do you have?"

A long pause passed before the trapped rat responded, "I could…"

"Cao ni ma, *go have sex your mother*," Wu said with venom dripping off his words as he hung up.

AIR SPACE - INDIAN OCEAN

Mark woke from his nightmare to find himself in the aisle, wedged between two of the seats. He quickly scanned the cabin, pulled up on the armrest to get up and sit down. *Damn! My left hand hurts like a bull stomped it.* Using his right, he gently massaged the other as he cleared his head.

307

Unable to focus enough to close down his mind, he got up and entered the lavatory and turned on the cold water. He took a thick green hand towel off the rack, placed it in the sink and saturated it while he removed his shirt. He wrung the towel and wrapped it around his head and neck.

A knock came through the lightweight door.

"Hey…Zorro…how hangs it?" Crank asked.

"Fine. Give me a minute."

"Take five if you need it. Just checkin' on you."

Mark stepped out of the lavatory to find Crank sitting across the aisle from Chikako, engaged in casual conversation. *Huh? Wonders never cease. She must have kicked his ass.* He walked down to galley, stopping at the wet bar to empty ice cubes into the damp hand towel before wrapping his throbbing hand with it.

"This bird have food on board?" she asked Mark.

"All of Hal's planes carry chow," Crank interjected. "Check the fridge…probably some precooked stuff to your left."

"Anyone else hungry?" She opened the cabinet.

"Yeah. That Mexican surprise there would do," Mark joked pointing at package marked *Enchiladas with Rice and Beans.*

"Crank?" Chikako asked as she continued her search.

"Make mine a double order of Mescan su-prise," he remarked as he passed by on the way to the head.

"You two seem to be getting along real friendly-like now," Mark commented.

"We had a little chit-chat while you were sleeping. Worked our differences out."

"About what? The chit-chat."

"Oh...dreams mostly." She gave Mark a knowing look before turning to the foil wrapped entrees. She opened them, placing each on the counter as she threw away the outermost layer of foil.

"Dreams?"

"Yes...You know about dreams, don't you?"

"Maybe."

Hummingbird entered the passenger compartment and moved to the crowded galley. "Chow? We're starving up front. Maybe you could fix us something to eat as well, sweetheart?"

Mark and Chikako shared a brief look, then burst into laughter.

"What?" the surprised slender balding man asked.

"Uh...she doesn't do domestic. She's just helping me because my hand is banged up..."

"How'd that happen?"

"Not sure. Felt fine when I took a nap..."

"Dreams," she remarked, giving Mark another look.

Mark again felt uncomfortable in her presence.

Crank returned and the tiny kitchen area became too crowded immediately. "What's the hold-up here? Where's the Mescan delight?"

"On the counter. I opened it...you cook it." She headed for the rest room.

"What the hell is she talking about...how'd you injure you hand in a dream?" the copilot asked as he studied Mark's towel wrapped hand.

Crank shot a concerned look at Mark. *Ahh man! Hope she didn't tell him I spilled the beans.* "Why don't you pick out whatever you three up front want…I'll heat it up and deliver."

"We were kinda hopin' the fox would make the delivery."

Mark and Crank said as one, "In your dreams!" Both broke into laughter.

"What the…you guys are…I don't know…Are you both doing her?"

Crank grabbed the copilot by his right bicep and lifted him up like he was a rag doll. "You piss her off? She could probably kill us all. So shut your *friggin'* pie hole…go back to your comfy seat and *I'll* bring your chow." Crank released the man and shoved him toward the cockpit.

"Whoa…easy now, Crank. "

"You making something of it?"

"Nope. Just commenting."

"Did you know she grew up in an orphanage?"

"She told you that?" Mark replied with surprise.

"No. I found a photo of her and that Raku girl…I think in uniforms…standing in front of an orphanage when I went through her stuff back at the Sarvoy.

"What else did you find of interest?"

"Some smokin' hot lingerie…that I suspect I'll never see her wearing…damn it to hell."

Mark started laughing at Crank's frustration. "Never forget…Confuciuos say…he who rides tiger…can never dismount."

Crank studied Mark for another moment and then chuckled. "Good one, Zorro. Very good...Don't *you* forget it either."

McCAMBELL ENTERPRISES, LLC
Dallas, Texas

Hal McCambell, at seventy-six...still an imposing 6'3" figure weighing 210 lbs...sat behind his heavy ornate walnut desk reviewing the list Harmonica had sent him. He entered numbers onto a Texas Instruments calculator as he read off the cost of each, the old school machine whizzed and clattered as it printed each number on the roll of paper. He ripped the tape off, read from it and reentered the numbers again. When the second calculation was completed, he compared the two for several minutes. *Damn! Didn't take that much inventory after all. I still have to charge him for landing at the safe vault without advance approval. Can't let 'im think he can make a habit of it.*

"Maggie! Get Zorro on the line!" he bellowed.

Five minutes later Maggie's voice came over the intercom, "Line three."

The inactive Marine colonel—having served in Korea and three tours in Vietnam before joining the US Secret Service—picked up the hand-set on his land line. "You owe me big, jarhead!"

"How big?"

"Haven't finished the tally just yet...but somewhere in the neighborhood of $200,000."

There was a pause. "Don't piss up my leg, you old coot. You're in the wrong neighborhood and..."

"Don't get smart-mouthed with me. I can still kick your ass all day and not break a damn sweat!"

"*And*…until I see the list Harmonica sent you…"

"You callin' me a liar? Where the hell are you now? I'm getting on a friggin' plane and coming…"

"Ease up, big dawg. Ain't callin' you a liar…I want to see what McCambell equipment I reportedly took…That's all," Mark replied with a hint of amusement in his voice. "Some of that equipment was personal gear left for safe keeping…"

"I calculated that! But you owe me a damn storage fee…and interest!" he said.

Maggie, a plump sixty-three year old woman with bright red hair, was Hal's wife and long time secretary. She opened the door and peered in. "Hal…calm down, sweetie. You're going to give yourself another heart attack."

He waved his hand to shut the door and leave him alone.

"With interest? You are a piece of work…you grumpy ol' leatherneck. Fax me the inventory list and I'll confirm your vault keeper's data."

"Bullshit! I'll hand it to you myself. Are you in HK yet? Cause if you are…" He broke his conversation with Mark and yelled at his wife, "Maggie! Get one of the jet jockeys suited up! I'm going to Hong Kong!"

"Bad idea, Colonel. I'm going to see some Triad folks and they are way over your game, old friend."

He paused for a moment considering the new information. "Maggie, cancel the jet jockey."

"I'll contact you when I'm done. Then we'll talk about Honduras…or whatever rock you want to put me under…Ciao."

Hal sat holding the handset to his ear for several moments considering what Mark had said. Maggie peeped back into his office.

"Everything all better now?" she asked with a knowing twinkle in her eyes. "Mark's a nice young man. You shouldn't talk to him that way, honey."

"Nice young man," the old Scotsman said mimicking her. "Dear God if you even had one clue about…"

"Sweetie…calm down now. You know he will do what's right by you…don't you?"

Hal sat fuming, but slowly began to cool. "You damn right he will. He owes me! Hell…I taught him everything he knows."

"Everything? Now don't forget…that nice young Senator Cruz is meeting you at the Bent Tree Country Club for a round of golf," Maggie said with a big smile as she closed the door, leaving her angry husband to contemplate his actions.

MOMBASA, KENYA

Injera Daar, the dejected Minister of Defense sat in the squalled shack of a distant nephew in the slums of Mombasa. In the tiny confines of his six by eight non air-conditioned room, he calculated his next move. In the other room of the tiny wooden shack with rusted corrugated tin roof, his relatives—all eight of them—waited anxiously for him to be on his way. Even the thousand dollars he had paid them to hide did not ease their concerns of what fate awaited them if he was found inside their home.

Once a respected and important man as head of the Kenyan Defense Department, he now found himself at the end of a long knot-less rope. Without a miracle…he would certainly be tried and hanged for treason.

He opened his brown leather shoulder bag and poured the money and documents he had taken from his wall safe onto the dirty sleeping pad he sat upon. The crisp new American dollars held hollow value for the traitor. Taking his service pistol from an expensive black leather-covered briefcase marked with the initials I.D. in real gold—he cocked it and held the weapon to his temple…

AIR SPACE - INDIAN OCEAN

Mark had just finished his meal when the on-board FAX machine began kicking out a message from Hal. Dropping his trash in the under-counter bin, he moved to the machine and waited until all the documents had arrived. Mark collected the pages. "Hal sent a bill for our stay at the Hotel Cement. Need to check it out…see what the damages are."

"Yeah, boss. Bet the interest rate is up."

Mark settled into the rearmost seat and started with the message page. 'You are one seriously insane Marine! Of all the crazy jarheads I've ever known…you take the cake, hands down. If I don't hear from you I will consider the tools you have stored in my safe vaults as a down payment on what you owe. I'll collect the rest when I see your raggedy ass in Hell.'

314

At the bottom of the page, in a hand written note Maggie wrote, 'He's over it now. Be careful young man. Our grandson, your God child, expects to see you at his graduation in May, Love Maggie.'

Mark could not help but grin. *Scottish madman you are, Hal McCambell.*

Looking at the second page showed nothing more than the items he had signed off for with Harmonica. Taking a pen from his travel bag, he made notes along the margin of the prices he would have had to pay for the items if he had not been able to get to Hal's safe vault. When he finished the list, he added the figures and noted the bottom line was well within prices incurred if buying off the black market. *Hal you are a piece of work.*

The total invoice was $110,973.54. *Well short of $200K you quoted over the phone. I'm bettin' on Maggie. Never rely on the math of a Scotsman.*

Hal had the first two pennies, both dated 1947, he claimed to earn, mounted on a scarlet felt background inside a glass covered frame. It sat on the credenza along with a dozens photos of he and Ike, Ronald Reagan, Oliver North, Stormin' Norman Schwarzkopf, Lewis "Chesty" Puller, Joe DiMaggio, both Bush Presidents, numerous dignitaries around the globe and his favorite…he and the Duke.

At the one end of the photo gallery hanging on the wall behind the credenza were three photos of Mark. One of him and Hal at a International Long Range shooting event. The Trophy standing between them nearly as tall as Mark. The second, an

315

image of Mark and the op team that extracted Belgium foreign aid workers from Nigeria. And the third showed Hal, his three grandsons and Mark deep sea fishing off the coast of Panama. *Yeah, they had a history.*

"What'd it come too?" Crank asked as he worked his way to the head.

"Reasonable amount. Didn't even add a tax."

"Not like the him to forget the tax…You must have blown him real good at the annual bonus party," Crank joked as he slipped into the rest room.

"Bite me."

HONG KONG INTERNATIONAL AIRPORT
Chek Lap Kok Island

Built on a large artificial island, formed by leveling Chek Lap Kok and Lam Chau islands and reclaiming nine point eight kilometers of the adjacent seabed, the 3,080 acre airport site added nearly one percent to Hong Kong's total surface area. It connected to the north side of Lantau Island near Tung Chung by an over-water bridge. Since it was open for business twenty-four hours a day, the arrival of Hal's Gulfstream raised no warning flags, considering the high volume of air traffic. As a major hub in Asia for business travel, one more personal jet landing was indiscernible from the next.

"I'll be driving a red and yellow cargo transport tractor. When I pass by, jump on the third baggage car and close the roll-up door. When we get to the helo pad, I'll stop long enough for you to offload. Pilots name, Tiger…"

"Have our own pilot, thank you very much," Mark said cutting the ICC—*in country consultant*—off. "Have it fueled and rotors turning."

"No comm to that effect. Tiger *will* be doing the tour."

"10/4. Jackass out."

"What's up with Jackass?" Crank asked.

"One of Hal's inside jokes…Changed my call sign for this rodeo. Part of the payback. One new difficulty…helo comes with a pilot."

"Hal's?"

"Yep. Have to lose him…or her along the way."

"Maybe I could help," Chikako interjected.

"How's that?" Mark asked.

"I keep a place here. Not much, but it's quiet. Have some knockout drugs on hand for…just for. We have to lay low 'til tomorrow night anyway…"

"Think you could…" Crank started.

"Do fish pee in the ocean?" Chikako asked.

"We go with plan…What plan are we on now? Had so many since we hit Kenya I've lost count," Mark remarked with a sly laugh. "Call it plan…Hong Kong *fung goo*."

When Sparrow pulled to a stop at the assigned parking site on a less used ramp, Mark, Crank and Chikako moved down the loading ladder carrying their personal tool bags. As they hit the deck, a cargo tractor pulling a dozen carts flashed its lights and turned toward their G550 and began to slow down as it made a arc past them.

"Door three," Mark shouted over the noise and started walking briskly toward the moving train of baggage carts—ever scanning the surrounding area for danger.

Crank threw his gear on first—except for the black shoulder bag containing his weapons—and jumped on board. He turned back around, grabbed Chikako by the wrist and pulled her inside—as if she were a hundred pound tow sack of potatoes—throwing her into the opposite closed roll-up door.

"Hey! Give a girl a break!" she shouted in good humor.

By the time it was Mark's turn, the cart had passed Hal's jet and he had to double-time it to stay up with the door. He tossed his bags in as he grabbed the top of the opening and leapt into the dark compartment, much the same as he often performed a running mount on a galloping horse. *Let the horse's...or in this instance, cart's momentum provide you with the mount.*

Once all were inside, Crank pulled the door down, leaving only inches of open space. He immediately laid down on the floor and took up watch through the crack as the ICC drove to Hal's waiting chopper.

"Once airborne, talk to the pilot and have him set us down as close to your place as possible," Mark ordered.

"That would be on Lantau Island. From the helo pad we can rent a car and get to my place at Discovery Bay. You two will have to hide 'til I can get us into the car park. I keep a really low profile...No one has visited me there."

"Understood. Better consider a small van...Surfer boy's kinda hard to hide in a compact," Mark joked.

"Eat me."

The three riders could feel the train slowing, and true to his word, the driver reduced his speed to a crawl as they approached the helo pad. Crank slid the door up a foot and scanned for Hal's chopper with decals denoting *McCambell Import~Export* on the side.

"We're here, ladies," he called out as he flung open the door, grabbed his bag, and stepped out onto the empty ramp. "Your bags, missy."

She complied and deftly tossed her bags, one after another before dropping down next to him.

Mark hit the deck last and made a quick 360 degree check. Seeing no one, he moved toward the waiting helicopter.

As they approached the midnight blue chopper, the blades began to rotate as Tiger powered up. He opened a small window on his side of the craft and called out, "Let's move it. Oi see a security patrol car coming 'round the terminal."

All three new arrivals to Hong Kong double-timed it into the chopper. Less than a minute later they were in the air. Their speed was fortuitous—the security patrol vehicle had turned on its rotating rack lights and was headed straight for the helo.

"Destination, mates?" Tiger, the lanky Australian pilot asked in a double thick Aussie accent, as he banked to the right and out over Victoria Bay.

"What's the closest drop site with access to a rental car?" Chikako asked.

"Naut much open neow…What's wrong with 'al's warehouse complex? Toike a vehicle from there."

"Done," Mark said.

"What's yer fional destination?"

"Need to know only," Mark replied.

"Roight."

The rest of the short flight was done in complete silence, as the team watched a kaleidoscope of Hong Kong lights fly by underneath.

"Toike what ever one you loike. Koiys under the floor mat," Tiger said as the engine spooled down. He pointed to a row of cars, vans and delivery trucks lined up below—parked next to the three story warehouse building upon which they had just landed.

"Gate code?" Mark asked.

"The goiate is over there...the one to the north with that ornate wroight iron. Code is letters rather than numbers...Yer access code is...Jackarse."

"Ow...that hurts," Crank said as he laughed.

"Never owe Hal," Mark replied.

"You got that roight, mate. Oi was told you need a lift once you got 'ere."

"Call you tomorrow...1700. Be ready to go vertical by 2000 hours."

"Roight, mate. 'Til then," Tiger said as he stepped out of the chopper and headed for the access door. "Yer codes the saime up 'ere."

Mark, Crank and Chikako stood silently for several minutes taking in the view. To the east they could see the busy air traffic coming and going from Chek Lap Kok Island. To the north lay the muted glimmering lights on the mainland. A stiff cool breeze that smelled like the China Sea blew off the bay, causing their clothing to flutter and flap.

Mark finally broke the silence, "Let's roll."

HONG KONG
Langham Hotel

Wu sat on a gold-trimmed Ming dynasty chair in his study reading a message that had just arrived via a secure line fax. When he finished he fed the paper into a shredder. As he contemplated the bad news, he moved to the French doors that opened onto the balcony and walked out to formulate his next move. Pulling his cell phone, he dialed. On the fourth ring the voice of his oldest advisor answered.

"Yes, master Wu."

"Roll the bones, Chia," the unsettled ivory dealer instructed.

"Let me lay out the bed. One moment," Chia, a shreviled Chinese man of 94 years, replied. He was a reader of the ancient art of I Ching, used long before astrology to predict the future.

Wu could hear the sound of the bones being shaken then tossed onto the leather bed as he waited. Several minutes passed as Chia studied the pattern and deduced the meaning.

"There is danger…three dark warriors approach…they scale a tower…I see…" The ancient reader paused.

Several heavy moments passed as Wu waited for the man to continue. "What else do you see?"

"Death."

"Who's death?"

"Many. Too many to ascertain exactly whose."

"Roll them again!" Ching ordered angrily.

Chia complied and collected the bones, shook them and rolled a second time. After a long pause, "I can not see who, master...again...only many deaths."

The frustrated gang lord disconnected the call and stood confused and angry as he gazed at the shimmering lights on the mainland across the bay.

"Zhang!"

"Yes, master," the head of security answered as he stepped onto the balcony.

"Reinforce our position. Double...no...triple the guard."

"Yes, master," Zhang responded. He moved to a land line and made the call. "Collect twenty soldiers. Have them here immediately. Position half on ground level. Send the others to Master Wu's suite."

DISCOVERY BAY
Lantau Island

Chikako drove the unmarked gray Ford delivery van through the main gates of Discovery Bay—located on the northeastern coast of Lantau Island—after entering her pin code. Weaving through the empty roadways, she then entered the La Serene subdivision and continued to a dead-end street. A light rain began to fall as she drove skillfully into the covered parking attached to her home.

"Stay here for...ten minutes. I'll make a show of arriving to let the snoops know it's me. Then join me through that side door next to my BMW." She exited the vehicle and moved to the sliding side door where she extracted her personal bags. Walking to the front entrance she picked up several items of trash in the front of the small house with a red clay tile roof before entering and turning on the interior lights.

"Not bad digs," Crank remarked. "Did you see the breaks out there before we turned in here?"

"Nope."

"Long and clean. Four to six footers...Even rolls. Wish I had the time."

"She just looked out that window near the door," Mark said as he opened the sliding door from the inside and stepped out in a fast fluid motion.

Both he and Crank were inside in less than twelve seconds.

"Through there...take a right. Last door on the left. Comfort room is the door at the end of the hall."

Mark noted many of the vases, paintings and tapestries were antiquities. *Nice taste.* Entering the bedroom, he chose the single sleeping floor mat closest to the door and laid his bags on it. A large brass ceiling fan came on when he hit the light switch, gently stirring the musty smelling air. As he looked through his bag for his shaving kit, he caught a glimpse of movement and turned to see a six foot Burmese python sliding toward the door.

Crank arrived, having stopped in the comfort room first, just in time to meet the snake moving into the hallway. "Oh damn...snakes give me the willies."

At that moment, Chikako called out from down the hall, "Hey! Forgot to tell you about Rambo…"

"No shit!" Crank yelled back.

"Don't worry…he's harmless. I'll put him in his aquarium before we go to sleep," she said with the hint of laughter in her voice.

"Damn straight she will. If that slithering cold blooded reptile slides across me in the dark…I'll decapitate it lickity split."

She arrived at the door just in time to hear the end of his statement. "That would be a mistake."

Crank whipped his head around at her, then slowly turned back to Mark, "If I have to sleep with snakes…you can add another…"

"Rambo will be in my bed or his aquarium tonight…Any body hungry?"

"Yup."

"I could eat a steer. That greaser box dinner was nasty."

"Get settled in…Then join me in the kitchen."

Mark and Crank rinsed off the trail dust, dried themselves and put on clean clothes with an endless stream of good-natured banter. Once they were presentable; they found the kitchen by smell.

"Vegi stir-fry's all we have. There's sake in that cabinet…and a bottle of red or white wine…Suit yourself." She felt like a different person in the confines of her nest—even found herself relaxing, much to her surprise.

"What would you like?" Mark asked as he moved to the cabinet and opened the door. *Good wine too*.

"White for me," she said as she minced some fresh garlic. "Don't want to wake up with a heavy head. Business before pleasure."

"You said that before. Just what do you consider pleasure?" Crank asked while leaning on the red marble counter top facing her as she worked. He detected a slight stiffening in Mark's back at the question and noticed she glanced at Mark as well. *Smooth operator*. Crank could hear Bert's off-key rendition of the song bouncing through his brain.

"White beach...palm trees...hammock...sailing sloop..."

Mark interrupted her, "You sail?"

"Sailed from Japan to Indonesia once. Thirty-nine foot sloop. Past Luzon on the western side and slid into the inner islands of the Visaya." She skillfully chopped, sliced and diced red bell pepper and bok choy as she relived the trip. "Spent a couple of weeks just cruising...Masbate, Cebu, Southern Leyte...passed back into the Pacific around..."

"Surigao del Norte," Crank added. "Love to surf Surigao."

Chikako and Crank shared a look. She smiled then continued, "Curled around Mindanao then into the Sulu Sea and on down to Borneo."

"How long did it take?" Mark asked as he handed her a glass of white wine and passed a small cup of sake to Crank.

"Six months...Give or take...Do you sail?"

"Novice only. Buddy of mine in the Marines..." an anguished look fleeted over Mark's face as he turned to fill his cup with sake. "He and his family were big into it. Took me out a few times. Lost him in Afghanistan…Sailing is very Zen…unless there's a storm."

"When this is done…I'm going to do it again. Maybe stop a little longer at Bohol. Amazing beaches and everything is cheap."

Mark was up at sunrise and moved into the living area to do his workout. He would have preferred to go out on the small tile patio, but did not, lest any of her neighbors see him.

Working within the confines of the limited space, he bumped a table, causing a rich red vase to teeter then tumble. He dove and caught the fragile artifact inches from the hardwood floor before sliding into the wall.

"Nice catch, Zorro," she called with a hint of laughter from the hallway. "It's a Qing dynasty piece worth about 90,000 dollars…and a personal favorite."

Mark rolled over cradling the treasure like a touchdown pass and looked over to her leaning against the wall with her arms crossed. She was wearing a short light blue silk robe covered with pink cherry blossoms. "Bull in a china shop, huh?"

"There's an exercise room…other end of the hall from your room. I'd prefer you bounce around in there," she said before turning and entering the kitchen. "Have to go for food today. Coffee or tea for now."

Mark placed the vase back on its black stone base and moved to the kitchen. "Tea's good. How's Rambo this morning? Crank thrashed around all night expecting to have him slither up his back," he said with a laugh.

"In his aquarium. You have a plan yet?" she asked while she set a pot of water on the stove and then prepared a sterling silver teapot with a mixture of black and green tea leaves.

"You ever do any chute work?"

"Yes…Thinking of dropping in from above?"

"Seems like our best option. I'll call Tiger and give him a list of needs to round up…Called Hal earlier. He gave the Aussie a green light to man the chopper. That would allow all three of us to…"

"Three's a good number. Wu will have learned of Hayato's death by now and taken measures to strengthen his defenses."

"Suggest you make a grocery run after tea. Crank eats like three men normally. Off to the exercise room…Call me when the tea is ready."

***

CHAPTER SEVENTEEN

HONG KONG
Langham Hotel

The head of Chinese ivory smuggling syndicate sat at his ornate desk as the morning sun streamed into the penthouse. He replaced the phone on the cradle; his face twisted up in a barely contained rage. *I hate telling people I cannot deliver what I have promised,* Ching thought as he reviewed the events of the week. *I will make amends as soon as I can pick a replacement for Hayato.*

LANTAU ISLAND
Chikako's Home

Mark, Crank and Chikako sat in the dining room, the remains of their grilled fish, shrimp and lobster brunch still on the table, going over the plan for the fifth time.

"Tiger said he could have all the gear by 1800 and meet us at the warehouses by 2000 hours tomorrow," Mark informed the other two as he hung up the phone.

"So now we sit for thirty-two hours and wait? Man, I'm dyin' to try those breaks," Crank said while popping his neck left and right.

"That will come back to haunt you late in life," Chikako mentioned at the sound of the cracking vertebrae.

"Like there's gonna be a late in life experience?" He laughed.

"There's a big group of tourists that stay over in the condos by the beach…Come here just for the surf. No idea why…pretty lame compared to Witch's Rock or Australia…You could blend in over there with all the other foreigners."

Mark studied her as she made a suggestion that he was certain his friend would take. *Strange brew you are, woman.* "You know Witch's Rock?"

"One of the places I visit when I need solace. I go to Costa Rica once a year and just vegetate."

"And you surf?"

She nodded. "Novice only. Picked it up on a contract in Hawaii."

"Um…what can't you do?" Crank asked with a boyish grin.

"Have a real relationship," she replied, causing the two men to pause.

"Curse of the lifestyle," Mark said after an uncomfortable moment around the table. "Once you get free…"

"Free?" she whispered. "Too many ghosts to ever be free…I fear."

The two men got up at the same time, both feeling slightly unsettled by the direction the conversation had taken.

"Ride me down to the foreigner beach. Couple of hours on a board and I'm good."

"I'll tag along…no board for me. Just some fresh sea air and the view," Mark added.

"Ten minutes to change into beach attire and we're off," she said with a warm smile. "I'll take the breeze…and the view."

THAI LONG WAN
Hong Kong

Mark and Chikako sat under a palm leaf thatch umbrella watching Crank work the surf at Sai Wan, one of the five pristine beaches in Tai Long Wan area of the Sai Kung East Country Park. She decided to take them to the best surfing on the island rather than the puny rolls they had seen the night before. The big American was an expert surfer and it was evident—though the waves were small compared to what he usually rode—that he was having a blast.

"How does your Hal help someone disappear?"

"I don't really know the details. He has access to a pretty impressive array of resources...worldwide. One day they're working...the next day...gone."

"If...you kill Wu there will be a bounty on your head...all our heads. The Triad has fingers everywhere."

"Get in line. Already bounties...Shining Path in Chile, Tupac in Peru, Inkatha in South Africa...Zetas in Mexico..."

"Tell me about Mexico," she asked casually before taking a long sip through her straw of ice cold green tea.

Mark, surprised by her request, waved to the waiter before he answered, "Not much to tell...I...ah..." A slight, but discernible quiver came over his voice before he paused to collect himself, "There was an incident...I took some positive action. The Zetas got their panties in a wad."

She sat quietly, not satisfied with his answer, and waited for him to continue, but he didn't. "What sort of incident?"

Mark looked directly at her. *What's she fishing for?* "That's it...An incident."

"You ever dream about it? I dream about incidents some times...Doesn't help...Always turns out the same."

"Now and then. Not so much any more," he lied, wanting to move on and change subjects. "What incidents do you dream about?"

"Dead people mostly. People who shouldn't have died...Like that...Who died in your Zeta incident?"

Not gonna let it go I see. "My wife and son," he said flatly as the waiter delivered the fresh teas.

And there you go, you big lunkhead. Opened up finally. "I'm sorry. I should not have pressed you. I did not know," she said perfidiously. "You still miss them?"

"Every minute of every day…I should have been there…"

His eyes rimmed with tears behind his shades. He turned his head down the beach to further mask his sensitivity.

"Guilt is a…a bitch."

Crank paddled in from the surf and unfastened the safety strap from his ankle. He tucked his rented board and started walking toward them—effectively ending the conversation.

"Piece of shit board!" he said, smiling from ear to ear.

"Great entertainment, bro. Especially like the head forward flip you did to avoid the young girl."

"Eat me. She was a accident waiting to happen…Kept finding a way to interrupt my rides."

"Did you get her number?" Chikako asked. "If she wasn't interested she wouldn't have been there over and over again."

"Not my type…From the states."

"Surprise, surprise…you have a type?" she asked as he sat down. "Mind if I use the board?"

"Help yourself."

She removed her sarong—revealing hard muscled legs, light six pack abs and amazingly firm breasts covered only by a skimpy bikini top—pulled the surf board up out of the sand where he had stuffed it and trotted off into the sea.

"Jesus! Did you notice the scar on her thigh? Wicked."

"Noticed it back at Sheldrick's…Definitely serious."

"How'd she get it?"

A small cone of wind whirled down the beach throwing a shower of fine sand onto the two as they watched her paddle out to the breaks.

"No idea," Mark replied as he removed his chrome-tinted aviator Bausch and Lomb sunglasses and brushed the grit from his eyes.

"Come on, man…you're holdin' out on me…I ain't blind."

"Meaning?"

Crank paused as a young Chinese waitress delivered a large pitcher of iced beer and a glass to their table, her silly childlike smile directed at the still wet surfer. He filled his glass and took a long drink before going on, "She digs you man. Ever since Sarova…Don't jerk me around…you did her didn't you."

Busted. Mark looked to Crank allowing his silver-coated sunglasses to hide his eyes. "We had a moment…Nothing more."

"Maybe for you, dickhead," Crank said with a grin. "Not for her."

The conversation ceased as they sat silently watching her carve the waves. Though not in the same league as he was, she rode well, even hanging ten on occasion.

McCAMBELL WAREHOUSE
Hong Kong

Tiger had just finished laying out the equipment Mark had requested when the three warriors entered the vast open first floor room. He walked out onto the steel-railed third floor walkway and called down, "Up 'ere, mates."

"You take us in about a mile out upwind and then do a holding pattern 'til we call for pickup. Any questions?" Mark asked the chopper pilot.

"The entire top floor of the Langham belongs to…"

"We know who it belongs to…Questions?" Mark said as he finished checking the equipment needed to cut and secure bulletproof glass.

"Yah go in…an' gettin' in is tha eoisy part…how long do Oi hold?"

"If we don't call in an hour?…Take it home…Call Hal and tell him I'll see his fat ass in hell."

"Ready here, boss," Crank announced as he pulled his parachute on and attached his gear bag.

"Ready here, boss," Chikako said, mimicking him with a note of humor as she attached her bag as well.

Mark pulled his hair back into a pony tail and tied it tightly using a ten inch strip of brown latigo. Lastly he rubbed his index and middle fingers in the camo face paint container and made three black stripes across his cheeks. He repeated the same process on the other side, recreating a look he had used many times—one that resembled the stripes of the fearsome Bengal Tiger. He snapped the lid down and stowed it back in his ruck. "Time to party," he said dryly as he moved toward the stairs leading to the helo pad above.

All three wore identical black jump suits under their MC-4 US military harnesses—with black helmets, gloves and boots as well. The black parachutes Mark had requested would make them nearly impossible to see as they floated to the roof of the hotel.

As instructed, Tiger took them to a position a mile from the intended target and well above it before he slowed the chopper. "'Ere's where yah wanted to be, mates. Wish yah luck," he calmly announced.

Without any discussion, they leapt from the helicopter with Crank, being the heaviest by far, leading the way. Tiger veered off to the east to avoid any unnecessary turbulence from the rotors.

Lights from the throbbing metropolis below were dazzling as the trio fell. Even after midnight, thousands of vehicles still coursed the streets below and late night revelers partied, unaware of the drama unfolding above them.

Thousand one, thousand two, thousand three, he counted before he tugged firmly on the D ring attached to the chute deployment cable. The rectangular ram air parachute snapped out with a muted pop, and yanked Crank abruptly to a vertical position. He glanced up and checked his canopy's proper deployment and located the two steering handles hanging above his shoulders. Pulling down on the right, he spun slowly and checked for his teammates. They were stacked nicely and evenly spaced. The wind hissed softly though the 370 square foot canopy as the sounds of the rapidly departing helo faded and finally disappeared altogether.

They silently steered until they were over the target and made shallow descending turns until they could pick out an exact spot to touch down. A single red obstruction light atop a short galvanized pole lit the area in a surrealistic macabre glow.

Without incident they dropped gently onto the block-long tar-covered roof, avoiding the three air conditioning systems. They hurriedly gathered their chutes and hid them under one of the massive cooling units in the middle of the roof deck.

Without any communications, the team prepared their rappelling ropes, attached them to one of the numerous steel pipes that crisscrossed the roof, and stepped off gently into the black void—it was a long fall to the parking lot below.

Halting at the top of a glass window, all three hung quietly as Mark rappelled, rotated 90 degrees and peered inside through the thick tinted glass. As anticipated from the blueprints of the hotel—gathered by Tiger as instructed—it was a bedroom on the west end of the top floor suite.

Being the smallest of four, Mark had gambled it would be empty and as luck would have it…the room was dark and seemingly empty. Giving the thumbs-up, he lowered himself a little further and applied a pair of four and one half inch suction cups to the glass by adjusting the lift levers. Each was fitted with a stainless steel handle.

He removed another taller cup and affixed it to the window directly between the other two devices, loosened a thumbscrew in the center of it and affixed a telescoping rod to the pivoting head and re-tightened it. Mark retrieved a final piece of equipment from the ballistic nylon bag. He attached it to the end of the telescoping rod with an external cam lock. Looking back up at the others, they flashed a thumbs-up. Each had been checking the roof for any sign of a security alarm activation.

He grabbed hold of one of the suction cup handles to provide downward pressure on the diamond-coated glass cutting wheel mounted in the tool at the end of the rod. He took a deep breath as he bore down hard, initiating a circular cut some sixty inches in diameter. *Here goes nothin'*.

The hardened wheel bit into the glass, making a scratching sound reminiscent of a old-time phonograph needle on the lead-in grove before the recorded music played. Ambient light was so low, he could barely see the line he was etching.

He switched to the other suction cup to complete the circle, slowly turning upside down as the bottom of the arc was finished. He glanced down twenty-nine floors to the street below. *Good thing heights don't bother me*.

Once he transitioned back to the first handhold, he finalized the tiny cut to its point of origin. Mark lost no time in dismantling the cutting assembly and stashing it inside his zippered bag. He slipped his K-Bar out of its sheath and tapped sharply on the glass in six places along the cut with the heavy butt of the knife. Every second suspended out in the open was another invitation to alert the security forces.

He motioned to his team—they lowered a length of paracord tied to their rappelling harnesses. Mark attached each section of black nylon to one of the cups with a bowline knot. With a tensile strength of 550 pounds, each cord would be able to support the weight of the glass cutout by itself—the second line was just for insurance. He moved into a standing position as the others took up some the slack and looked inside the bedroom one last time to insure the door connecting to the hallway was still closed. He let out a little more slack in his rappelling rig as he calculated geometry of the entry. His plan was to kick the glass inside the circle as his body returned from the apex of the pendulum-like arc, using both muscle and momentum to create a clean break. He took three deep breaths to oxygenate his blood and checked his partners one last time before he launched himself away from uncut portion of the window.

The impact with the glass was heavier than he had anticipated. He felt it though the heavy soles of his tactical boots—but the cutter had worked its magic. The five foot disc of glass broke away in one piece, and swung into the bedroom suspended by the two cords. He raised up one foot horizontally to catch its return before it smashed back into the rest of the window—his other foot was pressed against the inside of the window itself. Hanging partially inside and outside the building he caught a glimpse of a figure laying on the bed. His hand snaked to his thigh holster—in a flash he drew down on a pair of terrified brown eyes.

There was a small candle burning on a bedside stand allowing just enough light to make out the body of a young, gagged nude woman secured to the bed's four corner posters. Pressing his index finger to his lips, he indicated silence. With fear in her eyes, she nodded while glancing to the door and back to Mark.

He called on his headset to Crank and Chikako and advised them lower the glass disc until it rested upright on the floor.

Pushing out slightly, he slipped inside, released the hand brake and landed lightly on the lush carpeted floor.

He moved to the door and listened intently. Assured no one was coming, he returned to the opening and signaled his compatriots to join him. He moved to the bed and released her gag and bindings, and then placed a sheet over her exposed and bruised body.

Chikako entered next, released her rappelling rope, immediately moved to the dimly illuminated bed and spoke in whispered tones to the girl—first in Chinese, and then Siamese—trying to ascertain what language she spoke.

"English, please."

Chikako's eyes widened as she smiled.

Mark stepped back over from the doorway and whispered, "We are here to help...Be quiet. Get under the bed and stay there 'til one of us returns."

Without question or hesitation, she slid off the bed and crawled underneath as Crank popped through the opening.

After extracting themselves from the rappelling lines, the three intruders readied their silenced firearms with speed and dexterity. Everyone was ready—Mark indicated with hand signals the paths he wanted them to take—Crank to the left, Chikako to the right and he would press straight forward.

He said softly, "No one gets out alive."

With a nod, they took up positions behind him as he slowly turned the door handle.

Wu sat in his study with Zhang going over the pictures and profiles of seventy-five women he would ship to his associate in Argentina for the annual auction in March. The photos showed each female nude in frontal, side and back views. Beside the image was a date of birth and a catalog number.

"Reserve numbers seven, fourteen, twenty-six and sixty-three for my personal stable and have them delivered to the estate. Inform Li Yum to have them prepared for me in the usual fashion," the sexually depraved Dragon Master said.

"Yes, master. How many for the brothers?" Zhang asked, as he circled the numbers on the glossy photos.

"Chose two for yourself…and the ten oldest for the soldiers."

"You are very generous, master. The brothers will be most grateful."

"Fifty is enough this year. Last year's average per girl brought seventy-five thousand American…"

Wu froze as the silent alarm triggered a flashing orange light above the door in his luxurious suite.

Zhang turned and looked over his shoulder to see the signal light as well. In a smooth and swift motion, he leapt from his chair and dashed through the open door. As he stood in the hallway he heard the electronic lock being activated as it closed. Similar orange lights were flashing through out the entire floor. His subordinates were moving to their assigned positions as he strode through the hall and into the living area.

Pfsit! Pfsit! Crank encountered a guard exiting a rest room in the hallway and double tapped the surprised man as he was fastening his pants. The sound of the body falling was louder than the report of his silenced S&W 99 .40 caliber pistol. He chose the lighter higher round capacity weapon from Rhino's vault before departing Nairobi and left his favored S&W .44 magnum behind.

Chikako had barely entered a hallway to her right when she and Mark both heard the distinctive metallic slap of the slide cycling on the former Navy SEAL's weapon. She looked to the intensely focused Texan and nodded as she broke off on her own. She took only another few steps when a man appeared in the hall ten feet in front of her—*Pfsit! Pfsit! Pfsit!*

She paused over the body momentarily when a second soldier rushed through a door on her left and slammed into her viciously. She lost the grip on her H&K .45 as her head smashed hard against the celedon colored wall. Suddenly the interior lights went off on the entire floor of the hotel, leaving the her grappling with the Triad soldier in the flashing glow of orange on green.

Mark noted the sound of her gunfire as he advanced slowly, knees bent, shuffling his feet to maintain a evenly balanced stance. Suddenly, out of a darkened room at the far end of the hallway a pair of Shinobi throwing stars whirled toward him, the eerie orange light reflecting off the sharpened polished steel. He slipped down and sideways in a fluid blur, knelt on his right knee and emptied a full magazine of 9mm into the doorway and through both the walls on either side. The subsonic 147 grain hollowpoints found their unseen target.

A hulking figure staggered out into the doorway from behind the wall on the left, took three steps forward. He dropped a razor sharp meat cleaver and fell forward, bouncing once before lying still as blood flowed onto the gold colored carpet. *Gonna be a bitch to remove that stain.*

Mark quickly moved to his left while replacing his empty magazine and squatted—his back to the wall—and took a quick look behind him. Another Triad was attempting to sneak up on him with a short thick sword in each hand. Mark rotated slightly, switched the pistol to his left hand, put two rounds into center mass and a third to his head. The last shot took the muscular Triad off his feet. He landed against the wall and dropped like a sack of rice to the floor. *Four down...more to go.*

Zhang, hearing the constant *Pfsit*s of silenced gunfire, motioned to a half dozen men in the living area to split up and attack. As they moved he noted the floor indicator on the private elevator ascending from the lobby. In a matter of a few minutes reinforcements from below would be pouring out into the suite to assist with the, as yet unknown, force moving through like avenging angels.

Chikako, outweighed by forty pounds and taken by surprise, lay underneath her assailant as he raised a heavy meat cleaver over his head. She reached up to deflect it, realizing she had little chance of stopping the razor sharp blade from slicing through her face.

Pfsit! Pfsit! Pfsit!

The attacker's head exploded, raining tiny bits of flesh, brains, bone and blood onto her. She rolled out from under the body and saw Crank advancing.

He dropped a half-empty magazine to the floor and reloaded. *Always keep a full mag. Never know when the extra four or five rounds would be needed at a critical moment.* He extended his left hand and lifted her to her feet effortlessly. He whispered, "Up you go…back in the fight. Lucky for you…my hallway was a dead end."

"Just in time, wave runner." Locating her .45, she followed him down the hall, walking backwards to cover their six.

A sly smile crossed Crank's lips at her reference, but it was short-lived. A half dozen mini-cyclone Chinese throwing stars came rushing toward him. Three bounced off his Armor 500 chest plate but one impacted his left thigh as he whirled to push her from the path of the deadly weapons.

"Ahhh…Shit!" He grimaced as they hit the floor. Rolling to his back, he fired at the two advancing Triad, scoring nine hits from his twelve round magazine. After another quick mag change, he laid the pistol on his lap and pulled the star free. He took a length of rubber tourniquet from his thigh pocket—as well as a four-by-four square bandage impregnated with alum—and tied it down snugly to try to staunch the bleeding.

She extended her hand, leaned back and held steady as he pulled himself upright. "Back in the fight." She grinned and took the lead with him now covering their back.

Mark proceeded to the end of the hallway, squatted and took a pair of quick looks left and right—he saw no one. He eased up slowly to get a better view of the living area and the French doors leading to the balcony. Something in his gut told him, *Duck!* He immediately dropped back to a kneeling position as a double bladed meat cleaver passed mere inches above his head and buried into the wall.

He rolled across the floor and bounced up against the opposite wall just in time to hear the elevator bell chime. Looking to his left, he saw the doors open, revealing a dozen men inside. *Oh, shit!* He swung his weapon around and emptied all sixteen rounds into the crowd.

Screams of wounded and dying men echoed through the suite. He pressed the magazine release, dropping it, as four survivors dashed for cover.

Wu sat in his study behind the locked door listening to the melee outside. He had already called for another round of reinforcements before the chaos began and now waited confidently that whomever had invaded his sanctuary was either dead or would be dealt with long before they found him.

He had watched the monitors of his security cameras—carefully concealed in what appeared to be smoke detectors—as the battle unfolded. Three assassins were all he saw. No one, other than some fool with a death wish, would ever attempt to kill him in his own lair. The grisly images on the monitor covering the private elevator after the doors opened gave him reason to reconsider.

Chikako reached back and touched Crank on the shoulder. "Main room," she whispered into her headset.

He wheeled to his left and took the opposite wall. *Bitch can be my six any time.* He hand-signaled that he would provide cover while she moved into the room.

She nodded and stepped forward, barely avoiding the blade of a short sword by driving into the assailant rather than moving away from him. The handle of the weapon struck her a heavy blow on the left shoulder and she went down.

Pfsit! Pfsit!

Crank laid a pair of 180 grain .40's into the blade wielder's center mass as a volley of AK fire ripped around him causing him to dive forward and behind a gold ornamented dark brown leather couch.

Lying on the floor, she flipped to her left and emptied her weapon at the man, killing him instantly with five direct hits to chest and head—he face planted on the carpet and lay still.

"Oh…this shit is getting deep!" Crank blurted, no longer concerned about silence. "Behind you!"

She reloaded in one fluid motion, sat up and sprayed the hallway with lead. Two men danced the dance of death as bullets riddled their bodies before they collapsed in a twisted heap.

"You good?" Mark called out from his position in the other entrance to the living area.

"Yeah, boss," Crank responded. "Little seepage, but nothing serious."

"Good to go," she added.

"Four or five made it off the elevator...Scattered left and right."

"You're slippin', grandpa," Crank joked. "Any more good news?"

"Not exactly...the elevator is headed down for another load."

"Outstanding!" Crank said sarcastically.

"Cover...I'm going to set a surprise." Mark counted to five, and then sprinted toward the elevator—dropping and rolling to a halt on the floor next to the doors. Pulling flash and frag grenades, he set them upright, and then started back for the hall entrance.

A cleaver struck him squarely in the back and glanced off his rear armor strike plate. Although it did little more than propel him forward, it was a physical reminder that there were still unseen enemy to be dealt with.

Chikako popped up and nailed the cleaver thrower between the eyes—her .45 round taking the back of his head off, spraying the wall with blood and brain matter. As she dropped, she caught a glimpse of Zhang's reflection in the glass of the French doors leading to the balcony. *I know that bastard.*

"Who has a clear shot at the grenades?" Mark asked as he caught his breath. *Have to send the folks at Armor 500 a testimonial on the cleaver defeat.*

"I do," Crank responded.

"Let the doors open a little bit...not enough for anyone to get out...don't want any more monkeys runnin' amuck in here...then tap 'em."

"Done deal."

"Surprised the police haven't shown up yet," he mused aloud.

"Ha! Hong Kong police are Wu's bitches," she answered. "They will show up to take photos sometime next week."

Wu nervously opened the left top drawer on his desk and picked up a engraved gold-plated ivory-handled Colt Mk IV and checked the chamber to insure it was loaded. He glanced at his image reflected in the highly polished slide and watched as a bead of sweat rolled down his cheek. *It's not supposed to be like this...*

***

CHAPTER EIGHTEEN

AIRSPACE OVER HONG KONG

From a mile away, Tiger looked though a pair of sixteen power gyro stabilized binoculars. The image itself was clear—what was happening inside the high-rise den of vipers was not. He had watched the primary lights go out in most of the top floor. *The flashing orange lights must mean the team has been detected.* One room still had lights on, and he surmised that was where the target of the suicide raid was located. *Flickering images in the head honcho's office must be from security monitors. Can't believe those three really thought they could pull this harebrained scheme off and live to tell about it.*

He scanned back across the building, searching for any sign the team was still alive. Tiger set the field glasses down for a second in his lap as he check his watch. *Ten minutes. They have been inside less than ten bloomin' minutes.* He scanned the air for conflicting traffic and found none, and was glad his bird was equipped with TCAS, short for terminal collision avoidance system. He lifted the glasses once more and scrutinized the darkened hotel floor. Several seconds passed before a brilliant white flash illuminated a large room for an instant…

LANGHAM HOTEL

Crank, still prone behind the ornate couch, focused on the elevator door, while Chikako, kneeling in the hallway behind him, covered the rear. As he glanced at the floor numbers they indicated two left before the elevator would be arriving in the war-torn suite. He started singing, badly off key, "Oooh…they are buying an elevator to heaven…your head is humming and it won't go…"

Chikako began to laugh; that dry anxious laugh that comes when death is rushing toward you. "You crazy son of a bitch… It's stairway."

"Different time…different song," he said as he finished the verse. "…the piper's calling you to join him."

The indicator showed the arrival and as the elevator settled, the doors began to open. Two AK 47 barrels, low and high, slipped through the crack and began to spray the room. Indifferent to the value of the priceless antiques within, the Chinese rounds blew vases, statues, ivory carvings, paintings and tapestries into fragments and dust. As the first man started to exit, Crank shot the two grenades with a controlled burst of .40 cal, causing them to explode practically simultaneously.

Screams of the Triad in the elevator followed the dual explosions and increased further as Crank, and then Mark stood for a better view and then filled the air with death from their weapons.

"Loading!" Crank yelled.

When Crank resumed fire, Mark shouted, "Loading!" He dropped a fifteen round mag and replaced it fluidly with a twenty-five rounder from the personally designed mag carrier on his right thigh. Bringing the weapon to bear; a voice went off in the back of his head, *On your six*. He wheeled and saw two Triads running full speed toward him, blades held high.

Half a magazine of 9mm rounds halted their progress, ripping the right arm off one and practically tearing the left leg off the other. As they fell, a shot to the head of each canceled their membership with the Triad.

"Cover!" Mark yelled as he pulled the pin and threw a Willy Peter grenade into the elevator car. Those not already dead, burned in the intense heat of the exploding phosphorous.

Hearing the call for cover, Chikako darted into an open door on her left and hit the floor, ending up on her back. One of Wu's guards rushed her with a two foot double-bladed ax. Her .45 barked four times. The assailant was dead when he hit the floor, his ax buried in the wooden dresser above.

As the smoke cleared, Mark and Crank advanced throwing short two and three round bursts into the burning elevator. A

Triad charged Crank from behind only to have one of Mark's shots slice through his throat.

Crank never looked back. He continued to advance and spray the bodies stacked before him. "The 'vator is done…walls are buckled."

"Got it…I'm going to look for Wu…"

Chikako, covered with blood, walked into the smoke filled room. "I'll clear the balcony."

Mark looked at her. "You hit?"

"No."

Mark pulled a diagram of the suite from a pocket and orientated himself on the whereabouts of Wu's study. "Move it! Rally here when done."

Crank worked his way back along a corridor, limping slightly. He looked down and saw the bandage was beginning to loosen. Sliding his pistol back into its holster, he retied the rubber tourniquet. As he looked up, a Triad, was flying through the air directly at him. He ducked to avoid the full impact of the hurtling killer, sending him tumbling head first onto the carpet. Before his assailant could recover, he moved behind him and snapped his neck in a swift brutal motion learned from years of practice.

The impact of a meat cleaver into his Armor 500 back plate caused him to instinctively spin, whipping his arm over that of his attacker and then down with such force that the man's elbow snapped like a dry twig. Crank violently ran the man face first into the wall, lifted him above his head and slammed him down onto his uplifted knee, breaking his back.

Satisfied both men were finished, he pulled his pistol and began to search for others, like a hulking wounded bear.

Chikako moved slowly and silently onto the balcony in search of Zhang, ever watchful that there may be others. Scanning the portion of the patio that faced north toward the mainland, she eased toward a corner with her back to the wall, knelt and took a quick look around. *Nothing. Where the hell did he go?*

She took one more look behind her to insure she had not missed him, whirled around the corner. As she eased up to a standing position, she caught a flash of movement in the reflection from the glass wall.

Zhang had used his black waist sash—wrapped around the corner pole of the balcony railing—to hang out of sight below the deck. Thinking she would continue forward, he pulled himself up and flipped silently onto the patio behind her. As he rushed forward, she turned, but not soon enough to bring her weapon to bear. He landed a backhanded knife chop to her wrist, causing the pistol to fall clattering to the floor before sliding off the deck and hurtling to the ground below.

The man's momentum carried him on past her as she ducked below him and landed a knee on his left hip. Surprised, he bounced off the wall, wheeled about and assumed a defensive position. "You are the one Hayato spoke so highly of...especially in his bed," Zhang said through clenched teeth, attempting to infuriate the woman now standing relaxed, hands down in front of him.

"He said the same of you."

With her guard seemingly down and quick reply to his taunt, the former commando in the New Republic Army studied her closely with narrow slits for eyes. He circled slowly to his right, bumping into a metal framed glass top table, which he kicked away swiftly to clear his path. The table bounced down the balcony behind him as the heavy glass broke and scattered across the deck.

Chikako slowly advanced, hands still down by her side, carefully measuring the distance to her target. Unnerved by her actions, he retreated, waiting for an opening.

"Your brother, the stupid son of a drooling whore and monkey…what ever happened to him?"

He was puzzled and angered by her question. "He died in Java."

"Oh…yes…A wooden spear to his heart…right?"

How could she know this?

"It *was* a wooden spear wasn't it?…As I recall he squealed like a stuck pig…"

"Ahhh!" the furious Zhang screamed as he charged, throwing a series of vicious kicks at her legs and body, before he passed like a charging bull.

She easily maneuvered out of harm's way. He was far more powerful than Hayato, but lacked his grace and speed. "…Then he lay on his back calling for you…"

Again he charged, this time landing a solid side kick to her right hip sending her flying toward the railing. She bounced off falling to the shattered glass decking before rolling to safety.

"One for you...I often wondered if your baboon asshole brother preferred boys to women..."

"You will suffer before I finish you," he growled.

As he advanced she leapt high and landed a front snap kick to his face; the ball of her foot impacting him on the left check just below the eye. He staggered back on shaky legs. Seeing her opening, a series of lightening fast kicks impacted his sternum, chest, and then his groin.

He fell to one knee, covering his head with his arms as he struggled for breath. He peered at the woman who had struck him. He was surprised to see her standing back waiting once again, a twisted smile on her lips.

She taunted, "Take your time you stupid inbred stack of meat. Please enjoy the fullness of holy testicle Tuesday.

He staggered slowly to his feet pulling a short heavy bladed sword from behind his back. "Enough of this...let us see how you insult when your arms are cut off."

"Took you long enough you filthy fornicator of livestock," she taunted as she slipped a twenty-four inch wakizashi—a Samurai short sword—from the harness behind her back.

They circled, then attacked one another, the metal on metal sound of their blades singing in the night air as they met.

Crank heard the sword fight and moved onto the balcony. Not a user of swords himself, he stood in awe of the skill of both combatants. *Holy Shit*!

354

Zhang, through brute force, finally scored a decisive blow, slicing through her left shoulder, leaving her holding her blade with one hand as she stumbled back in shock.

Bang!

Zhang's face went slack, his eyes vacant as he fell forward hard and lay lifeless—a .40 caliber bullet through his brain.

"That looked personal," Crank said as he helped her sit down on the tile balcony floor.

"The lowest of the low. He made yearly trips to the…to an orphanage and bought young girls for Wu to sell."

"Let me see the wound," he said as he tore the sleeve open exposing the deep three inch cut. He pulled out items he needed to stop the flow of blood. "And you know this how?"

Tending to her wound diverted his attention. When she did not answer, he realized she had passed out.

Wu sat in stunned silence. In his thirty year reign as Dragon Master, several attempts had been made on his life, but none equaled the annihilation of his forces like the images on his monitors. A cold clammy sweat ran down his back. *There is no way they can get in here. It would take a…*his eyes widened as he saw a man with long silver hair pull a roll of detonation cord, and begin pressing it in the jam around the frame of his inner sanctum steel door.

Once he finished attaching the explosive as he wanted, Mark looked up at the fake fire alarm and smiled—he held up a silver metal blasting cap before pressing it to the plastic tube near the floor.

He backed off down the hall and stepped into the doorway of a room. The grim faced Texan drew his pistol and shot the cap, causing the det cord to explode at a rate of four miles per second.

The steel door was little damaged, but the jam and wall around it were destroyed, causing the heavy locked barrier to fall forward and crash solidly onto the floor.

Wu, had taken cover behind his desk and peeked over through the open doorway. He saw the invader half-way down the hall as he took quick look back at his handiwork. The frightened Chinese Dragon Master opened fire.

Mark fell back quickly behind cover and counted the pistol shots as they rang out in a rapid fire string. He didn't have long to wait—five, six, seven, eight. He recognized Wu's weapon at first sight and by the sound of the caliber being used, he took another look after the last round.

Wu hid behind the ornate desk, frantically attempting to reload—dropping a round on the floor for each one he stuffed in the lone seven round magazine.

Mark moved down the hall, like a US Marine with a single mission, into the dragon's lair. "Come out come out, where ever you are."

Wu fumbled his attempt to slip the half loaded magazine back into the magwell when he felt Mark's presence behind him. He turned and looked up—the open muzzle of the suppressor was only inches away and pointed directly at his head.

"Speakie English?" Mark asked. "Drop the weapon!"

Wu nervously complied. "We can negotiate something…"

"I'm certain we can…Where's the safe?"

"Safe?" Wu asked with trembling voice.

"S…A…F…E…the big box where you keep all the loot."

"I…I…it's there…" Wu responded with a shaking finger pointing at a floor-to-ceiling wooden cabinet filled with priceless artifacts.

Mark glanced over, then back to the kneeling man.

"You can have everything…"

"Mighty generous of you, Wu…Now open it."

Crank, with Chikako's unconscious body draped over one shoulder appeared at the doorway. "Want me to make the call?"

"Yeah…ETD fifteen minutes," he answered, all the while keeping a close eye on Wu and his pistol aimed at his head. "What's her status?"

"Be fine in a couple of weeks. Big ol' slice in her shoulder."

Wu used a secret lever, one that looked like just one of the many priceless vases, but when tilted, released the false front revealing a seven foot by three foot steel vault door.

"Last time, fat boy…Open it."

Anger boiled inside Wu, but he knew that his options were limited. He turned the tumbler left then right and once again left. The mechanism clicked; he turned the handle and pulled the door outward, revealing a massive amount of various international currencies—mostly new Chinese Yaun—neatly stacked in organized piles. In addition, rows of gold bullion bars gleamed on the bottom shelf.

"Get the girl from the back bedroom...find some bags... pillow cases, whatever...and load this up. Mr. Wu and I are going to have a little pow wow on the patio."

"Yeah, boss," Crank replied before depositing Chikako in Wu's chair and taking off.

"Outside." Mark motioned with his pistol.

On the balcony, Wu saw the body of his head of security.

"Turn around...put your back to the railing...hands behind your head!"

Though not tall, Mark seemed to tower over the defeated Asian as he advanced to him and placed the tip of his suppressor against his forehead. The two stood for several moments in the cool breeze coming off Victoria Bay.

Wu could see the seething anger raging in the blue eyes even on the unlit balcony. A deep fear rushed over him causing him to loose control of his bladder.

A wicked smile crossed Mark's face. Holding the weapon to his head, he reached down and grabbed the wet testicles of the quivering Chinese man. " My days of ivory are over...*say it*!"

"My...my...days of...ivory are over."

"Again!"

Repeating the phrase began to calm Wu and somehow seemed to restore his damaged sense of pride. Then anger began to return—but it was too late.

Mark lifted him over the railing and released him.

Wu made one feeble and unsuccessful attempt to grab hold before he tumbled end-over-end, screaming all the way to the parking lot three hundred feet below.

BLOOD BROTHERS

He stood for several moments staring at the red smear of the man responsible for the death of tens of thousands of African elephants and rhinoceros. A sense of relief mixed with sadness swept over him.

***

CHAPTER NINETEEN

LANGHAM HOTEL

Mark walked back into the destroyed luxury suite, the stench of smoldering flesh was so strong he nearly gagged. Not that he hadn't smelled it before—on the contrary—he had many times in Iraq and Afghanistan—just not so many burned bodies in such a confined space. Noting the destruction without any emotional attachment, he reentered Wu's study to find Crank and the young hostage girl, wearing baggy pants and a man's long sleeve blue shirt, stacking handfuls of paper currency into various bags. Chikako was going through the Dragon Master's desk drawers. She placed documents she deemed of interest in a small green shoulder bag—the rest were thrown into the corner.

"Wu?" she asked.

"He took a flyin' lesson…Didn't do so well."

"Hey boss man...there's some serious flow here. Gonna need a forklift to move the bullion," Crank joked with a smile as big as a five year old boy seeing his first bicycle on Christmas day.

"Take what paper we can...burn the rest...I'm gonna to take a look around for something to haul the gold in."

"Tiger said he'd be down in five," Crank added as he held up a pair of 20 ounce gold ingots gleaming office lights. He kissed them both before tossing them into a bag nearly filled with money.

"Hold out a couple of thousand for Tiger...Call it a bonus. Don't mention what's in the bags...Hal finds out...the greedy bastard will want a percentage."

Crank started laughing. "Hell...he'll want it all."

In a closet in the Wu's bedroom Mark found a pair of heavy canvas bags with stout brown leather bottoms. *These'll do just fine.* He was taken back by the opulence of the furnishings. *Wish I had more time...and a bigger chopper.*

Crank made the climb up to the roof first, going hand-over-hand with so little effort he could have carried a bag of money with him. However, Mark had nixed the idea lest he drop it—leaving it to be found by whomever passed by on the ground below.

The young rescued girl went second, sitting in a rope sling hastily crafted by Mark out of the lengths of cotton rope that had been used to tie her to the bed. Crank hauled her up rapidly as she only weighed one hundred and ten pounds. Mark sent Chikako up next and he remained alone in the smallest bedroom surrounded by a dozen assorted nylon and canvas bags filled with Wu's ill-gotten gains.

With Crank operating one rope and Chikako and the young rescue working the other, the bags were on the roof in a matter of minutes. Actually, Chikako wasn't much help with a good portion of her medial deltoid muscle sliced open.

Mark swung out of the five foot opening in the glass and dangled above the city of Hong Kong. As he felt Crank pulling, he began to climb hand-over-hand. When he reached the top, the big man reached down and took his hand, pulling him over the edge onto the roof effortlessly.

"Remember...say nothing about the loot," Mark spoke softly, but with authority.

"What's going to become of me?" the frightened young girl asked.

Chikako wrapped her good arm around the smaller girl and held her close. "We'll get you somewhere safe. Then we'll figure it out together...Where are you from? What's your name?"

"I'm from Georgia...My name is Kayla...Kayla King."

"How long you been held captive?" Mark asked as he watched Tiger beginning to descend.

"I don't...don't know for sure..." she began to cry. "I was in Aruba with friends...we went to a bar...called Carlos and Charlie's...when I woke up I was..." Uncontrollable sobbing overtook her and she was unable to go on.

Chikako held her closer, giving a look to Mark and Crank that said...*that's enough for now.*

McCAMBELL IMPORT/EXPORT
Harbor Docks

Tiger set the chopper down on top of a different warehouse, also leased by one of Hal's cover companies. He had been silent on the flight off the roof until now, "Oi never 'spected ta evah see ya crazy mooks again…But 'ere ye are."

Mark moved forward to converse with him while the others exited the helo. Crank tossed the money-filled bags onto the landing pad. "This is for you, Tiger…Hell of a job, mate." He handed a stack of Yuan to him, shook his hand and jumped from the chopper, joining the others hauling off the bags.

"We got to get off this rock…In another couple of hours every Triad monkey spanker and the law will be searching high and low for us," Mark said.

"I have a friend who keeps a yacht here. Flies in on business and takes his clients out on the open water to discuss details… Security concerns…Owes me big time. We should make for it," Chikako responded.

"Crank, get us a ride…clean, no decals or stickers…when we get to the marina, pull the plates."

"Yeah, boss."

ABERDEEN MARINA CLUB
Hong Kong

Membership at the Aberdeen Marina Club was more than exclusive, it was by invitation only. If cost was a concern the

Aberdeen was not the club to consider. Members could suggest someone for consideration or interested parties could submit a letter introducing themselves and indicate their desire for a specific type of membership, either individual or corporate. The club's board of directors decided whether an invitation would be extended. Usually a mere millionaire had little or no chance of being accepted without a cosignatory from an existing member—billionaires were the norm.

Crank parked near the entrance and shut off the headlights, but kept the van's motor running. The three exhausted warriors had changed out of their combat attire and into casual travel clothing.

"What next?" Mark asked as he glanced over at Chikako.

"Let me use your phone. The Triad may try to trace mine."

Mark unlocked and handed over his satellite phone.

"I need to step out to make this call," she said as she got out of the van and moved into the shadows. When she finished she reentered and returned the phone. "One hour. My contact will have his people arrange entry."

Forty-five minutes later, a Honda mini-SUV pulled up to the gates and flashed its lights twice.

"That's our cue," Chikako said.

Crank turned on the running lights and drove to the open gate—controlled by two security guards armed with pistols in flapped hip holsters—and entered the private club grounds. Inside, he was directed by one of the guards to pull over and wait. Once the gates were secured, the Honda backed up, allowed one of the guards to climb in and motioned for them to follow.

At dock fifty-one, the lead vehicle stopped and the security officer in the passenger seat exited, walking back to the van. Parked in the boat slip was a 117 foot long, gleaming white yacht named the *Pearl of the Orient*. Mark powered down his window and waved. His left hand held the suppressed S&W low beside the seat.

"Miss Woo?" The officer asked as he looked into the vehicle and craned his neck to view the occupants.

"Yes, officer…I'm Lucy Woo," she said with a warm smile.

"Mr. Riato sends his regards. He has authorized your use of the Pearl for the entire week. Call security if you have any issues for us, and of course the front desk for all of your other needs. Have a nice stay." He abruptly turned climbed back into the Honda and it departed.

"Pretty sweet service there, sake momma," Crank said.

"Let's get the gear and money on board," Mark ordered like the inactive Marine gunny he was.

VICTORIA BAY
Forty five minutes before Sunrise

Using a small, but powerful flashlight, Crank made his way into the main salon and located the generator control panel. He turned on the ventilation blower fans to clear the engine room of any dangerous fuel vapors and let them run for a full thirty seconds. Once he was assured the danger was past, he turned the key and remotely monitored the start. He checked to see that the engine instruments were operating in the green band for oil and RPM before he toggled the rocker switch to *ON*.

He opened the yacht's electrical system control panel and quickly began to flip on the lights for the interior bedrooms, galley and the main salon itself. *There, that's more like it.*

Mark stowed his flashlight as the ship's lights came on. He had already managed to get most of the bags stashed out of sight. He had Chikako park the van in a secluded place and remove the plates. The Demerol Mark had injected in her wounded shoulder helped ease the pain, but she was still only operating with one good arm. She returned from her assigned task as the first of the twin turbo diesels rumbled to life.

"Any problems?" he asked.

"Not really. One of the mounting screws was a bit rusty, but I managed. I dumped the plates in the water a hundred meters away."

"Good job. Check on Kayla, would you?"

"My pleasure."

The second engine started as Mark made his way up to the fly bridge. He could hear the sea water pouring out of the intercooler exhausts as the pumps did their necessary job. By the time he topped the ladderwell, the glow of the huge GPS navigation display lit up the brilliant white bridge.

Crank was at the helm—his SEAL training made him the obvious choice for designated driver.

"How we fixed for fuel?" Mark asked.

"We're good for fifteen hundred miles or so, depending on the weather."

366

"That's a start. What do you need me to do?"

Pull up the white rubber bumpers and stow them below. Secure the docking lines and bring them aboard...I'm sure they have extras, but I don't know where."

"Aye–aye, Cap'n."

Crank grinned as Mark went down the exterior ladder and began to make preparations for getting under way. He watched him untie the short lines from the highly polished deck cleats. *Hell, even the damned bumpers are pristine. The owner must spend a fortune maintaining this floating palace.*

Mark returned to the bridge almost simultaneously with Chikako. Crank eased both engines into reverse as he checked the rudder position display to insure it was centered amidships. A light onshore breeze forced him to use a differential power setting to maintain a steady course as he expertly backed away from the slip. He used a combination of bow thrusters and one engine in forward with the other in reverse to make the ninety degree turn into the channel between the dock and the line of smaller yachts anchored between telephone poles sunk into the marina harbor bottom.

"I see you do know your way around a boat."

"In another life I might have been a pirate," Crank said without even looking at her.

They stood in the pilothouse watching the sun come up as the yacht continued its way out of the huge marina, paying close attention to the posted no-wake signs, and finally into the bay itself.

"Agipito said to leave his boat in Singapore. He has meetings there next month."

"This is sweet! I could get used to this baby," Crank cooed admiringly as he steered the Azimit 116 craft toward the rising red ball. He turned on the ship's radar system as the ocean came alive with all manner of water craft—junks, speedboats, ferries, fishing vessels of all types, mixed with pleasure boats, tankers and container ships. Pushing the two throttles forward to 2,200 rpm, the boat slowly began to accelerate to a cruise speed of twenty knots. A greenish white line formed aft of the boat as twin propellers churned away at his beckoning. Seagulls and cormorants began to dive and feed on small fish just below the surface as they became visible in the early morning light.

With a spacious fly bridge, formal main deck, owner and guest staterooms for ten, and accommodations for a crew of seven, the yacht was indeed a ship to covet. The trip to Singapore would be made in style, depending on a undetected exit from Hong Kong.

"I put Kayla in the VIP suite...She deserves a little luxury after what she has been through," Chikako said. "She opened up a little before she fell asleep. Just another white slave headed into hell when Wu finished with her."

"There's a lot of that," Mark said as he studied the charts.

"Someone should do something about it," she added.

Mark and Crank exchanged a look. Both knew full well where the central hub for trafficking young girls was in the Southern Hemisphere—Argentina. It would be next to impossible to end it there as the big boss was the son of the

Argentinean Minister of Defense. The military involvement was practically impregnable with the entire Argentinean Air Force flying cover, if the need arrived.

"That would not only be incredibly expensive to undertake...impossible to accomplish...and suicide to attempt," Mark replied.

"Like taking out Wu?"

"Damn...she's good! Walked you right in and chopped you off at the knees, amigo." Crank laughed.

"You're turning into a regular comedian...After we make it clear of the outer islands, pick up a heading to Macau."

"What? I thought we were going to Singapore."

"We are...If anyone wants to track this boat's movement on the harbor police radar tapes, I want them looking for us up there. We're not exactly flying supersonic in our getaway vehicle, are we?"

"Damn...now I know how you got the nickname Zorro. You are one crafty sumbitch."

Mark smiled slightly. "Run us out past the radar's horizon, them make for Malaysia. Going down to the galley...What's your order there, yeoman?" He headed toward the ladderwell.

"Not even ten minutes at the wheel and I get busted down to yeoman...Bummer. Steak and eggs...medium rare...southern style hash browns...orange juice...and hot black Joe. Get it up here ASAP...My ass is draggin'."

"I'll give you a hand," Chikako said as she slipped off the Italian leather covered chair.

***

EPILOGUE

KOTA TINGGI ISLAND
Malaysia

Just before dark, the white yacht dropped anchor on the lee side of the tiny island north of the Singapore strait—some fifteen miles east of their planned destination. Crank toggled the electric windlass control to the lock position as the ship drifted slowly downwind of the anchor, once it settled on the sandy bottom and its flukes took hold.

"Give me a hand with the cover and we'll get our launch hooked up to the crane," he called to Mark.

Crank shut off the four-stoke outboard engine as the twenty foot inflatable Zodiac approached the beach outside the remote fishing village. The sand crunched under the semi-rigid's bow and it came to a stop. Mark stood and stepped up on the blunt nose, and then jumped down just a couple feet from the line of sea foam that had accumulated from the early evening high tide. He turned around and reached up for Kayla.

"Go ahead, I'll catch you."

She cautiously stepped atop the high-strength rubber tube and balanced herself for a second. She looked back at Chikako, who smiled and nodded. Taking in a deep breath, she leapt into his arms. He caught her around the waist and set her down gently.

"See? Look...I know you've been through hell, but you have to learn to trust me. We've gotta got to get you to the US embassy and request a replacement passport. I'll spring for your airfare back home. But we can't just motor on into Singapore harbor with no papers for you. They have customs and immigrations...Understand?"

"I...I think so."

"A little help here, if you please..."

Mark looked up and saw Chikako balancing on the Zodiac's nose with a small backpack in her right hand. Her left arm was still in a sling. "Sorry...haven't forgot about you." He stepped closer and placed his hands on either side of her waist. Lifting her up easily, he turned slightly and set her on the beach.

"Hey, boss," Crank said as he scanned the beach for activity and looked back at the yacht anchored four hundred yards off shore.

"Yeah, what?"

"If all you need is a stinkin' passport...why don't you just call up President Thompson? She can have one waiting for you."

"I can't just call her up. For one thing, I don't have her number..."

"Hey, hardhead...your senator pal back in DC had the juice to ring her directly...Right? So, seeing as how we saved the Kenyan prez and all...and rescued this damsel in distress, you would think she might be feeling a bit generous. Surely, she'd send a diplomatic request for something like a little old passport."

Mark studied him for a few seconds. Crank was grinning like a Cheshire cat.

"There a reason you didn't mention this until now?"

"Yeah...just thought of it."

"You can do that? Make a phone call and get to the President of the United States?" Chikako asked incredulously.

"Well, sure," Mark said somewhat sheepishly. "I try not to wear it out."

She and Kayla glanced at each other and simply shook their heads as Mark fumbled in his cargo pants pocket for his phone. He looked at his watch and did a quick computation of the time zone differential between Malaysia and Washington—*0725. At least I won't be waking him up. I hope he doesn't think I'm a complete ass for letting Sarah down.* The Iridium phone went through its warm-up cycle and located a satellite with which it could connect. He scrolled down his contact list and located the senator near the top. One touch and the call began its long journey. On the third ring, a male voice answered.

"Senator Breitbart."

"Sir, Mark Ingram calling from Malaysia."

"Mark?…My God, son! I never thought we'd hear from you again! Charging off into the Kenyan civil war like you did…"

"Yes, sir…it was…how should I put it?…A bit frenetic there for a while…But we got him out, safe and sound."

"I should say so! Secretary Baker and President Thompson briefed me on all the action. Heroic stuff, all told. America is in your debt for saving an ally."

"Thank you for the kind words, Senator. I had a lot of help… Some didn't make it out…"

"I was aware of that as well. My condolences…So, what may I do to help you?"

"There is this young lady…Kayla King from Georgia."

"I'm familiar with her disappearance…Devastating to her parents, I'm sure."

"I can't go into the details, but my team has rescued her from white slavers…"

"What? She's alive?"

"Yes, sir…What I need is a replacement passport or travel papers to get her out of Singapore."

"Singapore? And you need my help…"

"That's the long and short of it, sir. If you could contact the President, and ask her for a bit of…well, let's call it greasing the wheels through the State Department, I think I can get her headed back home as early as tomorrow."

"Damn! You are amazing! She'll be more than happy lend a hand, I can assure you...I'll get right on it...Is this number a good one to call back?"

"It is...One other thing, sir. We don't need any publicity about the rescue coming out that ties us directly to it. The folks that took her in the first place won't like what we did to their clients...If you know what I mean."

"Something a little more permanent than a cease and desist order, if I remember correctly how you said it in our safari camp."

"Right you are, Senator. They are most definitely not gonna be pleased with our handiwork...and we don't need to put our team members at additional risk."

"I understand fully. Permit me to make a call to the White House, and I'll be back to you as soon as possible."

"Thank you, Senator."

He disconnected the call and placed the phone on standby. He glanced over at the young girl from Georgia. "Kayla, that's about as good as it gets. I think we're getting all your ducks in a row to get you back home."

NAIROBI, KENYA

The phone rang late at night in the luxurious apartment. A long shapely arm slipped out of the silk sheets and lifted the cellular phone off the marble topped night stand. The woman glanced at the phone number and quickly recognized the country code as Hong Kong. She turned on the crystal lamp as she set up against the elegantly carved rosewood headboard. "Yes?"

"Our mutual friend has met and untimely end here."

"Is that so?"

"Yes. His body was identified today through DNA after a long fall from his suite. A team of professional thieves broke in and robbed him and also murdered his associates."

"That is so unfortunate. I do hope the police can catch the culprits and bring them to justice," she said dispassionately. "A mutual friend here suffered a similar attack several days ago. Whoever it was, proved to be quite violent as well. They destroyed all video surveillance tapes before they departed."

"I understand you control the flow of precious cargo from Kenya. I am prepared to send a representative to replace Hayato and supervise the collection of valuable artifacts as before."

"I expected to hear from you. Hayato provided a…necessary service, as did his brother before him. My costs have risen somewhat due to the massive disruption brought about by our civil war. I, however, can still provide all the military and law enforcement intelligence information needed to insure that only a small part of our shipments are intercepted. My fee will only rise to twenty-five percent of the cost of goods sold."

A brief moment of silence occurred following the announced increase in the illicit scheme. The male voice came back over line after a short pause.

"Five more percent will not negate our agreement. Demand is still quite high in China and Vietnam as well…I will require a duplicate set of the shipping bill-of-lading for the last container Hayato shipped. My predecessor's office here was burned and his computer records are presumed destroyed."

"An unfortunate event indeed. I will make sure you have the necessary paperwork. What will be you new man's name?"

"Chan. His name is Lee Chan. I found our former reliance on the Japanese to be...less than optimal. Therefore, I will replace him with one of my own."

"As you wish. I will have my representative initiate contact when he arrives."

"I understand your need for privacy, Madame X."

"Of course...I am looking forward to a long and profitable relationship together. Good bye."

The line went dead before the man could even bid farewell. *I wonder what she looks like.*

Lutto set the cell phone back on the night stand and smiled.

SINGAPORE CHANGI INTERNATIONAL AIRPORT

Just outside the security checkpoint inside the bustling terminal, four well dressed foreign travelers stood with luggage filled with a completely new wardrobe purchased the previous day. Mark looked at the beaming face of young Kayla one last time.

"Your folks are gonna be so happy to see you. I wish I could be there to see it."

She wrapped her arms around him as squeezed as hard as she could. Tears rimmed his eyes as he glanced over at Crank.

"I know. I...I just...don't see how I can ever repay you for your help...all of you. I understand the things you told me about security and I can keep a secret," she said as she released him. She turned and hugged Crank as best she could. Her arms barely reached around his well-developed chest. "You too, Mr. Crank. Thank you from the bottom of my heart."

"You betcha, little girl...Got a whole new life ahead of you now. Enjoy it, " he said as he flashed his best smile.

She nodded and turned to the former Chikako. "So, I'll see you on board the flight to LA, Kari?"

"Right, go ahead and get yourself checked in. I'll be across the aisle in First Class, but we don't know each other, do we?"

"No ma'am. But thank you...for everything. You were..."

"Like a big sister? I always wanted to have a sister."

Kayla nodded as tears began to fill her eyes.

"No crying," Kari admonished. "Happy times call for happy face." She held out her right hand and Kayla grasped it in both of hers. Their eyes met as Kayla let go and brushed back the tears streaming from her brown eyes. "I'll never forget you!"

Kari nodded and watched her slowly turn toward the international concourse, her head held high.

"We did a good thing, gentlemen," Kari said to Mark and Crank. "Thank you for my new identity your friend Hal set up."

"My pleasure...One other thing," he said reaching into his dove gray ultra-suede jacket. He produced a sealed white envelope and proffered it to her. "Your share of the Hong Kong raid...it's in a Cayman bank and your account number and password are in here."

She looked down at the envelope and Mark detected the slightest frown. She shook her head. "No...I don't want their money. It is unclean...I want to start anew."

He stared at her for a second as he processed the surprising reaction. He slipped it back into his jacket and smiled. "Never gonna figure you out completely, I reckon. But, I wish you the very best in life…Enjoy Costa Rica."

"I will," she said as she stepped in and kissed him tenderly.

Crank averted his eyes like a gentlemen.

As the kiss ended, she turned to Crank and extended her right hand. He took it and held it firmly as she smiled broadly. Her eyes lit up with a sparkle that he had only seen once before in Africa. She released his handshake, snaked her right hand behind the big man's neck, pulling his head down to hers and planting a passionate kiss upon his lips.

His eyes opened wide at the unanticipated gesture. She pressed her breasts against his muscled chest as he slipped his hands around her waist. He gasped slightly, feeling like a love-struck teenager at his first prom.

Mark grinned and shook his head slightly. Kari ended the kiss and pushed away gently.

"Did I ever tell you I just *love* surfer boys?" she said as she flashed a perfect smile and reached down for her rollaboard. She turned and walked away without another word.

They watched as she disappeared into a sea of travelers. Crank looked over at Mark with a puzzled look.

"What the *hell* just happened?"

"I don't know, man. Either she digs you or has one sweet way to say good bye."

"She slipped me the tongue!"

BLOOD BROTHERS

"Come on, ace...Buy you a beer...we still got two hours to kill before our flight to Bangkok. It's gonna take all that time and more to get her off your mind."

Crank looked back over his shoulder as they headed for the bar. All he could muster was a single word, "Women..."

****

TIMBER CREEK PRESS

PREVIEW OF

THE NEXT EXCITING NOVEL FROM

TIMBER CREEK PRESS

by

KEN FARMER & BUCK STIENKE

BLACK EAGLE FORCE:
Fourth Reich

CHAPTER ONE

AIRSPACE OVER BOLIVIA

The early morning sun made the rocky snow-capped tops of the Andes Mountains to the west scintillate like diamonds. Younger and much more rugged looking than the mountains of North America, they were almost completely devoid of trees and visible vegetation for the top 10,000 feet to their summits.

The small white and blue US Air Force C-37 Gulfstream flew south from San Diego enroute to Buenos Aires paralleling the mighty peaks. Secretary of Defense Harold Baker gazed out the window. *Unbelievable. They make the Rockies look almost like hills...but I really can't wait to get to my new home at Berthoud Pass. The contractor should be finishing erecting it, if the last shipment of western cedar logs from Montana came in,* he mused as he visualized his retirement home on the continental divide west of Denver. He looked around the cabin at the team his staff had put together for the Argentinian conference. *What a great bunch a talented people. Their new boss will be lucky to have 'em.*

WARBIRD RESTORATION, INC.
GRAYSON COUNTY AIRPORT
DENISON, TEXAS

The innocuous large gray '50s era hangar with the weathered WARBIRD RESTORATION sign above the big doors stood as mute testimony of times past—but it was not as it seemed. Underneath the three old hangars on the west side of the field used by WR, was twelve acres of aircraft parking, storage, a command center, offices and training facilities for the most deadly black ops organization in American history. It was a clandestine group founded by President Reagan in 1986 and contracted to the Department of Defense to protect America's interests where ever they might be—without restrictions. The group was created for missions that are not—and cannot be—officially approved and was comprised of the crème de la crème from all of America's special forces, top pilots, the CIA and the Secret Service. Their mantra was, 'You never saw us. This never happened. We don't exist. We are the Black Eagle Force' and their motto was 'Semper Paro Bellum', or always ready for war.

The Chief Executive Officer, retired Marine Colonel, Dare Phillips and the Chief Operating Officer, retired Air Force

General Jack 'Burner' Stewart were holding a briefing in the ready room seventy-five feet below the massive hangars.

Phillips, a tall, trim, salt and pepper-haired former *Super Cobra* pilot—sporting a new mustache—referenced a miniature jet turbine engine close to the size of a beer keg sitting on a metal table in front of a group of BEF pilots and weapons officers. "People, what you see here is the latest upgrade to our M200, 600 and 800 aircraft. It's similar to Williams International gas turbine used to power the cruise missiles...with some modifications by our own design team...Burner, you want to take it from here?"

"Can do, Dare," Stewart said as the crew-cut silver-headed slightly shorter former Air Force ace got to his feet. "We will be replacing the dual rotary engines in all craft in the next forty-eight hours. The crews have already changed out 'A' squadron. Our resident engineers, Gears and Blaze..." He nodded at Gears Formby and Blaze Hermann sitting in the group. "...have assured us that we now have enough engines to outfit all sixteen of our birds and will be able to carry two replacements per craft on board Mama and Sister Bird...They can be exchanged in less than thirty-five minutes."

A buzz tittered through the room from the twelve pilots and equal number of WSOs stationed at the home base in north Texas.

"Heater McElheney is briefing the Eagle Nest team as we speak. 'B' squadron with Sister Bird will be outfitted by 1300, since we have to maintain readiness...Never know when we might get a call from the DoD."

"What are the advantages of the new power plants, Burner?" asked Jill 'Lucky' Hermann. She had been a top test pilot for the F-22 and F-35 programs for the Air Force at Tonopah before being recruited for the BEF by Dare.

"Power...Put simply...Power. That gives us greater speed, lift and higher ceilings...and of course, it means we can carry more weight."

"A few more missiles, maybe?" asked Maria 'Double D' Williams, former F-18A pilot in the Marine Corps. Her dark brown eyes sparkled at the thought of more ordnance in the already deadly VTOLS.

"Ya think?" piped up Jill's husband, Mike 'Cowboy' Hermann. The former Marine infantry captain was all Texan, standing six feet four and still built like the linebacker he was in college. His natural flying abilities astounded even the seasoned fliers of the BEF.

"Could also help keep us from a CFIT the next time you do a strafing run at ten thousand feet," his WSO Maria quipped looking directly at him.

"Would you give it a rest, D? How many times did you buy the farm in the sim? Huh?"

"A few...but you did it for real...hammer hands."

"Alright, that's enough." Stewart grinned as he stopped the good-natured banter between the two. "The additional thrust will require some transition time in the simulator and practice launch and recoveries at altitude. We're not sure yet exactly how these babies are going to work from the Galaxies. We've already tinkered with the decking on the cargo ramps, but we need some hands-on…"

"I'll volunteer." The tall statuesque blond with dark blue, almost violet eyes stuck her hand in the air.

"You and Bug can try it after Dare and Bull give it a go, Jill," Burner said. "Pecking order, you know."

"Right now, the sim schedule is posted…Let's hop to it," said Dare. "Semper Paro Bellum."

The unit got to their feet and simultaneously repeated, "Semper Paro Bellum."

AIRSPACE OVER BOLIVIA

It was to be the last official trip for his country as Secretary of Defense. President Annette Henry Thompson-Hermann had begged him to stay until the end of her second term, but the stress of the last five years with all the world crises from the incident in the Gulf of Mexico; her own kidnapping; the attempted Chinese incursion and most recently, the elimination of the radical Islamic threat had worn on the former Marine general. Though he was thickening a bit around the middle, he still had the carriage of a line officer. *She needs some fresh blood, I'm going to recommend General Jack Stewart as a possible replacement, even though Dare Phillips will scream bloody murder at losing him from the Black Eagle Force…It's still the best recommendation I can give her, and she trusts him…A valuable, but rare commodity in DC.*

Baker sipped his coffee, leaned back and rolled his head to return his gaze at the mountains. He looked across the aisle at his aide, an Air Force Colonel, who was still asleep after the all-night flight from southern California. The SecDef decided to let the man sleep. He unbuckled his seat belt, stood up and retrieved his briefcase from the overhead bin. Returning to his seat, he opened it and got out his Iridium satellite phone. He powered up the device and looked at his Rolex. *0725 back in Texas. Burner should be up and at 'em by now.*

He scrolled through his contact list. The operations desk at the Black Eagle Force HQ was close to the top. He tapped the icon and waited for the transmission to connect.

"BEF Operatons, Tom Tallman speaking."

"Morning, Tom...Harold Baker here. Is Burner available for a private conversation?"

"Yes, sir, they just finished a briefing...He's down in the mess hall, sir. I'll get him for you."

"Appreciate it."

That's odd. Don't recall ever gettin' a call from him that's not related to a tasking, Tom mused.

Three minutes later, the BEF Chief Operating Officer made it back to his office and picked up a secure line. "Secretary Baker, nice to talk to you, sir...what's on your mind?"

"Burner, sorry to barge into your breakfast, but I wanted to discuss something important to me...and to you." He looked out his window again. "Ever flown over the Andes at thirty-three thousand feet at sunrise?"

"Actually...yes, sir, I have."

"An awesome sight. Absolutely awesome. We're just about to cross over the border between Bolivia and Argentina...it's breathtaking.... But, that's not really why I called."

"Go ahead, sir...I'm all ears."

"We haven't released the formal announcement from the DoD, but I wanted you to be one of the first to know...I'm resigning at the end on the month."

"My God, Harold...that's rather sudden. Your health doing okay?"

"Aw, hell, strong as an ox, but thanks for asking. Guess it's more of a wish to turn the whole shebang over to someone new. It's a challenging position and not everyone is cut out for the responsibility."

"You have done an absolutely stellar job, Harold, I'm proud to say. President Thompson will have a hard time finding someone half as qualified."

"I know...That's why I recommending you to fill the slot."

Burner was stunned by the news. For the first time in memory, he had nothing to say.

"Jack? You still there?"

"Yeah...sure, Harold. I'm...I'm...uh, flattered by the vote of confidence. But I already have a job...They just got me broken in here and things are..."

"I knew you were gonna say that, General...I put four stars on your shoulders when America needed a man with vision and abilities far beyond the back-benchers inside the beltway. You stepped up to the plate because you, sir...are a true patriot. America needs you...Can I count on you again?"

388

"When do you need my decision?"

"I'm enroute to Buenos Aires for a meeting with their Minister of Defense. It's a brief conference, with an agreement to transfer some military hardware in exchange for a anti-drug coalition involving our DEA and..."

The Gulfstream 550 was some ten thousand feet above the elevation of the twenty-two thousand feet peaks of the Andes when he saw a shimmer at the same flight level. He looked again at the area that he estimated to be between sixty and one hundred yards. *There it is again!* The shimmer stopped and a strange aircraft materialized off the Gulfstream's starboard wing. *Son of a bitch!* He blinked and rubbed his eyes. It was still there.

"Holy crap! That's a God damned German Horton 229 flying wing or I'm the Easter Bunny. Bigger than the WWII prototype we've got at the Smithsonian by almost two-thirds. Almost as big as the B-2...What the hell?" he said excitedly.

"What are you talkin' about, Harold?"

"There's a flying wing off our starboard side!" The retro looking aircraft was painted a dove gray color. Suddenly, the left wing dropped as the right rose. Baker could see the distinct symbol of a Nazi Iron Cross painted in black with a white outline on the upper surfaces of both wings. He had seen them in person at Washington Smithsonian Air and Space Museum and could scarcely believe his eyes. "Wait a second!...He's rolling in on us!"

The craft continued to bank toward the Gulfstream—an oddly aerodynamic glass bubble on her nose glowed red briefly, and then went out…

BLACK EAGLE FORCE HEADQUARTERS
DENISON, TEXAS

Stewart jerked the phone from his ear as a high-pitched squeal almost took out his eardrum. "Jesus!" He eased the instrument back to the side of his head—dead silence. "Mr. Secretary? Hello…hello?" He disconnected and clicked Tallman back. "Tom, I just got what sounded exactly like an EMP signal while I was talking with the SecDef. See if you can get him back on line."

"You got it boss." After a couple of seconds, he buzzed back. "Nothing, Burner…The signal is gone."

"Figured…Listen, I want any and all NEOS pictures available for the last thirty minutes of the area surrounding the Bolivia and Argentina border. Then contact the NSA with notification of a possible nuclear detonation, tell Dare I need to see him…and…get me the president."

"Yes, sir…but I can tell you right now, that we don't have any low level birds crossing over South America…There's no need. The only ones I know about belong to China, Russia and Japan. China is out, so that leaves Japan and Russia."

"Get what you can."

AIRSPACE OVER BOLIVIA

Simultaneously, the transport shuddered slightly and the whine of its engines spooled down. The muted rumble of the air flowing over the white and blue jet was the only sound that Baker could hear. The plane immediately began to slow as the much larger German aircraft swooped overhead, barely clearing the top of the C-37 T-tail.

"What in hell was that?" the SecDef shouted at an aide seated next to the cockpit bulkhead.

"I don't know, sir, but I'm damn sure going to find out," he said as he unbuckled, got to his feet and opened the cockpit door.

Inside, Lt. Col Bob Fuller, the aircraft commander and his copilot, Major Jamie Richards, were struggling with all four of the Honeywell PlaneView glass cockpit displays being completely blank. Each was trying a different method to resume electrical power. Fuller thumbed the sidewall-mounted cursor control device and was astounded that it was not working. Richards tried the center console-mounted multifunction control display units. All three screens were blank, and unresponsive.

"MCCUs are down!" he announced.

"I have the aircraft. Autopilot's off and the CCD's tits up!" Fuller responded as the aide opened the door.

"What happened?" he shouted at them.

"Don't know! We lost all power! Nothing's working, not even the radios!" the copilot hollered over his shoulder. "Better strap in, we're going down!"

"Mein Gott, Hans! Now you've done it for sure! What the hell were you thinking?" screamed the copilot in the Gotha 429 flying wing fighter bomber as they rolled out on a return heading for their clandestine base.

"Where is your backbone, Johan? You know as well as I that the cloaking device failed! That man saw us! I saw the look on his face in the window...You know the regulations about security..." the craft's commander, Major Hans Hauser replied.

"Don't go quoting regulations to me...we both know flying close to foreign aircraft is strictly prohibited, but no, you wouldn't listen to me..."

"Stifle yourself, Captain. How was I to know the damned cloak would fail? We haven't had that happen in over...what...six years?"

"Almost seven...That aircraft was from America, right? You could see the flag on its tail as clearly as I...Dumkopf! You just bought us a mountain of trouble...I can feel it."

"Watch you tongue, mister! You are this close being brought up on charges for insubordination." He held his gloved finger and thumb apart a half an inch. "The pulse weapon destroyed all their electronics on board, so there was absolutely no chance to radio their position or announce a sighting. They will all be dead when they crash somewhere in the jungle, and leave no trace...Just gone...If you are wondering why I didn't use the directed energy beam...I considered it. But it leaves physical evidence not easily explained if the aircraft is wreckage is, by some sort of miracle, ever found...They didn't promote me to major for being average. The sooner you accept that fact, the better. Now sit back and shut up. If I want an opinion out of you, I'll give you one."

"Oxygen masks on, regulator set 100 percent," yelled Richards as he pulled the mask from his face.

"Oxygen mask is on, regulator set," replied Fuller as the co-pilot ran through the Loss of Aircraft Pressurization emergency action checklist. The tiny cabin altitude gauge was mechanical and indicated the jet's interior pressure had risen from the ususal 4,500 feet to 14,000 feet, but the rest of the sleek Gulfstream's electronics, including the interphone were fried. Forced pressure breathing would make cockpit communications increasingly difficult as the bird's remaining pressurized atmosphere leaked out of tiny orifices such as the lavatory and galley sink drains.

"Passenger Emergency Oxygen system, deploy," Richards yelled.

Fuller glanced over his right shoulder. The overhead compartments stowing the O2 masks had worked as advertised. Every passenger had grabbed theirs and donned it as expected. Bob shot Jamie a thumbs-up as he noted his own breathing rate was already increasing rapidly. *Dammit! Calm down. You still have windmill RPM and flight hydraulics. What the hell is max L/D?* He glanced down instinctively to the Flight Management System screen on the center console. It was blank. *Shit!* All the aircraft's stored electronic data for weight and balance, endurance and approach speeds were located there. And it was stone cold dead.

He glanced at the backup indicated airspeed gauge, next to the standby altimeter. It was already dropping through 240 KIAS. *70,000 pounds gross weight, give or take. 205... Yeah...205, that's a good number.* With both hands on the yoke, he felt the nose getting heavier as the aircraft slowed. He clicked the trim button twice, but felt no change in the steadily increasing pressure. He tried a couple more inputs, each longer than the first. *Dummy, you don't have any electricity to run the trim motors.*

Major Richards pulled out the iPad where all the navigation and instrument arrival charts—as well as complete copies of the electronic versions of the pilot's operation manual, the C-37-1, and all the aircraft's emergency procedure checklists were stored. He laid it on his lap and pressed the tiny *On* switch. Nothing happened. *Jesus!* He tried it again with the same result. *I know it worked before we left San Diego. I checked it!* He felt this heart begin to pound as the severity of their plight became clearer. *Dammit! I wish the 89th Airlift Wing had not been so friggin' politically correct and green!* The Joint Base Andrews air wing had insisted all aircraft be switched to paperless electronics to *'save the trees, save the planet'*. Now all the two pilots could rely on were their memories.

Relax, Richards told himself. *You can do this.* He started to exhale, but found the natural effort blocked. "What the..." he began to say, but pressurized dry oxygen filled his lungs involuntarily. He grabbed his mask, pulled it aside and exhaled forcefully. When he replaced the mask, his lungs filled up as if he had stuck a water hose down his throat. He started to panic, but remember the lesson from twelve long years before. *The altitude chamber back in UPT!* He glanced at the standby altimeter—the skinny needle had begun to swing left off the 00 at the top of the case. The bird had begun to descend. His mind raced. *Loss of All Generators Checklist.*

"Master generator switch, reset," he said as he forced out the words against the full flow. He flipped the switch without result. He tried it again. No change. *Circuit Breakers! Yeah!* He spun around in the seat and glanced back at the panel. Over half were popped out, their white collars visible. He quickly scanned the rows of electronic control breakers until he found the two engine driven and single APU generator breakers. He pressed them hard, but none would reset itself to the proper position. *Crap! That ain't supposed to happen!*

He looked over at the aircraft commander. The sun streaming through the side window was blinding as he studied the silhouette of his friend. He glanced out at the endless vista of unbroken verdant green jungle below to the east and south. Fog filled the low lying areas of the distant river basin—the steep, craggy mountain sides of the unpopulated Andes were as foreboding and unforgiving as the mountains of the moon. *What the hell are we gonna do?*

His sullen reverie was short lived. Fuller pulled the quick donning mask away from his face for a second. "Give me a hand!...Trim's out! Hold two oh five indicated," he yelled as the oxygen hissed past his face. Jamie placed both hands on the copilot's controls and pulled back slightly.

Bob grabbed the manual trim wheel beside his right knee and rotated the wheel clockwise two turns. "How's that?" he called over to Jamie.

Give me a little more, his copilot signaled with his hands. Fuller gave the unit another half turn before Jamie signaled okay. Bob ran though the math in his head. *17 to 1 glide ratio at max lift over drag...that's 3.2 miles per thousand...33,000 feet works out to 105 miles...None of these damned switches work. That means we can't get in-flight ignition or FADEC electronic fuel control...How about the HMG?...Hell no, the hydraulic motor generator won't work with both engines windmilling! They want all the hydrauics for flight controls...No restarts...Son of a bitch!...What the hell happened to our electronics!*

BLACK EAGLE FORCE HEADQUARTERS
DENISON, TEXAS

"Yes, Madame President, that's what we have at this juncture. I wish I had more."

"Our hands are tied, General. The real reason Harold was going down to Argentina was to negotiate a comprehensive military cooperation treaty with their new Prime Minister. At this point, we can't officially put boots on the ground or even fly over it with armed military aircraft..."

"Yes, ma'am, I understand...I just need a standard protocol tasking from you."

"You have it, General Stewart. You have it."

"With your concurrence, BEF will take over operational responsibility of this incident...code name Anaconda, standard protocol on my mark. The time is now 1605 Zulu...Mark."

"Transfer acknowledged at 1605 Zulu. God speed."

Burner disconnected and looked at Dare. "Well here we go."

"Damn it! I just pray to God, it's just a communications problem...but my gut says otherwise." Phillips looked at the latest satellite weather photo of the region on the eighty inch flat screen on the wall. "It's going to be like looking for the proverbial needle in a haystack."

"A very, very big haystack."

***

TIMBER CREEK PRESS